Engaging Youth in Politics
Debating Democracy's Future

Engaging Youth in Politics
Debating Democracy's Future

Russell J. Dalton, editor

international debate education association
New York & Amsterdam

Published by
International Debate Education Association
400 West 59th Street
New York, NY 10019

Library of Congress Cataloging-in-Publication Data
Engaging youth in politics : debating democracy's future / edited by
Russell J. Dalton.
      p. cm.
  ISBN 978-1-61770-014-9
  1. Political participation. 2. Youth--Political activity. 3.
Democracy. I. Dalton, Russell J.
  JF799.E56 2011
  323'.0420835--dc22
                                    2010046638

Printed in the USA

 IDEBATE Press

IDEA SOURCEBOOKS
ON CONTEMPORARY CONTROVERSIES

The International Debate Education Association (IDEA) has dedicated itself to building open and democratic societies through teaching students how to debate. The IDEA Sourcebooks on Contemporary Controversies series is a natural outgrowth of that mission. By providing students with books that show opposing sides of hot button issues of the day as well as detailed background and source materials, the IDEA Sourcebooks on Contemporary Controversies give students the opportunity to research issues that concern our society and encourage them to debate these issues with others. IDEA is an independent membership organization of national debate programs and associations and other organizations and individuals that support debate. IDEA provides assistance to national debate associations and organizes an annual international summer camp.

Contents

Acknowledgments

I would like to thank all the authors who contributed their works to this volume, and especially to Peter Levine, Director of the Center for Information & Research on Civic Learning & Engagement (CIRCLE) at Tufts University. CIRCLE has become the primary source for research and policy discussion about youth participation in America, and several of the essays in this volume were originally published as CIRCLE research papers. Natalie Cook also provided assistance in assembling this collection. My thanks to Eleanora von Dehsen for her careful preparation of this manuscript.

This collection reflects the vision of Martin Greenwald of the Open Society Institute who saw the need for a book that collects the best scholarship on youth engagement in the United States and other nations. I hope that this book is valuable to young people trying to understand their changing role in contemporary politics, and adults who are puzzled by youth who don't act like their elders.

Introduction:
The Debates over Youth Participation

Russell J. Dalton

The patterns of political participation are changing in the United States and other advanced industrial democracies. This is important because the vitality of democracy largely depends on the participation and judgment of its citizens, who select government officials, contribute to community welfare, and pressure the government to represent public preferences. Thus changes in participation patterns can have fundamental implications for the democratic process. Researchers broadly agree on this point, but they disagree on how exactly participation is changing—and that is the theme of this book.

For much of U.S. history, analysts have stressed the participatory nature of Americans. Alexis de Tocqueville visited the United States in the 1830s and articulately credited the success of America's new democracy to its engaged citizens:

> The political activity that pervades the United States must be seen to be understood. No sooner do you set foot upon American ground than you are stunned by a kind of tumult; . . . here the people of one quarter of a town are meeting to decide upon the building of a church; there the election of a representative is going on; a little farther, the delegates of a district are hastening to the town in order to consult upon some local improvements; in another place, the laborers of a village quit their plows to deliberate upon a project of a road or a public school. . . . To take a hand in the regulation of society and to discuss it is [the] biggest concern and, so to speak, the only pleasure an American knows.[1]

The linkage between citizen participation and democracy became a foundation for democratic political theory. Sidney Verba and Norman Nie, the leading researchers on this topic, state that political participation "is at the heart of democratic theory and at the heart of the democratic political formula in the United States."[2] Without public involvement in the process, democracy lacks both its legitimacy and its guiding force. Furthermore, this image of an engaged public was a central part of the American political lore and described the American public up through the late twentieth century.[3]

In recent years, however, a growing chorus of political analysts and academic researchers claim that Americans and citizens in other established democracies are becoming politically disengaged. Election turnout has declined in most of these nations.[4] At least in the United States, the social and community involvement that Tocqueville so admired is seemingly waning.[5] This research argues that fewer of us seem to be working with local groups in the community, contacting politicians, or even engaging socially with our friends and neighbors. And there is a growing disenchantment with politicians and political institutions.[6]

These trends have led to very dire forecasts about the vitality of democracy in the United States and other established democracies. For example, a 2005 study cosponsored by the American Political Science Association and the Brookings Institution begins:

American democracy is at risk. The risk comes not from some external threat but from disturbing internal trends: an erosion of the activities and capacities of citizenship. Americans have turned away from politics and the public sphere in large numbers, leaving our civic life impoverished. Citizens participate in public affairs less frequently, with less knowledge and enthusiasm, in fewer venues, and less equally than is healthy for a vibrant democratic polity.[7]

If this is correct, the study identifies one of the most important political problems of our time. Moreover, the book boldly proclaims that its dire forecast represents the consensus of social science research. Imagine the newspaper headlines that this report might have generated: "Social Scientists Agree: The Sky Is Falling."

However, the topic of how participation is changing is still highly debated among social scientists, and this special collection of essays addressees the debate, which revolves around two key themes. First, scholars disagree on the level of the public's involvement in politics. Numerous studies provide evidence of a decline.[8] Political scientist Robert Putnam has summarized the critical position in stating "declining electoral participation is merely the most visible symptom of a broader disengagement from community life. Like a fever, electoral abstention is even more important as a sign of deeper trouble in the body politic than as a malady itself. It is not just from the voting booth that Americans are increasingly AWOL."[9]

In contrast, other research finds either mixed evidence on participation trends over time or argues that the patterns of participation are changing and that past research focused on the types that are in decline.[10] For example, Ronald

Inglehart, director of the World Values Survey, offers a much more optimistic image of contemporary citizen participation: "One frequently hears references to growing apathy on the part of the public . . . These allegations of apathy are misleading: mass publics are deserting the old-line oligarchic political organizations that mobilized them in the modernization era—but they are becoming more active in a wide range of elite-challenging forms of political action."[11] This view is starkly different from the decline in political participation literature.

Second, this debate focuses on youth as a primary source of political change. Political observers from Tom Brokaw to Robert Putnam extol the civic values and engagement of the older, "greatest generation" with great hyperbole—while claiming that young Americans are dropping out of politics, producing the decline in political activity.[12] Often the criticisms of youth are quite harsh, blaming them for the demise in contemporary society and politics for being uninformed, uninvolved, and narcissistic.[13] Some of the clearest evidence of decreasing political involvement comes from American elections. In the first election after the expansion of the vote to 18-year-olds (1972), more than half of young people under age thirty voted. This dropped to about 40–45 percent voting in the 1990s. With such a small minority of young people voting and otherwise participating in campaigns, the future vitality of democracy did seem at risk. William Damon, a contributor to this collection, summarized this general position:

> Young people across the world have been disengaging from civic and
> political activities to a degree unimaginable a mere generation ago.
> The lack of interest is greatest in mature democracies, but it is evident
> even in many emerging or troubled ones. Today there are no leaders, no
> causes, no legacy of past trials or accomplishments that inspire much
> more than apathy or cynicism from the young.[14]

Is the situation of youth really so dire? Other evidence points to increases in several forms of political action among the young.[15] Professor of public policy Cliff Zukin and his colleagues examined the full repertoire of political action among young Americans, and they rejected the general claim of youth disengagement: "First and foremost, simple claims that today's youth . . . are apathetic and disengaged from civic live are simply wrong."[16] Young people across the established democracies are generally less engaged with voting and cynical about electoral politics—although the increased youth participation in the 2008 U.S. elections challenges even this observation. Youth are still more likely to participate in contentious forms of political action and are the primary users of new Internet-based forms of action. Volunteerism among the young has greatly increased over the last two decades. Thus, there is counterevidence that young people are changing their style of political action rather than dropping out of politics entirely. From this perspective, America and other established democracies are witnessing a change in the nature of political involvement that is leading to a renaissance of democratic participation—rather than a general decline in participation.

This expansion of political activity also raises a question of what is political participation. Voting and participation in election campaigns are obviously examples of political action. So, too, are most forms of direct or contentious political action, such as contacting a politician, working with a group on a political issue in the community, and protesting or signing a petition. But is working with a nongovernmental organization, whether Common Cause or the Audubon Society, a form of political participation? Does it matter whether the activity is lobbying government on the protection of endangered species or joining in the annual Audubon bird census? Is debating the political role of youth a form of participation, because it develops tools of good citizenship and spreads information about politics? Is political consumerism a form of political participation? Organized boycotts against Nike sportswear, Walmart, and other retailers over products that were produced by child labor or by environmentally unfriendly practices have altered the marketplace and lead to changes in public policy. Even sending a text message can be political participation in the right circumstances, such as forwarding texts about the Obama campaign or grass-roots organizing of protests in developing nations. Clearly, the boundaries of what is political are expanding, and thus we use a broad definition of the political: "any activity, individual or collective, devoted to influencing the collective life of the polity."[17]

So much is being written on youth and politics today because most political observers agree that conditions are changing—they only disagree on the direction of change. Either democracy is at risk or it is on the verge of a renaissance. The young are disengaging from politics or they are expanding the boundaries of the political and empowering the citizenry in new ways. These are the important political debates we introduce in this volume.

THINKING ABOUT YOUTH

Part of the challenge in studying people is to identify general patterns from unique individual experiences. Young people come in all shapes and sizes, with different political skills and interests. So there is no single pattern that applies to all people in a generation. Furthermore, some of the comparisons in this book focus on the United States and others look at youth in different nations—and the experiences of youth can vary cross-nationally. Still, previous studies of youth and politics provide some general patterns that can guide the specific discussions in this book.

Some political science researchers expect that everyone should be interested and involved in politics, but in reality we know there are practical limits. People have many concerns in their lives, and politics frequently comes low on the list of priorities. This is especially the case for young people, who face the life challenges of attending school, dating, and eventually finding a life partner, getting a job and establishing a career, starting a home, and having a bit of fun at the same time. Changing life conditions with age make politics more relevant to people's lives, however. As students leave school and begin a career, they start paying significant taxes and contributing to Social Security and Medicare, which make government programs more visible. When young people purchase a home, they begin to pay property taxes and become aware of government policies that impact homeowners. Raising children brings couples into contact with schools and a host of other programs designed to benefit the young. In short, as we age we become more directly aware of how the government touches our lives in many ways, and this should stimulate interest in what the government is doing and how we can influence it. Thus, for a half century public opinion surveys across the established democracies have routinely found that interest in politics, knowledge of politics, and electoral participation is lowest among young people and grows as they age and become integrated into their political communities.

This is known as the "life cycle pattern" of political participation.[18] In every U.S. presidential election for the last fifty years, turnout has always been higher among the middle-aged than among the first-time voters. In addition, if we track a particular group of first-time voters across elections, their participation routinely increases. For instance, about half of 21–24-year-olds voted in the 1964 election, and their turnout increased by about 20 percent in the 2004 election.[19] The same general pattern applies for interest in politics: it starts at a modest level and then generally increases over time (although it also varies in reaction to political events). Consequently, all else being equal, we should expect young people will generally be less politically active than older adults, and their political involvement will increase as they age. So, when an older political analyst castigates the young for being less politically involved, this might be construed as a myopic view of political realities that applied even when the analyst was young.

Age group differences in an election can also reflect a "generational pattern" in political values and behavior. Successive generations were raised in different political and social conditions, which can leave an imprint on political views. For instance, many political observers have heaped great praise on the Greatest Generation that came of age during the Depression and fought in World War II.[20] Their values were shaped by wartime experiences, emphasizing duty, individual responsibility, and national pride. Those who came of age in the 1950s, the postwar Baby Boomers, were raised in a relatively conservative environment of economic growth and the return to normalcy in politics. The 1960s Flower Generation experienced the countercultural era as they came of age. More recently, Generation X reached adulthood in the 1990s in a post-Cold War world when the economy was growing and new global issues were transforming politics. The Millennial Generation enters the electorate in the decade when international terrorism and economic decline create new political uncertainties, but other social changes create new opportunities as well. Generations are the carriers of these historical experiences. In addition, each generation was raised with different political skills and interests that can shape their political behavior.

Researchers attribute part of the decline in turnout to generational change. Because of their changing social circumstances, younger generations today are less interested in elections, less knowledgeable, and less likely to participate out of a sense of duty. For instance, in his provocatively titled book Is Voting for Young People?, Martin Wattenberg observes the decreasing turnout of the youngest age group over successive elections: 51 percent of 21–24-year-olds voted in 1964 as compared to only 42 percent in 2004. The decline over time is even greater if we compare 18–21-year-olds. He explains these patterns in terms of changes in the social conditions and norms of the young, such as media usage and leisure time behavior.[21] Then, even if voting does subsequently increase through the life cycle, it presumably will not reach the level of previous middle-aged voters because of the lower starting point of more recent generations. Such differences across succeeding groups of young citizens are described as a generational pattern of political participation that affects birth groups differentially even at the same age.

The mix of life cycle and generational patterns is illustrated in Figure 1, which shows the relationship between age and voting in the 1972 and 2004 elections. The 1972 election was the first in which 18–20-year-olds could vote; and the voting age was also lowered in most other established democracies at about this same time. In 1972 about 55 percent of young Americans (under thirty) voted, but about 70 percent of 50-year-olds turned out to vote—a typical life cycle pattern. (Turnout decreases slightly among the very oldest citizens, partly because of health and mobility reasons.) In 2004, however, only about 45 percent of young Americans voted, which may lead to lower levels of participation as they age—a generational decline in participation. One can also observe that the first-time voters in 1972 were in their early fifties by the 2004 election, and their turnout had risen as they aged—the life cycle pattern. The patterns in the figure are central evidence in the indictment of youth disengagement, and they appear in many other established democracies.

Figure 1. U.S. Turnout by Age: 1972, 1996, and 2004

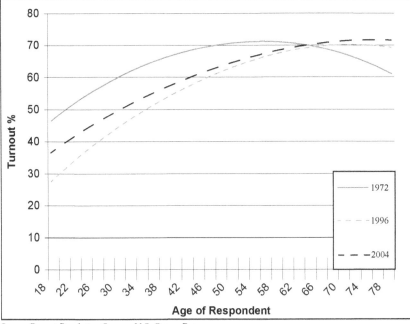

Source: Current Population Surveys, U.S. Census Bureau.

Of course, the 2008 U.S. presidential election demonstrated that generations can also move in a positive direction. The Obama campaign pursued an unconventional strategy of trying to mobilize young voters in the primaries in order to expand the electorate with new Obama supporters.[22] According to many experts who studied electoral participation, this was a strategy that was bound to fail, because few young people would turn out on Election Day. In fact, the Obama campaign was very successful in the primary elections, nearly doubling the percentage of young people that attended a caucus or voted in a primary compared to 2004.[23] Youth turnout in the general election was also up compared to several previous elections, more so than the increase in turnout among older Americans. Youth turnout grew because of the conscious efforts by the Obama campaign and political groups to engage youth—partially in response to the downward trend noted above. Several analysts also claim that the youngest generation, known as the Millennial Generation, is more politically engaged than its predecessor, Gen X. Even with this increase in youth turnout, however, the life cycle pattern still appears: young people participated at a lower rate than middle-aged Americans in 2008. Moreover, many factors made this a unique campaign, and it is not likely to be repeated in other U.S. elections or in other Western democracies.

Another aspect of generational change can be a shift in the patterns of political action. Contentious forms of political action, such as protests and demonstrations, have become more common, and these activities are typically embraced by younger generations. Similarly, new forms of Internet activism seem to be the domain of younger generations. Thus, several recent studies suggest that even as the young are turning away from electoral politics, their participation in these other political activities is increasing.[24] In other words, although fewer young people may be engaged in elections, they instead engage as volunteers in their community, active political consumers, or participants in other forms of direct action.

Even in these examples, however, generational and life cycle factors may be intermixed. If these new forms of direct action persist and perhaps increase as Gen X and the Millennials get older, this may represent a generational shift in overall participation patterns. It is also possible that some of these new forms of participation are the activities of youth. So, as the young age, they will be less likely to protest or boycott (but they may redirect their energies to other forms of participation).

In summary, there is an active debate on the changing patterns of political participation in established democracies. Even if analysts disagree on the specifics, they agree that this is a dynamic time in politics and something is changing in the fundamental relationship between citizens and their government. The resolution of this debate may take time; as we track participation over time, we can understand the dynamics of change that are affecting contemporary democracies. But debating these issues and their implications cannot wait until the research evidence is convincing.

PARTICIPATION AND DEMOCRACY

The debates over youth participation levels are built on a premise that participation matters—as it should in a true democracy. I believe that the level of youth participation matters in many ways. It matters because the policy priorities and policy opinions differ across generations. Part of Obama's appeal to young voters in the 2008 primaries was that he discussed issues of concern to youth that were typically overlooked by politicians of both parties: the high costs of college tuition, health insurance for young people who do not yet have jobs with benefits, the genocide in Darfur, and various environmental concerns. Young Americans also differ from their elders on a range of standard policy issues, such as support for social programs, issues of multiculturalism, international relations, and political tolerance. If youth do not participate, it should not be surprising that the government will devote greater attention to the demands of older voters who do vote and participate in conventional politics.

What would a youth-oriented political agenda look like? A striking example of the different priorities of the young comes from the United Kingdom Youth Parliament (UKYP). Members of the Youth Parliament are elected annually and serve as advocates for youth issues. They also hold an annual meeting in the House of Parliament to heighten the attention to their agenda. To highlight the issues important to youth, the UKYP produces a manifesto, which is reproduced in the Appendix to this book.[25] As you review it, you'll see some of the standard issues of national concern. In addition, there are a whole set of issues missing from most election campaigns: an end to fees for university students, development of sex and relationship courses in the high schools, jobs programs for youth, policies against bullying at school, and programs to aid children living in poverty. Moreover, through their activism the UKYP successfully seen some of their policy reforms enacted into law, most notably new standards for sex education in British schools. Without participation, these views would have no voice.

The lack of participation can also affect election outcomes. If young people do not participate in elections, they lose their voice at this crucial stage of the democratic process. To use the United States as an example, if young people voted at the same level as their parents in the 2000 and 2004 elections, the outcome of these two presidential elections would have been reversed. Similar patterns would appear in close elections in many other democracies because the partisan preferences of young voters often differ from those of their parents and grandparents. Voting matters. We should not overlook the decline in electoral turnout among younger citizens, and government and society should takes steps to engage the young in the electoral process if they want all their citizens—young and old—to be represented.

Youth participation is not only about youth having their say; democracy works best when all views are represented. This allows different social interests to be fully addressed, and it should make collective decisions better in the long run. One example of this imbalance is Social Security legislation. American policy makers are very sensitive to the views of senior citizens, because they vote regularly and actively participate in conventional politics (and the AARP is a very effective lobbying organization). However, this produces public policies that guarantee seniors benefits now, with mounting costs put off for future generations to pay. Current Social Security and Medicare benefits exceed the inflow for these programs from Social Security contributions and taxes. When this method of generational accounting is applied to government spending and financial commitments overall, it produces a fiscal imbalance of epic proportions.[26] As one retired U.S. senator humorously said when discussing this issue with students at the University of California, Irvine: "Watch out for your grandparents, they are trying to steal you blind." If young people are more active in the political process and aware of these issues, better public policy should be the result.

Participation among youth provides the foundation for political activity throughout the life cycle. A number of longitudinal studies indicate that politically active youth carry over this engagement to their adult years.[27] Civic volunteering in high school, for instance, does not end with graduation. It develops skills and norms that lead to higher levels of voting and volunteering in the adult years. Research on turnout argues that when more young people vote in their first elections, this will lead to continued higher levels of turnout as this generation ages. Political participation can be habit forming, and this is an argument to begin the habit early in life.

Finally, Director of the CIRCLE center, Peter Levine has described a range of other positive rewards for young activists.[28] Those who participate in civic activities during high school are less likely to use illegal drugs, to drop out of school, to be violent, or to have unprotected sex. Being engaged with others also provides personal and psychological support networks that can benefit young people in dealing with the challenges of life and the transition to adult roles. Indeed, Robert Putnam's influential book, Bowling Alone, maintains that the socially engaged are healthier, wealthier, and wiser.[29] Young people can benefit from the elixir of participation.

In the end, the nature of participation affects the vitality of the whole democratic process. Adlai Stevenson, twice the Democratic Party nominee for president, famously said that with democracy "people get the kind of government that they deserve." The issues of debate in this volume revolve around the question of what kind of democracy contemporary citizens deserve.

The Topics in This Book

The essays of this book generally focus on politics in the United States, but the broad trends of political change are often similar across other established democracies. Election turnout is generally down for youth in most established democracies; party attachments are also generally eroding among the young. Some of the same phenomena can even be observed in developing democracies. Therefore, we try to place the United States in comparative perspective when discussing changes in participation over time and the lessons that might be learned from other nations.

The essays address five key themes in the current debate on youth participation in contemporary democracies. Part I presents three essays that discuss the role of youth in society and how it is changing, which provide a foundation for the later essays in the book. William Damon presents the critical view toward the changing attitudes and behaviors of youth as eroding the basis of democratic politics, and argues for a change in youth as the solution. In contrast, the essays by Alison Byrne Fields and Siyka Kovacheva suggest that youth have the potential to be active political participants if society and political leaders realize this potential. One side argues the glass is half empty and declining, the other that the glass is half full and rising.

Does it matter when people don't vote? Part II focuses on youth voting in elections. Evidence of decreased participation is clearest in this area. Martin Wattenberg's essay documents the decline in turnout in the United States over the past quarter century, and the even larger drop off among the young. Eva Anduiza assembles evidence of similar declines in turnout from a wide range of established democracies. The U.S. experience is thus not a unique consequence of the specific institutions or processes of American politics, as some observers have claimed, but a general process affecting other democratic societies. Wattenberg and Perea largely point the blame at the changing political norms and expectations of youth. Cali Carlin offers a much different perspective, arguing that young people are turned off by the nature of electoral politics, and that politics itself must change if election participation is to increase.

Part III examines nonelectoral forms of political participation. Russell J. Dalton shows that participation in these forms has been increasing in the United States, partially counterbalancing the decrease in voting turnout. Moreover, young people who are turning away from elections participate more in direct forms of action and contentious politics. Abby Kiesa and her colleagues discuss the rise in volunteerism among the young, while Mark Kann and his colleagues discuss the growth of Internet-based activism. The World Wide Web seems to be the domain for social and political activity by the young. Michele Micheletti and Dietlind Stolle show how the spread of political consumerism is allowing individuals to express their views on a wide range of social and political concerns. This section suggests that youth are not necessarily disengaging from politics but appear to be shifting their efforts to nonelectoral forms of action.

Regardless of how much youth participate overall, there are also differences in engagement among young people—and these differences in activism translate into differences in influence. Part IV begins with James G. Gimpel and J. Celeste Lay discussing the special challenges of engaging at-risk groups, which often have great needs but are not politically involved. James Hyman and Peter Levine use surveys of youth to show how social status, race/ethnicity, and gender vary in their patterns in participation. Finally, Krista Jenkins describes the similarities and differences between men and women in their styles of political participation. These essays suggest that efforts to increase youth participation should pay special attention to the variations in participation that presently exist, and the challenges of engaging those at the margins of politics.

The debates about changing participation patterns reflect a shared concern that democracy should empower citizens to participate in the decisions affecting their lives. Therefore, the final set of essays discusses various options to expand citizen participation, with a special focus on youth. David Villano presents a variety of community reforms that can encourage greater political participation and change our expectations about politics. Peter Levine discusses how schools can be reformed to be centers of democratic learning and to develop stronger norms of citizenship. Finally, Dietlind Stolle and Cesi Cruz summarize a wide range of evidence showing best practices from other nations to promote a more participatory public. All three chapters show that there is much that can be done to improve the quality of citizenship.[30]

The strength of democracy is its ability to adapt and evolve. We are now in a period when change and reform are needed to meet the challenges of a changing society and public. The essays in this volume engage in a debate by first discussing the nature of the challenges facing us and then the possible solutions to these challenges.

ENDNOTES

1. Alexis de Tocqueville, *Democracy in America* (New York: Knopf, 1966), pp. 249—50.

2. Sidney Verba and Norman Nie, *Participation in America: Political Democracy and Social Equality* (New York: Harper and Row, 1972), 3.

3. Verba and Nie, *Participation in America*; Gabriel Almond and Sidney Verba, *The Civic Culture: Political Attitudes and Democracy in Five Nations* (Princeton: Princeton University Press, 1963); Sidney Verba,

Norman Nie, and Jae-on Kim, *Participation and Political Equality: A Seven Nation Comparison* (New York: Cambridge University Press, 1978).

4. Martin Wattenberg, *Where Have All the Voters Gone?* (Cambridge: Harvard University Press, 2002); Andre Blais, *To Vote or Not to Vote? The Merits and Limits of Rational Choice Theory* (Pittsburgh, PA: University of Pittsburgh Press, 2000).

5. Robert Putnam, *Bowling Alone: The Collapse and Renewal of American Community* (New York: Simon & Schuster, 2000).

6. Russell Dalton, *Democratic Challenges, Democratic Choices: The Erosion of Political Support in Advanced Industrial Democracies* (Oxford: Oxford University Press, 2004); Joseph Nye, Philip Zelikow, and David King, eds., *Why People Don't Trust Government* (Cambridge: Harvard University Press, 1997).

7. Stephen Macedo et al., *Democracy at Risk: How Political Choices Undermine Citizen Participation, and What We Can Do about It* (Washington, DC: Brookings Institution Press, 2005), 1. See Alan Wolfe, *Does American Democracy Still Work?* (New Haven: Yale University Press, 2006).

8. See the essays by Damon, Wattenberg, and Perea in this volume. See also Putnam, *Bowling Alone*; John Hibbing and Elizabeth Theiss-Morse, *Stealth Democracy: Americans' Beliefs about How Government Should Work* (New York: Cambridge University Press, 2002); Thomas Patterson, *The Vanishing Voter: Public Involvement in an Age of Uncertainty* (New York: Vintage Books, 2003); National Conference on Citizenship, *America's Civic Health Index: Broken Engagement* (Washington, DC: National Conference on Citizenship, 2006), http://www.ncoc.net/index.php?tray=content&tid=top5&cid=100.

9. Putnam, *Bowling Alone*, 35.

10. Russell Dalton, *Citizen Politics: Public Opinion and Political Parties in Advanced Industrial Democracies*, 5th ed. (Washington, DC: CQ Press, 2009), chap. 4; Cliff Zukin, Scott Keeter, Moly Andolina, Krista Jenkins, and Michael X. Delli Carpini, *A New Engagement? Political Participation, Civic Life, and the Changing American Citizen* (New York: Oxford University Press, 2006); Pippa Norris, *Democratic Phoenix: Reinventing Political Activism* (Cambridge: Cambridge University Press, 2002), chap. 10; Robert Putnam, *Democracies in Flux: The Evolution of Social Capital in Contemporary Society* (Oxford: Oxford University Press, 2002).

11. Ronald Inglehart, *Modernization and Post-modernization: Cultural, Economic and Political Change in 43 Nations* (Princeton: Princeton University Press, 1997), 307.

12. Putnam, *Bowling Alone*, chs 14–15; Wattenberg, *Is Voting for the Young?*; Macedo et al., *Democracy at Risk*, chap. 2.

13. Mark Bauerlein, *The Dumbest Generation: How the Digital Age Stupefies Young Americans and Jeopardizes Our Future (Or, Don't Trust Anyone Under 30)* (New York: Tarcher, 2009); Jean Twenge, *Generation Me: Why Today's Young Americans Are More Confident, Assertive, Entitled—and More Miserable Than Ever Before* (New York: Free Press, 2007).

14. William Damon, "To Not Fade Away: Restoring Civil Identity among the Young," in Diane Ravitch and Joseph Viteritti, eds., *Making Good Citizens: Education and Civil Society* (New Haven: Yale University Press, 2001), 123.

15. See the four essays in Part III of this book. See also Russell Dalton, *The Good Citizen: How a Younger Generation Is Reshaping American Politics*, revised ed. (Washington, DC: CQ Press, 2009), ch. 4; Norris, *Democratic Phoenix*. Neil Howe and William Strauss, *Millennials Rising: The Next Great Generation* (New York: Vintage Books, 2000).

16. Zukin et al., *A New Engagement?*, 189.

17. Macedo et al., *Democracy at Risk*, 16. See also Peter Levine, *The Future of Democracy: Developing the Next Generation of American Citizens* (Medford, MA: Tufts University Press, 2007), chap. 1.

18. Although this pattern of increasing electoral participation is widely documented, researchers have not fully explained the specific reasons for it. For example, see Benjamin Highton and Raymond Wolfinger, "The First Seven Years of the Political Life Cycle," *American Journal of Political Science* 45 (2001): 202–209; Laura Stoker and M. Kent Jennings, "Life-cycle Transitions and Political Participation: The Case of Marriage," *American Political Science Review* 89 (1995): 421–433.

19. These comparisons are based on the U.S. Census Bureau's Current Population Surveys for both years. See also Wattenberg, *Is Voting for Young People?*, chap. 4.

20. Tom Brokaw, *The Greatest Generation* (New York: Random House, 1998); Putnam, *Bowling Alone*.

21. Wattenberg, *Is Voting for Young People?*; see also Putnam, *Bowling Alone*.

22. David Plouffe, *The Audacity to Win: The Inside Story and Lessons of Barack Obama's Historic Victory* (New York: Viking, 2009); Dalton, *The Good Citizen*, Epilogue.

23. Emily Hoban Kirby, Karlo Barrios Marcelo, Joshua Gillerman, and Samantha Linkins, "The Youth Vote in the 2008 Primaries and Caucuses," CIRCLE (June 2008), http://www.civicyouth.org/PopUps/FactSheets/FS_08_primary_summary.pdf

24. See the essays by Dalton, Kiesa et al., and Bennet in this book; see also Zukin et al., *A New Engagement?*; Dalton, *The Good Citizen*, chap. 4.

25. See www.ukyouthparliament.org.uk.

26. Lurence Kotlikoff and Scott Burns, *The Coming Generational Storm: What You Need to Know about America's Economic Future* (Cambridge: MIT Press, 2004); Kent Smetters and Jagadeesh Gokhale, *Fiscal and Generational Imbalances: New Budget Measures for New Budget Priorities* (Washington, DC: American Enterprise Institute Press, 2003).

27. David Campbell, *Why We Vote: How Schools and Communities Shape Our Civic Life* (Princeton: Princeton University Press, 2008); Daniel Hart, Thomas Donnelly, James Youniss, and Robert Atkins, "High School Community Service as a Predictor of Adult Voting and Volunteering," *American Educational Research Journal* 44 (2007): 197–209; Daniel McFarland and Reuben Thomas, "Bowling Young: How Youth Voluntary Associations Influence Adult Political Participation," *American Sociological Review* 71 (2006): 401–425.

28. Levine, *The Future of Democracy*, 62–69.

29. Putnam, *Bowling Alone*.

30. See Stephen Macedo et al., *Democracy at Risk*; Daniel Shea and John Green, eds., *Fountain of Youth: Strategies and Tactics for Mobilizing America's Young Voters* (Lanham, MD: Rowman and Littlefield, 2007); James Youniss and Peter Levine, eds., *Engaging Young People in Civic Life* (Nashville: Vanderbilt University Press, 2009); Jane Eisner, *Taking Back the Vote: Getting American Youth Involved in Our Democracy* (Boston: Beacon Press, 2004).

Part 1:
Are Youth the Problem or the Solution?

This is a time of substantial social and political change in the United States and other advanced industrial democracies. At such times the focus of attention often shifts to youth as the agents of change. The essays in this section broadly describe the contrast between the way youth view politics and the way politics works in contemporary democracies. In "To Not Fade Away: Restoring Civil Identity among the Young," William Damon presents the critical view, seeing the changing norms and behaviors of youth as eroding the basis of politics, especially through their political disengagement and alienation. Alison Byrne Fields, in "The Youth Challenge: Participating in Democracy," presents a more moderate assessment, noting the potential of American youth to be politically involved if political leaders understand their values and orientations. The essay "Will Youth Rejuvenate the Patterns of Political Participation?" by Siyka Kovacheva, adds an international perspective that is much more positive, suggesting that new styles of citizenship and engagement among the young can be a force for democratic growth and renewal. In short, these three essays ask the broad question: Are youth the problem or are they the solution to improving the democratic process in modern societies?

To Not Fade Away: Restoring Civil Identity among the Young

by William Damon*

The death of democracy is not likely to be an assassination from
ambush. It will be a slow extinction from apathy, indifference and
undernourishment.

Robert Maynard Hutchins

Success often breeds the seeds of its own demise—just as, in coastal areas,
hot weather eventually consumes itself by raising a cooling fog from the sea.
Complacency is a common mechanism for success-born self-destruction in human affairs. It has the curious effect of creating conditions for eventual collapse
at the same time as fostering the delusion that it could never happen. The more
secure the sense of complacency, the more dense the reverie and the greater
the peril. Among the most hazardous and oblivious senses of complacency are
those that pile up across generations. Family histories come replete with stories
of younger generations who have squandered wealth out of the naively entitled
belief that their good fortune could never end.

The late twentieth century proved a triumphant time for democracy. Before
World War II, only 28 percent of the world's nations claimed to be democratic.
By century's end, after tyranny upon tyranny has fallen, this figure had risen to
62 percent. Perhaps this will prove to be the most important societal change
of our time: although contemporary social theorists tend to portray the late
twentieth century as an era of rapid technological innovation and economic
globalization, future historians may characterize it as the watershed period when
democracy became recognized as the world's governance model of choice.

But whether history will in fact be written this way will depend on a matter
that may seem insignificant in relation to the grand scale of international politics. It is on the inauspicious front of young people's minds and morals that the
battle for democracy will be won or lost in the coming years.

On this front, in contrast to the geopolitical one, the tide has not been turning the right way. Young people across the world have been disengaging from civic and political activities to a degree unimaginable a mere generation ago. The lack of interest is greatest in mature democracies, but it is evident even in many emerging or troubled ones. Today there are no leaders, no causes, no legacy of past trials or accomplishments that inspire much more than apathy or cynicism from the young.

In the United States, eighteen-year-olds were given voting privileges before the 1972 presidential election, and 47 percent of young people in the eighteen to twenty-four-year age range voted that year. With the exception of an insignificant blip in 1992, voting rates in this age group declined consistently until the 1996 presidential election, when only 27 percent voted—barely one in four. Early analyses from the national election of 2000 suggest a further decline from even this insubstantial rate—and this was a hotly contested race.

Nor is the disaffection confined to a national level—as if it were in reaction, say, to past presidential crimes and peccadilloes. There has never been a time in American history when so small a proportion of young people aged twenty to thirty have sought or accepted leadership roles in local civic organizations. On opinion surveys it is hard to find a public figure on any level whom the young admire, let along wish to emulate. In fact, many of today's young show little interest in civil life beyond the tight circles of their family and immediate friends. Their lack of interest is reflected in the sorry state of their knowledge. In recent Department of Education assessments, only 9 percent of U.S. high school students were able to cite two reasons why it is important for citizens to participate in a democracy, and only 6 percent could identify two reasons why having a constitution benefits a country.[1]

It would be misleading to paint too bleak a picture of today's young. Many are thriving, most are staying out of trouble, and some are positively engaged in the broader civil society. Even the vast majority who have little interest in civic affairs often discover pockets of civil concern. One shining light of youth civil engagement these days is community service. Young people are out helping those in need to an extent that is impressive by any standard: almost half of American high school students devote time to charitable works at least once a month; about half of those do so weekly.[2] Other members of youthful social affiliation still glow: family ties, peer friendships, sports teams, after-school clubs, communities of aesthetic, spiritual, and religious activity, study groups and other school-based organizations.

The problem is that a great many of today's young do not avail themselves of such opportunities. Far too many young people are drifting into *anti* social engagements, as I (among many others) have documented in recent writings.[3] But there is another problem, just as serious for the futures of the young and the society that they will inherit. Even for those youngsters who are staying on a positive track, there is something gone awry, something missing or fading away, from the seemingly propitious track that they are on. With astonishingly few exceptions, even the most positive of today's youth affiliations are unaligned, for the present and likely for later, with the public domain, where our democratic society is composed and sustained.

THE DEDICATION GAP

Periodically, my Center on Adolescence at Stanford conducts interviews with adolescents and young adults in order to explore their views about themselves and society. In spring 1999 we collected a few in-depth interviews with youngsters aged fourteen to eighteen living in some heartland American communities.[4] We also examined essays that these and hundreds of other students had written about the laws and purpose of life in today's world.

What struck us was not only what these young people said but also what they did not say. They showed little interest in people outside their immediate circles of friends and relatives (other than fictional media characters and entertainment or sports figures); little awareness of current events; and virtually no expressions of social concern, political opinion, civic duty, patriotic emotion, or sense of citizenship in any form.

For example, when asked what American citizenship meant to him, one student replied, "We just had that the other day in history. I forget what it was." Another said, "I mean being American is not really special. . . . I don't find being an American citizen very important," and yet another said, "I don't know, I figure everybody is a citizen so it really shouldn't mean nothing." One student said directly: "I don't want to belong to any country. It just feels like you are obligated to this country. I don't like the whole thing of citizen. . . . I don't like that whole thing. It's like, citizen, no citizen, it doesn't make sense to me. It's like to be a good citizen, I don't know. I don't want to be a citizen. . . . It's stupid to me." Although such statements are by no means universal, neither are they atypical. In fact, they are strikingly similar to sentiments that I hear from students in every formal or informal setting that I visit.

To the extent that political life showed up on these students' radar screens at all, it was viewed with suspicion and distaste. "Most [politicians] . . . are kind of crooked," one student declared. Another student, discussing national politics, said, "I feel like one person can't do that much, and I get the impression that [most people] don't think a group of people can do that much." The cynicism carried over to political action at all levels, even school. When talking about how school government works, one girl said, "The principal and vice principals probably make the decisions and say what is going on and don't worry about it." A palpable feeling of futility—a "what's the use?" sensibility—ran through all the students' attitudes about political participation. The following excerpt from one student's interview is illustrative. Before the statements below, the girl had been complaining that her school's dress code was arbitrary and unfair.

Q. Why do you think there's no action on it?

A. I guess because [the students] think that even if they do try to do it, they will not change it. It's a rule and it's going to be there forever. It's not going to change. We've always had that rule. You come here you have to abide by our rules. We're not going to change it just because you want to change it.

Q. Do you feel like there is any democracy at all at your school?

A. I don't know.

Q. Do you vote on anything other than electing representatives?

A. Nope.

Q. Do they vote on anything?

A. I have three representatives in my class, but I don't really ask them about this stuff and they don't really tell us about that. I mean, they might vote on stuff. I don't know that they do though.

When asked what they would like to change in the world, the students mentioned only such personal concerns as slowing down the pace of life, gaining good friends, either becoming more materially successful or less materially oriented (depending on the student's values), and being more respectful of the earth, animals, and other people. None of the students expressed concerns about the civic and political worlds, domestic or foreign. If they had expressed such interest, they would have few tools to pursue them: they lacked even minimal knowledge of topics in national and world affairs.

Although some of the students considered themselves to be leaders among their circles of close friends, almost none desired to be a civic leader. (There was a lone exception in our sample.) One boy, for example, dismissed the idea by saying, "It just doesn't seem like a very good job to me. I'd rather be concentrating on more artistic efforts rather than civic efforts or saving the world or something."

Is this unusual, or remarkable in any way? Hasn't youth always been a time for the pursuit of personal pleasures and intimate relationships rather than participation in the broader civil society? Have the young ever been driven by a sense of civic duty or dedicated to social and political purposes beyond their own everyday lives? Indeed, is there not plenty of time in later life to get interested in such things?

The uncomfortable answers to these rhetorical questions are: (1) yes, young people's current lack of dedication to broader civil purposes is unusual by any historical standards that we have; (2) no, youth traditionally has not been a time of exclusively personal and interpersonal goals to the exclusion of civic ones; and (3) yes, young people normally have been drawn to civic and political affairs by the time of late adolescence. In fact, there is reason to believe that a person's crucial orientations to life incubate during adolescence. If civic concern is not among them, it may never arise.

We all have memories, of course, about times in our own recent history when young people in numbers threw themselves into the political fray. They joined the civil rights movement, campaigned for political candidates, lobbied for environmental protection, and protested government actions that they did not like, such as the Vietnam war and the Watergate abuses. One sociological study has shown that young people who marched for civil rights in the 1960s were far more likely than their peers to later join civil associations, assume positions for civic leadership, and vote.[5] We also are aware (at least from old Hollywood films, if not from family lore) that in our country's more distant past young people have signed up with ardor for military and public service when wars and other threats to their society have emerged.

But there is far more evidence for a tradition of youthful civil engagement than these few scattered data points. Virtually all the classic theories of human development—of Jean Piaget, Erik Erikson, Jane Loevinger, and Harry Stack Sullivan, among many others—portray adolescence as a period when young people formulate their personal, social, and civil identities. A civil identity is an allegiance to a systematic set of moral and political beliefs, a personal ideology of sorts, to which a young person forges a commitment. The emotional and moral concomitants to the beliefs are a devotion to one's community and a sense of responsibility to the society at large. The specific beliefs and commitments, of course, may change over the subsequent years, but the initial formulation of them during adolescence always has ranked as a key landmark of human development. Piaget found evidence for this in the young people's diaries, Erikson and Sullivan in clinical encounters, Loevinger in psychometric measures and surveys. This is a part of a large data base spanning many countries and several generations of youngsters.

A civil identity is by no means the province of the privileged in society. Nor is it totally extinct in our own society. I quote here from an interview conducted a few years ago by my former student and frequent collaborator Daniel Hart. The interview was conducted with a seventeen-year-old African-American boy living in an extremely disadvantaged section of Camden, New Jersey. David, the subject, expresses an affiliation with his community and a sense of responsibility for it that still exists, though it has become increasingly rare among advantaged and disadvantaged youngsters alike.

Q. How would you describe yourself?

A. I am the kind of person who wants to get involved, who believes in getting involved. I just had this complex, I call it, where people think of Camden as being a bad place, which bothered me. Every city has its own bad places, you know. I just want to work with people, work to change that image that people have of Camden. You can't start with adults because they don't change. But if you can get into the minds of young children, show them what's wrong and let them know that you don't want them to be this way, then it could work because they're more persuadable.

A number of young people from all backgrounds still acquire a solid civil identity, and the possibility is still very much alive for the many who are not doing so. It is still the case that neurological and cognitive growth around the time of puberty, combined with the expansion of social roles and educational experience that the secondary school years brings, sets the stage for the adolescent's formulation of civil identity.

But what happens when young people choose not to walk upon the stage that has been set for them? To put it frankly, we do not know. We do not know how the abnegation of civic concern on the part of a young person will affect his or her later development; nor do we how it will shape the society that a cohort of similar young people will inhabit. It is as if we had launched two daring experiments, one psychological and one sociological, asking the twin questions: how will it turn out for the individual, and how will it turn out for the society, if we skip over (or perhaps try to postpone) the traditional developmental process of forming civil identity during the adolescent years?

As a social scientist, I generally welcome experiments, especially ones that explore the vagaries of human development and social change. But this is not an experiment that I can support. For the continued health of a democracy that counts on the dedication of a prepared citizenry, the stakes are simply too high. If the results are not to our liking, it might not be so easy to reverse the experimental conditions.

IMPOLITE WORDS AND YOUTH CHARACTER FORMATION

In earlier writings, I have made the case that an unfortunate combination of cultural forces in contemporary society has obstructed the formation of moral commitments among many young people.[6] I identified two conditions in particular: a failure to communicate high moral standards to the young at a time in their lives when their character development requires unambiguous guidance; and the isolation (or worse, division) among people and institutions who are responsible for providing coherent guidance to the next generation.

Civil identity is a part of youth character formation. It develops—or does not develop—through many of the same processes that shape moral character. If we are to foster civil identity among today's young, we must start by understanding what has gone wrong in our efforts to guide young people's character formation. I will start with a story. It was told to me by a Washington, D.C., mother who called in to a National Public Radio program on which I recently spoke.

The week before, the mother received a note from her son's school. In her son's class, someone had been taking lunch money out of students' backpacks, and the authorities had just caught the culprit—her son. Distressed, the woman called the boy's teacher to see what she could do to make sure that the boy did not continue to steal. According to this parent, the teacher said something to this effect:

> Mrs. Jones, we sent you a note because we must keep you informed, but now we must ask you to stay out of this. We held a teacher's conference to decide what to do, and we are handling the situation in a professional manner. We are not calling your son's behavior "stealing." That would only embarrass him. It would make him think of himself as a thief. We have told your son that this is "uncooperative behavior." We have explained to your son that he will not be popular with the other students if he continues to act this way.

Mrs. Jones reported that the boy now dismisses her efforts to communicate with him about the matter. In fact, she suspected that he had "blown the whole thing off" without learning anything from it at all.

Now, *stealing* is an impolite word, carrying with it a moral accusation that indeed should embarrass anyone with a sense of right and wrong. But that, of course, is the point—it *is* a matter of right and wrong. If we remove the moral meaning behind it, its potential to evoke shame or guilt, the concept carries nothing more than an instrumental meaning. If you get caught stealing, you may get punished or become unpopular. If you don't get caught . . . well, so what? This is the opposite of moral education—in fact, it qualifies as moral *mis*education.

An essential part of moral education is reaffirming the emotional sense of moral regret that young people naturally feel when they harm another person or violate a fundamental societal standard. Every child is born with a capacity to feel upset when another person is harmed (empathy), with a capacity to feel outrage when a social standard is violated, and with a capacity to feel shame or guilt when he or she has done something wrong.[7] This is the emotional basis for the child's moral character; but it will quickly atrophy without the right kinds of feedback—in particular, guidance that supports the moral sense and shows how it can be applied to the range of social concerns that one encounters in human affairs.

Yet there is hesitancy today to assert the moral sense, or to use a moral language at all, in many homes and schools. There are several reasons for this: some adults worry that shaming children wounds their self-esteem; some believe that moral teaching does not belong in schools; some believe that there are no moral truths anyway, or that it is hypocritical to preach them to the young when so many adults ignore them, or that in a diverse society one person's moral truth is another's moral falsehood.

The result of this hesitancy is a prevailing, and debilitating, climate of moral uncertainty in many of the places where young people look to adults for guidance. In recent visits to schools I have been increasingly struck by how readily a school can be paralyzed by a common breach of standards such as cheating. Over the past few years, I have been called into several secondary schools—many of them elite—to help resolve cheating scandals. In every case, the ambivalence of the teaching staff about the moral meaning of the incident was palpable at the time of my arrival. Many, if not most, of the teachers publicly expressed the opinion that it was hard for them to hold students to a no-cheating standard in a society in which people cheat on taxes, the president cheats on his spouse, and so on. Many sympathized with the cheaters because the tests were somehow flawed, or because the cheaters had been acting out of loyalty to their friends by secretly sharing the information. It can take days of intense discussion, and some arm-twisting, to get the teaching community solidly behind the moral bases for a no-cheating standard—namely, that cheating is wrong because (1) it violates trust between teacher and student, (2) it gives students who cheat an unfair advantage over those who do not, (3) it encourages dishonest behavior, and (4) it undermines the academic integrity, codes of conduct, and social order of the school.

Adult solidarity on the side of clear moral standards is precisely what guides character formation in the young. I am not referring to an arbitrary, imposed set of commands regarding debatable issues but rather a sense of shared values concerning fundamental norms of human behavior: honesty, fairness, common decency, respect for legitimate authority, compassion, and the like. I have worked with parents from just about every ethnic group and socioeconomic background, and I have yet to encounter groups that do not want to see their children behave according to such standards. Nor, in my reading of the anthropological literature, have I found significant variation from these shared standards across cultures.[8]

After all, what society could long exist if it explicitly promoted, say, dishonesty rather than honesty in human communications, cruelty instead of compassion, or disrespect rather than respect for legitimate authority? One reason that moral standards are not arbitrary is that they are deeply functional, at least in the long term. Another reason that they are not arbitrary is that they reflect a consensus, a living tradition of past and present judgments, about what people in society consider to represent the good in human affairs.

The belief that moral standards are not arbitrary, that they reflect basic human truths *and therefore merit a sense of certainty*, is the essential message that must be passed down across the generations if the ethical center of society is to be preserved. This is, in large part, an emotional message: it engages the heart as well as the mind and fosters the sustained devotion to society that, as Durkheim originally noted, is the necessary prerequisite of all moral education.[9]

Yet this is precisely what has been missing from a culture that has come to favor moral relativism over moral certainty. And this culture is very much present in the classroom: although it may seem that the average schoolteacher is a long way from the literary and academic circles where postmodern thinking holds sway, today's intellectual trends have reached every corner. Our teachers have eyes and ears, they are bright and curious, and most are right in tune with the prevailing cultural notes. Moreover, many of the teachers, and especially the younger ones, have studied education in current programs that promote what I have described as an "anything-goes constructivism."[10] This approach (a bastardized version of Piaget's theory) stresses the importance of the child's autonomous discovery and discourages discipline, external feedback, and objective standards: in short, it is ideologically in sync with postmodernist views on cultural transmission in general and moral learning in particular. Not surprisingly, the great majority of the teachers I meet believe that young people must work out their own values, and they question whether there are any solid moral truths that they ought to impart to students.

In this climate of moral relativism, expressions of moral sentiments become not only impolite but dangerous—they may in fact become fighting words. A teacher's reprimand to a student, when phrased in a moral language of right and wrong, can and does lead straight to litigation in today's school world. A growing number of public schools in the United States are being sued by parents who believe that their children have been unfairly accused of a moral infraction.[11] I have seen this happen in a number of cases—often in matters related to honesty (cheating, lying to a teacher, forging excuses from a parent), but also in matters related to seriously harmful behavior (racial or ethnic slurs, harassment, violent assault).

It is hard to imagine a young person learning a firm moral code in a society that embraces no common values; and yet this is precisely the condition that we offer young people when moral instruction in the school is hesitant, haphazard, and wholly uncoordinated with the core values of the home and the community. The development of moral commitment among young people thrives on coherence in the social environment. Studies of adolescents from a variety of American cities and towns have found high degrees of prosocial behavior and low degrees of antisocial behavior among youngsters from communities that are characterized by widespread consensus in moral standards for young people.[12] The opposite is true of communities characterized by conflict, divisiveness, and lack of shared standards for the young. For a young person's moral character, a coherent set of social influences that reflect a set of core common values is a far more telling condition than affluent material conditions.

Young people need to hear clear and consistent messages from all the respected people in their lives if they are to take the messages to heart. Enduring moral commitments—ones with an emotional as well as a cognitive foundation—are acquired through repeated exposures to core standards in multiple settings. Even though children are born with emotional predispositions toward empathy and other moral orientations, social guidance is needed for further growth. To have a lasting impact, the guidance must come from many sources and take many forms. A student best learns honesty when a teacher explains why cheating undermines the academic mission, a parent demonstrates the importance of telling the truth for family solidarity, a sports coach discourages deceit because it defeats the purpose of fair competition, and a friend shows why a lie undermines the trust necessary for a close relationship. The student then acquires a living, felt sense of why honesty is important to all the human relationships that the student cares about.

Because of increased public awareness that many young people's moral and behavioral standards are not what they should be, character education programs have proliferated in schools across the United States. There are more than 150 independent organizations producing materials, and the market for the materials is growing yearly. I am generally in favor of this effort. At the very least, it makes a public statement to young people that morality once again is an educational priority for our society. (Moral education "came with the territory" for the first century of American schooling.)

Still, in reviewing these programs, I have had to conclude that their effectiveness is undermined by mixed moral messages that students receive in other parts of the school day.[13] It does little good for students to discuss the virtues of honesty in a class on character development when one period later an English teacher looks the other way while students copy material for their papers from an encyclopedia. The moral atmosphere that students actually experience in their schools—the manner of their teachers, the integrity of the school codes, the quality of the peer relationships that they form—has more influence on character growth than do academic programs.[14] This is especially the case when these programs are at odds with the culture of the school. In the end, the school culture will overwhelm any isolated effort, because it is the culture that shapes the social relationships that students participate in. It is through these relationships that students acquire the norms and values that they eventually make part of themselves. A student's moral identity is forged from the felt reality of many such relationships, and the moral identity will be strongest when the relationships tend to support the same high standards of behavior.

The same can be said for the student's positive affiliation with civil society: to be learned, it must be felt as well as imagined, and it must be fostered through multiple relationships that all show the student why such an affiliation should play an important part in the student's life goals. Civil identity is a part of moral identity, acquired through similar developmental processes.

In my previous writings, I have discussed the problem of nurturing moral identity in young people growing up in a culture infused with moral relativism.[15] Here I turn to the equally urgent problem of fostering civil identity among young people growing up in a time of skepticism about public life and public service. The civil disaffection felt by many of our young resembles their moral confusion in many ways: it has led to a similar sense of indirection—indeed, paralysis—and it feeds on the same general sense of skepticism and uncertainty. But there are additional cultural currents that must be directly addressed if our civic engagement problem is to be solved. In order to do so, I will need to invoke another impolite word, *patriotism*, or the love of one's own society.

PATRIOTISM, THE EMOTIONAL ANCHOR OF CIVIL IDENTITY

Intellectual trends, as I have noted, do not confine themselves to circles of intellectuals, at least not these days. In this era of universal education and mass communication, the most cutting-edge trends reach into every corner of our culture. This includes, of course, the public schoolroom, where teachers impart, for better or for worse, the particular ways that they interpret the ideas of the day.

In many intellectual circles, including much of education, the notion of patriotism has been out of fashion since at least the days of the Vietnam war. This may be understandable, at least when patriotism is confused (as it has been) with the kinds of chauvinistic and supermilitaristic passions that have spawned such evil nationalisms as National Socialism. It is not that patriotism itself has been abandoned: most educators no doubt feel a sense of it in their own lives. But it is rarely advocated as a legitimate goal of education or promoted as an essential virtue to pass on to the younger generation. Much like the notion of moral truth, it is honored in personal practice but held on tenterhooks when talked about in professional circles. Most often, it is not talked about, at least not without doubt and skepticism.

When patriotism does come up in education, the goal is usually to find ways to guard against its dangers. Many educators see patriotism as antithetical to a more global perspective on humanity and thus as the enemy of such humane conditions as peace and justice. Influential educators have urged schools to teach children to become "cosmopolitan" or "citizens of the world" rather than to identify themselves with any particular nation-state. One prominent advocate of cosmopolitan education is the University of Chicago professor Martha Nussbaum, whose work has been celebrated in academic reviews and the popular press alike. Nussbaum has written that we must avoid instilling in students an "irrational" patriotism "full of color and intensity and passion." She writes that "through cosmopolitan education, we learn more about ourselves." Nussbaum goes on to explain: "One of the greatest barriers to rational deliberation in politics is the unexamined feeling that our own preferences and ways are neutral and natural. An education that takes national boundaries as morally salient too often reinforces this kind of irrationality, by lending to what is an accident of history a false air of moral weight and glory. By looking at ourselves through the lens of the other, we come to see what in our practices is local and nonessential, what is more broadly or deeply shared. Our nation is appallingly ignorant of the rest of the world. I think that this means that it is also, in many crucial ways, ignorant of itself."[16] For such reasons, Nussbaum wonders why we would ever teach American students to see themselves first and foremost as U.S. citizens, with all the rights and responsibilities that would then accrue: "Most important, should they [our students] be taught that they are, above all, citizens of the United States, or should they instead be taught that they are, above all, citizens of a world of human beings, and that, while they happen to be situated in the United States, they have to share this world with citizens of other countries?"[17]

The posture that one simply "happens to be situated in the United States" seems about as far away from a sense of national affiliation as one can get. But Nussbaum is no more extreme in her distaste for U.S. (or any other) citizenship than are many other prominent educators today. In a well-received book called *Banal Nationalism*, the social scientist Michael Billig warns against all messages, explicit or symbolic, that communicate a sense of national identity across generations: "Banal," Billig writes, "does not imply benign. . . . In the case of the Western nation-states, banal nationalism can hardly be innocent: it is reproducing institutions which possess vast armaments."[18] Such sentiments have drawn criticism from some, yet they are by no means anomalous.[19] More to the present point, they are widely shared by teachers in the ranks of our public and private schools. In fact, in my own informal observations, they set the tone for much of what is taught in social studies curricula across the United States.[20]

Why should this be troublesome? After all, the notion of global citizenship is a benign one, especially in a world that is growing closer together every day. Moreover, spirited criticism of our own country is healthy, absolutely in line with the best parts of our democratic tradition. My concerns are not with the ideology or criticism per se but rather with their uses in educating the young. Here I will make two assertions, based upon my own understanding of the developmental needs of young people during their primary and secondary school years:

1. A positive emotional attachment to a particular community is a necessary condition for sustained civic engagement in that community. For full participatory citizenship in a democratic society, a student needs to develop a love for the particular society, including its historical legacy and cultural traditions.

2. The capacity for constructive criticism is an essential requirement for civic engagement in a democratic society; but in the course of intellectual develop-

ment, this capacity must build upon a prior sympathetic understanding of that which is being criticized.

My first assertion stems from the same developmental perspective that I have used to discuss moral commitment and character formation in general.[21] My argument is that consistent moral action requires commitment; commitment is a function of identity; and identity is the way that a person organizes all the personal identifications, ideas, and feelings that have continuing importance in the person's life. Hence the importance of fostering a positive emotional attachment to a community, a sense that "I care about the community in the way that I care about myself," if we are to expect sustained moral action on its behalf.

In order to understand a person's behavior, we must know not only what he or she believes but also how important that belief is to the person's sense of self—that is, why (or even whether) it is important for the person to act according to the belief. All our studies of moral behavior have shown that a person's answers to the second set of questions, pertaining to self-identity, prove to be the best predictor of the person's actual conduct.[22] And a person's emotional experience is a central part of the person's self-identity, implicated in every decision about "who I am" and "who I want to be."

On the matter of civic engagement and civil identity, psychological research has been thin to date, but recent writings in the philosophical literature support the argument that I am making here. Reacting to the idea of educating students according to the "cosmopolitan ideal of world citizenship," my colleague Eamonn Callan writes:

> The patriotic sentiment runs deep in many contemporary societies, and in its liberal form it can mitigate against the civic alienation and ethnic chauvinism that are among the most serious threats to the viability of mass democracy. If the sentiment is somewhat weakened or, worse still, remains strong but comes to be regarded as a civic bond divorced from the principles of universal justice, our loss may be great. The USA is a revealing case because even though patriotism has commonly been implicated in the worst of American history, it has also had no small role in the best. The struggle against slavery, the Civil Rights movement, and even oppositions to the Vietnam war were animated by a commitment to a universal justice. But the commitment was commonly mediated by a love of American democracy and its founding principles. To give up on the task of perpetuating that love from one generation to the next in the name of world citizenship is to forego the moral power of a live tradition for the charms of an imaginative construction.[23]

The "task of perpetuating that love from one generation to the next" is the responsibility of adults who raise and educate the young. It is the central mission of civic education, or at least it should be. Regrettably, present-day civics instruction in our schools is not taking up this task; and, in any case, schools alone could never succeed in "perpetuating that love" in the face of a hostile or indifferent culture. Just as a child's moral identity is forged through direct experiences in multiple social settings that together reflect a coherent set of standards, a child's civil identity can be acquired only in the course of many actual encounters, and reasonably congruent reflections on those encounters, that touch the child deeply.

My second assertion also indicates a developmental reality not widely recognized in today's educational practice: teachers can be as egocentric as their students.[24] Often in their instruction, teachers will emphasize the issues that they themselves find problematic and have worked through in their own thinking as adults. A prototypical case of this is the beginning professor who dwells on a specialized dissertation topic while lecturing undergraduates. I have complained about the way that this egocentric error has distorted much teaching today. As one example, teachers often try to spur children's creativity by urging them to ignore structure, forgetting that the most wildly creative geniuses in all fields begin by mastering their disciplines. (Picasso drew horses that looked just like horses when he was a child.) As another example, so much effort in the humanities is directed toward deconstructing texts for purposes of social criticism that students are never taught the truth and beauty of the text itself—that is, the reasons why readers have loved the text and why educators have believed it worth teaching to the next generation. In all teaching, the first effort must be to give students reasons to cherish the material enough to invest their attention in it and, eventually, to pursue it on their own. Without this prior positive investment of attention, any critical exercise will be pointless.

Students need a positive exposure to the history, cultural heritage, core values, and operating principles of their society if they are to become motivated to participate as citizens in that society. They need to acquire a love of their society, a sense of pride in its best traditions, an emotional affiliation with the broader community of state, a sense of patriotism in the benevolent and inclusive senses of that word, if they are to develop a civil identity. What is more, students need to be given a sympathetic introduction to the workings of a democracy if they are to become good critics of the democracy. All this must be done through action as well as words, in multiple contexts, and in ways that inspire students on the emotional as well as the intellectual plane.

What Our Schools Can Do

The problems that I have been describing are ideational in origin and emotional in effect. In a sentence, we have been failing to impart to children the kinds of inspiring messages that they need to hear in order to develop strong civic commitments and an enduring civil identity. By "inspiring messages" I mean knowledge about their society set in a context of appreciation for the best contributions of their society over time. In the United States, some obvious themes would be our traditions of democracy, liberty, opportunity, justice for all, pluralism, optimism, and generosity. Although such themes show up in our popular culture and mass communications, they are rarely emphasized in the systematic school instruction that many children receive every day. In my observations of present school practices, these positive themes most often are buried beneath critical perspectives on the damage that our society has done, or is doing, to sectors of humanity or the planet as a whole.

If children are to take such messages seriously, in ways that move them emotionally, they need to encounter the messages in multiple settings, coming away with a sense that the messages are authentic and fundamentally true. It is not that children cannot handle critical perspectives. In fact, it is essential for their intellectual development that they learn to handle complexity, and it is essential for their moral development for them to learn that there are shades of gray. But there is a time and a place for everything. When students are introduced to an idea, they can make sense of it only if it is presented in a coherent way. If it is a powerful idea that we hope that they will live by—an idea that reflects our deepest beliefs about goodness, truth, and beauty—it is all the more important to convey a sense that the idea is in fact a part of what it means to acquire the culture, to become a full participant in the society.

Do we, in our pluralistic society, have ideas that we can impart to the young in such a wholehearted way? The answer is yes, we do, although we do not always realize it. As I have written on many occasions, our moral universe is full of shared values: parents everywhere want their children to be honest, respectful, kind, responsible, law-abiding, fair-minded, and so on.[25] There are differences in emphasis and interpretation, but these differences pale in comparison to the commonalities. A 1999 Public Agenda survey of eight hundred parents living in the United States, for example, reveals high levels of agreement about what the parents want children to learn about America. One-quarter of the parents were foreign-born, but this made little or no difference in their perspectives on what messages to give children about U.S. citizenship. Among the findings of the Public Agenda survey are:

- Foreign-born and native-born parents, including whites, African Americans, and Hispanics, share a belief that the United States is a special country and, in a number of findings, express thankfulness for being here. They voice a new patriotism that is calm and inclusive.
- The chief components of the American ideal—identified by all groups with very strong majorities—are individual freedom and opportunity, combined with a commitment to tolerance and respect for others.
- Parents also express somewhat submerged fears that others—and sometimes they themselves—take the country for granted and that there is too much emphasis on "the things that divide us."
- Large numbers of both U.S.- and foreign-born parents expect the schools to teach all children about the ideals and history of the country.[26]

If the Public Agenda survey is accurate, parental values concerning U.S. citizenship may be poorly aligned with what our schools are teaching on the subject. This is by no means the only place that such a gap exists. I have written about similar misalignments in the areas of language learning, academic achievement, and behavioral standards. Bellah and his colleagues have attributed such gaps to the increasing tendency of modern schools to position themselves as enclaves of expertise, separate from their communities.[27] In my view, this kind of separation does children no favor in any area of their development: in intellectual areas, for example, students will become most motivated to learn when their family and friends support their academic achievement. In the areas of moral and civil identity, where the student's relationship to the community is itself the subject matter to be mastered, separation can be especially detrimental to growth. Even more costly is the discord that often accompanies separation.

In order to foster civil identity in our young, schools must join with their communities in the effort to impart to young people a sympathetic understanding of our democracy and a deeply felt love of their country. Now I am aware that when I write this, I risk being accused of trying to indoctrinate children by brainwashing them with a whitewashed picture of America. But whitewashing is not at all what I have in mind. For one thing, it is a necessary part of character education to teach about the mistakes that have been made and the problems that persist. It is never helpful to pretend that any person or society is perfect: a far more useful message for a child's character formation is that none of us is perfect but we can always do better if we try. For another thing, dissent is one of democracy's proudest traditions—and it can be taught that way, enhancing rather than decreasing respect for the nation's heritage.

The point is not to paint for children a falsely glowing picture of their country but rather to present the country's shortcomings within a positive frame-work—that is, in perspective of its noblest aspirations (whether or not fulfilled), traditions, attainments, and ideals. For fostering true understanding, context is all. Students rely on guidance from their teachers to provide a context of meaning for all the otherwise disconnected bits of information that the world throws at them. A landmark civil rights demonstration can be presented either as an indicator of our society's racism or as a sign that there have been people in our society who have been determined—and permitted by our democratic system of governance—to correct that racism. Which orientation is more likely to encourage students themselves to get involved in constructive civil action? Which is more likely to instill civic affiliation rather than cynicism and apathy?

Educational guidance that helps students find enduring reasons to devote themselves to their vital communities—national as well as local—will promote affiliation, civic engagement, and participatory citizenship. A truthful render-ing of a society's successes and failures can always be presented in a context of appreciation for the society's highest ideals. This is especially true for one of the world's great democracies.

What forms can this kind of guidance take? The most effective character education programs blend opportunities for constructive action with guided re-flection. Civics education should follow the same principle. Schools and com-munities must work together to create opportunities for young people to partici-pate in civic and political events at every level, from the school to the broader society. In the classroom, coursework should make connections between these lived experiences and the challenges faced by historical or present-day civic leaders. Within and beyond the classroom, young people should be given a sense of their own potential roles in the continuing drama of their society's search for a more exemplary democracy. This will require conveying to the young a firm faith in the fundamental mission of democratic governance as well as high expectations for young people's capacities to improve it once they have gained their own understanding and commitment.

ENDNOTES

1. "35% of High School Seniors Fail National Civics Test," *New York Times*, November 21, 1999.

2. James Youniss and Miranda Yates, *Community Service and Social Responsibility in Youth*. Chicago: University of Chicago Press, 1997.

3. See William Damon, *Greater Expectations*. New York: Free Press, 1995. In the aggregate, young people's behavior has grown increasingly uncivil year by year according to practically every indicator that we can muster: physical assault, verbal aggression, cheating, lying, stealing, sexual harassment, vandalism, drunkenness, discourtesy, and so on, down a panoply of major and minor assaults on the social fabric. Of

course, these are normative trends and do not apply to every young person, many of whom continue to be exemplary citizens in every sense. Our sensationalistic media focus on the most horrific (and, fortunately, still rare) examples of this trend, such as the Columbine school shootings, but the problem goes far beyond such atypical incidents.

4. Susan Verducci and William Damon, The outlooks of today's teens. In Richard Lerner and Jacqueline Lerner, eds., *Adolescents A to Z*. New York: Oxford University Press, forthcoming.

5. Doug McAdam, *Freedom Summer*. Oxford: Oxford University Press, 1990.

6. Damon, *Greater Expectations*.

7. William Damon, *The Moral Child*. New York: Free Press, 1990.

8. Richard Shweder et al., The cultural psychology of development: One mind, many mentalities. In William Damon, ed., *Handbook of Child Psychology*, vol. 1. New York: Wiley, 1998; Richard Shweder, Milpitra Mahapatra, and Joan Miller, Culture and moral development. In Jerome Kagan and Sharon Lamb, eds., *The Emergence of Morality in Young Children*. Chicago: University of Chicago Press, 1987.

9. Emile Durkheim, *Moral Education: A Study in the Theory and Application of the Sociology of Education*. New York: Free Press, 1961.

10. Damon, *Greater Expectations*.

11. I have heard varied estimates of this, as high as one-third in the past decade, but I have not been able to come up with a reliable figure.

12. Francis Ianni, *The Search for Structure: A Report on American Youth Today*. New York: Free Press, 1989.

13. William Damon and Anne Gregory, The youth charter: Towards the formation of adolescent moral identity, *Journal of Moral Education* 26 (1997).

14. As for moral education programs, by far the most effective are those that engage students directly in action, with subsequent opportunities for reflection: community service, for example, has proven to be one of the most reliable means of triggering positive change in students' values and commitments; see Youniss and Yates, *Community Service and Social Responsibility in Youth*. The reason, again, is that students respond to experiences that touch their emotions and senses of self in a firsthand way.

15. William Damon, *The Youth Charter: How Communities Can Work Together to Raise Standards for All Our Children*. New York: Free Press, 1997.

16. Martha Nussbaum, with respondents, *For Love of Country: Debating the Limits of Patriotism*. Boston: Beacon, 1996, p. 11.

17. Ibid., p. 6.

18. Michael Billig, *Banal Nationalism*. Thousand Oaks, CA: Sage, 1995, p. 7.

19. In the book of essays responding to Nussbaum's notion of a cosmopolitan education (Nussbaum, *For Love of Country*), several scholars ended up defending the benefits of loving one's country, though the defense was ambivalent in most cases. The most unambivalent defense came not from a scholar but from the poet Robert Pinsky, who found Nussbaum's cosmopolitan position "arid" and "sterile." Pinsky wrote that the cosmopolitan formulation "fails to respect the nature of patriotism and similar forms of love" (p. 88).

20. I know of no data on teachers' views on this matter, but I have discussed it with many whom I have met in my visits to schools in many parts of the United States. Also, I have had my own unintended litmus test: every now and then in a lecture or conversation, I introduce the idea of patriotism. It is, invariably, the least popular thing I say—and I tend to make controversial statements. In professional circles, I cannot count the number of times that friends and colleagues have counseled me to rethink the idea or, at the very least, to "find a different word."

21. Damon and Gregory, The youth charter.

22. Anne Colby and William Damon, *Some Do Care: Contemporary Lives of Moral Commitment*. New York: Free Press, 1992.

23. Eamonn Callan, Reply, *Studies in Philosophy and Education* 18 (1999).

24. Jean Piaget, *The Child's Conception of the World*. London: Kegan Paul, 1928.

25. Damon, *The Youth Charter*.

26. A Lot to Be Thankful For, a report from Public Agenda, 1999.

27. Robert N. Bellah, Richard Madsen, William M. Sullivan, Ann Swidler, and Steven M. Tipton, *The Good Society*. New York: Vintage, 1992.

***William Damon** is professor of education and director of the Stanford Center on Adolescence, Stanford University, California.

DISCUSSION QUESTIONS

1. What is Damon's evidence that "young people's current lack of dedication to broader civic purposes is unusual by any historical standards"? Would this still apply today?

2. Damon says that many young people lack national pride and a civic identity. Do contemporary youth have less national pride than previous generations or just a different way of expressing these feelings? Is this a positive or a negative for democracy?

3. Should schools teach more about what is right in America so young people are not so cynical regarding politics?

The Youth Challenge: Participating in Democracy

*by Alison Byrne Fields**

In the eyes of many who are concerned about the future of our democracy, we have a crisis on our hands. Young people between the ages of 18 and 30 are now the largest voting bloc in the United States: 43 million individuals making up 25 percent of the electorate.[1] Yet, despite the strength that comes in numbers, this group of Americans is choosing not to participate in the electoral process. Since the elections of 1972, when young people between the ages of 18 and 21 were first eligible to vote, youth voter turnout has dropped by at least 13 percent, a higher rate of decline than the rate for older voters.[2] In November 2002, with a number of pivotal electoral contests to be decided, less than 13 percent of young people were expected to show up on Election Day.[3] This lack of representation at the polls is having an impact: young people's issues and young people themselves are being virtually ignored by candidates.

It's difficult to deny that this is a problem: if young people made better use of their right to vote there could be significant changes in the current political landscape of the country. While the same candidates might be elected to office, the issues that these officials invest their time and energy in could become more reflective of the concerns of our youngest citizens. Federal funding for grant money for college tuition—as opposed to the student loans that saddle young people for years after graduation—could become a higher priority than prescription drug benefits for seniors.[4] At the very least the two issues might share the public policy stage. Perhaps there would be more third-party candidates in office as the result of young people's growing disdain for bipartisan politics.[5]

The reality is that younger citizens are not voting in large numbers. But maybe "the problem" is not as clear-cut as it initially seems. Too often, the low voter turnout among young Americans is taken as conclusive evidence that they are not engaged in creating social or political change. Or, even worse, that young people don't care about their country or their communities.

The truth is more complex. Cynthia Gibson, a program officer at Carnegie Corporation who focuses on the question of youth civic engagement, suggests that young people today may be the most engaged generation ever.[6] Young people are volunteering at higher numbers today than in previous generations.[7]

College students are protesting more than their parents, the baby-boomer generation, did. According to the UCLA Higher Education Research Institute's annual survey of college freshmen, participation in organized demonstrations grew to an all time high in 2001.[8] Across the country, college students have organized demonstrations against and in support of the wars in Afghanistan and Iraq, including students at Hampshire College who passed a resolution condemning the civilian death toll in the war on terrorism. Students at the University of Michigan have organized rallies and petitions in support of affirmative action. Resident advisors at the University of Massachusetts established the first-ever undergraduate employee union to secure better pay and improved work conditions for themselves. Students at Harvard University continued their efforts from the previous year, organizing protests to establish a "living wage" for campus food workers and janitors. The anti-sweatshop movement—which spread nationwide three years ago—continues to have an impact, with students at Florida State University challenging their administrators to join a watchdog group that enforces labor standards for companies that manufacture university apparel, a multimillion dollar industry. Other issues being addressed on campuses include the Israeli-Palestinian conflict, racism in higher education and funding for school facilities.[9] The protests at colleges and universities are coming from the right side of the political spectrum as well, with students responding to anti-globalization protests from the left with their own pro-globalization and pro-capitalism demonstrations.[10]

And it's not just college students. Kids in high school are fighting to establish gay-straight alliances. Young people in the Bay Area of California are taking on the juvenile justice system.[11] High school students in New York City are walking out of their classes to demonstrate their anger over a lack of funding for education.[12] Students in Massachusetts are boycotting standardized tests that they see as being unfair to students in underresourced school districts.

Youth activism is being manifested in other ways as well. Students are organizing their peers to get teen centers and skateboard parks built in urban and suburban communities across the country. While many schools are not teaching young people what they need to know about electoral participation, some schools *are* requiring students to give their time to their communities through service learning programs and community service.[13] Whether they are being directed into volunteer activities by their school or making their own decision to get involved, large numbers of young people see volunteering as a more viable alternative to other forms of civic and political participation. Young people are also using their power as savvy consumers to "punish" companies that choose to implement unsafe or unjust practices by organizing boycotts and are rewarding those companies that make a commitment to social responsibility with "buy-cotts," giving them their business and their loyalty.[14] Young people are working together across lines of ethnic and racial difference. They are finding innovative ways to express their ideas and organize their communities and are redefining for their generation what it means to be a responsible citizen. All the evidence points to the fact that young people *do* care. So is there really a problem here?

Yes—and the problem is the disconnect: young people do not think that the electoral process generates any "tangible" results, particularly when it comes to the issues that they care about most.[15] Without suggesting that there is a hier-archy—that voting is a more important thing to do than protesting or boycot-ting or organizing your community—young people who make the choice not to vote aren't taking advantage of all the tools for creating change that have been made available to them. And by not using all of these tools, they are prevent-ing themselves from being as effective as they could be in their pursuit of better communities and social and political reform.

MISSED CONNECTIONS

Over the past thirty years, voter turnout for young people between the ages of 18 and 24 has declined by approximately one-third, with a minor upswing in 1992.[16] The impact of this lack of electoral participation has been that political candidates are rarely taking younger citizens' issues into consideration. On a broader scale, young people's lack of electoral participation has ramifications for the overall future of our democracy. Voting isn't something that a young Ameri-can will inevitably "grow into," like a sweater that's too big in the shoulders. According to the Aspen Institute's Democracy and Citizenship Program, "If Americans establish a pattern of voting when they are young they will be more likely to continue that pattern as they grow older."[17] The opposite is true as well: today's young people will not automatically "mature" into voters as they transi-tion into different age cohorts, as studies of previous generations have shown.[18]

If, then, young people are clearly not participating in the electoral process in large numbers, what is the reason—or reasons—why? Unfortunately, there's no simple answer. For some, their status as nonvoters relates to a lack of in-formation or a lack of the necessary confidence to ask the kinds of questions that would help them find out what they need to know. Many young people, for example, don't know how, when, or where to register to vote because the information is not being offered to them in school or at home. They don't know how or where to vote. They may not even know who the candidates are or what they stand for as politicians. (It is a problem that many older voters have as well.

Political advertising rarely helps even the most motivated voter get a clear picture of where a candidate stands). Some young people don't vote because their parents never voted. It may never even occur to them that they should register and show up at the polls.

For a large number of young people, refraining from voting is a conscious decision, though their reasons vary. Some reject "the system" because of their belief that it is non-egalitarian or corrupt. They may view other forms of participation as being a better use of their time, if only, for example, because they can see more immediate and personal results. Others can't recognize that their vote might have a direct impact on their lives because the candidates are not discussing the issues that they care about on the Sunday morning news shows or, more importantly, on the shows or stations that young people are actually watching.

During the 2000 presidential election, Third Millennium, a national, non-partisan, nonprofit organization and Carnegie Corporation grantee, launched in July 1993 by young adults,[19] conducted an analysis of media buys by both major party presidential candidates. Although people over the age of 50 make up just under 37 percent of the population in this country, almost 64 percent of the candidate's ads were placed during programming where these older voters were the likely viewing audience. In contrast, while people between the ages of 18 and 34 make up 31 percent of the electorate, just over 14 percent of the political ads were aired during shows that younger voters—or potential younger voters—would likely be viewing.[20] So, for example, you were much more likely to catch sight of George W. Bush or Al Gore if you were tuned into 60 Minutes than if you were watching Friends.

This situation has been described many times before as a chicken-and-egg dilemma: young people don't vote because candidates don't discuss their issues and candidates don't discuss their issues because young people don't vote. "We've got a real disconnect between the rational strategies for candidates to win elections and good strategies for maintaining a healthy democracy," says Thomas Patterson, a political scientist at Harvard University.[21] Candidates target their messages, their resources, and their time toward voters who are most likely to turn out at the polls on Election Day. Young people, candidates justifiably believe, are not those voters.

While on staff at Rock the Vote during the 2000 elections, I clearly remember sitting in the audience at the second presidential debate at Wake Forest University in Winston-Salem, North Carolina. By that time, with John McCain[22] and Bill Bradley out of the race, the only candidate who seemed to me to be willing to take a stand on issues of relevance to young people was Ralph

Nader, and he wasn't being let in the front door. As members of the live audience, we had been instructed to keep as quiet as possible so that our reactions did not influence the outcome of the debate. I was sitting in a row with Gideon Yago, a member of MTV's "Choose or Lose" news team, and Jeff Chang, a hi-phop writer who, at the time, was covering politics for rap mogul Russell Simmons' 360HipHop.com. All three of us were invested, on both a personal and professional level, in whether or not the candidates mentioned young people. Professionally, we were looking for a story for the young audience that we were going to report back to. But, as members of that age group ourselves, we were tired of being pushed to the sidelines. When George W. Bush made a statement of concern about the number of uninsured young people just out of school and trying to start their professional lives, I had to restrain myself from making any noise. I was excited by the fact that—for even a few brief minutes—an issue of importance to young people was taking center spotlight on the public policy stage. Considering the fact that it may have been the only time that either of the candidates bothered to mention young people that night, for my colleagues and myself, it was the highlight of the debate.

WHO ARE THEY?

Who are the young men and women who collectively make up the group I've been calling "young people"? They're Generation Y (as opposed to X), they're the Millennials, the DotNets,[23] or Generation 9-11.[24] They were born between 1977 and 1987. The oldest were babies in the Reagan-Bush era. The youngest went to kindergarten around the time that Bill Clinton first walked into the Oval Office. The climate in which they have been raised has been influenced by the atmosphere of political cynicism generated by the Watergate scandal and perpetuated by the Iran-Contra hearings, Whitewater, and Monica Lewinsky (or Kenneth Starr—it depends on whom you ask). For those with access to computers, the Internet is a given and a resource for school research, entertainment and friendships. Community can be found in their neighborhood, among their school friends, or in an online chat room.[25] They download their music. They are savvy consumers, highly aware of their value to marketers. The majority of them identify neither as liberal nor conservative, preferring to identify as moderates. Those who are willing to align themselves with a major political party tend to be those who have more positive views about politics.[26] Regardless of these labels, young people, on the whole, are more socially tolerant than past generations and have higher levels of respect for the rights of gays and lesbians and immigrants. Their own racial diversity influences their willingness and ability to surmount racial and ethnic barriers in order to work together, as well as their desire to influence others to do the same.[27] By and large, they don't watch the news,[28] but they *were* tuned in on the morning of September 11, 2001. It was a day when their lives were shaken in much the same way that the lives of those belonging to previous generations were turned upside down by the assassinations of John F. Kennedy, Robert F. Kennedy, Martin Luther King, Jr. and Malcolm X or by the bombing of Pearl Harbor.

In the late 1960s, young people were confronted with a different kind of harsh reality when they, their friends, their brothers, their husbands and their boyfriends were being sent overseas to fight in the Vietnam War, a conflict that many of them did not understand or support. Many began asking why, if they were old enough to fight and die for their country, they were not old enough to vote and make decisions about who was making decisions about their lives. These young people chose to organize their peers—and appeal to older generations. It was this sentiment that eventually led to the ratification of the 26th amendment, giving people between the ages of 18 and 21 the right to vote.

I recently attended a discussion during which it was suggested that one of the distinctions between young people today and those of the baby boom generation is that the baby boomers had more respect for authority. Confronted with images of young people from the late 1960s and early 1970s—climbing over the fences at Woodstock, taking to the streets to oppose the war or to show their support for civil or women's rights—it is difficult to think of this group as being particularly mindful of authority. But perhaps there is something to this idea.

In the 1960s, when young Americans recognized that they were not being heard on an issue that was impacting their generation, they fought to gain the right to vote: they looked to the traditional political process as a mechanism for addressing their concerns. Today, young people have that same mechanism at their disposal but, lacking respect for the impact of the political process and for the authority of elected leaders, they choose to look elsewhere to find solutions for the issues that affect their lives.

In that first election after the 26th amendment was passed, American voters re-elected Richard Nixon to the presidency. Just a short time later, after the Watergate revelations, he became the first president forced to leave the White House under humiliating circumstances. In the following years there have been many more scandals and sensationalized events. Young people have seen their president's sex life plastered across their television screens. They have heard about elected officials accepting illegal campaign contributions and have seen a number of them resign in disgrace. They have watched major corporations and other monied interests hijack the political process by buying influence and power. In the last presidential election, young Americans saw our nation's leadership at the highest level come down to the question of whether or not a chad was dimpled, pregnant or hanging. They have heard candidates and elected officials tell them to "Just say no"—or suffer the consequences—while excusing their own former drug use as "youthful indiscretion." In this atmosphere it is not difficult to understand young people's distrust and their need to ask, "What exactly am I meant to respect?"

Where Do We Go from Here?

Those who are concerned with and committed to youth civic engagement are divided among themselves about which strategies are most effective for increasing engagement and about the outcomes that might actually constitute success. In other words, what does an engaged young person look like? Is he the high school student who volunteers at the soup kitchen every Saturday? How about the 18-year-old who is proudly wearing her red, white, and blue "I Voted" sticker on Election Day? What about the kids who chain themselves to the front door of the local Starbucks to protest globalization?

According to a recent report that synthesizes the literature and views of various constituencies and experts on these issues, the approaches to fostering youth civic engagement tend to fall into four general categories:[29]

1) **Civic Education.** Those who advocate for school-based civic education as a tool for increasing youth engagement believe that there is a need to develop innovative new courses that teach the "fundamental processes and instruments of democracy and government." They point out that as schools have de-emphasized civic education over the past thirty years, there has been a parallel decrease in young people's level of civic engagement over the same time period.[30] And many believe it is particularly necessary to provide civic education in both elementary and high school because a significant number of young people do not attend college. The discrepancy in voter turnout between college students and young people of the same age who do not go on to higher education emphasizes this need.[31] No matter when it is taught, advocates believe that a rich and relevant civic education curricula must be developed or students will be turned off and will be unable to see the connection between what is happening in the classroom and what is happening around them in the community and the broader world.

2) **Service-Leaning.** Service-learning is a form of civic education in which

"lessons from volunteer work are integrated into school work on democracy and public policy." Its advocates believe that the strategy encourages young people to get involved in their communities while helping them to make the connection to public policy and more long-term systemic change.[32] Proponents of this strategy also believe that through service-learning, students can be encouraged to make the leap from "simply reading and talking about democracy to actually participating in it."[33]

3) **Political Action, Advocacy, and Social/Community Change.** Those who are committed to increasing political action—particularly voter turnout—include the Youth Vote Coalition, which is focusing on trying to get candidates and elected officials to pay more attention to young people and their issues.[34] With the same goal in mind, the Aspen Institute's Democracy and Citizenship Program has developed a toolkit to better enable candidates to reach young voters with effective messages that might encourage them to make it to the polls.

Some of the suggested strategies for reaching young voters include committing to using a minimum level of resources to conduct outreach to young voters; learning how to relate issues to young people in a way that makes them relevant; taking electoral campaigns to where young people spend their time; and making information about campaigns available on web sites and in places where young people hang out with their friends. Finally, candidates are asked to come right out and ask young people to vote.[35] The strategy for both Youth Vote and the Democracy and Citizenship program is to transfer some of the onus onto candidates to address the issue of low youth voter turnout. Young people can no longer be the sole source of the blame.

4) **Youth Development.** Youth development experts view civic engagement as a developmental process—one in which developing a "strong sense of personal identity, responsibility, caring, compassion and tolerance" is an essential first step toward being engaged politically or at the community level. Youth development relies heavily on young people being directly involved in providing the solutions to their own disengagement, rather than a more "top-down" approach that blames young people rather than supports them as individuals with a wide range of assets and strengths.[36]

A growing number of experts believe that, in order to truly achieve the goal of ensuring that young people are participating in the democratic process, it is necessary for civic engagement advocates to work together to integrate their approaches. Combining strategies could also help to achieve greater consensus on what engagement looks like and might go a long way toward dismantling a hierarchy in which volunteering shows up on one end of the spectrum, nonviolent civil disobedience on the other, and both are considered to be just fine for the time being—until we can get young people to vote.

Young people who do consider themselves to be engaged and who do vote will tell you that having parents who talked about public affairs in the home or took them to the polls as children has increased their own interest and participation in politics. (The fact that previous generations' voter participation is in decline has, therefore, had a diminishing effect on the level of young people's participation.) In addition to having engaged parents, students who have been exposed to civic education in school report that it had a positive impact on them.[37] Having friends who participate can also be influential. Finally, for many young people, the mere fact that someone bothered to ask them to was enough of a reason to get involved—including myself. My own impetus for becoming interested in political change occurred when I was 15 years old and Father Richard Carderelli, the priest at my Catholic high school, asked me to attend a conference on nuclear disarmament being run by college students at Yale. His request instilled in me an amazing sense of pride and confidence because a man that I admired thought that I was important and capable enough to participate.

ACCEPTING THE CHALLENGE

Clearly, there is great concern on the part of many about the low numbers of young people who turn up at the polls on any given Election Day. But while it may be simply human nature to want young people to share the political values of preceding generations—at least as far as using the right to vote—perhaps the time has come to recognize that they are not participating in this seemingly fundamental aspect of democracy because, in their eyes, it does not help them to achieve the goals that they view as important: improving their communities and generating positive social and political change. To achieve these goals, young people, instead, are volunteering, organizing their communities, protesting, and boycotting in record numbers. Young people are using media and technology and working across lines of racial and ethnic difference to redefine what it means to be an engaged citizen in the 21st century.

The challenge, therefore, that we face as a society, is how we can help young Americans to link the issues that they care about with their desire to have a tangible impact on improving their world and help them see that their participation in our democracy can be the key to bringing about social and political change. How can we best provide them with the support that they need? How can we strengthen young people's effectiveness and help them to grow confident enough to take on new challenges? How can we influence candidates and others in positions of leadership to take up their portion of the responsibility for engaging youth in issues of social, civic and political importance?

There are other challenges at hand. If young people continue to reject the electoral process as a useless tool and retain their nonvoting behavior as they grow older, what impact will this have on the future of our democracy? How will the attitudes of today's young people influence their children's attitudes toward electoral participation?

Young people today are unique in their experiences and in their resulting approaches to creating stronger communities and political and social change. The time has come to commit ourselves—as a country and as a society—to making them, in every way possible, full partners in shaping the future of our democracy and our world.

ENDNOTES

1. Data from the Center for Information and Research on Civic Learning and Engagement (CIRCLE), as reported by the Youth Vote Coalition web site. www.youthvote.org/info/factsheet.htm.

2. Center for Information and Research on Civic Learning and Engagement (CIRCLE), Research and information: Political participation and voting. www.civicyouth.org/research/areas/pol_partic.htm.

3. Youth vote coalition, Terrorism, economy and crime weigh heaviest on minds of young voters. Balance of Congress may hang on efforts to turn out youth vote in November, September 30, 2002. www.youthvote.org/news/pressreleases/pr100302-oct3event.htm.

4. The average graduate of a four-year private institution, graduating with a B.A., has more than $17,000 in student loan debt. American Council on Education, How much student loan debt does the average student accumulate? 1999–2000 National Post-secondary Student Aid Study. www.acenet.edu/faq/viewInfo.cfm?faqID=21.

5. According to a survey conducted prior to the 2000 presidential elections, 64 percent of young people believe that the United States "should have a third major political party." Howard Fineman, Generation Y's first vote, *Newsweek*, July 17, 2000, page 26.

6. Cynthia Gibson, *From Inspiration to Participation: A Review of Perspectives on Youth Civic Engagement*. The Grantmaker Forum on Community and National Service, November 2001.

7. Scott Keeter et al., *The Civic and Political Health of the Nation: A Generational Portrait*. Center for Information and Research on Civic Learning and Engagement, September 19, 2002.

8. Higher Education Research Institute, College freshman more politically liberal than in the past, UCLA survey reveals, January 28, 2002. www.gseis.ucla.edu/heri/01_press_release.htm.

9. Toumani, et al., Protests that make the grade, *Mother Jones*, September/October 2002.

10. Tricia Cowen, Student activists: Still a strong force, *The Christian Science Monitor*, March 27, 2001, page 17.

11. William Wimsatt and Young Visionaries, *Utne Reader*, September 2002. www.utne.com/Youngvisionaries.

12. Miriam Markowitz, Stephen Baxter, and T. Eve Greenaway, 9.11-9.11: The Year in Youth Activism, *Wiretap*, September 10, 2002. www.wiretapmag.org/print.html?StoryID=14081&wiretap=yes.

13. Michael DeCourcy Hinds, Youth vote 2000: They'd rather volunteer, *Carnegie Reporter* 1 (Spring 2001). www.carnegie.org/reporter/02/vote2000/index.html.

14. Keeter, et al., *The Civic and Political Health of the Nation*.

15. Institute of Politics, *Campus Attitudes towards Politics and Public Service (CAPPS) Survey*. Harvard University, Kennedy School for Government, October 2001. www.ksg.harvard.edu/iop/2001-IOP-Survey.pdf.

16. Peter Levine and Mark Hugo, Youth voter turnout has declined, by any measure, Center for Information and Research on Civic Learning and Engagement (CIRCLE), September 2002.

17. Democracy and Citizenship Program, *30 Million Missing Voters: A Candidate's Toolkit for Reaching Young Americans*. Aspen Institute, 2000.

18. Carnegie Corporation of New York, The youth vote: Defining the problem and possible solutions, *Carnegie Reporter* (Spring 2001) 1, www.carnegie.org/reporter/02/vote2000/vote.html.

19. Third Millennium, Advocates for the Future. www.thirdmil.org.

20. Third Millennium, *Neglection 2000*. www.neglection2000.org.

21. Goldstein and Morin, Young voters' disengagement skews politics, *Washington Post*, October 20, 2002, page A1.

22. John McCain's appeal to young people was due in part to the fact that he was fighting the influence of "big money" in politics—a concern of young people because of its capacity to diminish their own power and influence. His appeal also resulted from his ability to tap into the concerns of both liberal and conservative young voters. Prior to the Republican presidential primary in California, I personally recall registering a number of young people who were switching their party affiliation from Democrat to Republican due to their desire to show their support for McCain.

23. Keeter et al., *The Civic and Political Health of the Nation*.

24. Kantrowitz and Naughton, Generation 9-11, *Newsweek*, November 12, 2001.

25. Keeter et al., *The Civic and Political Health of the Nation*.

26. Lake Snell Perry and Associates, The Tarrance Group, Inc., *Short Term Impacts, Long Term Opportunities: The Political and Civic Engagement of Young Adults in America*. Center for Information and Research in Civic Learning and Engagement (CIRCLE), 2002.

27. Higher Education Research Institute, College freshman more politically liberal than in the past.

28. Keeter et al., *The Civic and Political Health of the Nation*.

29. Gibson, *From Inspiration to Participation*.

30. Richard Niemi, Trends in political science as they relate to pre-college curriculum and teaching. Paper presented at the Social Science Education Consortium, Woods Hole, Massachusetts, 2000.

31. National Association of Secretaries of State, *New Millennium Survey: American Youth Attitudes on Politics, Citizenship, Government, and Voting*, Section four: Political socialization, 1998. www.stateofthevote.org/survey/sect4.htm.

32. Carnegie Corporation of New York, The youth vote: Defining the problem and possible solutions, 33. Gibson, *From Inspiration to Participation*.

34. Craig D'Entrone, Voting strategy: With traditional efforts to get young people to vote a dismal failure, organizers say it's time for a new approach, *Newsday*, November 1, 2000, Part II, page B6.

35. Democracy and Citizenship Program, *30 Million Missing Voters: A Candidate's Toolkit for Reaching Young Americans*. Aspen Institute. 2000.

36. Gibson, *From Inspiration to Participation*.

37. Keeter et al., *The Civic and Political Health of the Nation*.

*Alison Byrne Fields** is a writer and communications consultant who served as the creative director and chief strategist for Rock the Vote.

Fields, Alison Byrne. *The Youth Challenge: Participating in Democracy*. New York: Carnegie Corporation of New York, 2002.

Used by permission.

DISCUSSION QUESTIONS

1. What is the youth challenge that Fields presents, and does this pose a real problem for American politics?

2. Do young Americans not participate because politicians don't listen to young people, or because young people don't listen to politicians?

3. Is there evidence to support the claim that "young people today are the most engaged generation ever"?

Will Youth Rejuvenate the Patterns of Political Participation?

by Siyka Kovacheva*

The low numbers of young people voting in the European Parliament elec-tions in western Europe or in the local elections in central and eastern Europe, the decline in youth membership in such traditional institutions as political parties, trade unions and even youth organizations in north-western or south-east Europe in comparison with only fifteen or twenty years ago are all signs of accumulating problems in the realm of youth political participation. They are often interpreted as youth "disenfranchisement," "decline of social capital," young people's "de-politization," "social vulnerability," "marginalization," and "anomie."[1] Is this a trend toward a lasting youth disengagement from politics and society or a sign that these traditional forms are being replaced by new pat-terns of civic involvement invented by young people?

Research-based evidence of youth's non-involvement in politics is contro-versial and its evaluations debatable. One of the main reasons for the diverging visions of present-day political participation is the growing fragmentation and partiality of research perspectives. As Norris argues, while political scientists who remain uncritically trapped within 1960s concepts mourn eroding party membership, international relations scholars celebrate the birth of global civil society and communications researchers welcome the rise of Internet activism.[2] Methodological fallacies also contribute to this situation through the lack of truly longitudinal data series and, more importantly, through inadequate designs of comparative multi-country surveys. The latter often miss young people's own understandings and even, as O'Toole et al. point out, impose researchers' con-ceptions of politics and political participation upon respondents.[3] Comparative survey research tends to neglect the social context in which political participa-tion is set, and hence cannot fully conceive of and explain the differences in its forms.

For its part, youth policy at a European level regards youth political participa-tion with both concern and hope. The [European] Commission's White Paper "A New Impetus for European Youth" defines youth participation in public life as a priority of European and national youth policies.[4] The follow-up to the White Paper, together with the Council of Europe's Revised European Charter on the Participation of Young People in Local and Regional Life express growing anxiety about the hazards for the practice of youth active citizenship and firmly assert the crucial role of youth involvement in the process of democratization and European integration.[5] Young people's engagement in public life holds out great promises, but what social trends are conducive to, or impede, their fulfillment?

This chapter examines the development of the concept of participation from two main theoretical and research perspectives: political science and youth studies. It then addresses some significant challenges to youth participation in the new context of an enlarging Europe. On this basis it attempts to outline new avenues for the growing agenda of research into youth political participation.

The Changing Concept of Political Participation

Participation is not a static concept but has been recurring and changing with developments in social theory and research. The varying practices of civic engagement have also affected the ways in which participation has been understood and conceptualized.

One of the channels for elaborating the concept has been the broader theory of democracy and governance. Classic political concepts postulate participation as an integral part of a democratic system of governance. In the abundant literature on democracy there tend to be two basic understandings of citizen participation: a narrow and a broader understanding. The former limits civic participation to voting, and the latter provides a more substantial definition of the term, linking it to a broader range of citizens' involvement in politics.[6] While initially Dahl considers elections and political participation as two logically independent dimensions of democracy, later he combines them in a global measure of polyarchy.[7] For Dalton the success of democracy is largely measured by the public's participation in the process of decision making and responsiveness of the system to popular demands.[8] Multiparty elections are not the single prerequisite for democracy, as they can be used by the winning party to rule without respect to the law.[9] While they accept that the factors bringing democracy into existence are not the same as those for keeping it stable,[10] Rose, Mishler and Haerpfer stress the importance of popular support for democratization in central and Eastern Europe.[11] They perceive popular demands for freedom and democracy in post-communist societies as a guarantee against the establishment of undemocratic regimes.

Political theory offers various classifications of the forms of citizen participation in solving social problems.[12] The concept of the modes of democratic participation is highly relevant to the study of youth involvement in politics.[13] It distinguishes between conventional or institutional participation and unconventional or protest politics. The first mode confines participation to activities within established political institutions while the second is a direct action, outside institutions and confronting the political elite. Many studies show a growing diversification of the patterns of political participation.[14] Norris claims that political participation has undergone a significant transformation—from the involvement of interest groups to new social movements, from conventional repertoires to protest politics, and from state orientation to a multiplicity of target agencies, both non-profit and private.[15]

Modern developments in democratic theory link the rise of new patterns of political participation to post-materialism, civil society, and democratic governance. The post-materialist thesis links the changing dimensions of political participation to a cultural shift in society. Inglehart argues that social trends in postindustrial society have brought about the replacement of the old materialist values, associated with security and authority, by post-materialist values associated with a higher concern for the environment, human rights, gender equality, individual autonomy and self-expression.[16] For him, while voter turnout has declined together with support for the old-type hierarchical and bureaucratic organizations, younger generations have become more inclined to participate in issue politics, new social movements, transnational advocacy networks and other "elite challenging forms of political participation."[17] The strife for subjective well-being and higher quality of life leads to newer and non-traditional forms of self-expression in politics.

A useful conceptual tool for understanding the new forms of political participation is the theory of civil society and social capital. In the post-war era the systematic trend toward erosion in party identification is accompanied by the flourishing of various types of agencies and social networks, which encourage political participation: voluntary associations, community groups, and private organizations.[18] The social relations and horizontal links that arise among people form a social capital, which is the basis of citizens' public engagement. Despite the fact that these organizations are heterogeneous and not all of them directly target political power, they create "social networks, norms of reciprocity and trustworthiness,"[19] stimulating a shared concern for the public good which in turn influences political participation.

The development of social capital is closely linked to trust, which is understood as both general interpersonal trust and political trust, that is, confidence in institutions.[20] Being a significant prerequisite for collective action, trust and solidarity are not a constant value but differ among different regions in the world and different stages in the development of each society. Putnam considers that social trust and civic engagement have declined significantly in the United States toward the end of the twentieth century. In contrast with this interpretation, Salamon et al. argue, based on research evidence from twenty-two countries, for the rise of a global civil society, through a global associational revolution, a massive upsurge of organized voluntary activity in the unique sphere outside the state and the market.[21]

Fresh impetus for the concept of participation comes from the newly placed focus on governance in democratic theory. The United Nations Development Programme (UNDP) defines democratic governance as a system in which all people can participate in the debates and decisions that shape their lives. The participation of citizens, as well as that of political and economic actors, guarantees the systemic management of market, democracy and equity. The idea of governance developed from its limited understanding as the exercise of authority and control in the institutional economics school into the concept of participatory or joint governance.[22]

Joint governance creates a form of participatory democracy adapted to the present-day realities of global interdependence. Participatory democracy is not a substitute for representative democracy but acknowledges the need for more participation and accountability in global decision making.[23] Global governance based on participatory mechanisms is possible not only through interstate efforts but also through a global civil society, an alliance between the new and the old social movements. The anti- or alter-globalization protests dominated by young people represent an attempt to put powerful economic forces under social control. Sobhan states that the involuntary constraint on the sovereignty of decision making in the nation state can be overcome by giving a stake to all citizens in the outcomes of the globalization process, as well as by an increased participation of global civil-society groups in the workings of multilateral institutions.[24]

The new developments in the concept of participation from the perspective of political theory are strongly linked to the understanding of values and behaviors dominant among youth. Political science most often interprets youth as an age group, a cohort like others or at best the least experienced cohort. It is young people who are most likely to see politics as boring and irrelevant to their lives.[25] It is the youngest age group among eligible voters who are the least likely to vote in elections.[26] Youth is the age cohort predisposed to unconventional political participation.[27] Another interpretation of the specificity of youth, popular with political science researchers, is that of generation. According to Inglehart, the young generation is leading the way to the value change toward post-materialism in advanced societies.[28] Similarly, Putnam explains the decline in civic participation and social capital as a generation change.[29] Sinnott and Lyons identify age as an indicator of generational mobilization or demobilization.[30] They argue that different generations acquire habits of political participation or non-participation early in life and carry those habits forward into later life. This ties in with Mannheim's concept of generations.[31] Young people are influenced by the significant historic events which took place during their formative years—the period when they became politically aware.

THE EVOLUTION OF THE CONCEPT OF YOUTH PARTICIPATION

If age is a strong predictor of political behavior for political scientists who do not agree whether this is an age cohort or a generation effect, participation is a central concept in youth studies and has risen to the top of research and policy agendas.[32] In the youth field the idea has also evolved considerably, although following a different path.

The classical approach to the idea arises from the socialization theories of Eisenstadt and Coleman.[33] Parsons conceptualizes the participation of young people as their integration into the structure of society through internalizing dominant social norms.[34] The social position of youth is accomplished through their involvement in existing institutions and arrangements. Thus participation turns out to be more about controlling young people and regulating their activities in concordance with the requirements of the state system than about their autonomy or self-fulfillment. This understanding has been criticized as biased toward preserving the status quo, perceiving the young only as passive acceptants of adult values and practices.[35]

A later perspective has as its departure point the concept of citizenship as formulated by T. H. Marshall.[36] According to this concept, youth participation is seen as the problem of young people's access to the wide range of civil, political and social rights in a given community. Citizenship rights, gradually acquired during youth, and the transition to civil, political and social citizenship together produce the right to full participation in society. It is also about "belonging" to one's nation and having the responsibility to contribute to its well-being. Following T. H. Marshall's explanation of the relationship between citizenship and social class, as well as other dimensions of stratification (such as gender, race, ethnicity, etc.), the debate on citizenship links the concept of participation with the issues of social exclusion and inclusion. The notion of social participation of individuals and groups offers a framework for examining the opposite process of social exclusion.

Citizenship theory has important consequences for the understanding of political participation. The new understanding of citizenship envisages it not as a passive conferring of social rights and responsibilities but as their active appropriation by the groups previously excluded from them. Citizenship is a wider concept than a legal or civil status and is linked to people's willingness and ability to actively participate in society.[37] Also, citizenship is no longer limited to the structures of the nation state,[38] but is performed when citizens take responsibility in their relations to a wide range of private and public institutions. Applying the broader approach to citizenship, Roker and Eden develop a concept of constructive social participation. It encompasses various social actions: formal voluntary work, informal community networks, neighborliness, informal political action, awareness raising, altruistic acts, and caring work at home and in the community, through which young people "participate in their communities and influence policies and practices in the world around them."[39]

In the 1990s, the Council of Europe's European Steering Committee for Intergovernmental Co-operation in the Youth Field (CDEJ) developed a new proactive understanding of youth participation, postulating that "participation is not an aim in itself, but an approach to becoming an active citizen, [a means of] taking an active role both in the development of one's own environment and in European co-operation."[40] Such an approach was accepted in the design of the study of youth experiments in European Union member states.[41] The operational definition used in this study accepts Golubovic's ample interpretation: "power based on the possibility of exerting influence on the economic and social aspects of life in the broad community."[42]

Unlike the classic notions of youth participation as a passive process of development and integration into societal structures, youth researchers in communist Eastern Europe in the 1980s linked it to the concept of "juventization." Mahler and Mitev offered an understanding of youth as an active and committed group and described participation as a two-way process: interaction rather than integration, a development of both young people and society.[43] From this perspective young people were seen as the group who produced new values and who, through their active participation in social life, changed and "rejuvenated" society. The effect of youth participation was societal innovation. In the political context of the societies with one-party regimes, however, this concept was soon blended into the dominant constructs of the official ideology, leaving aside and subduing its critical dimension towards the status quo.

Breaking with the ideological myth about the "great mission of youth" in building the classless communist society, youth research under post-communism turned from the concept of "juventization" to "youth citizenship." Following T.H. Marshall, some authors shifted the conceptualization of participation back to the more passive notion of integration into existing social structures.[44] Others embraced a more proactive understanding, linking it to involvement in associational life and social capital more generally.[45] In a study of youth participation in Eastern Europe, Kovacheva implied a proactive, problem-solving approach to youth participation, perceiving it as the active involvement of young people in the social transformation of their societies.[46] Defining participation as youth initiatives to solve various social problems, the study examined the process of implementation of youth participation projects, focusing on three major indicators: a well-defined problem situation (acute and unjust conditions in need of changing); resources for participation (individual participants, group structures, influential allies) and outcomes (on individuals, organizations, community and society).

Youth research generally focuses on three basic forms of political participation:[47]
• involvement in institutional politics (elections, campaigns and membership);
• protest activities (demonstrations and new social movements);
• civic engagement (associative life, community participation, voluntary work).

There are new developments in all three forms brought about by young people—in the way they participate in election campaigns or launch protest demonstrations, act collectively in the community or on the global arena. Significant innovation might be sought in the realm of the third pattern, which expands the notion of political participation to encompass wider issues and arenas that have become foci of the particular demands of young people. Siurala defines these types of participation as "postmodern" types, including expressive, emotional, aesthetic, casual, virtual and digital participation.[48]

To explain young people's civic activities youth studies employ a more substantial definition of youth than that used by political science. From this perspective young people do not form just another age group in the population but a group with a specific social position in each society. Youth research offers at least three approaches to conceptualize youth: as a generation, as a life stage and as a social group. The first concept is similar to the one applied by political science, departing from Mannheim's seminal essay.[49] It is highly relevant in times of the rapid social changes Europe is enduring now.[50] The second approach starts from the social psychological specificity of this life stage—the search for self-identity—and explores the values that shape its consciousness.[51] The third understanding conceptualizes youth as a group in a process of transition from dependence into autonomy, while moving between the spheres of education and employment, from the parental home to an independent housing and family formation.[52]

The exploration of the new formative experiences in a transforming Europe at the bridge between the two centuries, the new points of identification in the globalizing world and the new social context in which youth transitions are made are all points of departure for a heuristic understanding of political participation.

YOUTH POLITICAL PARTICIPATION IN A CHANGING EUROPE: CHALLENGES TO DEMOCRACY

Conceptual debates in political science and youth studies have to consider various emerging trends in youth political participation in the context of an enlarging Europe. They pose significant challenges to the creation of a citizens' Europe and to democracy more generally. Many of them fully merit the interpretation of changing forms of youth political participation instead of its erosion.

While voting levels have started to decline in many European countries, this trend is not all-pervasive. When young people feel democratic development in their countries threatened, they enter the ballot boxes in great numbers, as in Bulgaria in 1997 and Slovakia in 1998. Youth participation in voting is usually high when combined with the other two forms of activities: unconventional and civic. Young people quickly mobilize around single issues, such as the spill from the Prestige oil tanker in Spain or the protests against the war in Iraq, which were particularly widespread in countries such as the United Kingdom and Spain, whose governments supported the war efforts. Political self-expression through the arts and sport, voicing environmental concerns, human rights, gay and lesbian politics, and consumer boycotts have spread to post-communist countries.[53] Youth in Nordic countries, and in Estonia, is playing a leading role in using the Internet for renovating the forms of institutional participation, for example contacting government officials, online consultations, and policy discussions.

The spread of consumerism among young people might be a serious challenge to their civic participation, as it presents a shift away from collective solidarity and ideological engagement. For Putnam, the civic disengagement observed in the United States of America has been the result of the trend towards the privatization of leisure, particularly among the young generation.[54] In central and eastern Europe, the anti-state connotation of leisure typical of the communist regimes no longer exists.[55] Whereas under communism youth consumption was rendered political by the oppressive state, which politicized and punished all youth autonomous activities aimed at self-expression, at present consumption is seen as being led by the market only and encouraged by the state. Some authors interpret the spectacular consumption of the affluent groups among youth as behavior that ignores politics and the rest of society.[56] Others explain this pursuit of pleasure by the encouragement of parents who try to open a generational umbrella over their offspring and provide them with fashionable clothes or the latest mobile phones, willingly limiting their own personal consumption.[57] However, it might also be seen as a form of new, more individualized and flexible political participation.[58]

Individualization is another global trend affecting the political participation of young people in Europe. Attitudinal surveys have documented the growing inclination to search for individual solutions and the dislike of collective action.[59] Not only opportunities but also risks are being fragmented.[60] One of the consequences of this trend is the widespread unwillingness among young people to participate in formal youth organizations with regular membership and routine activities. There is still a need for more flexible models of participatory microstructures that will appeal to young people in Europe.

It is not so much individualization as the continuing centralization of political and social life in many European regions—in south-western and most of Eastern Europe—which inhibits young people's experiences of participation in politics and civil society. The short-term financing of youth projects, the invisibility of youth initiatives in the regions, outside the metropolitan areas, the low level of co-operation within the third sector also contribute to young people's preferences for participation through more flexible and informal structures.[61]

Mobility in Europe usually enhances the civic engagement of youth, being a form of experiential learning from other cultures and institutions. While Western cities become more and more multicultural, the exposure of rural youth to "otherness" remains limited. Young people in the United Kingdom and in Mediterranean countries also have a low "European competence" in terms of experience and language skills.[62] For most young people, however, challenging racism and ethnic intolerance has come to the fore in their participatory actions. In Eastern Europe, a lot of the participatory potential of young people in the region is lost because of emigration. Youth emigration from South-Eastern and Eastern Europe is mostly for economic reasons—the wish to participate in

Western markets and welfare systems. At the same time, young emigrants are more disappointed and critical of the current situation in Bulgaria, Romania, Ukraine and Belarus, and more impatient with respect to their countries opening up to the West. The desire to leave is not a totally apolitical stand and might be interpreted as striving for individual integration in cases where the young are weary of the slow and ineffective efforts of their country's integration into the European community.[63]

The above trends in youth political participation arise from the changing experiences and predicaments faced by young people in Europe. Their efforts to solve current problems contribute to the rejuvenation of political participation by developing original participatory forms, and give fewer grounds to be interpreted as political disengagement or apathy of participation.

THE EMERGING AGENDA OF YOUTH PARTICIPATION RESEARCH

The short synopsis of the conceptual development in political science and youth studies, combined with the overview of emerging trends in youth participation, provides valuable insights into the mutual enriching of the two perspectives. This section focuses upon some issues that cast brighter spots in the mosaic of youth participation research.

The Concept of the Political

First of all, youth participation research needs to question the concept of the political in the same way as gender researchers have done previously by disputing the established border between the public and the private.[64] Youth researchers should go further and create a broader concept of politics relevant to young people's own definitions. More studies may add additional details but the overview of existing literature suggests that for young people politics encompasses not only those actions attempting to influence government policy but also issues of wider social concern. A political action is every action that challenges the established hierarchies of values and norms, institutions and authorities. Norris speaks about lifestyle politics, which breaks down the dividing line between the "social" and the "political" even further.[65]

The Scope of Political Participation

At the same time, and under the conditions of decentralization and globalization, political actions are not actions directed towards the nation state but also towards smaller and wider constituencies—towards regional and local communities, as well as those at European and global level. We need to widen our research coverage across the full range of national and cultural contexts and study participation patterns in the "consolidated democracies" of central Europe, the emerging democracies in south-eastern and north-eastern Europe to the "insecure democracies" further east in the Commonwealth of Independent States (CIS) countries.[66]

Youth research has to become more receptive to differences in young people's participation caused not only by European enlargement but also by the growth of social inequalities in the process of globalization and in the prolongation of the youth phase. Youth has long stopped being a short sip of happiness, which it was in pre-industrial Europe or indeed in the early decades of modern societies. Different groups among youth might have different definitions of politics and different forms of political expression.

The Forms of Participation

Researchers have to develop concepts that are more sensitive to the political aspects of such forms of youth participation as leisure activities. Stolle, Hooghe and Micheletti reveal the possible ethical and political repercussions of consumer behavior.[67] They see the political nature of such participation in the fact that young people's actions to boycott certain goods and services and buy others on moral grounds target issues, values and institutions that concern the authoritative allocation of values in society. De Leseleuc, Gleyse and Marcellini envision sport as a theatre of social concerns, which surpasses the practice of sport itself.[68] Sports such as cliff climbing present a symbolized and ritualized way of relating "one" to "another." It has a truly political mission—to create new civic links and integrate participants into a community. The cliff climbers construct "territories" which challenge the existing order of social relationships, the very political balance in society. Research should not underestimate the political implications of other types of leisure activities, of volunteering and social work, mobility and migration.

The Resources of Youth Participation

Political action is also not only the action structured through political institutions and non-governmental organizations (NGOs) but also involvement in less structured, looser networks and friendship circles, and even individual action, such as political consumerism. Inglehart points to the preference of younger generations for participation in loose, less hierarchical informal networks and various lifestyle-related sporadic mobilization efforts.[69] Stolle, Hooghe and Micheletti also stress young people's inclination to participate in less bureaucratic and hierarchical organizations or to pursue individualistic and unconventional action, such as political consumerism.[70]

The Internet has become another innovative resource for youth participation.[71] Until now it has been used mostly in advancing both traditional and unconventional forms of participation and new social movements: E-mail lobbying, networking, mobilizing, raising funds, recruiting supporters, communicating their message to the public. However, it is too early yet to predict what alternative avenues for political expression this resource is giving to young people.

The Methods of Studying Participation

We need to renovate our research methods to make them more sensitive to new trends in political participation. One avenue for such development is the collection of good quality data for comparative and intercultural analysis, which acknowledges variations across national, regional and local contexts in Europe. Another route is to widen the scope of research methods used to study youth participation patterns, which up to now seem to be dominated by quantitative designs. There should be more case studies of youth participation projects, in-depth interviews and group discussions, as well as representative surveys and multi-country comparative studies. Action research merits particular attention in the investigation of youth participation. The innovation potential of focus group interviews is particularly relevant to the study of young people's understanding and experience.[72] This methodology allows participants to present and argue concepts in their own terms in a more equal and democratic dialogue, avoiding dominance by the researcher.

Summing up the new developments in young people's political participation and studies thereof, we might argue that youth political participation has become an attractive concept in political theory and youth research, promising democratic innovation in society. It is also appealing to young people themselves as an effective way to influence social change in Europe. When studying participation, however, there should be a degree of caution against simplistic assumptions of participation being always "a good thing," because intolerance and xenophobia, terrorism, and the "ethnicization" of politics also occur among youth groups.

Whether youth is rejuvenating the forms of political participation is not only a theoretical question. Systematic research-based evidence will confirm or refute such a hypothesis. A more flexible and reflexive methodology will contribute to a better understanding of youth political participation. Only by developing and implementing a comprehensive research agenda can we provide a conclusive answer to the question about the forms and avenues for the renovation of participation and democracy.

ENDNOTES

1. The respective sources are M. Adsett, "Change in Political Era and Demographic Weight as Explanations of Youth 'Disenfranchisement'," *Journal of Youth Studies* 6 (2003): 247–264; Robert Putnam, *Bowling Alone: The Collapse and Revival of American Community* (New York: Simon and Schuster, 2000); Srdjan Vrcan, "Youth: Politics, Sub-politics and Anti-politics: The Case of Croatia Since the Mid-eighties," in *Flying Over or Falling Through the Cracks? Young People in the Risk Society*, eds. Blanka Tivadar and Mrvar Polona (Ljubljana: Office for Youth of the Republic of Slovenia, 2002); Arseniy Svynarenko, "National, Political and Cultural Identities of Youth: Tendencies in Post-Soviet Ukraine," in *Youth, Citizenship and Empowerment*, eds. Helena Helve and Claire Wallace (Aldershot, UK: Ashgate, 2001); and Marian Adnanes, "Social Upheavals, Anomie and Coping: Bulgarian Youth in the Nineties," in *Balkan Youth and Perception of the Other*, ed. Petar-Emil Mitev (Sofia: LIK, 2000).

2. Pippa Norris, *Democratic Phoenix: Reinventing Political Activism* (New York: Cambridge University Press, 2002).

3. Therese O'Toole et al., "Tuning Out or Left Out? Participation and Non-participation Among Young People," *Contemporary Politics* 9 (2003): 45–61.

4. EC Commission of the European Communities, *White Paper on a New Impetus for European Youth*, COM 681 final. Brussels: Commission of the European Communities, Directorate General for Education and Culture, 2001.

5. EC Commission of the European Communities, Follow-up to the White Paper on a New Impetus for European Youth: Proposed Common Objectives for the Participation and Information of Young People, in Response to the Council Resolution of 27 June 2000 Regarding the Framework of European Co-operation in the Youth Field, COM 184 final. Brussels: Commission of the European Communities, Directorate General for Education and Culture, 2003; Council of Europe, *Revised European Charter on the Participation of Young People in Local and Regional Life* (Strasbourg, France: Council of Europe, 2003).

6. Josef Schumpeter, *Capitalism, Socialism and Democracy* (London: Allen and Unwin, 1952); Juan Linz, "Totalitarian and Authoritarian Regimes," in *Handbook of Political Science*, Vol. 3, eds. Fred Greenshtein and Nelson Polsby (Reading, Mass.: Addison-Wesley, 1975).

7. Robert Dahl, *Polyarchy: Participation and Opposition* (New Haven: Yale University Press, 1971), 7; Robert Dahl, *Democracy and Its Critics* (New Haven: Yale University Press, 1989).

8. Russell Dalton, *Citizen Politics in Advanced Industrial Democracies* (Chatham, NJ: Chatham House, 1998).

9. Guillermo O'Donnell, "Delegative Democracy," *Journal of Democracy* 5 (1994): 55–69.

10. Dankwart Rustow, "Transitions to Democracy," *Comparative Politics* 2 (1970): 337–363.

11. Richard Rose, William Mishler, and Christian Haerpfer, *Democracy and Its Alternatives: Understanding Post-Communist Societies* (Baltimore: Johns Hopkins University Press, 1998).

12. Tom Bottomore, *Political Sociology* (Minneapolis: University of Minnesota Press, 1993); Sidney Verba, Norman Nie, and Jae-On Kim, *Participation and Political Equality: A Seven Nation Comparison* (New York: Cambridge University Press, 1978).

13. Max Kaase, "Mass Participation," in *Continuities in Political Action. A Longitudinal Study of Political Orientations in Three Western Democracies*, eds. M. Kent Jennings and Jan van Deth (Berlin and New York: Walter de Gruyter, 1990).

14. Steven Rosenstone and John Hansen, *Mobilization, Participation and Democracy in America* (New York: Macmillan, 1993); Nancy Burns, Kay Lehmann Schlozman, and Sidney Verba, *The Private Roots of Public Action* (Cambridge: Harvard University Press, 2001); Michele Micheletti, Andreas Follesdal, and Dietlind Stolle, *Politics, Products, and Markets: Exploring Political Consumerism Past and Present* (New Brunswick, NJ: Transaction Press, 2003).

15. Norris, *Democratic Phoenix.*

16. Ronald Inglehart, *Modernization and Postmodernization: Cultural, Economic and Political Change in 43 Societies* (Princeton: Princeton University Press, 1997).

17. Ibid. 296.

18. Russell Dalton and Martin Wattenberg, eds., *Parties without Partisans* (Oxford: Oxford University Press, 2000).

19. Putnam, *Bowling Alone,* 19.

20. Susan Pharr and Robert Putnam, *Disaffected Democracies: What's Troubling the Trilateral Countries?* (Princeton: Princeton University Press, 2000).

21. Lester Salamon et al., *Global Civil Society: Dimensions of the Nonprofit Sector* (Baltimore: Johns Hopkins Center for Civil Society Studies, 1999).

22. Francesca Beausang, "Democratising Global Governance: The Challenges of the World Social Forum," MOST Discussion Paper No. 59 (2002), http://www.unesco.org/most; John Kay, *Foundations of Corporate Success* (Oxford: Oxford University Press, 1996); UNESCO, *Governance and Democracy: UNESCO as an Ethical Organization and a Critical Think Tank* (Paris: UNESCO, 2001).

23. Gilberto Dupas, "The Logic of Globalisation: Tensions and Governability" *in Contemporary Society,* MOST Discussion Paper No. 52 (2001), http://www.unesco.org/ most/dsp52.htm

24. Rehman Sobhan, "The Impact of Globalisation on New and Restored Democracies," paper presented at the Fifth International Conference of New or Restored Democracies, Ulaanbaater, Mongolia, 2003, http://www.icnrd5-mongolia.mn/papers/paper7.pdf.

25. Clarissa White, Sara Bruce, and Jane Ritchie, *Young People's Politics: Political Interest and Engagement amongst 14- to 24-year-olds* (York, England: York Publishing Services, 2000).

26. Richard Sinnott and Pat Lyons, *Democratic Participation and Political Communication in Systems of Multi-level Governance.* Report prepared for the European Parliament Task Force on Voter Participation in 2004 elections to the European Parliament, 2003.

27. Dalton, *Citizen Politics in Advanced Industrial Democracies;* Kaase, "Mass Participation."

28. Inglehart, *Modernization and Postmodernization.*

29. Putnam, *Bowling Alone,* 19.

30. Sinnott and Lyons, *Democratic Participation.*

31. Karl Mannheim, "The Problem of Generations," in *Essays on the Sociology of Knowledge,* ed. P. Kecskemeti (London: Sage, 1952).

32. Lynn Chisholm and Siyka Kovacheva, *Exploring the European Youth Mosaic: The Social Situation of Young People in Europe* (Strasbourg, France: Council of Europe, 2002), 45.

33. Samuel Eisenstadt, "From Generation to Generation," in *The Sociology of Youth: Evolution and Revolution,* ed. Harry Silverstein (New York: Macmillan, 1965), 6; James Coleman, *The Adolescent Society* (Glencoe, IL: Free Press, 1961).

34. Talcott Parsons, *The Social System* (Glencoe, IL: Free Press, 1952).

35. Jürgen Hartmann and Sylvia Trnka, *Democratic Youth Participation in Society: A Concept Revisited* (Uppsala, Sweden: Uppsala University Press, 1985).

36. Thomas Marshall, *Citizenship and Social Class* (Cambridge: Cambridge University, 1952).

37. Peter Dwyer, *Responsibilities: Contesting Social Citizenship* (London: Policy Press, 2000).

38. Gerald Delanty, *Citizenship in a Global Age. Society, Culture, Politics* (Buckingham: Open University Press, 2000).

39. Debbie Roker and Karen Eden, *A Longitudinal Study of Young People's Involvement in Social Action.* Report to the ESRC (Award number: L 134 251 041) (2002).

40. CDEJ, *The Participation of Young People* (Strasbourg, France: Council of Europe Publishing, 1997), 45.

41. Eric Boukobza, *Keys to Participation: A Practitioner's Guide* (Strasbourg, France: Council of Europe Publishing, 1997).

42. Zagora Golubovic, "Worker Participation and Dealienation of Labour Relations," *Socioloski Pregled* 16 (1982): 1–10.

43. Fred Mahler, *Introducere in Juventologie* (Bucharest, 1983); English summary in IBYR-Newsletter No. 1/1984; Peter-Emil Mitev, "Sociology Facing Youth Problems," *Youth Problems* 34 (1982): 1–274.

44. Marshall, *Citizenship and Social Class*; Vladimir Chuprov, Julia Zubok, and Christopher Williams, *Youth in a Risk Society* (Moscow: Nauka, 2001); Mirjana Ule et al., *Social Vulnerability of Youth* (Ljubljana: Office for Youth of the Republic of Slovenia, 2000).

45. Ladislav Macháček, "Youth and Creation of Civil Society," in *Youth, Citizenship and Empowerment*, eds. Helena Helve and Claire Wallace (Aldershot, UK: Ashgate, 2001); Reingard Spannring, Clarie Wallace, and Christian Haerpfer, "Civic Participation Among Young People in Europe," in *Youth, Citizenship and Empowerment*, eds. Helena Helve and Claire Wallace (Aldershot, UK: Ashgate, 2001).

46. Siyka Kovacheva, *Keys to Youth Participation in Eastern Europe* (Strasbourg, France: Council of Europe, 2000).

47. Lynn Chisholm and Siyka Kovacheva, *Exploring the European Youth Mosaic: The Social Situation of Young People in Europe* (Strasbourg, France: Council of Europe, 2002).

48. Lasse Siurala, "Changing Forms of Youth Participation," paper presented at the Roundtable on new forms of youth participation, Biel, Switzerland, 2000, www.coe.fr/youth/research/participation.

49. Karl Mannheim, "The Problem of Generations," in *Essays on the Sociology of Knowledge*, ed. P. Kecskemeti (London: Sage, 1952).

50. Hank Becker, ed., *Dynamics of Cohort and Generation Research* (Amsterdam: Thesis Publishers, 1992); Victoria Semenova, "The Social Portrait of Generations," in *Russia in Transformation* (Moscow: Academia, 2002).

51. J. Cote, "The Role of Identity Capital in the Transition to Adulthood: The Individualisation Thesis Examined," *Journal of Youth Studies* 5 (2002): 117–134; Helena Helve, "Values, Worldviews and Gender Differences Among Young People," in *Youth and Life Management: Research Perspectives*, eds. Helena Helve and John Bynner (Helsinki: University Press, 1996).

52. John Bynner and Kenneth Roberts, *Youth and Work: Transitions to Employment in England and Germany* (London: Anglo-German Foundation, 1991); Claire Wallace and Siyka Kovacheva, *Youth in Society: The Construction and Deconstruction of Youth in East and West Europe* (London: Macmillan, 1998).

53. Kenneth Roberts and Bohdan Jung, *Poland's First Post-Communist Generation* (Aldershot, UK: Avebury, 1995); Ule et al., *Social Vulnerability of Youth*.

54. Putnam, *Bowling Alone*.

55. Wallace and Kovacheva, *Youth in Society*.

56. A. Meier, "'Jeunesse Doree'—Polarization Tendencies in an Emerging Capitalist Society on the Balkans," paper presented at the International Conference Non-violence and Dialogue Culture among the Younger Generation, Sofia, Bulgaria, 2002.

57. Mitev, "Sociology Facing Youth Problems."

58. Michele Micheletti, *Political Virtue and Shopping. Individuals, Consumerism, and Collective Action* (New York: Palgrave, 2003).

59. Maria Iacovou and Richard Berthoud, *Young People's Lives: A Map of Europe* (Colchester, UK: University of Essex, 2001); Siyka Kovacheva et al., "Democratic Culture and Political Involvement of Central/Eastern European Youth," in *Democratic Citizenship in Comparative Perspective*, ed. Martina Klicperova-Baker (San Diego, CA: San Diego State University, 2003); Macháček, "Youth and Creation of Civil Society."

60. Andrew Furlong, Barbara Stalder, and Anthony Azzopardi, *Vulnerable Youth. European Youth Trends 2000* (Strasbourg: Council of Europe Publishing, 2000).

61. Roker and Eden, *A Longitudinal Study*; Kovacheva, *Keys to Youth Participation*.

62. IARD, Study on the State of Young People and Youth Policy in Europe, final report for the Commission of the European Communities, Directorate General for Education and Culture, 2001, http://europe.eu.int/comm/education/youth/studies.html.

63. Siyka Kovacheva, "Emigration Attitudes of Bulgarian Students," in *Balkan Youth and Perception of the Other*, ed. Peter-Emil Mitev (Sofia, Bulgaria: LIK, 2000).

64. Janet Siltanen and Michelle Stanworth, *Women and the Public Sphere* (London: Routledge and Kegan Paul, 1984); Victoria Goddard, ed., *Gender, Agency and Change* (London: Routledge, 2000.)

65. Norris, *Democratic Phoenix*.

66. Christian Haerpfer, "A New Index of Democracy: The Democratisation of Mass Public in Five Central European Countries," unpublished manuscript. Vienna: Institute of Advanced Studies, 2001.

67. Dietlind Stolle, Marc Hooghe, and Michele Micheletti, "Political Consumerism: A New Phenomenon of Political Participation?" paper presented at the ECPR Joint Sessions, Edinburgh, 2003.

68. Eric De Leseleuc, Jacques Gleyse, and Anne Marcellini, "The Practice of Sport as Political Expression? Rock Climbing at Claret, France." *International Sociology* 17 (2002): 73–90.

69. Inglehart, *Modernization and Postmodernization*.

70. Stolle, Hooghe, and Micheletti, "Political Consumerism."

71. Norris, *Democratic Phoenix*.

72. J. Brannen et al., eds., *Young Europeans: Work and Family Life: Futures in Transition* (London: Routledge, 2002); O'Toole et al., "Tuning Out or Left Out?"

*Siyka Kovacheva** is director of the New Europe Centre for Regional Studies in Plovdiv, Bulgaria, and associate professor of sociology at the University of Plovdiv.

Siyka Kovacheva. "Will Youth Rejuvenate the Patterns of Political Participation," in Joerg Frobrig, ed., *Revisiting Youth Participation: Challenges for Research and Democratic Practice in Europe*. Strasbourg, France: Council of Europe, 2005. © Council of Europe.

Used by permission.

DISCUSSION QUESTIONS

1. Why are young people participating in different political activities than their parents, and does this improve or lessen their influence on politics?

2. If you were trying to influence the government, what method of political participation would you use, and why?

3. Is the situation of youth participation in the United States different from the experience of European youth?

Part 2:
The Decline in Electoral Participation

Even with the surge of interest in the 2008 U.S. presidential elections, nearly 40 percent of the eligible public stayed home on Election Day. A similar pattern of declining turnout in elections has occurred in almost all advanced industrial democracies. Research on these trends generally finds that turnout has decreased the most among the young, and this is the theme of the three essays in this section. Martin Wattenberg's "Electoral Turnout: The New Generation Gap" focuses on the decline in election turnout in the United States, which he attributes to the political apathy of youth who were raised in a new media environment where celebrity matters more than information. If young people will not change, and he is not optimistic that they will, his provocative solution is to make voting mandatory for all citizens. In "Youth Turnout in Europe," Eva Anduiza presents evidence that a similar pattern of decreasing election turnout is increasing in European democracies, and again the young are leading this decline. She suggests that the structure of the electoral system and the politicization of youth are important predictors of youth turnout in elections. Finally, in "The Young Vote: Engaging America's Youth in the 2008 Elections and Beyond," Cali Carlin offers a different perspective. She suggests that the problem of decreasing electoral participation does not lie solely with the young but also reflects the unwillingness or inability of political elites to engage the changing values and citizenship norms of the young. For her, the solution is not that young people should change, but that politics needs to better understand their new citizens and respond to them. Since elections are so important in selecting government leaders, the decline of turnout and the ways to address this decline are central themes in the current debates about youth and political engagement.

Electoral Turnout: The New Generation Gap

*by Martin P. Wattenberg**

In November of 1998 I did not vote. Like many of my fellow baby-boomers, I was relatively nonchalant about failing to participate. In my own mind, I felt that I had a pretty good excuse. About a week before the election my father had undergone heart bypass surgery. I had flown across the country on short notice to be there, and the thought of getting an absentee ballot before I left California was not something that crossed my mind. (By the time I arrived on the East Coast it was too late to request an absentee ballot by mail, but I later realized I could have requested one in person just before I left.) Ironically, I was able to keep a few commitments on election day to do radio interviews on the topic of non-voting by simply emailing the producers that I would be at a different phone number. The fact that I wasn't voting that day came up a couple times on the air and led to further interesting discussion, but no real embarrassment on my part.

My father, by contrast, took a different view regarding not voting. He had just gotten out of the hospital a couple of days before the election, and had scarcely been able to walk 10 yards outside the house, but nevertheless said on Tuesday morning that he wanted to be driven to the polls. This idea did not sound so wise to me under the circumstances. I proposed an alternative: given that my parents were going to vote for different candidates for Governor, I suggested that neither one vote rather than going to the trouble of canceling each other out. This suggestion met with resistance from both my parents, who reminded me that there were many offices on the ballot besides Governor and that they probably would agree on some of them. Yet, they acknowledged that without the use of a wheelchair it would be very difficult for my father to make it from the curb to the High School gym where their community votes. We agreed that I would first go to the polling place and see if there was a wheelchair there. When I returned from my scouting trip I reported that the biggest problem we'd be up against was competition for the wheelchair—there were an awful lot of very elderly people there. But all went well, and as I waited for my parents to punch their ballots it occurred to me that the average age of the people then voting around them was clearly above retirement age. When I mentioned this observation on the way out, my mother replied that elderly people naturally realize they have a lot at stake on election day.

The fact that young people are so much less likely to vote is now so readily apparent that it hardly takes a Ph.D. in Political Science to notice it when observing activity at a typical polling place. In the summer of 1998, a Chinese delegation observing a primary election in Georgia expressed amazement that so few people had shown up at the polls, and particularly noted that very few young people had cast ballots. Xu Liugen, the leader of the delegation, summarized his observations to the Associated Press as follows: "I would have some doubts about the representativeness of those who are elected. Why such a low interest? Why don't the young people come to the polls?"[1]

To understand America's current turnout problems, one must answer the questions posed by Xu Liugen. My father's insistence that he really wanted to vote, my casual baby-boomer attitude, and the outright political apathy I frequently see among today's college students are apparently all representative of current generational attitudes toward voting. How, when, and why these generational differences developed are the challenging questions that this paper seeks to address.

A COMPARATIVE PERSPECTIVE

The phenomenon of relatively low turnout among young people is one that has drawn attention from political analysts in many countries. Recently, the International Institute for Democracy and Electoral Assistance (IDEA) issued a report showing problem to be common throughout the democratic world, and described various voter education programs targeted at young people that countries have adopted to try to combat it.[2] The data presented in the IDEA report are less than ideal for the task, however. They are derived from a hodgepodge of studies that differ widely in terms of the time elapsed since the last election, and some refer to a nation's most important election whereas others do not. Fortunately, the Comparative Study of Electoral Systems project (CSES) now provides an ideal set of comparable national election studies from which generational differences can be assessed.

Unlike the almost unique tendency of Americans with lower degrees of education to be substantially less likely to vote, the United States does not stand out so dramatically in terms of a generation gap in electoral participation. Table 1 shows that among the advanced industrialized democracies included in the CSES thus far, Americans under the age of thirty report the second-lowest level of turnout, with only Swiss youth turning out at lower rates. The largest turnout gap between the young and the old is found in Japan, but the United Kingdom, USA, Japan and Switzerland are not far behind in this respect. Overall, the problem of getting young people to the polls is fairly common. Leaving aside the Australian case, where compulsory election attendance eliminates any substantial turnout rate differences, people under 30 are at least 10 percent less likely to vote in 7 out of the 9 cases.

Table 1. Turnout by Age in Advanced Industrialized Democracies in Recent Years (%)

	18–29	30–44	45–64	65+	Difference between < 30 and >65
Japan	55	82	89	92	-37
United Kingdom	55	67	81	87	-32
USA	53	72	80	84	-31
Switzerland	46	56	75	76	-30
New Zealand*	76	83	90	94	-18
Norway	73	85	94	90	-17
Germany	86	92	95	97	-11
Spain	85	90	92	93	-8
Netherlands	88	91	92	94	-6
Australia	98	99	99	100	-2

Note: * New Zealand data were validated by checking the public records of participation by the respondents.

Source: Comparative Study of Electoral Systems; 2001 British Election Study; 2000 American National Election Study. Validated New Zealand data provided by Jack Vowles.

It might be thought that young people today, having grown up in an age free of nuclear threats and the Cold War, are satisfied with the way that democracy is working and are therefore less concerned about participating than previous generations. The cross-national data do not support this theory, however. Of the ten countries represented in Table 1, young people report significantly higher rates of satisfaction with how democracy is working compared with senior citizens in just two—New Zealand and the Netherlands. In three other countries there was no significant difference, and in five countries those under thirty expressed a substantially higher rate of dissatisfaction. Given that the relationship between turnout and dissatisfaction with democracy is not that strong, one shouldn't jump to the conclusion that many young people are abstaining from the electoral process because they are alienated. But the theory that young people are not voting because they are satisfied can be ruled out.

Of course, there is nothing in the CSES data to indicate that declining turnout rates in advanced industrial democracies are due to increasing levels of non-voting among young people. The simple cross-sectional data shown here could be due to life-cycle and/or generational factors; time series data would be necessary to sort this out. Thus far, such research has been done on Canada and Japan;[3] findings indicate strong generational effects in the decline of turnout in these countries. In the United States, a wealth of comparable data over time exists, making it possible to investigate this question in detail.

The Political Know-Nothing Generation

There is little doubt that life-cycle factors play at least some role in explaining the low turnout rates of young people in the United States. National surveys over the last half century have consistently found that electoral participation tends to increase with age. Benjamin Highton and Raymond Wolfinger outline a series of major life changes that young people commonly go through, each of which might make it less likely for them to vote while they sort out their lives.[4] Their analysis of the 1996 Census turnout dataset, however, demonstrates that only a small portion of the age differential in turnout can be accounted for by such lifestyle transitions.

A more general reason that may explain some of the steady rise in turnout rates throughout the life cycle is what Donald Green and Ron Shachar call "consuetude."[5] They write that "an act may be said to be subject to consuetude if, other things being equal, merely engaging in the activity today makes it more likely that one will engage in the same activity in the future."[6] Their analysis of the NES panel surveys shows that people are more likely to vote if they have voted in the previous election, even after a host of individual factors that typically predict turnout are controlled for. People who vote regularly learn to feel comfortable with the activity, they argue. And given that American ballots are extraordinarily long and complicated by international standards, this familiarity is likely to be of special importance in the United States. Furthermore, because Americans are asked to vote so often, the process of doing so repeatedly eventually leads to what Green and Shachar describe as an attitude that going to the polls is "what people like me do on election day."[7] The story at the outset of this paper about my father insisting on voting reflects just such an attitude; obviously young people need time to develop this feeling.

The problems of youth turnout in America today, however, go well beyond the normal life-cycle factors. An analyst looking at the various data from 1972, when eighteen- to twenty-one-year-olds were first enfranchised, could have reasonably concluded that young people were interested in politics, but many just hadn't yet got around to clearing the registration hurdles and getting into the habit of voting. Today, the situation is clearly different. A tremendous gap has opened up between the young and the elderly on measures of political interest, media consumption about politics, political knowledge, and, of course, turnout.

The high level of political apathy among young people today is unexpected given that their educational achievement levels are so high. Even those who have made it into college are expressing remarkably little concern for politics. A yearly nationwide study of college freshmen recently found that among the class of 2002 only 26 percent said that "keeping up with politics" was an important priority for them, compared with 58 percent among the class of 1970—their parents' generation.[8] If one looks more broadly at all people under the age of thirty, the NES data on "following what's going on in government and public affairs" displays a striking decline in political attentiveness among young people since 1964. Table 2 shows that from 1964 through 1976 there was little difference between those under thirty and those over sixty-five in terms of this measure of general political interest, with young people actually showing a bit more interest in 1968 and 1972. Since 1980, however, the youngest voting-age citizens have consistently expressed the least interest in public affairs by a substantial margin. The 2000 survey findings, in particular, mark a new low in political interest among young people. Only 33 percent of respondents under thirty said they followed government and public affairs most or some of the time; among senior citizens, the figure was 73 percent. As expected, campaign interest was also at a new low for young people in 2000—only 11 percent said they were very interested in the campaign as opposed to 39 percent among the elderly.

Table 2. General Interest in Public Affairs in the United States by Age, 1964–2000

	18–29	30–44	45–64	65+	Difference between < 30 and >65
1964	56	67	64	63	-7
1968	58	60	63	53	+5
1972	65	68	67	62	+3
1976	58	67	70	65	-7
1980	48	56	62	64	-16
1984	50	57	62	64	-14
1988	46	54	58	63	-17
1992	53	60	65	65	-12
1996	45	51	64	64	-19
2000	38	50	60	64	-26

Note: There are four possible response categories to the general political interest question: hardly at all, only now and then, some of the time, and most of the time. These four response categories have been recoded as follows: hardly at all = 0; only now and then = 33; some of the time = 66; most of the time = 100. Cell entries are averages for each age group.

Source: American National Election Studies.

Why young people today are not interested in public affairs is a difficult question to answer. Since I started asking my students for their opinion on this nearly a decade ago, I have gotten more possible answers than I ever could have dreamed of. Typically, the first response I get is something to the effect that politics just hasn't affected their generation the way it did previous generations. Certainly, today's youth have not had any policy touch their lives the way the draft and the Vietnam War affected their parents, or the way Medicare has benefitted their grandparents. Mark Gray and I asked a question regarding people's perceptions of this in our post-2000 election survey of 4 Southern California counties. The question went as follows: "Some of the issues discussed during the campaigns for the November election directly related to policies affecting people of your generation. Do you think that politicians pay too much attention to these issues, about the right amount or too little?" Sixty-two percent of respondents under the age of 30 said "too little," 21 percent said "about the right amount," and 9 percent said "too much." The percentages for those 65 and over were 33, 41, and 11 percent, respectively.

However, I believe that the cause of young people's apathy runs much deeper than a sense that the issues aren't relevant to them and that the politicians ignore them. Central to any generational hypothesis are changes in socialization experiences. For the last two decades, young people have been socialized in a rapidly changing media environment that has been radically different from that experienced by the past couple of generations. Political Scientists were slow to realize the impact of television—as late as 1980 there was surprisingly little literature on this subject. Today, a similar shortcoming is the lack of research concerning how the shift from broadcasting to narrowcasting has dramatically altered how much exposure a young adult has received to politics while growing up. The first major networks—ABC, NBC, and CBS—chose to use the term "broadcasting" in the names of their companies because their signal was being sent out to a broad audience. As long as these networks dominated the industry, each would have to deal with general topics that the public as a whole was concerned with, such as politics and government. But with the development of cable TV, market segmentation has taken hold. Sports buffs can watch ESPN all day, music buffs can tune to MTV or VH1, history buffs can go to the History Channel, and so forth. Rather than appealing to a general audience, channels such as ESPN, MTV, and C-SPAN focus on a narrow particular interest. Hence, their mission has often been termed "narrowcasting," rather than the traditional "broadcasting." This is even more true for Web sites, which require far less in start-up costs than a television channel and hence can be successful with a very small and specific audience.

Because of the narrowcasting revolution, today's youth have grown up in an environment in which public affairs news has not been as readily visible as it has been in the past. It has become particularly difficult to convince members of a generation that has channel surfed all their lives that politics really does matter. Major political events were once shared national experiences. The current generation of young adults is the first to grow up in a media environment in which there are few such shared experiences. When CBS, NBC, and ABC dominated the airwaves, their blanket coverage of presidential speeches, political conventions, and presidential debates sometimes left little else to watch on

TV. As channels have proliferated over the last two decades, though, it has become much easier to avoid exposure to politics altogether by simply grabbing the remote control. Whereas President Nixon got an average rating of 50 for his televised addresses to the nation (meaning that half the population was watching), President Clinton averaged only about 30 in his first term.[9] Political conventions, which once received more television coverage than the Summer Olympics, have been relegated to an hour per night, and even this highly condensed coverage gets poor ratings. The presidential debates of 1996 and 2000 drew respectable average ratings of 28, but this was only half the typical level of viewers drawn by debates held between 1960 and 1980. In sum, young people today have never known a time when most citizens paid attention to major political events. This is one of the key reasons why so many of them have yet to get into the habit of following and participating in politics.

More specifically, one key media consumption habit that young people have not developed is reading the daily newspaper. As Teixeria shows, newspaper reading is particularly predictive of who votes, even after controlling for a host of demographic and attitudinal variables.[10] Table 3 displays percentages of people reading campaign stories in the newspaper since 1960 by age group. From 1960 to 1976, there was no consistent difference in this measure between the youngest and oldest citizens. Since 1980, though, those under thirty have been substantially less likely to pick up a newspaper and read about the presidential race. In both 1996 and 2000, senior citizens were more than twice as likely to say they had read campaign articles in newspapers as those under thirty.

Table 3. Percent Reading Newspapers about the Campaign by Age, 1960–2000

	18–29	30–44	45–64	65+	Difference between < 30 and >65
1960	84	80	81	74	+10
1964	75	80	80	77	-2
1968	68	81	76	72	-4
1972	49	59	62	61	-11
1976	68	78	77	70	-2
1980	56	78	76	72	-16
1984	62	77	77	70	-8
1988*	35	47	57	57	-22
1992	35	50	57	60	-25
1996	28	39	52	60	-32
2000	27	35	48	56	-29

Note: *major change in question format occurred here.

Source: American National Election Studies.

Because of the media environment that young people have been socialized in, they have learned much less about politics than their elders. The current pattern of political knowledge increasing with age has become well known in recent years.

But it was not always that way. The 1964 and 2000 National Election Studies each contain a substantial battery of political knowledge questions that enable this point to be clearly demonstrated. Table 4 shows the percentage of correct answers to eight questions in 1964 and nine questions in 2000 by age category. (Because the level of difficulty of the questions differed somewhat, one should only examine the differences within a year and not necessarily infer that political knowledge as a whole has gone down.) In 1964, there was virtually no pattern by age, with those under 30 actually scoring 5 percent higher on this test than senior citizens. By contrast, in 2000 young people provided the correct answer to only one out of every three questions, whereas people over 65 were correct half the time. Regardless of whether the question concerned identifying current political leaders, information about the presidential candidates, or partisan control of the Congress, the result was the same: young people were less knowledgeable than the elderly.

Table 4. Age and Political Knowledge: 1964 and 2000 Compared

	1964	2000
18-29	66	34
30-44	71	43
45-64	69	51
65+	61	50

Note: Entries are based on the percentage of accurate responses to a series of 8 questions in 1964 and 9 questions in 2000. In 1964, respondents were given credit for knowing that Goldwater was from Arizona, Johnson was from Texas, Goldwater and Johnson were Protestants, Democrats had the majority in Congress both before and after the election, Johnson had supported civil rights legislation, and Goldwater had opposed it. In 2000, respondents were given credit for knowing that Bush was from Texas, Gore was from Tennessee, Republicans had the majority in the House and Senate before the election, Lieberman was Jewish, and for identifying William Rehnquist, Tony Blair, Janet Reno, and Trent Lott.

Source: 1964 and 2000 National Election Studies.

Given that today's youth has not been exposed to politics through the broadcasting of national shared experiences, the label of the "know-nothing generation" ought to be considered descriptive, not pejorative. It is not their fault. But nevertheless, the consequences are real and important. Thomas Jefferson once said that there has never been, nor ever will be, a people who are politically ignorant and free. If this is indeed the case, write Stephen Bennett and Eric Rademacher, then "we can legitimately wonder what the future holds if Xers remain as uninformed as they are about government and public affairs."[11] Although this worry may well be an overreaction, important consequences ensue when citizens lack political information. In *What Americans Know About Politics and Why It Matters*, Michael Delli Carpini and Scott Keeter make a strong case for the importance of staying informed about public affairs.[12] Political knowledge, they argue: 1) fosters civic virtues, such as political tolerance; 2) helps citizens to identify what policies would truly benefit them and to incorporate this information in their voting behavior; and 3) promotes active participation in politics. It is certainly the case that lacking information about politics in comparison with their elders, fewer young Americans are heading to the polls compared with previous generations—a development that has pulled the nationwide turnout rate down substantially in recent years.

THE AGE-TURNOUT RELATIONSHIP OVER TIME AND IN DIFFERENT TYPES OF ELECTIONS

The standard source for information on the precise relationship between age and turnout in the United States has long been that displayed in Wolfinger and Rosenstone's (1980) classic work based on 1972 data.[13] These data are displayed in Table 5, along with comparable data from the 1996 Census survey. There have been several striking changes in the age-turnout pattern. The data for ages 18 to 60 show a noticeable decline in turnout from 1972 to 1996; importantly, the rate of decline increases as one moves downwards in age. In contrast, it is readily apparent that turnout has actually gone up for ages 66 and above. Political Scientists used to write that the frailties of old age led to a decline in turnout after one became eligible for Social Security; now an examination of the Census survey data shows that such a decline occurs only after 80 years of age. The greater access to medical care provided to today's seniors must surely be given some of the credit for this change. Because senior citizens can perceive personal benefits from government programs like Medicare it is therefore particularly easy for them to believe that politics does indeed make a difference.

Table 5. Age and Turnout Percentage in Presidential Elections: 1972 and 1996 Compared

	1972	1996
18–24	49.6	32.4
25–30	58.4	40.3
31–35	62.2	47.1
36–40	65.1	54.1
41–45	68.5	58.5
46–50	70.8	62.6
51–55	71.5	63.2
56–60	71.0	66.9
61–65	70.0	68.7
66–70	69.5	70.9
71–75	65.2	69.4
76–80	61.0	68.1
81+	46.2	56.1

Note: All figures are percentages.
Source: U.S. Census Bureau Studies.

This phenomenon can also be seen in public records of turnout rates by age in primaries and special elections. Table 6 presents data on such elections from a variety of U.S. localities that have posted such information on the Internet. These percentages are based on registered voters only, because the local election officials who compiled the data are strictly interested in who on their registration rolls has turned out. If one were to take into account the lower registration rates of young people, then the generational differences would be even greater. The results just for registered voters, however, are disturbing enough. Young registrants, being more likely to be Independents, rarely participate in primaries. Their single-digit primary participation is dwarfed by margins ranging from 4:1 to 12:1 in the localities shown in Table 6. Young people are thus taking a very small part in the choosing of party nominees. The situation with regard to special elections held to decide referenda questions does not seem to be quite as bad. Nevertheless, it is clear that separating such policy decisions from high-salience elections gives extra weight to the opinions of the elderly, who are much more likely to turn out in such circumstances.

Table 6. Turnout Among Registered Voters by Age in Special Elections and Primaries for Various Counties and States (%)

	Pierce County, Washington State 1999 referendum		Alaska 1999 referendum		Johnson County, Kansas 2000 primary
18–25	26.3	18–24	22.3	18–24	3.2
26–35	40.2	25–34	27.9	25–39	15.0
36–50	60.4	35–54	45.4	40–59	44.8
51–65	76.8	55–64	56.3	60+	37.0
66+	81.4	65+	61.8	–	–
	Brevard County, Florida 1st 1998 primary		Tri-County, Oregon 1998 primary		South Carolina 2000 primary
18–29	5.5	18–29	10.0	18–21	8.8
30–39	13.8	30–39	19.0	22–44	11.0
40–49	19.3	40–49	32.9	45–64	23.9
50–59	24.0	50–59	44.2	65+	31.1
60–69	29.7	60–69	58.8	–	–
70–79	30.5	70–79	66.0	–	–
80+	23.6	–	–	–	–

Source: Composed from secretary of state websites in each state.

WHY LOW YOUTH TURNOUT MATTERS

Although many young people seem to think it doesn't matter if they don't vote, it does. Harold Lasswell wrote many years ago that "Politics is who gets what, when, and how." As long as young people have low rates of participation in the electoral process, then they should expect to be getting relatively little of whatever there is to get from government. Yet, until they start showing up in greater numbers at the polls, there will be little incentive for politicians to focus on programs that will help them. Politicians are not fools; they know who their customers are. Why should they worry about young nonvoters any more than the makers of denture cream worry about people with healthy teeth?

Of course, most everyone can look forward to getting older eventually. Those who were neglected in the 2000 presidential campaign will probably be seriously courted in the campaign of 2040. From this perspective, it could be argued that most people will one day get the chance to be heard in the electoral process and to reap the political benefits. Such a perspective, however, assumes that there are not generational differences in attitudes that can influence the course of public policy. Who gets what does not just involve material goods, but has also been increasingly about basic non-material values in recent years. Ronald Inglehart has documented a shift from materialist to post-materialist values throughout the advanced industrialized world, which has been largely driven by generational change and replacement.[14]

Table 7. Young vs. Elderly Opinion on the Issues in the 1990s

	Under 30	65 and over
Liberal	23	11
Moderate	25	28
Conservative	26	31
Don't know	27	29
Favor government help to get people jobs	35	19
In-between	19	23
People must get ahead on their own	35	43
Don't know	11	16
Favor more government spending for things like education and health care	39	21
In-between	22	30
Prefer less domestic spending	23	30
Don't know	16	19
Favor increased spending for public schools	80	54
Same	17	41
Want decreased school spending	3	6
Favor increased spending to protect the environment	61	41
Same	34	53
Want decreased environmental spending	5	6
Favor equal role for women	67	44
In-between	15	20
Women's place is in the home	14	25
Don't know	4	12
Never permit abortion	11	14
OK for rape, incest, health	28	34
OK for other reasons	15	14
Abortion should be a matter of personal choice	45	36
Don't know	1	3

Note: All figures are percentages.

Source: Combined data from the 1992–1998 National Election Studies.

There are indeed sharp differences between younger and older Americans on both material and non-material issue questions, as displayed in Table 7. In order to have plenty of cases for analysis, data from the 1992 through 1998 National Election Studies were combined, yielding 1,526 respondents under the age of 30 and 1,252 respondents who were at least 65. As expected, young people are substantially more supportive of government spending that would particularly help them, such as for public schools and jobs programs. Roughly similar differences in terms of magnitude can also be found for value questions. Young people are more in favor of spending to protect the environment, an equal role for women in society, and abortion rights. In terms of general ideological labeling, young people are virtually as likely to say they are liberals as conservatives on the ideological scale, whereas among senior citizens conservatives outnumber liberals by 20 percent. In sum, if young people had turnout rates equal to those of older people, voting behavior and public policy would probably be shifted noticeably to the left.

CONCLUSION

It is not young people's fault that they have not been exposed much to politics while growing up and hence are less informed about politics than previous generations. Their low turnout rates are understandable in light of their unique socialization experience.

American politicians are not really to blame for this inequitable pattern of generational representation, either. They didn't consciously try to create a situation that would greatly benefit older people. It is only natural for them to study who has voted in the past and to focus on these people, thereby leaving most young adults out of the picture. But if politicians were to ponder the principles universally valued in any democracy they might be moved to try to address this problem. If official election observers in a third world country noticed that older people were three times as likely as younger people to vote, they would no doubt call this fact to the attention of local authorities, and suggest there an imbalance ought to be looked into.

A well-established democracy like the United States ironically has fewer options than a third world country for dealing with such a problem. In a new democracy, for example, it would be easier to change the electoral system to facilitate the emergence of a party that would particularly appeal to young people. It seems unlikely, however, that there will ever be any serious consideration of changing the single-member district system in the United States. A strong independent candidacy, such as that of Ross Perot in 1992, may emerge from time to time to energize young people a bit, but an enduring viable third party is nowhere on the horizon. Of course, nothing precludes one of the existing two major parties from strongly targeting this large block of unmobilized young adults. Given young people's opinions on policy questions, however, there is little reason to expect the Republicans to do so. And the Democrats, having spent decades building up their image as creators and protectors of Social Security and Medicare, would find it difficult to switch gears and try to make themselves the party of the young.

It would theoretically be easier to make additions to the modern television campaign so that everyone, especially young people, would be more likely to be exposed to the discussion of the issues. In 1992, the presidential candidates were suddenly everywhere on the television dial, appearing on MTV, the Nashville Network, the "Arsenio Hall Show," and many forums. Voters seemed to like the idea of candidates cutting through the journalistic filters and talking to them on programs they regularly watched. This election marked the only one since 1960 when turnout went up substantially, a pattern that was especially evident among young people. Such broad-based exposure for the candidates needs to be somehow institutionalized for the narrowcasting age.

Although the solution to the new generation gap in voting participation in the United States is going to be difficult to find, the consequences for the present are readily apparent. Major issues that affect young adults are not even making it on to the public agenda, and young people's opinions on the issues are not being faithfully represented through the political process.

ENDNOTES

1. June Preston, "Chinese Observers Slam U.S. Voter Turnout," Associated Press, August 12, 1998.

2. International Institute for Democracy and Electoral Assistance, *Youth Voter Participation: Involving Today's Young in Tomorrow's Democracy* (Stockholm: International IDEA, 1999).

3. Andre Blais, Elisabeth Gidengil, Neil Nevitte, and Richard Nadeau, "The Evolving Nature of Non-voting: Evidence from Canada." Paper prepared for delivery at the Annual Meeting of the American Political Science Association, 2001; Karen Cox and John Creighton Campbell, "Generational Change or Periodic Fluctuation? Age and Political Attitudes in the US and Japan." Paper prepared for delivery at the annual meeting of the American Political Science Association, 2001.

4. Benjamin Highton and Raymond Wolfinger, "The First Seven Years of the Political Life Cycle," *American Journal of Political Science* 45 (2001): 202–209.

5. Donald Green and Ron Shachar, "Habit Formation and Political Behaviour: Evidence of Consuetude in Voter Behaviour," *British Journal of Political Science* 30 (2000): 561–573.

6. Green and Shachar, "Habit Formation and Political Behaviour," 562.

7. Ibid.

8. George Edwards, Martin Wattenberg, and Robert Lineberry, *Government in America*, 10th ed. (New York: Longman, 2002), 3.

9. Samuel Kernell, *Going Public: New Strategies of Presidential Leadership*, 3rd ed. (Washington, DC: Congressional Quarterly Press, 1997), 132.

10. Ruy Teixeira, *The Disappearing American Vote* (Washington, DC: Brookings Institution Press, 1992).

11. Stephen Bennett and Eric Rademacher, "The Age of Indifference Revisited: Patterns of Political Interest, Media Exposure, and Knowledge Among Generation X," in *After the Boom: The Politics of Generation X*, eds. Stephen Craig and Stephen Earl Bennett (Lanham, MD: Rowman and Littlefield, 1997), 39.

12. Michael Delli Carpini and Scott Keeter, *What Americans Know about Politics and Why It Matters* (New Haven, CT: Yale University Press, 1996), chap. 6.

13. Raymond Wolfinger and Steven Rosenstone, *Who Votes?* (New Haven: Yale University Press, 1980).

14. Ronald Inglehart, *Modernization and Postmodernization: Cultural, Economic and Political Change in 43 Societies* (Princeton: Princeton University Press, 1997).

Martin P. Wattenberg is professor of political science at the University of California, Irvine.

Martin P. Wattenberg. "Electoral Turnout: The New Generation Gap." *Journal of Elections, Public Opinion and Parties Review* 13 (2003): 159–173.

DISCUSSION QUESTIONS

1. If young people fail to vote, don't they lose their best opportunity to affect the issues that concern them most?

2. How much political knowledge do citizens need to make choices that represent their interests? Are the knowledge tests discussed by Wattenberg an appropriate measure of the necessary knowledge?

3. What suggestions does Wattenberg offer to increase youth turnout? How effective do you think these changes would be?

Youth Turnout in Europe

by Eva Anduiza*

This chapter analyses youth turnout in European national parliamentary elections. It seeks to provide answers to the following questions: Is the level of turnout always lower for the youngest age groups of the electorate? If so, why is this the case? Which factors explain the participation rates of young citizens? To what extent are low youth turnout rates responsible for turnout decline in elections?

Before addressing these issues, it is worth looking at average turnout rates in Europe and their evolution over time.[1] On average, between 1945 and 2009, 77 out of 100 voters participated in parliamentary elections. However, there are quite a few remarkable variations from this general pattern. Countries vary to a large degree in their average turnout rates and in changes in turnout over time. Eastern European countries and Switzerland tend to have low turnout levels, between 50 and 70 percent. Northern European countries like Belgium, the Netherlands, Germany, or the Scandinavian nations—except Finland—tend to have high turnout levels, averaging over 85 percent.

Turnout has dropped significantly, particularly during the last two decades. Between the 1940s and the 1980s, average turnout in Europe exceeded 80 percent of the electorate. However, in the 1990s the average dropped below 75 percent and fell to 67 percent in the 2000s. The fact that Eastern European countries have started to vote in competitive elections in the 1990s with low participation rates explains some of this turnout decline. However, it is remarkable how turnout has plummeted, decreasing by more than 10 points (and often by more than 15) between the 1990s and the 2000s in a large majority of these countries (Bulgaria, the Czech Republic, Latvia, Lithuania, Poland, Romania, Slovakia, Slovenia, and Ukraine). In Croatia and Estonia this decline has been more moderate. Only Hungary and the Russian Federation have experienced an increase, although slight.

In older European democracies turnout has also declined in the last two decades. In most of the nations this decline is between 5 and 10 percentage points, but in some cases it surpasses reaches over 10 points (see for instance Portugal or the United Kingdom). In Belgium, Denmark, and the Netherlands the decline is relatively minor. Only Spain and Switzerland show no decline in the 2000s. In the case of Switzerland the major decline had already occurred in the 1980s, after women were given the right to vote and many older women entered the electorate who had no history of voting.

As we will see later in the chapter, one of the main explanations given for this rather generalized turnout decline is the fact that younger cohorts are voting less. Let us then have a look at what the relationship between age and turnout is like.

THE RELATIONSHIP BETWEEN AGE AND TURNOUT

Almost every study of the relationship between age and electoral participation shows a similar pattern in Figure 1.[2] Turnout is usually low among the youngest age category (just over 60 percent in the selected countries); then increases more or less markedly as voters approach middle age, with the highest levels of participation among people between 60 and 69 years of age (about 87 percent); and finally decreases slightly for the eldest age group. We call this a positive curvilinear relationship. Note that in this case we are using survey data, which generally overestimates turnout levels for two main reasons. On the one hand, voters are more likely to be sampled and to answer surveys on politics. On the other hand, voting is a socially desirable behavior that encourages over-reporting (people may be reluctant to acknowledge that they have not complied with a civic duty such as voting in elections).

Figure 1. Turnout by Age in Europe

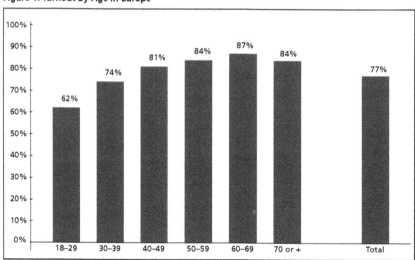

Source: 2007–08 European Social Survey round 4 including 31 European countries. Data are weighted so that each country has an equal weight, N=50,685.

If we look at what happens within each specific country (data not shown), the picture may vary slightly, but it is essentially confirmed. In some nations the relationship between age and turnout is very pronounced, in others it is weaker. But it is always there. As a consequence, young voters between 18 and 29 show the lowest level of turnout in all countries, with the exception of Belgium and Poland, where the elderly have similar rates. Then turnout increases as age increases. The maximum level of turnout may be reached at different ages depending on the country: early (40 to 49 years of age) in Poland or Turkey, later in other countries such as Belgium, the Czech Republic, Denmark, Greece, the Netherlands, Portugal, Sweden, and Ukraine, typically between 60 and 69 years of age. Then, turnout declines slightly among older citizens. Beyond a certain age, voters start having limitations associated with old age and retirement: less social networks due to retirement, health or mobility problems, etc. Thus, the decline in electoral participation among elderly people can be interpreted as the result of decreasing resources and less integration in social and community life. In addition, it can also be due to the lower educational level of elderly groups. Traditionally, researchers have argued that highest levels of education increase the level of electoral participation.

Since those between 18- and 29-years-old now are probably the cohort with the highest level of education in history, we would expect them to vote more. It is puzzling to see how the generation with the highest level of formal education and probably the highest levels of accessible political information drops out from voting in such a generalized way, showing below average turnout rates in every country analyzed. Some authors have warned about the political disenfranchisement of the young.[3] When younger citizens do not participate in elections, it is less likely that their preferences will be taken into account within the political system. This is a problem for political equality, just as it is when there are lower turnout levels of people with low levels of resources.[4] However, the turnout level of young people varies quite significantly among countries, which means that youth turnout does not *need* to be low. It is thus important to understand under what conditions youth turnout may increase.

If young people continue to have this low turnout level as they age, then as generational replacement occurs, we can anticipate plummeting levels of average electoral participation. The turnout decline in the last two decades would be only a small proportion of the decline to come. Low turnout rates are often considered as an indicator of poor democratic quality. The extent to which youth turnout poses a problem for future turnout levels depends on whether the younger generations will continue to vote infrequently or will increase their turnout levels as they grow older.

CROSS-COUNTRY DIFFERENCES IN YOUTH TURNOUT

Table 1 presents a comparison of turnout rates among voters under 30 and those 30 or older. Although youth are always less likely to vote, their turnout levels vary widely, from 40 percent or less in the United Kingdom, Latvia, and the Czech Republic to almost 90 percent in Belgium, Sweden, and Denmark. Considering all countries, the average turnout level for voters between 18 and 29 is just over 62 percent: 4 out of each 10 young voters do not vote in parliamentary elections in Europe.

Table 1. Youth Turnout Compared to Adult Turnout by Country

	Turnout of electors 30 years old or more (A)	Turnout of electors 18 to 29 years old (B)	Ratio (A/B)	Difference (A–B)
Czech Rep.	63	35	1,79	28
Latvia	69	39	1,77	30
United Kingdom	76	40	1,90	36
Switzerland	68	48	1,43	21
Estonia	70	48	1,45	22
Bulgaria	76	51	1,50	26
Romania	73	51	1,41	21
France	81	56	1,44	25
Israel	84	57	1,47	27
Slovenia	78	58	1,35	20
Slovakia	81	60	1,35	21
Portugal	75	60	1,25	15
Russia	77	62	1,24	15
Turkey	93	62	1,49	31
Ukraine	86	66	1,30	20
Germany	86	66	1,31	20
Norway	89	67	1,32	22
Poland	74	68	1,09	6
Croatia	82	70	1,17	12
Finland	85	71	1,19	13
Netherlands	89	72	1,23	16
Hungary	82	73	1,12	9
Spain	83	75	1,11	8
Greece	91	79	1,15	12
Sweden	93	80	1,16	13
Denmark	96	88	1,09	8
Belgium	93	89	1,04	4
Cyprus	97	89	1,08	7
Average	82	62	1,32	20

Source: 2007–08 European Social Survey round 4, data are weighted to correct for within-country sampling deviations and so that all countries have an equal weight in the average. Sample sizes vary between 1,118 cases in Cyprus, and 2,369 in Israel.

Turnout among people 30 or older is about 20 points higher than among those between 18 and 29. This means that on average, adults are more likely to vote than youth. However, this figure also varies quite importantly. In some countries, such as Cyprus, Belgium, or Denmark, the difference in turnout between the two age groups is relatively small. However, in countries like the United Kingdom, the older group is almost twice as likely to vote as the younger, a differing by over 35 percentage points. In general, the higher the average level of turnout in a country, the smaller the difference between the two groups.

The fact that the pattern of cross-country turnout variation is similar for young voters and for the whole electorates leads us to think that the factors explaining levels of youth turnout cross-national are likely to be those cited as explanations for overall turnout. A large number of factors affect turnout levels. Individual resources, motivations and exposure to mobilization stimuli make a person more likely to vote. The probability of voting depends on socioeconomic characteristics, such as income or education, that act as resources.[5] Among the most important predictors of voting are political attitudes that motivate political involvement: being close to a party, feeling that voting is a civic duty, being interested in politics and able to understand political issues.[6] People are also more likely to vote if they are asked to do so,[7] that is, if they receive mobilization stimuli, for instance, through social networks.[8]

The context in which an election takes place also influences turnout.[9] First, there are institutional features.[10] Compulsory voting—as in Belgium—significantly increases electoral participation. Other factors related to the electoral system, such as the size of parliament, the degree of proportionality, or the structure of the ballot, may also affect turnout. Turnout, for instance, is higher in systems with proportional representation than in majoritarian electoral systems, like the United States or Britain. Parties and candidates mobilize voters more in systems where their efforts are likely to have consequences in the number of votes and seats, and this is more likely to happen in large districts with proportional representation.

Second, there are factors related to the political offerings in an election. The degree of competitiveness of an election is strongly related to turnout, as citizens may feel their vote is more important for the result, and parties mobilize more intensely in a close election.[11] This competitiveness effects holds particularly for young voters.[12] Parties and trade unions have played an important role as mobilization agents, whose decline also may account for turnout decline.[13]

All these factors affect turnout and are interrelated, making it difficult to disentangle their relative effects on the level of electoral participation. As a result, some multivariate analysis is required to estimate their relative importance. Table 2 reports the result of such analysis, which estimates the expected turnout for different potential explanatory factors, while holding constant all others.[14] The table shows that education as a cognitive resource, party identification and interest in politics as motivations, and compulsory voting as an incentive produce the largest changes in the percentage of turnout.

Another significant finding is that young voters seem to vote more in new democracies, although the difference is not statistically significant. However, turnout in new democracies is slightly lower than in older ones, which indicates that young voters are not responsible for the decline in turnout seen in most Eastern European countries.

Table 2. Expected Changes in Youth Turnout

	Expected turnout when variable is at its lowest value	Expected turnout when variable is at its highest value	Difference
Age (18 to 29)	33	55	+22
Years of formal education (0 to 26)	30	66	+35
Interest in politics (very low to very high)	37	61	+24
Party identification (no/yes)	46	72	+26
New democracy (no/yes)	46	54	+8
Compulsory voting (no/yes)	46	67	+21
Average district magnitude (1 to 150)	44	59	+16

Note: These percentages are calculated from multivariate analyses described in appendix. The right-hand column includes the expected change in turnout among the young due to an increase in the explanatory factor of the left-hand column, while holding all other variables at their averages.

Source: European Social Survey, 2008.

LIFE CYCLE VS. GENERATIONAL EFFECTS

We know that youth turnout may be increased by a number of individual and contextual characteristics, but we still would like to know if young nonvoters will eventually start voting as they grow older, or whether they will persist in their low turnout levels throughout their lives. In other words, is youth turnout a result of the specific situation of young voters in their life cycle—which will change—or a result of belonging to a generation that has little interest in voting—which will not change.

The first cross-sectional analyses of the relationship between age and turnout appealed to the *life cycle hypothesis*.[15] According to this theory, young people vote less because they are in a specific situation of their life cycle that does not encourage electoral participation. They lack experience with the electoral process and in general with political matters, and they are not familiar with the electoral system or the party alternatives. Therefore, youth are also less likely to have party attachments, and they may have fewer social ties that favor mobilization and thus participation (a partner, an employment, a permanent residence, school-age children). According to this life-cycle explanation, if age represents experience and political integration, it is not surprising that young inexperienced citizens have lower levels of participation. However, as they grow older, they become experienced and integrated and thus increase their turnout levels. As people enter middle age, they acquire many resources and motivations that facilitate participation.

Middle-age people are more integrated into the community and are also more exposed to mobilization efforts by social groups. They are also familiar with political parties, candidates, and electoral processes and thus can more easily follow the campaign and vote in the elections. They tend to be more opinionated and to have higher levels of interest in politics and political knowledge and thus more motivations to vote. These voters also tend to become more attached to parties and to internalize ideologies more deeply.[16] For all these reasons the low turnout of the young is expected to increase as these individuals age. Further analysis on the life cycle hypothesis shows that although transitions into adult roles do not always increase turnout as expected,[17] there is evidence supporting the idea that voting is a habit that develops throughout life.[18]

The *generational explanation* maintains that the reason for low turnout among young voters is not their lack of political experience and integration, but that they belong to a generation that does not attach enough importance to the electoral process, or feels excluded or alienated from politics. When enough longitudinal data were available to test this, several studies emphasized the importance of this generational effect.[19] This would be a more worrying explanation, for it implies that this young generation of voters will not start to participate in elections later in their life cycle, and will show low turnout levels in the years to come. Generational replacement will bring overall turnout levels down, unless newer cohorts differ from previous ones and start having high turnout rates, which is probably unlikely considering all accounts of political disaffection.[20]

In fact, life cycle and generational effects are both present simultaneously in most nations.[21] Another consideration is period effects: the characteristics of the immediate political context that may demobilize voters. This is what happens, when, as some have argued, turnout declines because current elections are less decisive and less competitive than they were before.[22] Unfortunately, it is quite difficult (or nearly impossible) to completely separate period, life cycle, and cohort effects. We can, however, approach the question of generational and life cycle change in a somewhat simplified way. If the life cycle hypothesis is correct, those that were young (between 18 and 29) in the early 1990s are now between 38 and 49, and should be voting significantly more than they were 20 years ago. This is roughly what Table 3 shows, by comparing turnout levels of the same cohort at two time periods for some Western European democracies. There is some evidence of the life cycle effect, particularly in France, Norway,

Finland, Switzerland, and Denmark, where the turnout rate of this cohort has increased. Other influences—probably period effects—are evident, as this generation in Belgium and the United Kingdom is significantly less likely to vote now than 20 years ago. Of course, there is no guarantee that turnout will eventually increase for the generation that is young today.

Table 3. Life Cycle Effects in Some European Countries

Country	Turnout of the cohort that was 18 to 29 years in 1989–93	Turnout of this cohort, which is 38 to 49 years in 2008	Difference
Belgium	97	93	-4
Denmark	86	96	10
Finland	69	82	13
France	63	78	15
Germany	85	87	2
Greece	89	88	-1
Netherlands	86	85	-1
Norway	76	89	13
Portugal	64	74	10
Spain	81	85	4
Sweden	89	91	2
Switzerland	50	62	12
UK	81	73	-8

Sources: Author's elaboration from data in Anduiza 1999 and the European Social Survey, 2008.

If the generational hypothesis is correct, young voters should be voting less now than young voters 20 years ago. This generational decline in turnout may also show a period effect: turnout levels may have declined for all age groups. In any case, in Table 4 we observe that turnout among the youngest age group has halved in the United Kingdom, and declined significantly in Germany, the Netherlands, Greece, Norway, Sweden, and Belgium, and to a smaller extent in all other countries considered. The new generation of young voters votes significantly less than the same age group 20 years ago.

Some authors argue that these differences in turnout levels across different cohorts are due to the fact that younger cohorts are more sensitive than other cohorts to contextual factors and period effects. For instance, they may be more affected by the decline in electoral competitiveness that reduces mobilization efforts by parties and also voters' interest in the election. This occurs because young voters have not yet developed the habit of voting.[23] Thus, such period effects may influence the younger cohorts more.[24] However, other authors argue that young electors have different values, and that the sense of voting as a civic duty that characterizes older generations is far weaker among the young.[25] This interpretation is supported by the increasing gap between young and old in terms of political interest, media consumption (particularly newspaper reading), and political knowledge.[26]

Table 4. Turnout among Two Generations of Youth

Country	Turnout among electors 18- to 29-years-old in 1989–93	Turnout among electors 18- to 29-years-old in 2008	Difference
Belgium	97	89	-8
Denmark	86	88	2
Finland	69	71	2
France	63	56	-7
Germany	85	66	-19
Greece	89	79	-10
Netherlands	86	72	-14
Norway	76	67	-9
Portugal	64	60	-4
Spain	81	75	-6
Sweden	89	80	-9
Switzerland	50	48	-2
UK	81	40	-41

Sources: Author's elaboration from data in Anduiza 1999 and European Social Survey 2008.

CONCLUSION

Turnout among the youth is low compared with the older voting groups in all European democracies, reflecting the positive relationship between age and turnout that is found nearly everywhere. But beyond this general pattern, there are substantive differences across countries in the level of youth turnout and also in the gap between youth and older-age groups. Turnout levels of the young are *always* relatively low compared to the older age groups but are *not always* low in absolute terms. Individual resources, motivations, and contextual incentives may increase turnout. However, there are no magical solutions to increase voting and a very important amount of variance in individual turnout remains unexplained.

The relatively low levels of youth turnout are partially the result of a life cycle effect, but they also have a generational component: younger cohorts seem to be less compelled to vote. Thus, low turnout among young voters is important for several reasons, but quite crucially because it may be one of the main reasons for turnout decline. The higher educational levels of the younger cohorts have attenuated the decline in turnout. But younger electors, at least in some Western democracies, are less likely to be interested in politics, to feel that voting is a civic duty, and thus less likely to vote. However, not all the decline in turnout is attributable to the younger cohorts. Gallego finds for instance that turnout decline in Germany and Sweden is concentrated among the poorly educated, and that the voting rates of the highly educated remain high even for the young.[27] Moreover, in Eastern Europe youth participation does not seem to be responsible for the sharp decline in turnout during the last two decades.

In spite of these nuances, youth seem to be voting less than 20 years ago, and seem to be less prone to experience life cycle effects that would increase their participation levels. Since elections continue to be a central piece of the institutional structure of democracies through which citizens express their political preferences, this is serious problem, even if young people are participating in other ways when deciding to get involved.[28]

APPENDIX

For average official turnout rates we used the voter turnout database compiled by the International Institute for Democracy and Electoral Assistance (http://www.idea.int/vt/index.cfm). The analysis of participation in elections of different age groups is based on data from public opinion surveys. For most of the article our source was the European Social Survey (ESS) (http://www.europeansocialsurvey.org/index.php). The ESS includes representative samples of 28 European countries surveyed in 2008. For the comparisons with turnout in the early 1990s, we examined the postelectoral surveys found in Anduiza.[29] Data on the contextual characteristics of the different countries are from the Quality of Government Dataset (http://www.qog.pol.gu.se).

The data reported in Table 5 are based on the following logistic regression with clustered standard errors that combines ESS and QoG data.

Table 5. Multivariate Analysis of Youth Voter Turnout

	B coef.	Standard error
Age	0.084*	0.045
Education	0.051*	0.030
Interest in politics	0.325**	0.137
Party closeness	1.128***	0.213
Party membership	0.652**	0.252
Compulsory voting	0.883**	0.357
New democracy	0.337	0.250
Mean district size	0.004**	0.002
Effective N of parties	-0.066	0.086
Organizational density	-4.239	5.639
Constant	-2.809***	1.056
N	7.807	
Pseudo R2	0.09	

* Significant at 90%, ** Significant at 95%, *** Significant at 99%

Note: Age is the number of years of the respondents for those aged 18 to 29. Education is the number of years of formal education, ranging from 0 to 26. Interest in politics ranks from 0 to 3 (very little, little, some, very much). Party closeness and party membership are two dummy variables that identify those who feel close to a party and those that are party members. Compulsory voting and new democracy are two dummies that identify the relevant countries.

Source: Individual data from European Social Survey, 2008; mean district size is based on the variable "jw_mdist" of the QoG database and reports the average district magnitude of the districts for lower house elections. Effective number of parties is based on the variable "gol_enep" of the QoG database. Organizational density is the proportion of citizens that are members of a political party according to the ESS.

ENDNOTES

1. See, for instance, Eva Anduiza, "Youth Turnout in National Parliamentary Elections," in *Youth Voter Participation: Involving Today's Young in Tomorrow's Democracy* (Stockholm: International IDEA, 1999).

2. Eva Anduiza, "Youth Turnout in National Parliamentary Elections."

3. Kathy Edwards, "From Deficit to Disenfranchisement: Reframing Youth Electoral Participation," *Journal of Youth Studies* 10 (2007): 539.

4. Aina Gallego, "Understanding Unequal Turnout: Education and Voting in Comparative Perspective," *Electoral Studies* 29 (2010): 239–248.

5. Sidney Verba and Norman Nie, *Participation in America: Political Democracy and Social Equality* (New York: Harper & Row, 1972); Sidney Verba, Kay Schlozman, and Henry Brady, *Voice and Equality: Civic Voluntarism in American Politics* (Cambridge, MA: Harvard University Press, 1995).

6. André Blais and Chris Achen, "Duty, Preferences, and Turnout." Paper presented at the General Conference of the European Consortium for Political Research, Potsdam, September 10–12, 2009.

7. Steven Rosenstone and John Mark Hansen, *Mobilization, Participation, and Democracy in America* (New York: Macmillan, 1993); Alan Gerber and Donald Green, "The Effects of Canvassing, Phone Calls, and Direct Mail on Voter Turnout: A Field Experiment," *American Political Science Review* 94 (2000): 653–663.

8. Diana Mutz, "The Consequences of Cross-cutting Networks for Political Participation," *American Journal of Political Science* 46 (2002): 838–855.

9. André Blais, "What Affects Voter Turnout?" *Annual Review of Political Science* 9 (2006): 111–125; Benny Geys, "Explaining Voter Turnout: A Review of Aggregate-level Research," *Electoral Studies* 25 (2006): 637–663.

10. Robert Jackman and Ross Miller, "Voter Turnout in the Industrial Democracies during the 1980s," *Comparative Political Studies* 27 (1995): 467–492; Eva Anduiza, "Individual Characteristics, Institutional Incentives and Electoral Abstention in Western Europe," *European Journal of Political Research* 41(2002): 643–673.

11. André Blais, *To Vote or Not to Vote: The Merits and Limits of Rational Choice Theory* (Pittsburgh: University of Pittsburgh Press, 2000).

12. Julianna Sandell, "Political Socialization in Context: The Effect of Political Competition on Youth Voter Turnout," *Political Behavior* 30 (2008): 415–436.

13. Mark Gray and Miki Caul, "Declining Voter Turnout in Advanced Industrial Democracies, 1950 to 1997: The Effects of Declining Group Mobilization," *Comparative Political Studies* 33 (2000): 1091–1122.

14. The multivariate analysis is presented in the Appendix.

15. Lester Milbrath, *Political Participation: How and Why do People Get Involved in Politics?* (Chicago: Rand McNally, 1967); Raymond Wolfinger and Steven Rosenstone, *Who Votes?* (New Haven: Yale University Press, 1980).

16. Philip Converse, *The Dynamics of Party Support: Cohort-analyzing Party Identification* (London: Sage, 1976); Paul Abramson, "Developing Party Identification: A Further Examination of Life-cycle, Generational, and Period Effects," *American Journal of Political Science* 23 (1979): 78–96.

17. Benjamin Highton and Raymond Wolfinger, "The First Seven Years of the Political Life Cycle," *American Journal of Political Science* 45 (2001): 202–209.

18. Donald Green and Ron Shachar, "Habit Formation and Political Behaviour: Evidence of Consuetude in Voter Behaviour," *British Journal of Political Science* 30 (2000): 561–573; Alan Gerber, Donald Green, and Ron Shachar, "Voting May Be Habit-forming: Evidence from a Randomized Field Experiment," *American Journal of Political Science* 47 (2003): 540–550.

19. See Wattenberg essay in this book; André Blais, Elisabeth Gidengil, and Neil Nevitte, "Where Does Turnout Decline Come From?" *European Journal of Political Research* 43 (2004): 221–236; Hanna Wass, "The Effects of Age, Generation and Period on Turnout in Finland, 1975–2003," *Electoral Studies* 26 (2007): 648–659.

20. See, for instance, Russell Dalton, *Democratic Challenges, Democratic Choices: The Erosion of Political Support in Advanced Industrial Democracies* (Oxford: Oxford University Press, 2004).

21. Wass, "The Effects of Age, Generation and Period on Turnout in Finland 1975–2003"; Blais et al., "Where Does Turnout Decline Come From?"

22. Mark Franklin, *Voter Turnout and the Dynamics of Electoral Competition in Established Democracies since 1945* (Cambridge: Cambridge University Press, 2004).

23. Ibid.

24. Edward Phelps, "Young Citizens and Changing Electoral Turnout, 1964–2001," *Political Quarterly* 75 (2004): 238–248.

25. André Blais and Daniel Rubenson, "Turnout Decline: Generational Value Change or New Cohorts' Response to Electoral Competition" (unpublished manuscript, 2008).

26. Martin Wattenberg, *Is Voting for Young People?* (New York: Longman, 2006).

27. Gallego, "Understanding Unequal Turnout."

28. David Marsh, Therese O'Toole, and Su Jones, *Young People and Politics in the UK: Apathy or Alienation?* (Houndmills, UK: Palgrave, 2007).

29. Anduiza, "Youth Turnout in National Parliamentary Elections."

*Eva Anduiza is associate professor of political science at the Autonomous University of Barcelona.

DISCUSSION QUESTIONS

1. Does decreasing turnout among young people in most nations mean they are dropping out of politics in general?

2. If turnout is decreasing in almost every nation, with different institutions and political experiences, does this suggest that there is nothing that can be done to increase turnout? Does this mean that specific explanations for the decline in turnout in your nation are incorrect, if this is happening in most nations?

3. What is the evidence that lower turnout among young is a sign of generational change versus life cycle effects? What are the implications if the decrease in turnout is due to one or the other factor?

The Young Vote: Engaging America's Youth in the 2008 Elections and Beyond

by Cali Carlin*

SUMMARY

Young Americans express great interest in the upcoming presidential elections and are concerned about the future of this country. Adults ages 18 to 30 are nearly one quarter of the eligible voter pool, yet this group is not well defined along party lines; nearly two out of five 18 to 24 year olds identify themselves as "independents."[1] While the lack of party affiliation will prevent a significant number of young voters from voting in the primaries, the large number of independent young voters makes their vote both interesting and unpredictable when played out in general elections.

It is in the best interest of campaigns to engage and leverage the potential of this unpredictable group. Young people offer a significant source of vitality and grass-roots organizing ability, as well as tangible votes. Presidential candidates should carefully consider this younger demographic as they decide how to allocate their time and resources in the months ahead. Also, aside from individual candidates, an investment in young voters provides an opportunity to instill partisan affiliation and devotion; long-term loyalty is largely founded in the early years of voting.

While the 2008 campaign season is still in its early stages, at this point many young people believe the presidential candidates have not tried very hard to engage them. Presidential candidates should address issues of particular concern to younger voters and commit to campaign tactics that will specifically reach them. Issues of key concern for young adults are similar to those of older Americans—including the Iraq war, education, the economy, and health care—but, generally speaking, younger voters are more optimistic and idealistic.

Engaging younger voters does not stop when the polls close. To truly involve them over the long term, they have to believe that their efforts, their views, and their votes "make a difference." Some of the tactics that benefit candidates and campaigns also may make sense as an approach to the Presidency itself. Courting younger voters then ignoring their issues will quickly be viewed as a cynical ploy, and young adults will dis-engage, to the great detriment of the nation.

Specifically, presidential candidates and their campaigns—and Presidents—should make concerted efforts to:

- Address the policies and issues of key concern to younger Americans
- Hold events that specifically speak to and target young citizens
- Provide an opportunity for young people to ask candidates and the President questions through websites, in-person forums, and town hall meetings
- Widen the base of young people participating in campaign activities, fundraisers, and events and provide volunteer opportunities for a greater number of youth
- Continue to involve young adults and seek their opinions in creative ways once in office and
- Leverage the "new media"—the internet, social networking web sites, and mobile phone networks—for all of these efforts.

Nexters, Millennials, Gens Y and X

Boundaries and definitions for the young generation often overlap. Members of Generation X are widely accepted to be those born between 1966 and 1980, Generation Y those born between 1978 and 1996, and Generation Next those born from 1981 to 1988. The term "Millennials" is simply a sleeker name for Generation Y. For the 2008 election campaign, portions of all these groups fall into the "young voter" category. In this chapter, references to young adults or young voters signify the nearly 24 million Americans who are 18 to 30 years old.

Clearly, many individuals in these large categories are near or in their prime adult years. Candidates can engage them in the ways described below, and a President can keep them interested in government by making its relevance to their lives clear and by continuing to seek their views—not as a campaign tactic, but in a sincere effort to be the leader of *all* the American people.

This report is based on national surveys and independent studies of young adults. The author also conducted dozens of interviews over the course of a year and moderated several focus groups on topic in the summer of 2007.

Tap into the Power of Young People

When surveyed, twice as many young people say they are paying attention to the 2008 presidential election, as did for 2004.[2] This past summer, nearly 60 percent of young people indicated they were paying a lot or some attention to it. As a journalist, I have spent the last few years interviewing, corresponding with, and reporting on young people all across the country. From first-hand experience, I have observed that young adults sincerely care about the direction of this country and are vitally interested in who is elected President as well as what that person does once in office.

Young adults, especially students, are familiar with working hard for little or no pay and have proved their worth in campaigns. The current generation of young adults is very engaged: nearly a third of 17 to 29-year-olds reports having engaged in politics.[3] They bring essential vitality to grassroots organizing. From precinct-walking to phonebanking, young volunteers can help fuel the efforts of a campaign by making direct contact with voters. A visit inside the "war room" at the Arnold Schwarzenegger campaign headquarters revealed the campaign's core strength: not a single staffer looked over the age of 25. The operation was run by low-paid interns and volunteers impassioned by their work and their candidate.

When campaigns empower young people, young people in turn empower campaigns. Both the Schwarzenegger and Phil Angelides gubernatorial campaigns in California tapped the power of youth. College students are the quintessential activists, willing to spend time and energy on what they believe in. Students can and will participate in causes that ignite them. Candidates should not discount a school or community because of the generally prevailing stereotype of its "liberal" or "conservative" views. The minority of students who counter the prevailing view can be a rich pool for recruiting committed volunteers.

The campaign tactics young people develop can be both new and fearless. Again in the 2006 California gubernatorial race, a young volunteer discreetly filmed the opposing candidate's speeches and then posted unflattering clips to the video website YouTube. He was engaged in a classic guerrilla-style campaign activity, updated (and having more impact) for the internet. This generation of young people is independent minded, technologically savvy, and incredibly resourceful—who would not want them on their campaign team? Who would want to fight against them without the same resources?

Not only does tapping into the power of young people provide inexpensive and plentiful labor, but it also cultivates in young voters a deep sense of loyalty to the candidate and party. This is an opportunity the newly elected President should continue to nurture. Our leaders should reach beyond having a handful of highly committed young staffers on their campaigns and in the West Wing; they should expand their reach to include a broad base of young supporters.

Similarly, they should plan fundraising events and public appearances affordable for and targeted towards younger Americans. When campaigns effectively harness the competitive spirit of young people and focus this force on concrete campaign goals, the results can be remarkable, and can evolve into support for the new administration.

Ride and Support the Momentum

Young voter turnout has been steadily increasing in recent elections: this healthy trend should be both leveraged and sustained. Turnout for the most recent presidential elections rose nine points among 18 to 29-year-old voters—from 40 percent in 2000 to 49 percent in 2004. Among voters ages 18 to 24, participation was 11 percent higher in 2004.[4] In the 2006 mid-term elections, the number of young voters increased by 2 million voters from the previous mid-terms in 2002. In order to sustain this momentum through 2008 and beyond, parties, candidates, and elected leaders must take an interest in and nourish young citizens.

Generally speaking, young adults do not believe that presidential candidates have as yet shown sufficient interest in their issues. As of June 2007, 65 percent of 17 to 29-year-olds surveyed said they did not believe that candidates have made enough effort to reach them.[5] This opinion was largely based on young people's perceptions of campaign activities. If they constantly see media reports of candidates at events, luncheons, and town hall meetings attended by older adults—their parents' and grandparents' generations—but rarely see participants their own age, this view will persist. While Generations X and Y may be the children of cyberspace, they still want some "face time" with candidates. Young voters desire more events, like town hall meetings or rallies, where they have the chance to ask questions on topics of interest to them. To the credit of the campaigns, in recent months there has been a flurry of creative events seemingly geared towards reaching young America; however, they are mainly technology based.

Connect through Young Americans' Media

Recently, a wide variety of tactics has been employed in an effort to reach the young demographic. These techniques are not only promising campaign tactics, but can be used by the new President to maintain a network for ongoing, cost-effective communication and engagement of young people.

Internet

The internet is literally the ultimate platform for reaching Millennials. The following are tactics that can be effectively and efficiently leveraged:

Candidates' Official Sites

This summer [2007], roughly 31 percent of young adults surveyed reported they had already visited a candidate's official website or a general political website.[6] This is a substantial percentage, especially given that the survey was conducted 17 months before the general election. By November 2008, the large majority of young America may have visited a candidate's official pages, making a well crafted site with areas geared towards the young vote essential. This is the venue where candidates can make their case to the individual, clearly and convincingly, without competing voices. Candidate sites are one of the few places young voters say they trust to find factual information on the candidates as well as where they stand on matters of policy.

Blogs

While blogging sites are generally viewed as a biased source of information by Generation Nexters, they still can have a subconscious effect. The young generation is skeptical about online postings, especially blogs. Focus group participants recognized that political blogs are often infiltrated by individuals with agendas and maybe even connections to political organizations and campaigns, so generally trust few of them. Credible media outlets and candidates' official pages are seen as more trustworthy.

Social Networking

While they can be tricky terrain, social networking websites can offer a candidate fertile ground in which to grow support among young voters. To date, social networking pages have been underutilized. As of June 2007, only 10 percent of 18 to 29-year-olds reported visiting a candidate's social networking page,[7] yet 97 percent of college students report having visited the social networking site Facebook in the previous month.[8]

To use social networking sites more effectively, campaigns must be creative, using young "influencers" to make information about their candidate more widely available. One way to do this is through applications like virtual campaign buttons. For example, a Massachusetts high school student put a virtual

"I support Obama" button on his Facebook page, and within 24 hours, 400 other students had followed suit. This is not surprising, considering that Barack Obama has more than a quarter-million virtual friends on social networking sites. Other candidates also should pursue "internet friends," recruit campaign volunteers, and leverage the "influentials" through this medium.

Focus groups reveal it is far more meaningful if candidates personally seek out and request someone to become a virtual friend than if the individual has to seek them out. Candidates can do this by using young volunteers, interns, and college groups to recommend people who would likely support their campaigns. Staffers can then find the recommended people on social networking sites and ask whether they want be added to the candidate's friends list.

Once elected, this network of virtual friends would afford a prime opportunity for the new President to build on a base of interested young people. These are individuals to stay in touch with, to query regarding issues of concern, and to help reach other young Americans. On their issues, especially, they are a prime audience in efforts to create support for administration policies.

Online Innovation

The internet is constantly being utilized in different and unpredictable ways by campaigns and media outlets—from the CNN-YouTube debate to the Yahoo News Candidate Mash-up to the MySpace/MTV Dialogues. Buzz about the CNN-YouTube debate was overwhelmingly positive, with a definite "Wow, you're talking to me and really you do care about us!" response from Millennials. These sorts of events and outreach efforts are on the right track. They speak specifically to young people and portray the candidates as modern and savvy communicators.

Events

Young people also have a desire for old-fashioned, direct contact with their candidates and leaders. Events like the MySpace/MTV dialogues do a great job of merging technology with physical tangibility. These events are hosted on college campuses and streamed on MTV.com and MySpace, allowing viewers to ask questions in real time, via instant messaging. Our next administration should continue use of these types of platforms to keep young adults informed and involved in policy matters.

Cell Phones

Mobile communication is an exceptionally effective and efficient medium for mobilizing young voters and is likely to be one of the most revolutionary tactics in 2008. A study by Princeton University and University of Michigan students shows voter turnout in 2006 increased 4 percent when people received voting reminders via text messages.[9] Simple, to-the-point messages yielded a 5 percent increase. Even more impressive is the cost-effectiveness of this approach. Using phone banks also yields a 4 to 5 percent increase in turnout, but is much more expensive ($20 per vote generated versus $1.56 per vote).

Further, more than half of 18 to 24-year-olds do not even have a land-line phone, so are unreachable by a phone bank, yet 89 percent own a cell phone.[10] Sixty-three percent of young people with a cell phone regularly use text messaging (compared to only 15 percent of Baby Boomers), which makes mobile reminders potentially pivotal in mobilizing young voters. However, the messages should be carefully constructed and selectively sent. While 59 percent of the 4,000 participants in the study said the text messages were helpful, nearly a quarter found them annoying.[11] Young people may appreciate a text reminder near voting day if they have requested it, but resent a barrage of them. So far, only a few campaigns have developed communications strategies involving mobile phones or are registering participants for messages and notifications.

Connect with Young Americans' Concerns

Several topics are of primary concern among young Americans. Similar to older voters, they are most interested in policy on Iraq, the environment, the economy, health care, and immigration, but tend to be a little more optimistic and idealistic on these issues. Young people are more concerned about the present state of education than are older Americans and less concerned about the future of Social Security. Young people are also somewhat more open on social issues, like gay marriage. Candidates should explain their ideas and positions on these issues when targeting young adults, and the next President should take young people's views and priorities into account in developing—and explaining—new administration policies.

KEY FACTS

- Twice as many young people say they are paying attention to the 2008 election as were doing so prior to the 2004 election.[12]
- Young voters largely identify as independent, at 40 percent.[13]
- The overwhelming majority of young adults, 85 percent, say they are interested in following national affairs–up 14 points from 1999 and close to the interest reported by adults of all ages.[14]
- Young voter turnout increased significantly in recent elections. Among 18 to 24-year-olds, it jumped 11 points, from 36 percent in 2000 to 47 percent in 2004. Among 18 to 29-year-olds, turnout increased from 40 percent in 2000, to 49 percent in 2004.[15]
- Iraq, education, health care, and the environment rank as the most critical concerns for young Americans.

Iraq

Similar to the rest of the adult population, the war in Iraq is the chief issue of concern among young Americans: 32 percent say it is the most important problem facing the country.[16] Another survey shows 50 percent believing either "Iraq" the "War" the "War on Terror" or "Domestic Security" is the most pressing issue.[17] This young generation is closely connected to the troops serving in the Middle East, who are their peers, friends, and immediate family members.

The young generation is moderately more hopeful than older Americans about the potential for success in Iraq. Of the 17 to 29-year-olds surveyed, 51 percent said it is likely or somewhat likely that the United States will succeed in Iraq, compared to only 45 percent of all Americans.[18]

As far as what actions they would like to see taken, opinions are extremely varied and generally follow established lines. Some would like to see an immediate end to the war, because of its many costs, and others worry that a too-abrupt end will translate into future problems in the region that they may have to grapple with. Iraq is not a conflict young Americans want to see continue through their adult life, yet they are well aware that it could. What young adults do agree on is the desire to see a comprehensive plan. They say they want their next commander-in-chief to have a plan they describe as "intelligent," "well thought out," and "flexible." While they admit they don't have the answer to Iraq, they want a President who does.

Education

The overwhelming majority of young adults say issues surrounding education are important to them, and, since many of them are students or recent graduates, this is not surprising. On average, college students carry $20,000 in debt on graduation day, which makes federal policies on student aid particularly important to them.[19]

Beyond the financial burden of higher education, young people express concern about the nation's primary and secondary schools. One worry is that U.S. students are not globally competitive. Lack of foreign language instruction is a particular problem. They believe it should begin earlier and be offered in a broader range of languages. A focus group also revealed frustration over tenure, which participants believed forces out favorite young, enthusiastic teachers, while preserving jobs for teachers perceived as "apathetic and cynical." While these are very specific examples and opinions, they illustrate the depth of the ideas and concern from young adults regarding our education system, as well as a desire for our next President to propose specific solutions.

Economy

Because of bills racked up in college, being new to the workforce, and having higher rates of unemployment, young Americans are very interested in the well-being of the U.S. economy. One of the challenges for this generation is that, while overall they are more educated than their parents' generation, their college degrees were more expensive to attain and do not portend as great an increase in earning potential. Higher education is still important, however, because the gap in earning is even greater for those without it. On top of the relative drop in earnings, unemployment rates are two to three times greater among young adults today, and their bankruptcy rates and credit card debt are both high.

Given their uncertain financial future, young adults are extremely interested in what the next President will do for our economy. The most basic desire is for good employment and career advancement opportunities. A huge majority—88 percent—say job training and opportunities for younger workers are important. Unemployment rates and weak benefits also play into the younger generation's views regarding their next major area of concern—health care.

Health Care

About a third of young adults lack health insurance.[20] As a result, they are more in favor of a comprehensive national health care system than are adult as a whole. About 62 percent of young adults support a national plan, compared to only 47 percent of the population at large.[21] Uninsured youth support a national health care plan at the rate of 75 percent. Young adults admit to not understanding the nuances of the health reform plans proposed—a communications challenge for every candidate and administration—but they do understand that health care is something they need.

Environment

An overwhelming majority of young people feel Americans should do whatever it takes to protect the environment. Overall, they are more concerned about the environment than are their parents and grandparents. Some 90 percent of 17 to 29-year-olds say government policies that promote reduced oil and gas use are important,[22] and Gen Nexters are similar to Baby Boomers when it comes to a willingness to pay higher prices to protect the environment. A new President who wanted to take dramatic action on environmental issues would be able to build on this strong support.

Immigration

Young Americans generally have a more positive and open-minded attitude toward immigration issues than do older adults. When surveyed, 67 percent of Nexters say they believe today's immigrants strengthen the country with their hard work and talents, while only 30 percent of adults over 61 share this view. Similarly, only 30 percent of younger adults say immigrants are a burden, compared to 50 percent of older adults.[23] Young people do worry about potential strain on government programs and resources, like education. Still, they are much more likely to believe the number of people allowed to immigrate to the United States should be increased or kept the same, while older Americans are more likely to want a decrease.

These opinions likely reflect the current generation's remarkable diversity. Many of them have grown up in a multiracial, multicultural society. (According to a Gallup Poll, 95 percent of 18 to 29-year-olds approve of dating between blacks and whites, while only about 30 percent of their grandparents share that view.[24]) Young people perceive current immigration policy as pointless, since it is not enforced, and would like to see comprehensive immigration reform. As part of this, they would like to see the corollary issues of employment, education, and security addressed. Again, the next administration may find support for immigration reform among younger Americans.

Social Issues

Stances on social issues follow a very similar pattern. Millennials are more progressive than the generations which preceded them, especially on the issue of gay marriage. The under-30 population is the only age group with a relatively favorable view on gay marriage, and their views are largely shaped by personal experience, not so much by whether they are liberal or conservative or even religious. (Young adults are religious for the most part—seven out of 10 college students say religion is somewhat or very important in their lives.) Americans who know personally someone who is gay are about twice as likely to favor gay marriage, and young people more often have gay acquaintances.

Most young Americans value free agency and would like the government to avoid interfering in personal choices whenever possible. Millennials' stance on social issues underscores the fact that this group is largely independent and does not necessarily correspond to traditional labels.

Social Security

Young people are quite apathetic and uninformed when it comes to the topic of Social Security. Many have written off Social Security as a lost cause and figure there is no chance of any money being left in the pot for them upon retirement. This widespread ignorance seems irrational, since the issue *will* directly affect them, but young people believe they have many more pressing issues to worry about. In fact 60 percent of 18 to 24-year-olds surveyed said they haven't heard *anything* about a plan to privatize Social Security.[25] For the minority of Nexters who were even *slightly* aware of the idea, 74 percent are in favor, possibly again reflecting their independent streak. By contrast, only 48 percent of adults 41 and over support privatization. Still, the large majority of young adults see the issues of Social Security as vague, distant, and not directly applicable to their current or future lives.

Concluding Observations

Forty percent of young adults currently identify themselves as politically independent,[26] which could mean one of two things: they remain unaffiliated with a particular party but could be lured either way, or they feel utterly dissatisfied with both the Republican and Democratic parties and have no interest in joining either. Both possibilities should pique the interest of candidates, political parties, and the next President.

Democrats have been the frontrunners in reaching the younger demographic. In the mid-term elections of 2006, the Democrats' largest marginal win was with the youth, who voted 60 to 38 percent in favor of Democratic congressional candidates.[27] This 22-point margin made the crucial difference in several close Senate races and contributed to the Democrats' current majority in both houses. Similarly, the young vote could give Democrats the winning edge in the 2008 presidential elections, if the party continues to explore ways to cultivate it. Clearly, Republicans should seriously reconsider current lackluster efforts to target younger participation. Not only could this make a critical difference in 2008, but it could also prove vital to the party's future growth and viability.

Parties and individual candidates should invest in youth, not just to win particular elections, but because partisan loyalty is largely formed in the younger years. Utilizing young people as organizers, interns, and volunteers will be beneficial for both young people and the campaigns that engage them. With fresh minds, ample energy, and technological sophistication, younger voters can be a significant force in driving a candidate towards victory.

Encouraging young voter participation creates new responsibilities for candidates, campaigns, and our entire political system. Young Americans cannot be entirely accessed or engaged through the traditional tactics of phone banks, leaflets, television advertisements, and newspaper editorials. Social networking, text messaging, internet postings, and other "new media" must be deployed to bring young Americans to the political table.

Most of all, engaging young people in campaigns places added responsibilities for those elected, especially our new President. Engaging young America in the democratic process—and in governance—is in the interest of everyone in this country. Investments that our political leaders can make now in engaging this large segment of our citizenry will inevitably provide this country with a more intelligent, more connected, and more thoughtful government for years to come.

ENDNOTES

1. Harvard University Institute of Politics, Young Voters and Participation, April 2007.

2. CBS/MTV/NY Times Poll, The State of the Youth Nation: 2007, June 2007.

3. Ibid.

4. Tabulated from U.S. Census Bureau Data by Center for Information and Research on Civic Learning and Engagement (CIRCLE).

5. CBS/MTV/NY Times Poll, The State of the Youth Nation: 2007. June 2007.

6. Ibid.

7. Ibid.

8. Harvard University Institute of Politics, Redefining Political Attitudes and Activism. April 2006.

9. Dale, Allison, and Strauss, Aaron. Mobilizing the mobiles: How Text Messaging Can Boost Youth Voter Turnout, September 2007. Available at: www.newvotersproject.org/uploads/jX/a4/jXa4y7Q3JFWhnPsmdQcGfw/Youth-Vote-and-Text-Messaging.pdf.

10. Harvard University Institute of Politics, Young Voters and Participation. April 2007.

11. Dale, Allison, and Strauss, Aaron. Mobilizing the Mobiles: How Text Messaging Can Boost Youth Voter Turnout.

12. CBS/MTV/NY Times Poll, The State of the Youth Nation: 2007.

13. Harvard University Institute of Politics, Young Voters and Participation, April 2007.

14. Harvard University Institute of Politics, Redefining Political Attitudes and Activism. April 2006.

15. Tabulated from U.S. Census Bureau Data by Center for Information and Research on Civic Learning and Engagement (CIRCLE).

16. CBS/MTV/NY Times Poll, The State of the Youth Nation: 2007.

17. Harvard University Institute of Politics, Young Voters and Participation, April 2007.

18. CBS/MTV/NY Times Poll, The State of the Youth Nation: 2007.

19. Center for Education Statistics, Debt Burden, March 2007.

20. Kaiser Family Foundation, Uninsured Workers in America, July 2004.

21. Tabulated from U.S. Census Bureau Data by Center for Information and Research on Civic Learning and Engagement (CIRCLE).

22. CBS/MTV/NY Times Poll, The State of the Youth Nation: 2007.

23. Pew Research Center for the People and the Press, A Portrait of "Generation Next": How Young People View Their Lives, Futures and Politics, 2007.

24. The Gallup Organization, "Most Americans Approve of Interracial Dating," October 2005.

25. Pew Research Center for the People and the Press, A Portrait of "Generation Next."

26. Harvard University Institute of Politics, Young Voters and Participation.

27. Tabulated from U.S. Census Bureau Data by Center for Information and Research on Civic Learning and Engagement (CIRCLE).

*Cali Carlin currently works for CBS News in New York.

Carlin, Cali. The Young Vote: Engaging America's Youth in the 2008 Elections and Beyond. Washington, D.C.: Brookings Institution Press, 2007.

Used by permission.

DISCUSSION QUESTIONS

1. What are the major lessons of the 2008 election for increasing youth voting in other elections?

2. What are the best ways for politicians to communicate with young people?

3. Why don't political parties pay more attention to the issues of interest to young voters?

Part 3:
Participation beyond Elections

One explanation for why youth turnout in elections is decreasing maintains that young people have shifted their efforts to other types of political engagement. In "Youth and Participation beyond Elections," Russell J. Dalton provides an overview of the many forms of political participation available to citizens and describes how the styles of political action vary across generations. He maintains that total participation has actually increased in the United States, as new forms of political action have been added to the old. Moreover, youth are often more active in these new forms of action, which partially counterbalance their decline in electoral participation. For instance, in "Millennials Are Involved Locally with Others but Are Ambivalent about Formal Politics," Abby Kiesa and her colleagues discuss the substantial increase in voluntary activity among young Americans in recent decades and the factors that motivate this form of participation. In "The Internet and Youth Political Participation," Mark Kann and his colleagues turn the spotlight on Internet activism, which seems to be the special domain of the young. In a rapidly changing area, they discuss how the Internet has the potential to strengthen past forms of political activism and open new channels of citizen influence. "The Market as an Arena for Transnational Politics," by Michele Micheletti and Dietlind Stolle, describes the rise of political consumerism as a new method of action, in which people buy or boycott products in order to shape the social and political actions of businesses, and thereby pressure government to enact legislation. These findings raise two important questions. First, how has the growth of new forms of political action changed the citizen's ability to influence government actions? Second, do these new forms of action allow those already participating to find additional means of citizen influence and possibly produce a growing inequality among the politically active and inactive?

Youth and Participation beyond Elections

by Russell J. Dalton*

Sylvia is a senior citizen who lives in Orange County, California. She is deeply interested in politics and votes in every election after studying the candidates and propositions on the ballot. Moreover, she continues her activity between elections. On Monday, Wednesday, and Friday she rises at 6 AM to call the White House to leave her comments for the president on the issues of the day. On Tuesday and Thursday she calls either the senators from California or the leadership of the House or Senate.

Alix lives in northern California. She switched shampoos over animal testing and will not buy clothes produced by child labor. She yells at people who do not recycle. During her last year in high school, she helped organize a protest over the genocide in the Sudan that raised $13,000 for Darfur relief. All this was before she was even eligible to vote.

These two individuals show some of the diverse ways in which Americans are politically active. Participation means more than just voting. As previous essays have argued, a participatory public has been a defining feature of American politics and historically a strength of the political system. Social scientists maintain that political participation "is at the heart of democratic theory and at the heart of the democratic political formula in the United States."[1] Without public involvement in the process, democracy lacks both its legitimacy and its guiding force.

In the 1960s and 1970s Americans were actively engaged in voluntary associations, interested in politics, and involved in political discussion. Turnout in presidential elections reached a modern highpoint in the 1960s. Despite this heritage, many contemporary political analysts believe that the foundations of citizenship and democracy in America are crumbling.[2] Numerous pundits and political analysts proclaim that too few of us are voting, we are disconnected from our fellow citizens, we lack social capital, and we are losing faith in our government.

Moreover, as expressed in the other essays of this book, many analysts view the young as a primary source of this decline.[3] Authors from Tom Brokaw to Robert Putnam extol the civic values and engagement of the older, Greatest Generation with great hyperbole. At the same time, the young are described as the Doofus Generation or the Invisible Generation, even by sympathetic political observers. These analysts see young Americans as dropping out of politics, and thereby eroding political activity.

Is the situation really so dire? We agree that the American public has undergone profound changes in the past half-century, and this has changed participation patterns and citizens' relationship with government. However, this essay argues that prior studies misdiagnosed the situation by focusing on only a portion of political activity and by mistaking the sources of these changes. Many nonelectoral forms of political participation have been increasing, especially among the young. Cliff Zukin and his colleagues recently surveyed political action among the young, and they rejected the general claim of youth disengagement: "First and foremost, simple claims that today's youth . . . are apathetic and disengaged from civic life are simply wrong."[4] This description is starkly different from the decline in political participation literature.

Many political causes motivate today's youth, such as helping the less fortunate in the United States, addressing poverty in Africa (and the United States), improving the global (and U.S.) environment, as well as addressing their own political and economic needs. Consequently, Americans are changing their style of political action rather than dropping out from politics entirely—and these trends are most apparent among the young. From this perspective, the United States is witnessing a change in the nature of citizenship and political participation that can lead to a renaissance of democratic participation—rather than a general decline.

This essay first examines how political participation patterns are changing over time. Then, we describe how the participation patterns differ across generations, as younger Americans turn to alternative nonelectoral forms of action. Finally, we discuss the implications of our findings.

WHAT COULD YOU DO TO INFLUENCE THE GOVERNMENT?

Instead of starting with the common assumption that participation is synonymous with voting in elections, let's begin with a citizen-centered view of participation. How do people think of their participation options? How can they influence politics? Answers to this question reflect a combination of which tools the individual thinks will be effective and what they feel prepared to do.

As the examples at the start of this chapter show, people can be politically active in many ways, and our understanding of contemporary politics has to have an inclusive (and changeable) definition of what is political. And you might see your own connection to politics as very different from these two people. To go beyond these two individuals, public opinion surveys have asked people about their participation options:

Suppose a regulation was being considered by (your local community) which you considered very unjust or harmful; what do you think you could do? Suppose a law was being considered by Congress which you considered to be very unjust or harmful: what do you think you could do?

This question was first asked in 1959, and most Americans felt they could affect politics; only 18 percent said they could do nothing about a bad local regulation and only 22 percent said they could do nothing about a bad national law. When this question was repeated in the 1980s, the percentage of people who said they could do nothing held stable for local politics and decreased by another 7 percent for national politics. This is a first suggestion that political engagement is not decreasing in America. We suspect a more recent survey would find people even more engaged.

The expanding forms of political action are even more apparent in responses to how people would try to influence the government. Many people say they would work through informal groups, neighbors or friends to influence policy, especially at the local level, where the possibility of face-to-face cooperation is greater. This is the type of collective action that represents Tocqueville's image of participation in America. Although responses are slightly less frequent in 1981, this remains a common form of proposed political action.[5]

By the second time point, participation means more avenues of influence. In 1959, protests, demonstrations, petitions, and other examples of contentious politics were barely mentioned by 1 percent of the public. In 1981, 33 percent mention some direct action related to local government and 16 percent for national government. Most of these responses involved signing of petitions, but a substantial percentage also cited protests, demonstrations, and boycotts as a means of political influence.

The tendency to think of political influence as direct contacting has grown even more over this time span. Both contacting a local government official or a national government official has increased by more than 20 percent across the two decades. Direct contacting becomes the most frequently proposed method of political action for local government (55 percent) and national government (84 percent). This trend reflects two reinforcing patterns. First, people today are less deferential to elites and more likely to assert their own political views. Second, more people possess the resources and skills to take direct, individual action, such as writing a letter to an official or calling his or her office.

This question about methods of influence also illustrates the role of voting. In 1959, voting or working with a party was the third most frequently cited means of influence for both local and national government. The percentages citing elections and parties did not change dramatically in the next two decades—but other forms of action expanded. Voting is very important, but citizens are now much more likely to say they would turn to other methods when trying to influence government.

These findings are now a bit dated, however. In the modern context of e-mail and faxes, direct contacting has become even simpler for the individual.[6] Moreover, new forms of Internet-based participation have emerged as a result of technological change. And protest campaigns have expanded to include new forms of political consumerism and online activism. The boundaries of political action are now much wider than they were a few decades ago.

In summary, people see expanding options for how they can influence government. Moreover, the growth in the participation repertoire has come primarily in forms of direct action—such as contacting and protesting—that typify a style of participation that is much different from the institutionalized and infrequent means of electoral participation. If more recent data were available, we suspect these trends would be even stronger.

The Trends in Political Participation beyond Voting

American citizens see new avenues of political action available to them—but do they use these opportunities? Comprehensive longitudinal data on the participation patterns of Americans are surprisingly rare.[7] Most academic longitudinal studies examine only one aspect of political participation over time. Furthermore, even when a survey includes a large set of participation items, the question wording often varies, which limits our ability to compare surveys. Consequently, there is no single definitive source for data on U.S. participation patterns over the last several decades, and thus we must combine a variety of sources to track activity patterns.

We want to start our analyses as early as possible in order to describe patterns before the point in the early 1970s when previous research claims that participation generally began to erode. Moreover, with a long time span we can better see the long-term consequences of social change in the American public, which can be separated from the ebb and flow of specific events or specific election campaigns. Since the previous section of this book discussed voting trends, we focus on five other types of participation that partially overlap with the subsequent chapters in this section: participation in campaigns, involvement in community groups, contacting political figures, various forms of contentious political action, and Internet-based activism.

Campaign Activity

Participation in campaigns can be an exciting activity. People debate about the nation's future, learn new skills in educating others about how to vote, and find that attending a good campaign rally can be better than a night at the movies. Imagine all the young volunteers in Iowa in 2007–08 who now have a picture with President Obama in their Facebook photo album.

Fewer people are routinely active in campaigns, however, because this requires more initiative, more time, and arguably more political sophistication than the act of voting. Yet campaign activity can do more to influence political outcomes than voting, in part because one is influencing other voters. Campaign activities are also important to parties and candidates; candidates generally are more sensitive to, and aware of, the policy interests of their activists. Several analysts argue, however, that campaign activity has followed a downward spiral in parallel to voting turnout.[8]

The American National Election Study (ANES) has the most extensive time trends on campaign activity (Figure 1). The ANES asks about working for a party, going to a meeting, giving money, displaying campaign material, and persuading others how to vote. There are ebbs and flows in campaign involvement related to specific campaigns, with a slight downward drift in the 1990s.[9] Displaying a campaign button or a bumper sticker was popular in the 1950s and

Figure 1. Trend in American Campaign Activity

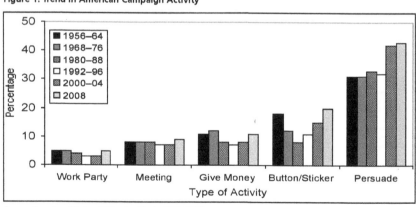

Source: American National Election Study, 1956–2008.

early 1960s, but one suspects that in contemporary elections more people forward election-related emails and display voting preferences through their Facebook affiliations than place placards on their lawns. Moreover, campaign activity has increased in the last few elections, even before the historic 2008 elections. In summary, campaign activity has ebbed and flowed over this half century period—and participation in election campaigns still engages a significant share of the American public.

Group Activity

The wellspring of democracy, according to Tocqueville, was Americans' involvement in their communities. Communal participation can take many forms. It often involves group efforts to deal with social or community problems, ranging from issues of schools or roads to protecting the local environment. From the PTA to local neighborhood-watch committees, this is democracy in action. The existence of such autonomous group action defines the character of a civil society that democratic theorists consider a foundation of the democratic process. Today, participation in citizen groups can include involvement in public interest groups with broad policy concerns, such as environmental interest groups, women's groups, or consumer protection groups.

Group-based participation has long been cited as a distinctive aspect of the American political culture, but it is difficult to measure without representative survey data. Several political participation studies have asked people if they had worked with others in their community to solve some local problem; 30 percent were active in 1967 and this increased to 34 percent in 1987.[10] A 2004 survey asked about community activity in only the last five years, and 36 percent reported working a community project. Similarly, the World Values Survey found that American membership in civic associations, environmental groups, women's groups, or peace groups increased from 6 percent in 1980, to 18 percent in 1990, to 33 percent in 1999.

These activities are perhaps the closest to the Tocquevillian image of grassroots democracy in America; thus it is very significant that informal collective action has become more common among Americans.

Contacting about Politics

Another type of political action is personally contacting a politician, government official, or the media about a political issue. This is a fairly demanding form of action, requiring that the individual identify a target and formulate a statement of their policy preferences. Sidney Verba and Norman Nie studied participation in 1967 and found a fifth of the public had contacted a member of the local, state or national government. When they repeated the survey in 1987, a third of the public had contacted politicians at one of these levels.[11] Indeed, other evidence suggests that more and more people use this method of individualized participation, which allows them to select the issue, the timing and means of communication, and the content of the message to policy makers.[12] A century ago, active citizens marched en masse to the polls with their ballots held high over the heads, and voted as their ward captain or union leader told them. Today, they sit in the comfort of their home and write politicians about the issues of the community and the nation.

Contentious Participation

Protest is another form of participation. Protest not only expands the repertoire of political participation, but it is a style of action that differs markedly from electoral politics. Protest can focus on specific issues or policy goals—from protecting whales to protesting the policies of a local government—and can convey a high level of political information with real political force. Voting and campaign work seldom focus on a single issue, because parties represent a package of policies. Sustained and effective protest is a demanding activity that requires initiative, political skills, and cooperation with others. Thus, the advocates of protest argue that citizens can increase their political influence by adopting a strategy of direct action.

Although protest and similar forms of action are part of democratic politics, early participation surveys did not ask these items. This partially reflected the low level of protest in the 1950s and early 1960s, as well as the contentious nature of these activities. The 1967 Verba/Nie participation survey, for instance, did not include a question on protest—even though it occurred in the midst of one of the most turbulent periods of modern American history. In the 1987 survey 6 percent said they had participated in a demonstration, protest, or boycott in the past two years.[13] More than a decade later (2004), 7 percent said they had participated in a protest in the past five years.

Another survey series has asked about participation in several types of contentious action (see Figure 2).[14] In the mid-1970s about half of Americans said they had signed a petition; now this group is about three-quarters of the public. Participation in demonstrations, boycotts, and unofficial strikes has roughly doubled over this time span. This series may exaggerate the trend in protest because it asks if the respondent had ever participated in these activities, instead of asking about participation over a discrete time span. However, if we could extend our time series back to the quieter times of the 1950s and early 1960s, the growth of protest activity would undoubtedly be dramatic. Protest has become so common that is now the extension of conventional political action by other means.

Figure 2. Trend in American Protest Activity

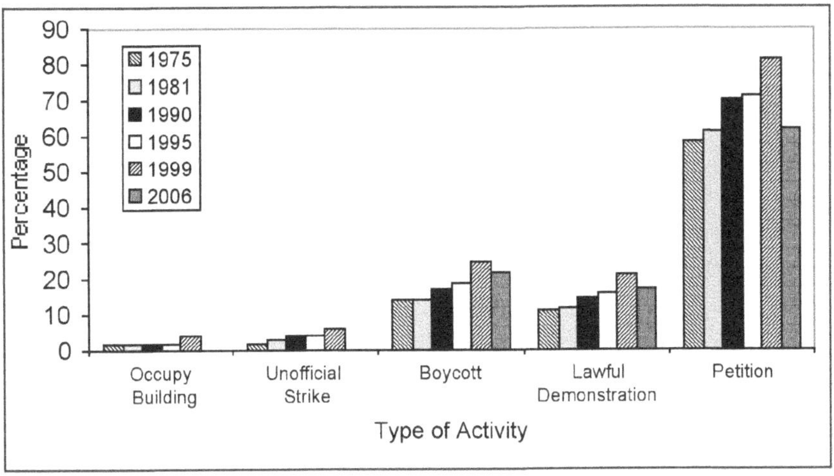

Note: The questions on occupying buildings and unofficial strikes were not asked in 2006.

Source: 1975 Political Action Study and World Values Survey, 1981–2006.

If we expand the definition of protest to include political consumerism, the increase in contentious politics is even more dramatic.[15] Political consumerism—buying or boycotting a product for a political reason—appears to be an increasingly common activity in most contemporary democracies, and something missing from earlier participation studies. The 2005 CDACS Survey found that roughly a fifth of Americans reported boycotting or buying a product for political reasons or ethnical reasons in the previous 12 months.[16] Political consumerism is at the border of politics and economics, but it has been effective in stimulating political change in areas ranging from treatment of third world labor to animal rights issues, to the certification of free trade coffee in your nearest coffee house.

Thus, most people in established democracies participate in some form of contentious action, if only by signing a petition. Participation in stronger forms of protest—such as joining in a lawful demonstration or boycott—actually rivals the levels of campaign activity.

Wired Activism

Finally, the Internet provides a new way for people to do traditional political activities: to connect with others, to gather and share information, and to attempt to influence the political process. For instance, people are now more likely to send an e-mail to an elected official or a media outlet than to mail a traditional letter through the U.S. Postal Service. While Web sites were unheard of in the early 1990s, they are now a standard and expanding feature of electoral politics. A wide range of political groups, parties, and interest groups use the Internet to disseminate information. The 2005 CDACS survey, for example, found that 17 percent of Americans had visited a political Web site in the previous year to gain political information. The blogosphere is another new source of political information that potentially empowers individuals as a rival to the established media. The Internet can also be a source of political activism that occurs electronically through online petitions or cyber-protests. There are even experiments in Internet voting.[17]

In addition, the Internet is creating new political opportunities that had not previously existed. For instance, Moveon.org became a vital tool to connect like-minded individuals during the 2004 Democratic primaries. The Obama campaign brought this to a new level in the 2008 election, when their Web site became a source of information on the campaign, a potent tool for fund-raising, and a means for individuals to connect to other Obama supporters through their own social networking site (MyBo). The potential of the Internet is also illustrated on MySpace, Facebook, and other social networking sites, where people communicate and can link themselves to affinity groups that reflect their values as a way to meet other like-minded individuals.

A number of recent surveys document the growing political activity on the Internet. The 2005 CDACS survey found that 17 percent of Americans had visited a political Web site in the past year, 13 percent had forwarded a political e-mail, and 7 percent had participated in other political activities over the Internet. The percentage of those who had engaged in any of these activities exceeded the percentage of those who had donated money to a political group, worked for a party or candidate, or displayed campaign materials over the same time period. The 2008 Pew Internet Survey found that significant numbers had done some political activity online (such as signing an "e-petition" or forwarding political e-mails), had used social networking for some form of social or political engagement, and made political contributions online.[18] The numbers are still modest and the uses are still growing, but the Internet is adding to the tools of political activism, especially among the young.

PARTICIPATION NOW AND THEN

It is clear that Americans now have access to an expanding range of different forms of political action. Moreover, such patterns have become institutionalized as the structure of political process has changed to accommodate a more participatory public. Governments now reach out to engage their citizens in new ways, and some citizens—though not all—are making use of these opportunities. For instance, the 2008 Pew Internet Survey estimated that two-thirds of the public had performed at least one political activity in the previous year, even excluding voting![19]

Unfortunately, there is not a single pair of surveys or other data source that documents all these changes in the framework of participation. Yet we can assemble suggestive evidence from the above discussion to illustrate how the public's total activity has changed over time. The first column in Figure 3 displays the patterns of participation described by the classic Verba/Nie participation study and other participation studies in the mid-1960s, when political activity was supposedly at its modern highpoint. About three-fifths of the public voted in the presidential elections of the 1960s, a fifth was active in presidential election campaigns, a quarter had contacted political officials, and a third was active in their community. This was the idyllic image of participatory America.

Figure 3. Estimate of Changing Participation Patterns over Time

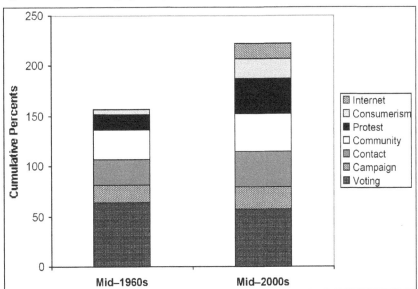

Source: Estimates by the author.

Four decades later, the situation has changed. Turnout in presidential elections has decreased by a few percentage points, which stimulated concerns about a disengaged public. But the best available evidence suggests that other forms of action have held steady or increased—and new forms of action have been added to the participatory repertoire. Just as many people are active in political campaigns based on the American National Election Studies. Several studies indicate that direct political contacting has increased, as well as community activity. In addition, political protest has dramatically grown from an unconventional and infrequent form of action to an extension of normal politics by other means. In a typical year, up to a third of the public reports signing a petition, participating in a demonstration, or joining in some other contentious action. In addition, political consumerism and Internet activism now have broadened the agenda of action, each involving 15–20 percent of Americans on an annual basis.

Again, these are suggestive estimates rather than precise calculations based on identical survey data from each time point, but the trend is obvious. Political participation in the United States has expanded over this period. The public's total activity is now more than a third greater than in the 1960s. Equally important, the patterns of action have also changed significantly.

YOUTH AND CHANGING PARTICIPATION PATTERNS

The explanation for changing participation patterns is complex, and many factors are involved. It partially reflects the growing political skills and resources of the citizenry, as education levels have risen and access to political information has increased. It partially reflects technological changes, such as the importance of television in informing the public and the growth of the Internet. Both of these technologies have had positive and negative consequences on the nature of political discourse. In addition, the growth of self-expressive values encourages participation in activities that are citizen initiated, directly linked to government, and more policy oriented.[20] In short, changing skills and norms encourage Americans to engage in more demanding and more assertive means of political action.

Age is another factor that is typically linked to participation patterns. Since the advent of public opinion research, studies have routinely found that young people are less interested in politics and less likely to participate in elections. Then, political involvement increases as individuals establish careers, begin raising families, and become integrated into their communities. This is generally known as the "life cycle model" of participation (see introduction to this book). Based on such age patterns, and especially the declining levels of electoral participation among the young over time, several scholars have argued that youth are dropping out of politics. The criticisms of youth and the perils for democracy are often harshly stated, as reflected in many of the contributions to this volume.

However, there is also a generational aspect to age differences in political participation. Generations are the carriers of these changing experiences and social conditions. Younger Americans are better educated than their grandparents, and more likely to have self-expressive values that lead to more challenging forms of action. Generations are also raised in different political conditions with different norms about politics. Younger generations have become more critical of political parties and elected politicians and thus are less attracted to conventional electoral politics. As a result, some alternative forms of nonelectoral participation appear especially appealing to young people. In contrast, research routinely proclaims that electoral politics is the domain of older Americans.

The complication, therefore, is that participation patterns across age groups reflect a combination of life cycle and generational effects. When life cycle and generational effects are reinforcing—such as for voting or belonging to a political party—older Americans are more likely to participate. However, in other instances a generational shift toward nonelectoral forms of participation among the young may be so strong that it may lessen or even reverse the normal life cycle pattern. Thus, rather than generalize about the overall political disengagement of youth based primarily on electoral participation, we need to compare patterns across the full range of possible political activities.

Our age comparisons are based on the 2005 CDACS survey that included the largest number of participation items in a recent nationally representative in-person survey.[21] As benchmark, we begin by comparing age groups in their electoral participation. Figure 4 presents the patterns of voting and party activity for five age groups, beginning with those under age 30. The top line in the figure displays the familiar pattern of significantly lower voting turnout among the young, and then increasing turnout with age. In this survey, there is a 26-percentage point difference in turnout between 18–29-year-olds and people in their 60s. Similarly, a summary of campaign activity—working for a candidate, displaying a button or sticker, or contributing money—shows a slight increase with age. These age differences reflect the general pattern of lower electoral engagement among the young. Moreover, other studies have shown that age differences in turnout have increased over time, which implies that more than just a basic life cycle pattern is involved.

Figure 4. Age Differences in Electoral Activity

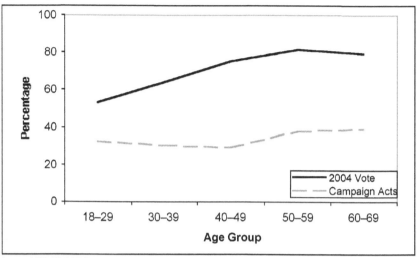

Source: 2005 CDACS Survey.

Beyond electoral politics, some of the most common political activities in-volve contacting officials on political matters and working with a group on a political topic. Figure 5 indicates that both of these forms of political activity are more common among older Americans, a pattern consistent with a life cycle increase in political involvement. Furthermore, Martin Wattenberg compares participation in community groups across three surveys (1967, 1987, and 2002)

Figure 5. Contacting and Working with a Group by Age

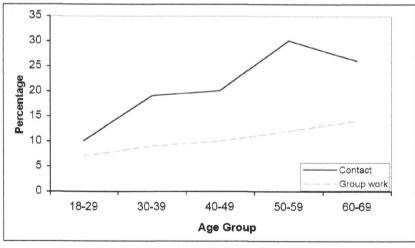

Source: 2005 CDACS Survey.

and finds that all age groups have become more active by roughly the same margin.[22] However, he finds that contacting has grown disproportionately among older Americans over time, with young people remaining constant in this activity between 1967 and 2004.

Figure 6 shows examples of more contentious and elite-challenging participation options—and they follow a much different pattern. The lower line in the figure displays the percentage that has participated in either a legal or illegal protest in the past year. While this is a relatively infrequent activity on an annual basis, it is still several times more common among the young than among the oldest cohort. Furthermore, there is evidence that this age pattern reflects generational changes, with younger Americans today more likely to use this method when compared to their parents' generation.[23] Similarly, the middle line is the percentage that has used the Internet in one of three political activities (visiting a political Web site, forwarding political messages, or participating in Internet-based political activities). Here the contrast between the youngest and oldest age groups is the clearest. The top line displays the percentage of each age group that has boycotted a product or bought a product for political reasons or ethical reasons in the past year. This activity is also slightly more common among the younger two age groups.

Figure 6. Unconventional Action by Age

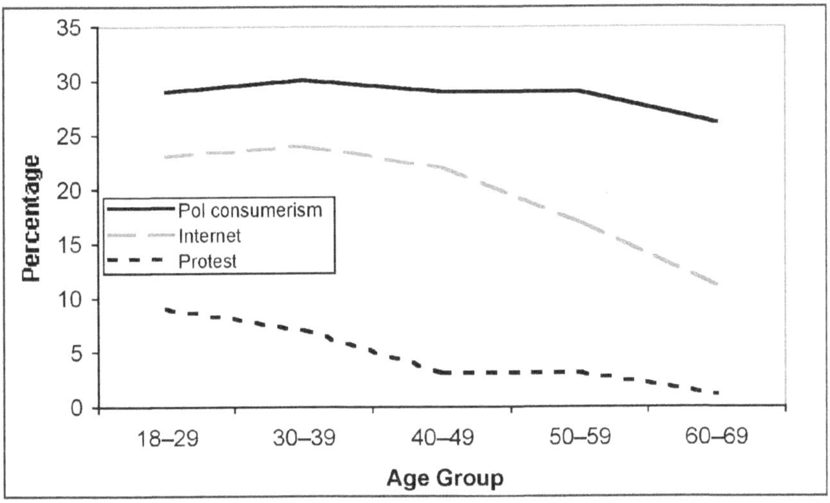

Source: 2005 CDACS Survey.

These age patterns across different activities fail to show a consistent decline in participation among the young; instead they suggest that social and political changes are transforming the way younger people are linked to politics.

Fewer young people vote, but they are more likely to volunteer, protest, or connect to politics through the Web—and all of these methods were often overlooked by studies of traditional forms of political participation. Furthermore, there are substantial differences even among those under age 30. For instance, the better-educated youth and those with more assertive norms of citizenship accentuate these trends—with higher levels of protest, political consumerism, Internet-based activism, and even participation in more conventional forms. Social change, therefore, affects young people differently depending on their own political skills and norms.

ENGAGED DEMOCRATS

Some of the leading political experts in the United States have asserted that Americans are disengaging from the political process, which may undermine the bases of American democracy. John Hibbing and Elisabeth Theiss-Morse claim that Americans have become politically disengaged and want to stay that way: "The last thing people want is to be more involved in political decision making: They do not want to make political decisions themselves; they do not want to provide much input to those who are assigned to make these decisions; and they would rather not know all the details of the decision-making process."[24] This theme is vividly represented by many of the contributions to this book.

This chapter has argued that the reality of American politics is much different. Few members of Congress, for instance, complain that they receive less input from their constituents than in the past; few government administrators yearn for a lobbyist to break the dullness of their daily routine. Instead, they see individual citizens, lobby organizations, and public interest groups as part of an expanding network of activism that has developed in Washington over the previous generation. In short, the good news is . . . the bad news is wrong. America remains a participatory society.

Election turnout has declined, but this is not typical of all political activity. The repertoire of action has actually expanded, and people are now more engaged in more forms of political participation. Participation in election campaigns is still common. People are working with informal groups in their community to address local problems—and this has grown over time. More people today make the effort to directly contact their elected representative or other government officials. The repertoire of political action now includes a variety of protest activities. When one adds political consumerism and Internet activism, the forms of action are even more diverse.

Thus, there are four major lessons from our findings. First, turnout rates in elections are a poor indicator of the overall political involvement of Americans. It is the most easily available statistic for local, state, and national politics—and it extends back in time. However, there is more to democracy than elections. Other nonelectoral modes of individualized or direct political action have increased over time. Rather than disengagement, the repertoire of political action has broadened.

Changes in political participation are analogous to changes in the contemporary media environment. Compared to a generation ago, Americans are consuming much more information about politics, society, and other topics. People are also consuming information from a greater diversity of media sources, some of which did not exist a generation ago. If one only tracked the viewership of the news programs on the major television networks, however, the statistics would show a downward trend in viewership over time. The declining viewership for ABC, CBS, and NBC is not because people are watching less television—they are watching more hours per day—but because there are more alternatives today. This is the same with participation: people are more active in more varied forms of action.

Certainly we should not dismiss the decrease in voting turnout. Elections are important because they select political elites, provide a source of democratic legitimacy, and engage the mass public in the democratic process. If large proportions of young (and older) Americans do not vote, their representation in the political process decreases (and may change election outcomes). It is not healthy for democracy when half or more of the public voluntarily abstains from electing government officials. This is especially problematic when the elected government does not represent all the people—and makes decisions that a full majority of Americans do not support. For instance, given these differential turnout rates, it is not surprising that the government devotes increasing resources to programs benefitting seniors while providing proportionately less support for the young. This realization has stimulated efforts to re-engage young people in elections.[25] However, the goal of participation reforms should be not only to encourage young people to act like their grandparents (and vote out of a sense of duty) but also to show how one can exert meaningful political influence through voting as well as through new forms of participation.

Second, the shifting patterns of political action reflect ongoing trends in the skills and political norms of the American public. The political skills and resources of the public have increased and, in turn, altered the calculus of participation. Turning out to vote is a relatively simple political act that is often mobilized by social or political groups through "get out the vote" drives. More people today can engage in more demanding forms of political action, such as individualized activity and direct action. Writing letters to a government official, for example, is less likely when three-fifths of the public has less than a high school education (the electorate of 1952) than when three-fifths have some college education (the electorate of 2008). Similarly, changing norms of what it means to be a good citizen are affecting participation styles. People want to be active in methods that give them more direct say and influence in politics and society. Many citizens will still vote because of the importance of elections to the democratic process. However, their participation repertoire includes more direct and individualized forms of action.

Third, the changing mix of participation activities has implications for the quality of citizen influence. Verba and Nie, for example, described voting as a high-pressure activity because government officials are being chosen, but it has limited specific policy information or influence because elections involve a diverse range of issues.[26] Therefore, the infrequent opportunity to cast a vote for a prepackaged party is a limited tool of influence. In contrast, direct action methods allow citizens to focus on their own issue interests, select the means of influencing policy makers, and choose the timing of influence. The issue might be as broad as nuclear disarmament or as narrow as the policies of the local school district—citizens, not elites, decide. Control over the framework of participation means that people can convey more information and exert more political pressure than is possible with only election campaigns. These new forms of action thus have the potential to increase the quantity and quality of democratic influence.

Finally, many discussions of democratic reform look to recreate an earlier period in American politics when campaigns and elections were more central to politics. But with the style of citizen participation changing, democratic institutions need to adjust. Over the past quarter century, campaigns, legislatures, and the courts have undergone reforms to make them more accessible, transparent, and accountable.[27] In addition, even the new forms of action described in this chapter understate the expanding forms of democratic participation.[28] Scores of cities are developing citizen panels or citizen juries to discuss issues ranging from city budgets to urban development to the schools. "E-democracy" is providing new opportunities for discussion and decision making. Deliberative assemblies are another new tool of citizen action. When taken together with the changes discussed in this chapter, America is arguably experiencing the greatest expansion of citizen participation since the Populist Movement of the early 1900s. Rather than a period of democratic decline, we face the opportunity for a new era of democratic expansion but we must realize the challenges of a changing citizenry and respond to them positively.

ENDNOTES

1. Sidney Verba and Norman Nie, *Participation in America: Political Democracy and Social Equality* (New York: Harper and Row, 1972), 3.

2. Robert Putnam, *Bowling Alone: The Collapse and Renewal of American Community* (New York: Simon and Schuster, 2000); Stephen Macedo et al., *Democracy at Risk: How Political Choices Undermine Citizen Participation, and What We Can Do about It* (Washington, DC: Brookings Institution Press, 2005); Alan Wolfe, *Does American Democracy Still Work?* (New Haven: Yale University Press, 2006); Martin Wattenberg, *Where Have All the Voters Gone?* (Cambridge: Harvard University Press, 2002).

3. See the essays by William Damon, Martin P. Wattenberg, and Eva Anduiza in this book. See also Mark Bauerlain, *The Dumbest Generation: How the Digital Age Stupefies Young Americans and Jeopardizes Our Future* (New York: Penguin, 2008).

4. Cliff Zukin, Scott Keeter, Moly Andolina, Krista Jenkins, and Michael X. Delli Carpini, *A New Engagement? Political Participation, Civic Life, and the Changing American Citizen* (New York: Oxford University Press, 2006), 189; see Ronald Inglehart, *Modernization and Post-modernization: Cultural, Economic and Political Change in 43 Societies* (Princeton: Princeton University Press, 1997), 307; see also Russell Dalton, *The Good Citizen: How a Younger Generation Is Transforming American Politics*, rev. ed. (Washington, DC: CQ Press, 2009).

5. For the full comparison of both surveys, see Dalton, *The Good Citizen*, chap. 4. There is a slight decrease in informal activity over time, although this might be due to the ambiguity of coding responses to such an open-ended question. Some of the examples of individual contacting in 1981 may also fit as examples of collective action involving an informal group.

6. Jeffrey Birnbaum, "On Capitol Hill, the Inboxes Are Overflowing," *Washington Post*, July 11, 2005, D01.

7. Putnam, *Bowling Alone* and Macedo et al., *Democracy at Risk* present trends in a wide variety of political activities, but many of these trends are from commercial marketing polls of uncertain quality. Other participation surveys change the time reference or the wording of the participation questions. The 1967 Verba/Nie survey, for example, did not have a clear time reference; their 1990 survey asked about activity over the previous twelve months. Other questionnaires vary the focus of activity or combine different activities in a single question. Neither the 1987 nor the 1989 survey has been systematically replicated.

8. Putnam, *Bowling Alone*, chap. 2; Macedo et al., *Democracy at Risk*.

9. Changes in campaign finance laws have altered the way that people give money to campaigns. Figure 1 presents only those who have given money to a party or a candidate in the campaign. However, other contributions go to political action groups. In 2004, for instance, 15 percent of the public gave to at least one of these sources, so the percentage in the table is a conservative estimate.

10. Sidney Verba, Kay Schlozman, and Henry Brady, *Voice and Equality: Civic Voluntarism in American Politics* (Cambridge: Harvard University Press, 1995), 72.

11. Verba, Schlozman, and Brady, *Voice and Equality*, 72.

12. Dalton, *Citizen Politics*, chap. 3.

13. Verba, Schlozman, and Brady, *Voice and Equality*, 72.

14. Inglehart, *Culture Shift in Advanced Industrial Society* (Princeton: Princeton University Press, 1989).

15. See essay by Micheletti and Stolle in this book. See also Dietlind Stolle, Marc Hooghe, and Michele Micheletti, "Politics in the Supermarket: Political Consumerism as a Form of Political Participation," *International Political Science Review* 26 (2005): 245–270.

16. The Citizens, Involvement and Democracy survey was conducted by the Center for Democracy and Civil Society (CDACS) at Georgetown University under the direction of Marc Howard. The data and associated materials are located at http://www.uscidsurvey.org.

17. Michael Alvarez and Thad Hall, *Point, Click and Vote: The Future of Internet Voting* (Washington, DC: Brookings Institution Press, 2004).

18. Aaron Smith, Kay Schlozman, Sidney Verba, and Henry Brady, *The Internet and Civic Engagement*, (Pew Internet & American Life Project: 2009), www.pewinternet.org/Reports/2009/15—The-Internet-and-Civic-Engagement.aspx.

19. Smith, Schlozman, Verba, and Brady, *The Internet and Civic Engagement*, 16.

20. Dalton, *The Good Citizen*; Inglehart, *Modernization and Post-modernization*.

21. The general patterns in Figures 4 through 6 were broadly replicated in an analysis of the 2004 General Social Survey, which has a shorter list of participation items. See Dalton, *The Good Citizen*, chap. 4. Additional information on the CDACS survey is in endnote 16.

22. Wattenberg, epilogue to *Is Voting for Young People?*, tables 8.3, 8.4a.

23. Wattenberg, epilogue to *Is Voting for Young People?*, table 8.6b. As critics argue that a lower baseline in youth turnout foretells a continuing lag as these citizens age, the higher group participation of youth may foretell continuing increases as they age.

24. John Hibbing and Elizabeth Theiss-Morse, *Stealth Democracy: Americans' Beliefs about How Government Should Work* (New York: Cambridge University Press), 1–2.

25. For a discussion of the implications of lower turnout among the young, see the essays in the previous section.

26. Verba and Nie, *Participation in America*, 52.

27. Bruce Cain, Russell Dalton, and Susan Scarrow, eds., *Democracy Transformed? Expanding Political Access in Advanced Industrial Democracies* (Oxford: Oxford University Press, 2003).

28. Graham Smith, *Democratic Innovations: Designing Institutions for Citizen Participation* (New York: Cambridge University Press, 2009).

*Russell J. Dalton is a professor of political science at the University of California, Irvine.

DISCUSSION QUESTIONS

1. Why are the patterns of participation changing in America? Is it due to the changes in technology and other institutional factors, or due to changes in the citizens themselves?

2. Will young people who protest or participate in online activism today remain politically active when they get older, or just drop their unconventional style of activity?

3. If Americans are changing the way they participate in politics, is this increasing or decreasing their ability to influence the government?

4. Is the growth in political activism a good thing for democracy if it comes at increasing inequality in who participates?

Millennials Are Involved Locally with Others but Are Ambivalent About Formal Politics

by Abby Kiesa, Alexander P. Orlowski, Peter Levine, Deborah Both, Emily Hoban Kirby, Mark Hugo Lopez, and Karlo Barrios Marcelo*

A large majority of college students are volunteering in a wide spectrum of areas (although some of the volunteering we perceive to be episodic). The most common fields in which students are volunteering are education, youth, health-care, and poverty/welfare issues; however, students also report volunteering in many other areas, such as the environment, technology, and human rights. Students most often report that their volunteer work is through an educational institution, such as their high school or college.

WHY THEY ENGAGE

Most students think it is their responsibility to get involved to make things better for society. A Minnesota student says, "There are a lot of places in the world that are really nasty, where you could get killed by the government if you do something they don't like. So it's like, I better get out there and do my part to keep this country a good place." And a Providence student says, "I kind of feel obligated to do service."

When asked for the fundamental purpose, or reason, for their engagement activities, the most popular response is "to help others." A Maryland student says, "I think volunteering is beneficial because you take it upon yourself to go out and do something then and there, and it's every person on their own actually trying to do something ..." Similarly, a Kansas State student says, "Out of volunteering comes good. Period." A Dayton student says, "I'm just trying to give somebody else the same things that I had in life." A UMass Boston student says, "This whole world, the whole reason for this world is not just about ourselves, it's never just me for me to grow, for me to this, for me to that. But it's what about my neighbor; what about the people after me ..."

CIRCLE's 2006 *Civic and Political Health of the Nation Survey* (CPHS) also showed that a majority of college students volunteer to help others (not to address a social or political problem).

Reason for Volunteering Among 18-to-25-year-old College Students

To Address a Social or Political Problem	11%
To Help Other People	74%
Some Other Reason	14%
Don't Know	1%

Source: 2006 Civic and Political Health of the Nation Survey.

However, many students in our study also note that they volunteer to change something. A Bowdoin student points out, "I feel as though we're all very lucky to be here and life is pretty great most of the time, but at the same time there's a lot of stuff that can be improved, and I think it's kind of my rent for living on earth to try and do stuff when I see problems and make it a little bit better."

Students use the language of "change," however, in two distinct ways: the first is a desire to effect systemic change, and the second (which is more common) is to address immediate needs in the community.

Some trace their civic engagement in college back to high school civics requirements such as required community service and required civics and government courses. A Providence student says, "Most [high]schools now have community service requirements and it's come to the point where they've trained you so much into it, it becomes second nature and habit to do service." That is a favorable view of high school service requirements. About equal numbers of students report positive experiences and negative experiences in high school civics and government classes. Both the positive and negative experiences influence their likelihood of being civically engaged, but in opposite ways. A Kansas State student says, "As a senior in high school I took a government class and I also took a global affairs class and that really got me started thinking about the way our government is working and the way it's affecting the issues that are going on in the world today. So that really got me started thinking and I've been able to recognize those same stories and follow them throughout college and that's really been helpful." However, another Kansas State student says, "I think back in high school about my history classes. Our history teacher had us do essay exams. And so I'd go home and memorize the information and stuff and then spit it back out. And, of course, the next day it was gone."

Students were asked if there is anything in their life that makes them more or less likely to follow or participate in the political system. In response, almost one in six students say that their parents' engagement has made them more likely to engage in the political system. Students also bring up, though to a lesser extent, personal experience as a reason they are more likely to follow or participate in the political system.

Volunteering and Public Policy

When given the opportunity, students can make links between their volunteer activities and public policy, some very passionately. Some students say that they volunteer to correct problems caused by public policy. Concerned with education, some students argue that specific No Child Left Behind policies negatively affect some schools around the country. Students also mention the inadequate amount of governmental aid after Hurricane Katrina. One Dayton student says, "I think a lot of the issues we're coping with across any sphere, have a lot to do with bad law and bad public policy." A Kansas State student says, "Whenever I volunteer, help, or sign a petition, or donate money, it may not always be for, I hope this directly changes the law. But there is that kind of notion of something is not quite, either not quite right or maybe not as good as it could be. So hopefully that, you know, the volunteering or some measure[d] action will help rectify the policy." But for the majority of students, their original motivation for volunteer work is not a concern about specific public policies.

Students See Organizing People as the Most Beneficial Strategy for Addressing Public Issues

Throughout the focus groups a theme began to emerge that was only reinforced by each consecutive conversation: Students seek to be involved *with others* and believe in the power of collective actions to address public issues.

In the focus groups students were asked whether they believe volunteering, advocating for policy change, voting, organizing people, or giving money is most beneficial to address public issues. The "organizing people" option was meant to be broad and generic and was not intended to imply only historic "community organizing" practices often used by the political left. That being said, we did not ask students to explain in detail what they meant when using the term.

Students maintain that organizing people is the best first-step to social change. A UMass Boston student says, "The more people you get, the more awareness you raise, and then comes the money, and then comes the policy changes, so organizing the people is the most important one, hands down." Other students make the same point, stating that once people are organized, it is easier to get financial and volunteer support, and therefore easier to advocate for policy change.

When presented with a large pile of images and asked to choose one that most represents the term "politics," a Maryland student picks a photograph of citizens. He says, "This, to me, like, grassroots little local town, you know, doing their thing, to me, that's like the heart of politics....Whereas they might not have the same kind of power, you know, each person individually as someone who is sitting there, but, you know, as a whole, they can make it change, and they can do it themselves."

According to the survey given at the end of the focus groups, while most students believe that they individually can make some difference in their community, a larger percentage of students believe that groups of people working together can make a great deal of difference.

How much difference do you believe you can personally make in working to solve problems?		How much difference do you believe that people working together as a group can make in solving problems?	
Great Deal of Difference	18%	Great Deal of Difference	62%
Some Difference	45%	Some Difference	30%
A Little Difference	33%	A Little Difference	7%
No Difference at all	2%	No Difference at all	1%
Don't Know	1%	Don't Know	1%

Source: Survey of Millennials Talk Politics Focus Group Participants 2007.

Students note that finding groups to volunteer with is a big motivator for them. A Dayton student says, "What I found to be really helpful, especially here, is just that there are so many service clubs. If you have something that you want to get involved in, there are opportunities." Students sometimes perceive a lack of something concrete to do or believe their individual efforts cannot have a significant impact, but believe people working in groups can create a great deal of difference.

STUDENTS DO NOT SEE VOTING AS AN EFFECTIVE WAY OF INFLUENCING CHANGE

Very few students say that voting is the most beneficial vehicle for addressing public issues; in fact, voting by far receives the least support. Students overwhelmingly testify that voting is not a vehicle for change. A Bowdoin student argues, "It's funny, when you're little you learn about the 'one vote' and this is how democracy works, but when you get older and you actually go and vote, you feel like those votes do not matter." Students think that voting is necessary, but view it more as a "symbolic gesture" than a means of creating change. A Wake Forest student says, "I think voting is important, but I think it would probably be the least beneficial if you wanted to make a change happen." A Berkeley student says, "I think voting is the least you can do in terms of showing that you're political."

Another Wake Forest student says, "I don't know how it should be changed, but I think it should be changed that when people vote, that their vote actually counts. You know, that people who vote actually feel like change can be made. I think it should be set up so that voting actually changes things ... Because maybe more people would vote, and then maybe what goes on in the government would be a reflection of what the common people wanted." A Dayton student says, "Your one vote isn't enough to change anything." Perhaps students' conception of voting can be best expressed by a Maryland student who reports, "I have voted every time I've been given an opportunity, but I do it more as a symbolic gesture than an actual means of changing something."

DISSATISFACTION WITH POLITICS

A Princeton student summarizes college students' general frustrations with the political system by stating, "Politics to me has, no I wouldn't call it a negative connotation, but it does not have an idealistic connotation; whereas rallying and activism and going for a cause has more of that idealistic undertone, while politics is marred by bad deals."

Today's college students express dissatisfaction and irritation with the current political system, which they find inefficient, corrupt, inaccessible, and counter to the genuine welfare of the nation's citizens. On the other hand, as mentioned previously, students have not given up on the potential of the political system to address public issues. They find and make their own civic opportunities and some make connections between these experiences and public policy.

After a free-association activity where students were asked to write or draw on a poster whatever came to their minds when they heard the word "government," a Princeton student reflects, "There's more negative under government, but, I mean that's to be expected." A classmate added, "Government is something that's very bureaucratic. It's sort of stale. It's not moving. It's there. It's frustrating." In most focus groups, "government" prompted such comments. The students noted their own frustration and sometimes observed that they would like to engage the system but find it disappointing.

Adding to students' frustrations with politics is a belief that the government is not currently fulfilling its proper role, and therefore should not be trusted; a Kansas State student says, "Government should be [about the] common good. I don't think we naturally feel that fit right now." A Princeton student similarly says, "Politics should be people's voices being heard, but I don't really feel like it is being heard right now." Consequently, students seem to look at the current political system with skepticism. As a Berkeley student says, "I think politics is seen as untrustworthy, and might be something that always has to be taken with a grain of salt. Double-check your race card, your resources, and always question. I think college students question politics." A Tougaloo student says, "Let's stop looking at some of these petty issues. Let's look upon what's really affecting us."

However, this is not to say that students completely disregard politics. In fact, many students differentiate between politics as it is currently practiced and their ideal practice of politics. A Minnesota student says, "When I think of politics, I think it has to do with humanity, the common good, the government, and all those things really."

DESPITE THEIR DISSATISFACTION, STUDENTS WANT TO ENGAGE

Combating a negative perception of collegiate student civic engagement, a Berkeley student says, "I think college students are really actively involved in politics, actually. I think we're led to think that they don't [participate], when in fact everything that I've witnessed has shown me otherwise."

We heard many stories of action related to public policy. A strong minority of students is engaged in various facets of political life. A Kansas State student says, "Our school district here in town, was just, they've been debating for a couple years whether to start a new administrative position called a diversity coordinator, which would be the first one in Kansas. And I had a professor on campus ask me to come speak on behalf of the position and talk about the benefits it would have on the community and the school district." A UMass Boston student told us about how he has "been working on housing issues for three years now," and, "got a friend of [his] to put up a bill in front of the State House."

Some students do prefer individual acts of service to politics. For instance, a student from Dayton says, "But in everything I have to do in a school day, the last thing I'm going to care about is politics. Like, that—that's just the way I am. I mean, I'd rather go and help that kid read than, than see what's going on." A New Mexico student says, "Like, the government is, like, really far away and something that you can't really affect or change, but something that you can actually do in your community and see the results of might be more, like, motivating, like, for people."

However, we also met students who say, in the words of a Minnesota undergraduate, "I think 'politics' is talking to one another and strategically organizing, working together to a common goal." A Tougaloo student says: "We're our own politics."

The students we spoke with are frustrated with the political system and with the media. But although they do not trust these major institutions, they try to engage with them. This finding is consistent with trends in national surveys. For example, youth have consistently lost trust in the news industry, yet their actual consumption of newspapers and other media has risen since 2000 (see Graph below). A Minnesota student says, "People are talking about the whole system is screwed up, it doesn't represent us. On some I agree, but on the other hand, I also definitely have confidence that there are mechanisms built in the system to change it, move it."

News Consumption and Confidence among 18-to-25 Year Olds

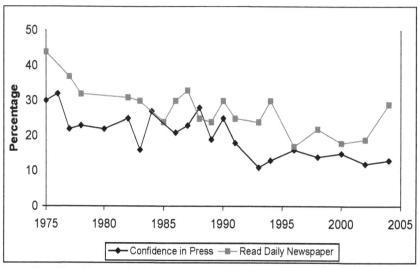

Source: General Social Survey analyzed by CIRCLE.

STUDENTS DO NOT VIEW THE POLITICAL SYSTEM AS ACCESSIBLE

Despite any convictions that the political system is corrupt, inefficient, and bureaucratic, college students do not completely dismiss politics from their lives. In fact, students want to engage the political system, but largely find it inaccessible. A Wake Forest student says, "I just get this feeling about politics as this inaccessible realm that people don't really have that much participation in." In the survey given at the end of the focus groups, most students (42 percent) indicate that they view politics as a way for the powerful to keep power to themselves. Only 12 percent indicate that politics is a way for the less powerful to compete on equal footing with the powerful.

Students express two reasons why they feel that the political system is inaccessible to them: a lack of resources and a lack of perceived importance. A Providence student says, "As college students, we don't really have a lot of the resources that you need to get your voice heard." A classmate agrees, adding, "We just feel like there's almost no point in trying when you can only do so much and you don't have the essential resources to actually make a big cause."

Students also feel that their representatives and other government officials do not consider them important. A Berkeley student explains, "Politicians really don't see students as a very viable or active population, simply because they're not the donors." A Maryland student feels the university's Student Government Association better represents him than any other political body because it is composed of students: "SGA is for the students, and I'm a student. I feel like presidents and delegates [are] for people older than me, younger than me, they have a broad range of people they have to serve." Some students also note that if they could make one change to the political system, they would like to be able to speak and interact with elected officials or have politicians pay more attention to young people.

The survey accompanying the focus group discussions affirms that students feel that the public is distant from the political process. When asked whether or not they feel the political system is responsive to the genuine needs of the public, an overwhelming 58 percent of students respond that the political system is not responsive to the genuine needs of the public, compared to only 28 percent of students who feel that it is responsive. Students are also more likely to feel that the government needs to do more to solve problems (42 percent) rather than feel that the government does too many things that should be left to businesses and individuals (12 percent).

FRUSTRATIONS WITH POLITICIANS

Students see no shortage of corruption within the halls of government, beginning with politicians. A Berkeley student explains that, as individuals climb the rungs of the political ladder, they forget why they began climbing in the first place: "When people are running for city council, you find people who really are interested in doing good for the community. When you get to statewide or national politics, you find people trying to better themselves to get to the top, to get this one more promotion, on their way to having a career in politics, and that is very disappointing to someone who's younger and more idealistic." A UMass Boston student adds, "Once that person that['s] in charge...once that person gets to that place, their eyes are, like, covered and, like, they see something else…Their mind is totally changed and they forget about the little people who want[ed] to help him get there."

Students also blame politicians for the inaccessibility of the political system. They assert that because they lack the financial resources to contribute to political campaigns, politicians often turn a deaf ear to the college population. Students view politicians as self-serving, rather than true representatives of the people. A Maryland student says, "I think oftentimes policy-makers and politicians set the issues for the public rather than the public setting the issues for the policy-makers and politicians."

As mentioned earlier, in the middle of each discussion, we offered a large set of visual images to the group and asked them to find the one that most represents politics to them. Many students describe their chosen picture as an exclusive conversation at a table composed of people whom they describe as white men, and often as overweight and bald. As one Bowdoin student says, "I chose this [picture] because I've always imagined politics as something that rich, white, slightly plump men do." They see a few powerful people making decisions for the entire nation behind closed doors, inaccessible to the general public. As a Dayton student says, "I think a lot of students feel very disconnected."

UNDERSTANDING THE SYSTEM

In the focus groups, students readily discuss issues that concern them. A Tougaloo student shares concern about Hurricane Katrina: "I never seem to see how we could always go over there and help other countries, but really our own country here, I mean, our own brothers and sisters here suffer[ed] for three days without any food." They are often aware of the role that policy plays related to issues that they care about, either contributing to or attempting to resolve the issue.

Yet many students are not able to articulate how those policies are put into place and what levels of government have authority in a given area. Some are forthright with their lack of knowledge in how the system works. A UMass Boston student says, "My cousins, they're all in the Boston Public School System. They don't have textbooks. The books that they have are photocopies of things or they have textbooks that they have to keep inside the classroom to then pass back, you know, to the next group of kids but they can't take them home. I don't understand that. It's all the money, all the taxes that they're taking from us, where's it going?" The students who are not involved civically or politically are the least likely to have knowledge of how the political system works.

Students do pick up on various aspects of the political process and many, though not all, have learned basic information about Congress and elections in high school. A Tougaloo student says, "Republican always wins in Mississippi, it's a Republican state." They know about the electoral college and the predisposition of a state's electoral votes to go Republican or Democratic in an election, they know that constructing policy is a long-term process and can identify political "spin" when they hear it. A Berkeley student explains to the rest of the group the details of her work related to Darfur, Sudan: "The idea is if enough people divest, then there will be a lot of government pressure on the Sudanese government and they'll have to take some sort of action and some sort of reaction to the international community, as opposed to what's going on right now."

At the conclusion of each focus group we asked students what would make the political system more appealing for them to participate in or follow. A range of ideas surfaced that included:

- "If change could be more attainable, good change, that would affect people positively"
- "Sincerity"
- "Making politics less commercialized"
- "I'd like my voice to be heard on more than just election day"
- "If it felt more close to us than far away"
- "A really easy way to give your input"

However these ideas more often than not lacked specificity. While some students did apply their comment to a particular process, system, or policy, more did not.

This lack of specific knowledge about how the political system works probably decreases students' likeliness to engage in the system because they do not know where or how to plug in and try to make an impact.

The Gap between Issue Concerns and Action

Even though students report volunteering in a large variety of areas, only a very small handful of participants note any volunteer experience related to the war in Iraq or the current genocide in Darfur, Sudan. However, when asked what current issues spark their attention, both of these topics are common responses. It seems that these issues are a deep concern among college students, but there is a gap between their noticing such problems and taking personal action.

Other issues that frequently spark students' attention—but not necessarily their personal action—include healthcare, HIV/AIDS, access to college, immigration, the environment, poverty/welfare issues, and (above all) education (including everything from college tuition to the No Child Left Behind Act). A Kansas State student says that, "For me, like focus in on such a global issue, it's, like, where do you begin, you know, because the problem is so huge." Many students list national or international issues as sparking their attention, but many more report taking volunteer action in local areas.

Volunteering as a Way to Become Informed

In an era when numerous media sources inundate students with an excess of information, some students indicate, in looking back on their volunteer activities, that community service is a way to filter information and gain more informed perspectives on public issues. A Maryland student says, "I think that civic engagement is very important whether you help others or to make a statement about society or helping a culture or a group or an organization. That engagement brings with it an awareness of issues in society that makes us all better citizens." A Dayton student says, "I think the more you are involved in things, the more you understand what's going on."

Volunteering as a Complement to Politics

In 2002, a statement entitled The New Student Politics suggested that some college students defined their volunteer or community service work as political, that their activity was a form of politics. This report, published by Campus Compact, was based on a conversation among a select group of engaged students from across the country.

In hopes of shedding light on this relationship several years later, we asked students in our survey whether they viewed volunteering and community service as a form of politics, an alternative to politics, a complement to politics, or as something unrelated to politics. A majority of the students respond that volunteering is a complement to politics.

Students also say that because they view the political system as inefficient and inaccessible, they turn to volunteering. A Minnesota student says, "I know for me in some ways it's about challenging the system in a lot of ways, and that's why I volunteer." A Princeton student says, "Policy and politics is this thing that's kind of hard to move, it's very easy to get fed up and just turn to something like volunteer work." And a Providence student says, "So obviously, this is an issue and a concern for Americans. I think community service has sort of taken the spot of politics for a lot of people."

However, when asked, students overwhelmingly maintain that their volunteer efforts do relate to public policy. Some students seem to talk themselves, in a circular fashion, into believing that their volunteer activities relate to public policy. In this section of the focus groups, it was clear that some students are still piecing their experiences and knowledge together, and that these students do not have many experiences to reflect on this aspect of their volunteer activities. In the end, very few college students said their volunteer activities did not relate to public policy. A Kansas State student says that, "When you volunteer it's kind of like you're pointing out a space that's not being addressed by public policy, almost."

Do You View Volunteering/Community Service as...

A Form of Politics	16%
An Alternative to Politics	10%
A Complement to Politics	51%
Has Nothing to do with Politics	22%

Source: Survey of Millennials Talk Politics Focus Group Participants 2007.

Students are seeking civic opportunities that are authentic, rather than competitive or partisan. For many, volunteering is an outlet to help others and "make change" on an individual level. They also see it as a neutral activity that is unlikely to provoke conflict. Students do not enter into volunteer activities with the intention of becoming involved politically. In hindsight, they report that volunteering has helped them to become aware of issues and learn how issues affect people, yet often do not know what they can do with this new awareness.

BARRIERS TO MORE POLITICAL ENGAGEMENT

While a significant majority of students can list the community service activities that they are or have been involved in, there is a solid minority of students who are also engaged in activities focused on public policy and/or elections. The focus groups shed light on several barriers students perceive to political engagement.

In several of the focus groups, students were directly asked to help explain why community service is common and political engagement is not. For many, the answer is clear and they provide a variety of reasons. As one student from Dayton says, "When I see a senator for the U.S. government, I see someone who has never served in a soup kitchen before. So if he's talking about an increase in minimum wage or something, he's not going to know exactly what he's talking about. So that's motivation for me to not be like that at all." A Princeton student says, "I just thought it was so boring and dull and that the entire government was corrupt, so why bother?"

Some students' answers suggest that they are not faced with a choice. For many, political engagement is not as available an opportunity as volunteering and other civic activities. Students are not eschewing politics as much as they do not see politics as an option. They see no clear access points, and their perceptions and experiences with the political system suggest to them that they cannot have an impact, which is what they seek.

WANTING TO HAVE AN IMPACT

Second only to the time they have available to get involved, students report that the most important factor in deciding whether or not to get involved in an activity is the impact they think it will yield. A New Mexico student says, "One thing that, I guess kind of dissuades me from taking action is, I guess I would call it impatience or just general frustration…If I work at it, if I volunteer, if I join a group—a progressive group, you know—is it going to make a dent, is it going to make a difference? And it feels like it won't. And I feel like, for me, if I'm going to do something I want it to have a dramatic effect. I want to change, you know, a lot of people's lives, make them better, but it feels like I'm working from the bottom and you know it's like this drastic inverted pyramid." Students want to know that the time they spend is productive and will directly assist others or directly change something—often, the life of one individual. They do not see how they can influence issues and even doubt that someone with access to the system will hear their opinions. Overwhelmingly, they perceive politics as slow-moving as well as messy and hard to understand.

A Providence student says, "If you were to write a letter to the President, it's probably not going to make a big difference. But when I can just sit and talk to a kid, then I feel like I'm actually doing something." A Maryland student says, "So for me, if I volunteer and help this child out, that's a little step, and I know I've made a little bit of effect in somebody's life." And a Princeton student says, "If I don't think I can influence the change, then I feel like there is no point in getting involved."

Again, while many students report that they are concerned about various international issues like the war in Iraq or the genocide in Darfur, their involvement most often focuses on the U.S., and largely on a local and regional level. Students do not see how they can influence international issues.

"A Lot of Talk, No Action"

Students believe public issues can be solved by people taking action and being engaged with others. They are frustrated with what they perceive as just "sitting around talking" and want to see more action being taken by public figures. A Tougaloo student summarizes this by saying, "Politics right now, a lot of talk, no action." Action, in students' perspectives, seems to center around decisiveness and activities that will have an immediate impact on alleviating problems. As one student from Wake Forest says, "The government has all these things going on, and it's kind of like—I don't know. They kind of play hot potato. They just kind of, like, pass it around while the people are suffering, so people just have to—that's why volunteering is important."

A New Mexico student says, "Like the government is, like, really far away and something that you can't really affect or change, but something that you can actually do in your community and see the results of might be more, like, motivating, like, for people and more of the focus."

Today's college students, having grown up with fast-paced electronic entertainment, hate being bored, are frustrated with inefficiency, and want the instant gratification of seeing the results of their actions. As one Princeton student says, "People in our generation grew up getting really used to immediacy. You know, video games, everything coming at you all the time…here, [in college] I had one friend who just worked her butt off in the 2004 election. She worked so hard and then the side she was working for lost, and she just became really disenchanted with politics after that."

Finding Opportunities

Students report that while opportunities to participate in political activities exist, they are not often widely known. A student's major, focus group participants reported, has a significant influence on whether he or she is exposed to discussions of other issues and to other students who are passionate about political issues and causes. More often than not, if students want to get involved or want to know more about an issue they do not find easy entry points on their campus. A New Mexico student says, "[College students] don't know where the access is to get involved with the government in a sense. So they don't want to get involved in politics because they don't really know where to go."

When students do find out about issues and causes, they tend to hear about them through friends, flyers, chalking (writing information on the sidewalk with chalk) or stories about an issue as it affects someone they know. They also report that they learn about issues and the political system through courses.

Many students also perceive political involvement to be intimidating because it is complicated and they do not feel qualified, they do not know enough, and they are not in a position to be listened to. A personal connection to an issue has a strong influence on students' likelihood to get involved in work related to that issue. Those who are engaged politically have had the opportunity to take concrete action. A Kansas State student says, "In high school I had the experience of being in my dorky service clubs and like [student government] and that kind of stuff…that kind of gave me faith in something larger, like I could, you know, be involved in [student government] and get, I don't know colder water in the water fountains. And then so when I see a larger government I feel like I can make an actual change in that." Another Kansas State student adds, "I think even on a small scale when you see that a voice can make a difference, I think that instills that feeling that I can continue this and then grow into larger incidences of making change."

Regardless of the campus, many students talk about "living in the now" or just trying to keep up with classes, in addition to work and family responsibilities. A Minnesota student says, "It is difficult to actually get out there and take political action when there are so many other things that you have to deal with and you can't ignore them." While students want to be informed and want to be involved, they often do not know how to integrate more regular civic or political involvement into their schedules beyond one-day projects. A Providence student says, "You go to high school, you go to college, you get a job and sometimes you just feel so trapped by that." A disconnect does exist in a few places as students, however, also do not seem to be fully aware of all of the opportunities on campus to be engaged and take action, though less of these opportunities are related to the political system.

*Abby Kiesa is a youth coordinator and researcher at The Center for Information & Research on Civic Learning & Engagement (CIRCLE). She is the lead author on this study.

Kiesa, Abby, Alexander P. Orlowski, Peter Levine, Deborah Both, Emily Hoban Kirby, Mark Hugo Lopez, and Karlo Barrios Marcelo, "Millennials Are Involved Locally with Others but Are Ambivalent About Formal Politics." In *Millennials Talk Politics*, Abby Kiesa et al. eds. (Medford, MA: Center for Information & Research on Civic Learning & Engagement, Tufts University, 2007), pp. 12–23.

DISCUSSION QUESTIONS

1. Instead of volunteering, couldn't young people have more political influence if they took the time to vote and select the politicians who actually make public policy?

2. Is volunteering primarily a way to affect public policy or a way to make the individual feel good about the work they are doing?

3. Are the opportunities and needs to volunteer equal across different types of young people? If there are differences, what are the consequences of these differences?

The Internet and Youth Political Participation

*by Mark E. Kann, Jeff Berry, Connor Gant, and Phil Zager**

Long-term declines in voter turnout in American elections seemed to end after the September 11, 2001, terrorist attacks.[1] In particular, youth voting rates increased. Approximately 36 percent of 18–24 year olds cast ballots in 2000, but more than 42 percent voted in 2004.[2] While it is uncertain if youths' online involvements contributed to this increase, it is evident that young Americans' presence on the Web has the potential to enhance their engagement in public life. In this article, we examine how American youths' contributions to three online worlds—participatory culture, political consumerism, and civic engagement—function as possible gateways to increased political participation. We suggest that American youths have never before had so many low-threshold opportunities for political participation, although we are uncertain whether, over time, substantial numbers will take advantage of those opportunities.

POLITICAL CONSUMERISM AND ONLINE POLITICS

Science-fiction author and A-list blogger Cory Doctorow offers two definitions of "participatory culture." The first focuses on fans as more than passive consumers in their relationship to the media they love. His second definition, drawn from the Participatory Culture Foundation, is more multifaceted.[3] It spans individuals listing their favorite music on their Facebook pages to anti-war activists posting photos of flag-draped coffins on the Web. Here, participatory culture is an online world, such as YouTube, where anyone can share nearly anything with nearly anyone.

With a sales price of US$1.65 billion, YouTube received *Time* magazine's "Invention of the Year" award. For all the career-ending gaffes, graphic cell phone hanging videos, and exploding diet coke fountains that it has hosted, nothing has been more popular on YouTube than "The Evolution of Dance," a six-minute, single camera video of a man dancing to a medley of songs.[4] As of this writing, this video has over 47 million views, more than twice the number of any other YouTube video. A critic looked at the video's mass appeal and commented, "It's a stunning shift when a single low-budget viral video can reach roughly the same number of people as an episode of 'Seinfeld.'"[5] Let us suggest four possibilities for how this world of participatory culture has the potential to increase youth involvement in public life.

First, online participatory culture promotes values that are conducive to democracy. A fundamental democratic value is citizen involvement, the basis for consent of the governed, the exercise of popular sovereignty, and vigilance against tyranny. Henry Jenkins suggests that youth involvement in participatory culture's social networking sites produced higher levels of political engagement. He reports that, among MySpace participants, "Only 21 percent of poll respondents ages 18 to 24 said they had voted for an American Idol contestant. But 53 percent said they had voted for a candidate for public office."[6] Apparently, young online social networkers care less about who America loves and more about who governs.

Another democratic value advanced by participatory culture is openness. Appeals Court Judge Damon Keith notes, "Democracies die behind closed doors." Involvement in participatory culture may motivate youths to keep the doors open.[7] Consider Video the Vote, a group of citizens armed with video cameras and YouTube accounts. Members shoot videos of polling places and interview disenfranchised voters for immediate Web posting. Someone in Los Angeles can find out about an Ohio voter who faced a faulty voting machine the same day.[8] By monitoring and documenting election practices, Video the Vote strengthens electoral openness and honesty.

Second, youths' involvement in participatory culture teaches citizenship skills. For example, participatory culture generally exposes young people to political information and ideas. A Pew Foundation study questioned whether people use the Internet merely to reflect and reinforce their own preconceived views. Its conclusion was that the opposite is true: "It is clear that their Internet use alone is a factor in their wide exposure to political arguments."[9] This conclusion applies particularly well to the world of participatory culture, where many political advocates use culture as a means to disseminate their particular viewpoints.

Participatory culture also teaches youths to apply knowledge to political problem-solving. Jenkins examines the world of Massive Multiplayer Online Role Playing games and identifies a "knowledge culture" where players cooperate to solve problems in a fictional universe. When someone encounters a dilemma, he or she consults with other online participants for help and technical support. Jenkins suggests that we apply the same strategy to politics. He writes, "If we learn to do this through our play, perhaps we can learn to extend those experiences into actual political culture."[10] Here, the line from participatory culture to participatory democracy is a relatively straight one.

Third, participatory culture invites political mobilization. Doctorow notes, "There's a bunch of costs incorporated with political action ... and the Internet is pretty good at knocking the hell out of those."[11] Participatory culture facilitates efforts to bring people together for political action. For example, when social networking site Facebook decided to change its interface and add a "feed" that was widely condemned as invasive, more than 750,000 students used Facebook to organize a protest against Facebook.[12] *Time* magazine reported, "Gen Y has unexpectedly found a way to organize."[13] Participatory culture facilitates political mobilization.

Perhaps the most famous usage of the Internet for political mobilizing was Howard Dean's 2004 presidential campaign. Joe Trippi, Dean's campaign manager, summarized the impact of participatory culture on politics: "There is no way to understate the importance of what MoveOn and its members proved—that the net can be used to mobilize huge numbers of grassroots to take local action beyond their monitors."[14] Trippi saw the Internet as a means to mobilize youthful, grassroots coalitions for a political cause. Although Dean's campaign had a spectacular crash, accelerated by Internet remixes of his infamous "Dean Scream," the impact of participatory culture persists in the 2008 presidential election cycle. Leading candidates announced their presidential bids over the Internet.[15] Virtually every presidential campaign employs online participatory culture and do-it-yourself toolkits to gain supporters, interact with them, and motivate them to organize and act in behalf of their particular candidate.[16]

Fourth, we should acknowledge that, for the moment, participatory culture tends to favor progressive or liberal politics. A survey of the YouTube homepage on 18 September 2006, offers an indication of political bias. YouTube highlighted a video of Ted Kennedy speaking about Internet neutrality as protection for "freedom of speech."[17] Certainly, an Internet culture that favors free expression, if not anarchist disdain for all restraints on liberty, lends itself to left-of-center politics. Note, however, that right-wing bloggers and faithbloggers have done their part to adapt participatory culture to conservative politics.[18]

Participatory culture also lends itself to "gotcha" politics. In the 2006 midterm election, the balance of U.S. Senate power came down to a seat in Virginia. Incumbent Republican George Allen was certain to defeat former Navy Secretary (and former Republican) Jim Webb as a steppingstone to a bid for the White House. However, participatory culture trumped certainty. University of Virginia student S.R. Sidarth videoed Allen's speeches for Jim Webb's campaign. At one rally, Allen pointed to Sidarth and referred to him as "macaca."[19] Sidarth uploaded the clip onto YouTube, where it became a nationwide phenomenon. Sidarth later recalled, "Nothing made me happier on election night than finding out the results from Dickenson County, where Allen and I had our encounter."[20] Allen lost that county, lost the Senate seat, and lost the Republican majority in the Senate.

When asked about the online potential for Internet mudslinging, Doctorow responds, "Don't focus on the mudslinging! Focus on the mud! The problem is not that leaders are being 'outed' as scumbags, the problem is that leaders are scumbags."[21] One democratic hope for participatory culture is that by surveilling public officials, it can drive corrupt politicians out of positions of authority and, by implication, reward political honesty and integrity.

In sum, participatory culture has the potential to enhance youth participation in politics. It promotes the key democratic values of involvement and openness. It teaches young citizens vital skills involving the acquisition of knowledge and collaborative problem-solving. It facilitates political mobilizations. And it tends to favor a progressive politics that values free expression and public integrity. Participatory culture provides both motives and opportunities for political engagement.

POLITICAL CONSUMERISM AND ONLINE POLITICS

"Political consumerism" is a political manifestation of participatory culture. It involves purchasing or refusing to purchase goods and services based on political, social, or ethical considerations rather than solely on price and quality. Dietlind Stolle, Marc Hooghe, and Michele Micheletti highlight three components of political consumerism: behavior, motivation, and frequency.[22] Behavior refers to the actual act of purchasing or refusing to purchase a product. The motivation component requires the behavior to be based on political, social, or ethical values as opposed to traditional consumer considerations. Frequency demands the behavior be repeated, ensuring its relevance and durability. Defining political consumerism in practical terms, the Organic Consumers Association (OCA) wants members to ask several questions before making a purchase:

Who profits from this sale? Are you buying this product from a national chain, or buying locally from an independent business, coop, or family farm? ... Were farmers' or workers' rights protected? Did the producer receive a living wage? Is it certified organic or fair trade? Is the company making or selling this item socially responsible?[23]

This form of political participation is enticing to youths, a demographic group commonly distrustful of government, because it is a less institutionalized, non-governmental approach to addressing public goals and grievances.[24]

Youth engagement in online political consumerism has several focuses. The most prevalent involves labor practices and human rights issues. Many students have formed activist groups, for example, urging their universities to ban Coca-Cola due to allegations of mistreatment of workers.[25] Youths have targeted Taco Bell for exploiting the labor of the Immokalee American Indian tribe in Florida.[26] A student-led boycott of Nike spawned a broad Internet protest against sweatshop labor.[27] Youths are also active in online political consumerism for anti-corporate, pro-environmental causes. They have boycotted Starbucks (on grounds of globalization and food safety), and supported organic foods (for benefiting the environment and public health).[28]

The Internet lowers the threshold for consumer participation. At the organizational level, the Internet facilitates dissemination of "Action Kits" and "Starter Resources" for initiating local campaigns. It also makes accessible articles and data for posting on blogs and Web sites as well as e-mail reminders about meetings, actions, and so forth. At the individual level, the Internet provides access to buying guides and e-mail listserves that educate participants and sustain their involvement in the movement. Note that these Internet tools make it easier for people to get involved but they do not independently generate involvement.

Typical "Action Kits" provide students useful resources for organizing a consumer group. One of the nation's largest youth-led political consumerism organizations, Sweatshop Watch, offers an online Action Kit for a nominal cost. The kit includes pamphlets, posters, and flyers as well as guidelines and tips for everything from maintaining intragroup communication to obtaining recognition from universities.[29] Another youth-led consumer organization is the Student-Farmworker Alliance, which maintains an online information kit with similar materials. It also provides links to a grassroots activism Web site which has a local media finder, organized by zip codes, that churns out the names of local newspapers, political publications, columnists, magazines, radio and television stations, and news services.[30] The Campaign for a Coca-Cola Free Campus publishes a detailed online action guide that spells out the case against Coca-Cola (including Coca-Cola's response and the Campaign's rebuttal) plus a guide for taking action, for example, by locating the university's contract with Coca-Cola, contacting competitors, and providing viable options.[31]

More examples include a student-led effort to foster university divestment from corporations that "support" the crisis in Darfur. The students' Web site offers a customizable proposal for use at any college. New student groups simply download the proposal, replace the generic "YOUR INSTITUTION" with the name of their own school, and the rest is pre-packaged.[32] In effect, online action guides lower the threshold for student involvement in the consumer movement by demystifying the process of creating new, student-led boycott organizations. With online resources, almost any student who is passionate about the issue can become a campus leader for the cause and network with other groups pursuing similar causes.

The Internet also lowers the threshold for individual youth engagement in political consumerism. Consider Internet access to buying guides. Buying guides are databases of manufacturers, producers, and stores that have met the criteria of online consumer groups. For example, an organic food site might include in its database farms that do not use hormones or pesticides. Many buying guides are searchable by zip code, making it easy for consumers to determine what they can "ethically" purchase in their area. Sweatshop Watch's Web site features a buying guide based on four "Shop with a Conscience" criteria.[33] While this guide is not searchable by zip code, it is differentiated by types of goods and features links to stores' Web sites. Young political consumers can use their home computers to research and purchase goods based on political considerations. A striking example of anti-corporatism aimed primarily at the Starbucks franchise is the Delocator. By typing in a zip code, the Delocator generates a list of cafes, bookstores, or cinemas not owned by the corporation. The site also contains information on why "Delocate," decrying the corporate "invasion" of American neighborhoods.[34] A growing trend on college campuses is a "Fair Trade Certified" online movement that urges "fair" prices for growers of coffee, tea, chocolate, and tropical fruit. The movement Web site prominently features a "Where to Buy" section that allows users to input a zip code and locate Fair Trade Certified retailers in their area.[35] These buying guides lower the threshold for youths political participation in two ways: they allow users to participate by making ethical online purchases and they help youths identify and locate nearby retailers that sell "ethical" goods.

Another online tool to encourage consumer participation is the e-mail listserve. A listserve is a simple way for organizations to e-mail people. This mechanism makes it easy for organizations to remind members about meetings or forward news clippings and newsletters. Perhaps the greatest effect of the listserv is to boost viewership of the organization's Web site and thereby remind users of the ease and necessity of their participation. OCA distributes a biweekly newsletter called "Organic Bytes." According to an OCA staffer, the group's Web site receives a boost in traffic by as much as 33 percent in the days immediately after the newsletter is sent out.[36] Other organic food Web sites, such as Local Harvest and Eat Well Guide, report similar increases in Web traffic following distribution of their newsletters.[37] By using listserves for periodic communications with members, listserves lower the threshold for participation, actively engage members in the movement, and link them to resources intended to promote further participation.

In sum, at both the organizational and individual level, the Internet lowers the threshold for youth participation in political consumerism. Action guides and blogs assist student organizers in creating and managing local movement chapters while buying guides, searchable databases, and listserves make it easy for individuals to find "ethical" products and sustain their involvement in the politics of the marketplace. The Internet also has the potential to increase youths' engagement in other aspects of civic life.

CIVIC ENGAGEMENTS

Digital technology can facilitate innovative forms of civic engagement. Political text messaging is a new version of the old tradition of person-to-person politics. This type of interpersonal political communication/conversation may soon surpass e-mail in its effectiveness in connecting with young citizens. Only 15 percent to 25 percent of solicited political e-mail messages are opened but approximately 95 percent of text messages are opened.[38] This suggests that young people, our primary text messagers, may be more receptive to receiving and responding to political text messages from friends than to e-mail messages from political organizations. This practice has already having a discernible effect in participatory culture. When the television show *American Idol* first asked viewers to vote for their favorite contestant by text message at the end of the 2004 season, 13.5 million people obliged. One year later, the number text message votes soared to 41.5 million.[39] Conceivably, a text messaging option could also increase young voter registration and turnout. Several youth voter registration efforts through text messaging appeared in 2006. For example, Voto Latino emerged from immigration protests that were organized through text messaging and social networking. The group is working to register 50,000 young Latino voters through text messages.[40]

Meanwhile, the Internet has helped revive the concept of the town hall meeting, the public square, and public discourse. The Democratic and Republican National Committees have embraced the idea of online communities as a means to disseminate their messages, engage citizens in dialogue, and expand the universe of potential voters through innovative outreach efforts. For example, Republicans' MyGOP facilitates online user efforts to plan a house party, conduct surveys, contact elected officials, call talk radio shows, help register voters, draft letters to local newspapers, and raise money.[41] By joining old political methods with a new technology that is more familiar to younger citizens than to older ones, both political parties are hoping to attract young Americans' interest, support, and loyalty.

Non-partisan Web sites also have experimented with online public discourse. Both Essembly.com and Hotsoup.com invite virtual contact between users to promote political engagement. Essembly was founded by a 23-year-old staffer from Senator John Kerry's presidential campaign. It invites users to generate debate topics. Hotsoup uses the lure well-known political figures to entice users to engage in online debate. Senators John McCain and Barack Obama agreed to create profiles prior to the site's launch.[42] Young people now have the ability to communicate with policy-makers and power brokers. Potentially, Essembly and Hotsoup could serve as robust conduits for public discussion.

Leading social networking sites Facebook and MySpace now allow political candidates to post their profiles. They also host advocacy and issue-oriented groups for discussion, organization and mobilization. This merging of social networking and online politics has the potential to integrate political discourse into youths' everyday lives. Democratic media strategist Chris Lehane comments, "Campaigns are still finding ways to tap the sites' potential." He claims that that the marriage of social networking and electoral campaigns may revolutionize politics.[43]

The Internet also facilitates and hastens growing rates of youth participation in service learning, community service, and national service programs. We have seen soaring rates of volunteerism among high school and college students in the new century.[44] The U.S. Bureau of Labor Statistics finds that 15.5 million teenagers volunteered for some cause in 2004.[45] Institutions of higher education such as Arizona State University provide academic credit to college students who tutor and mentor elementary school children and incarcerated young women. In 2005, some 32 percent of American elementary and secondary schools incorporated service learning into their curricula.[46] Young people's applications for national programs, including Teach for America, Peace Corps, and AmeriCorps, have risen dramatically in recent years.[47] The Internet has been useful in publicizing these programs and in allowing online applications, which lowers the threshold for youths' civic engagement.

An interesting program that promotes civic engagement is Wall Street Volunteers, an online clearinghouse for connecting young professionals to non-profit volunteer opportunities.[48] What distinguishes this program from other volunteer vehicles is its Internet component. The Wall Street Volunteers, in effect, have created a social networking site to connect young professionals to volunteer opportunities that fit into the demands of their personal lives and careers. The better the fit, the lower the threshold for participation, the more likely the civic engagement.

Let us emphasize that the Internet enhances the potential of young people to develop an interest in politics, take part in public discourse, show support for causes and candidates, and contribute to the public good by means of service learning or community and national service. It enhances this potential by opening up innovative means to pursue old political strategies and by lowering the threshold for youth engagement. To an extent, we expect young people to fulfill that potential. One of the most important means for increasing young people's political involvement is to invite them to participate (rather than to write them off as non-participants).[49] Because youths disproportionately participate and congregate online, and because the cost of contacting them (through Web sites, e-mail and text messages) is quite low, we are just beginning to see more cultural activists, consumer organizations, citizens, and candidates use digital technology as a means to promote political participation. The outstanding question is whether increased youth participation will be more or less robust, widespread, and significant.

CONCLUSION

Hope for a new age of youth participation in American politics, spurred by the growth of the Internet, must be tempered by the fact that *virtual* space is not *actual* space. Online activism—indeed, digital democracy—amounts to very little without manifestations of political activism in street demonstrations, polling places, political commissions, and the halls of government. Familiarity with online participatory culture, low thresholds for online political consumerism, and invitations for online civic participation do not address problems related to youths' political alienation and apathy or their relative lack of concern and commitment to the public realm. Nor does youth familiarity and facility with digital technology and the Internet address social, racial, and economic inequalities that have a dramatic influence on the distribution and application of power in the United States today. That said, we believe that youth participation on the Internet does have some potential to increase young people's political involvement.

Participatory culture allows and encourages the creation of media and meanings. It provides youths with the opportunity to become directly and immediately involved in public discourse. Political consumerism's online manifestations dramatically lower the costs for acquiring political information and testing the waters of participation. Additionally, the Internet broadens the field of civic engagement. Young people from across the nation are invited to engage in community and public service and they do so in significant numbers. Taken together, these three modes of online participation suggest that the Internet creates opportunities for youth involvement in politics and provides a measure of motivation, facilitation, and invitation for that involvement. Ultimately, however, the responsibility rests with young people themselves to determine whether to take advantage of online opportunities as well as to explore offline politics.

ENDNOTES

1. Will Lester, "Voter excitement level highest in years," accessed 11 October 2006, from http://news.yahoo.com/s/ap/20061011/ap_on_el_ge/motivated_voters_ap_poll.

2. W. Lance Bennett and Michael Xenos, "Young voters and the web of politics 2004: The youth political web sphere comes of age" (October 2005), p. 3.

3. Cory Doctorow, interviewed by Phil Zager on 9 December 2006.

4. "Michael Richards racist," accessed 23 November 2006, from www.YouTube.com/watch?v=9sEUIZsmTOE; "Saddam Hussein Execution, WARNING—GRAPHIC," accessed 2 January 2007, from www.YouTube.com/watch?v=MHzqUllh_c8; "Diet Coke + Mentos," accessed 2 March 2007, from www.YouTube.com/watch?v=hKoB0MHVBvM; "Evolution of Dance," accessed 30 April 2007, from www.YouTube.com/watch?v=dMHObHeiRNg.

5. Scott Kirsner, "Low-budget viral videos attract TV-sized audiences" (30 July 2006), §7, accessed 18 September 2006, from www.boston.com/business/personaltech/articles/2006/07/30/low_budget_viral_videos_attact_tv_sized_audiences/.

6. Henry Jenkins, "Tracking the MySpace generation" (29 August 2006), §3, accessed 26 September 2006, from www.henryjenkins.org/2006/08/tracking_the_MySpace_generatio.html.

7. Judge Damon J. Keith, *Detroit Free Press v. Ashcroft* 303 F. 3d 681 (26 August 2002), accessed 2 February 2007, from keithcollection.wayne.edu/pdfs/djkeith_031204.pdf.

8. "Video the vote, voting equipment failures," accessed 7 November 2006, from www.videothevote.org/stories/machinefailures.html.

9. John Horrigan, Kelly Garrett, and Paul Resnick, "The Internet and democratic debate" (27 October 2004), 25, accessed 7 November 2006, from www.pewinternet.org/pdfs/PIP_Political_Info_Report.pdf.

10. Henry Jenkins, *Convergence Culture*. New York: New York University Press, 2006, p. 347.

11. Doctorow interviewed by Phil Zager on 9 December 2006.

12. Tracy Samantha Schmidt, "Facebook's about-face: Signs of a Gen-Y revolution?" *Time* (8 September 2006).

13. Tracy Samantha Schmidt, "Inside the backlash against Facebook," *Time* (6 September 2006).

14. Joe Trippi, "The perfect storm" (June 2003), accessed 10 October 2006, from joetrippi.com/?page_id=1378.

15. Hillary Clinton, "I'm In," accessed 3 February 2007, from http://www.hillaryclinton.com/video/2.aspx; Barack Obama, "A Message from Barack," accessed 3 February 2007, from http://www.barackobama.com/video/.

16. Undergraduate researcher Jenna Hootstein has traced the efforts of 16 Democratic and Republican presidential candidates to use participatory culture in the 2008 campaign in "Do-it-yourself culture and the 2008 presidential campaign," April 2007, unpublished paper.

17. "Sen. Ted Kennedy supports net neutrality," accessed 18 September 2006, from www.YouTube.com/watch?v=6UlCXXZTTh8.

18. See Hugh Hewitt, *Blog: Understanding the Information Revolution That's Changing Your World*. Nashville: Nelson Books, 2005.

19. "Allen's listening tour," accessed 5 October 2006, from www.YouTube.com/watch?v=9G7gq7GQ71c.

20. S.R. Sidarth, "I am Macaca" (12 November 2006), accessed 17 November 2006, from www.washingtonpost.com/wp-dyn/content/article/2006/11/10/AR2006111001381.html.

21. Doctorow interviewed by Phil Zager on 9 December 2006.

22. Dietlind Stolle, Marc Hooghe, and Michele Micheletti, "Politics in the supermarket: Political consumerism as a form of political participation," *International Political Science Review* (2005) 26: 245–269.

23. "Organic Consumers Association," accessed 15 October 2006, from www.organicconsumers.org.

24. Madeleine Brand, "Protecting your privacy in the virtual world," *Day to Day* (2 January 2007), National Public Radio, Accessed from www.npr.org/templates/story/story.php?storyId=6710445.

25. Javier Correa, "Killer Coke," accessed 10 October 2006, from corporatecampaign.org/killer-coke/resolutions.htm.

26. Coalition of Immokalee Workers, "Boycott the Bell," accessed 3 October 2006, from www.ciw-online.org/tz_site-revision/home/home/html.

27. Michael Blanding, "Coke: The new Nike," *The Nation* (11 April 2005); "Sweatshop Watch," accessed 6 October 2006, from sweatshopwatch.org.

28. "Organic Consumers Association," accessed 15 October 2006, from www.organicconsumers.org.

29. "Sweatshop Watch," accessed 6 October 2006, from sweatshopwatch.org.

30. "Progressive Democrats of America," accessed 30 October 2006, from capwiz.com/pdamerica/dbq/media.

31. Correa, "Killer Coke," accessed 15 October 2006, from corporatecampaign.org/killer-coke/resolutions.htm.

32. "Sudan divestment task force," accessed 30 October 2006, from sudandivestment.org.

33. "Sweatshop watch," accessed 6 October 2006, from sweatshopwatch.org.

34. "Delocator," accessed 15 October 2006, from delocator.net.

35. "Fair trade certified," accessed 6 November 2006, from www.transfairusa.org/; *On Your Campus*, accessed 6 November 2006, from www.transfairusa.org/content/support/campus.php.

36. Anonymous Organic Consumers Association staff member, telephone interview conducted by Connor Gant, 27 October 2006.

37. Gwen Schantz, of the Eat Well Guide, e-mail interview conducted by Connor Gant on 16 November 2006; Guillermo Payet, owner/operator of Local Harvest, e-mail interview conducted by Connor Gant on 11 November 2006.

38. Lee Hudson Teslik and Robbie Brown, "Vote 4 me," *Newsweek Online* (3 August 2006), accessed 26 September 2006, from www.msnbc.msn.com/id/14141365/.

39. "Getting the message," *The Economist* (4 March 2006).

40. Rebekah Dryden "4 easy voter geg, txt me," *Arizona Reporter* (11 November 2006), accessed 27 November 2006, from www.azreporter.com.

41. "The hotline: On the download" (20 September 2006), accessed 20 September 2006, from hotlineblog.nationaljournal.com.

42. Jessica E. Vascellaro, "Campaign 2006 online: New sites aim to capitalize on social-networking craze to spark political involvement," *Wall Street Journal* (21 September 2006).

43. Emily Goodin, "Hotline extra—Click here," *National Journal* (21 October 2006), 70–71.

44. Mark Hugo Lopez, "Volunteering among young people," Center for Information & Research on Civic Learning and Engagement (June 2003), accessed 2 October 2006, from www.civicyouth.org.

45. "First Lady Laura Bush releases new study showing high levels of teen volunteering" (30 November 2005), accessed 3 October 2006, from www.usafreedomcorps.gov.

46. "Academic community engagement services at Arizona State University," accessed 17 October 2006 from uc.asu.edu/servicelearning/index/php; "Fact Sheet: Learn and Serve America" (June 2006), accessed 3 October 2006 from www.nationalservice.gov.

47. Beth Walton, "Volunteer rates hit record numbers; Peace Corps and others see surge," *USA Today* (7 July 2006), accessed 17 October 2006, from web.lexisnexis.com/universe/document?_m=020aa5648dd1c4c90085 3068f8280708&_docnum=21&wchp=dGLbVtzzSkVA&_md5=6f606cc582484b0767ccbbd8fa75bad9.

48. "Wall Street Volunteers," 2005, accessed 2 October 2006, from http://www.wallstreetvolunteers.org.

49. See Cliff Zukin et al., *A New Engagement: Political Participation, Civic Life, and the Changing American Citizen*. Oxford: Oxford University Press, 2006, p. 146.

*Mark E. Kann, professor of political science and history, holds the USC associates chair in social science at the University of Southern California. Jeff Berry, Connor Gant, and Phil Zager are undergraduate students and research assistants who collaborated on the research and writing that went into this article.

Kann, Mark E., Jeff Berry, Connor Gant, and Phil Zager. "The Internet and Youth Political Participation." *First Monday* 12, no. 8 (August 2007). http://firstmonday.org/issues/issue12_8/kann/index.html.

Used by permission.

DISCUSSION QUESTIONS

1. Does Internet activism represent a new means of political activism, or is it just traditional political activity by other means? What is new?

2. Is Internet activism inherently unfair because it empowers those who are better educated and have easy access to computers, while further limiting the options of the less educated and less affluent?

3. Should governments introduce systems of Internet voting to increase the participation of the young?

The Market as an Arena for Transnational Politics

*by Michele Micheletti and Dietlind Stolle**

December is the season of giving. Streets and shopping windows are decorated in holiday colors, and Christmas music and spirit fill shopping malls. For retail stores, it is a most lucrative time of year. Newspaper, television, radio, and now even Internet advertisements try to convince people that they truly can show their loved ones how much they really care by giving them special gifts at Christmas time. A particular focus of marketing attention is the younger generation, a group seen as easy prey for marketing strategists because of their concern over personal appearance and the social status accompanying brand name clothing, shoes, and other consumer-oriented material goods. But this characterization does not apply to all young people. The Christmas season is also when the political consumerism movement gears up for focused action to question the basis of consumer society. Many young people are involved in this reevaluation of Western consumer-driven society which, at the same time, links them to the lives of people in other parts of the world—principally the developing world which is increasingly home to "outsourced" production of consumer goods.

A few holiday seasons ago, BehindTheLabel.org, an on-line advocacy network, put out an urgent appeal against The Gap, a large clothing chain with stores in several nations that markets its clothes to young people. It urged consumers not to patronize GAP stores, claiming on its on-line slideshow: "The Gap uses sweatshop labor, if you buy Gap you do too. Make a difference. Be the generation that stops sweatshops. Tell your family and friends: Don't buy me GAP this holiday season." In Canada, advocates wearing Santa outfits appeared in shopping malls to call attention to the effects of our commercial society in other parts of the world. In other countries, activists against sweatshops have taken to the streets; in the Netherlands, for example, Dutch protesters dressed themselves as angels to attract consumer attention on a busy public street lined with clothing stores and asked shoppers to send the company of their choice a Christmas card asking about its offshore production practices and codes of conduct.

These examples tell the stories of many young people who are conscientious consumers. They use the marketplace to challenge how we live, work, and do politics in the world today. These young activists urge us to think about consumer society in new ways by confronting what they consider to be an ethically blind and consumption-crazed society. They encourage individual consumers to fight for the rights of workers and animals, and against unleashed free trade, the power of transnational corporations, and the use of pesticides and genetically modified organisms in our food. Much of this concern is directed toward the working conditions and environments of people living elsewhere, reflecting a transnational political awareness that transcends national issues. Targets for this form of political engagement are not only the policies of young people's own governments in the developing world, but also developing countries governments themselves and, most of all, powerful transnational corporations. This type of engagement stands in seeming contrast to the common critique of today's young people as materialistically oriented. Although the numbers indicate that, for example, college freshmen have an increased interest in becoming financially well off,[1] the trend-lines also show that they attach more importance to contributing to society.[2]

People who use the market in this fashion are political consumers. Formally defined, political consumerism is the choice of producers and products with the aim of changing ethically or politically objectionable institutional or market practices. Their choices are informed by attitudes and values regarding issues of justice, fairness, non-economic issues that concern personal and family well-being, and ethical or political assessment of favorable and unfavorable business and government practice.

Although the concept is fairly new, political consumerism is an old phenomenon. Historical studies of the United States and Europe have shown how the market has frequently been used as an arena for political activism. Women, marginalized groups, and young people have, for instance, employed their purchasing power to help put an end to domestic American sweatshop labor in the early 1900s by buying "White Label" goods, to combat various kinds of discrimination through boycotts, and to fight for peace by encouraging their parents to be socially responsible when they invest in the stock market. In more recent times, the goals, targets and alliances of political consumerism have gone global. Citizens both young and old from different nations have joined together in international boycotts to protest governmental or corporate policy. Well-known examples include those against Nestlé, South Africa, and grape producers. Recently France and the U.S. have been the focus of grassroots international boycotts because of their positions on the Iraq war in the spring of 2003.

Political consumerism comes in different forms. Citizens *boycott* to express political sentiment and they *buycott* or use labeling schemes to support corporations that represent values—environmentalism, fair trade, and sustainable development, for example—that they support. While not only about environmental, labor, gender and child welfare issues abroad, these techniques represent one powerful way for young people to express views on global inequalities and other justice issues.

Young people are engaged in all forms of political consumerism. Survey research from different countries shows that they are more interested in grassroots engagements and in using the market than other channels for political participation. When asked in 2002 if they had ever "not bought something because of the conditions under which it was made," 51.4 percent of young Americans between the ages of 15 and 25 said "yes" and a majority stated they had done so in the last year. The same survey reports that 43.7 percent of young Americans said they *had* bought a certain product because they liked the values of the company that made it.[3] According to the report, political consumerism ranked by far the highest for young people out of a range of political activities including contacting a public official, writing a letter to a newspaper editor, and participating in protests and rallies. About two thirds of the respondents said that they were not involved in any kind of conventional political engagement. Clearly, the high percentage of political consumers among young people is partially caused by the fact that those below eighteen years of age are not yet allowed to vote; however, in the remainder of the paper we will show why and how political consumerism might be a new and important tool for political engagement especially for young people.

Swedish and Danish national surveys confirm the importance of the marketplace as an arena for young people to engage in politics. Nearly 28 percent of all Swedes between the ages of 16 and 29 have boycotted for a political reason within a recent twelve-month period, and over 40 percent indicate that they have actively chosen a product for similar reasons. Many claim that they act as political consumers more than just once, whereby particularly those youngsters who have enjoyed extensive education are most involved.[4] Yet political consumerism has the potential to evolve into a widespread phenomenon, which might include also those usually left out of conventional politics. A study conducted by the Swedish National Board for Youth Affairs shows that almost everyone in this age group has sometime in their life boycotted or would consider boycotting for a political reason. What is particularly interesting is that this high level of appeal (just under 100 percent) can be compared with a bit fewer than 70 percent who stated that they were generally interested in politics.[5] Also, Danish youth (18 to 29 years of age) said in a 2000 national survey that they were active as political consumers,[6] although their general interest in politics tended to be rather low. The attractiveness of the market as an arena for politics for young people who are not interested in or enthused about traditional or conventional politics is also confirmed in a non-random cross-national student survey. About 70 percent of university students in the social sciences surveyed in 2003 at a Canadian, Belgian, and Swedish university think that it is one's personal responsibility to buy products from the "right" company. And roughly 72 percent of them stated that they have chosen products based on ethical considerations in the last year.[7]

What is particularly interesting is that young citizens' market-based political strategies go beyond boycotting and buycotting, which are commonly targeted in survey research. Young people are also activists in internet campaigns, mobilize their schools, universities or fellow-students to take actions regarding consumer issues, engage in culture jamming, and use the Internet to voice their individual opinions on consumer society and transnational corporations. Most frequently, young people use these means of involvement in their fight for workers' rights in developing and western countries and the treatment of animals. This engagement is channeled through a variety of opportunities for activism that are offered by the "no sweat" and animal rights' movements, two global advocacy movements that developed strongly in the 1990s and 2000s. The "no sweat" movement, represented by North American anti-sweatshop advocacy networks and the European Clean Clothes Campaign, fights for fair working conditions in the global garment industry. The crusade for proper animal welfare, while less directly concerned with global issues, includes bans on fur trading as well as animal testing.

A fairly new tool for these advocacy movements and even individual young citizens who support them is culture jamming/adbusting. This tool turns "corporate power against itself by co-opting, hacking, mocking, and re-contextualizing meaning."[8] Culture jamming involves activities that generally fall under the categories of media hacking, information warfare, terror-art, and guerrilla semiotics. They are individualized types of actions that can be performed alone but that help a common cause. The most famous case of culture jamming was incited by former MIT graduate student Jonah Peretti, who ordered a pair of customizable Nike shoes with the word "sweatshop" on them. This request turned him into a global celebrity. The emails—completely independent of his control or encouragement—reached an estimated 11.4 million people around the globe. This is an example of culture jamming in the classical sense, in that he utilized Nike's own marketing strategy to argue for his request. Peretti's story shows that the Internet is an important tool for global social activist network-building, and it illustrates how individualized life-style choices can dovetail with responsibility-taking for global social justice.[9]

Postcard campaigns are another important form of culture jamming that is used frequently by the anti-sweatshop movement. Typically, activists pass out postcards in front of targeted clothing stores and at music concerts, movement events, and other public happenings that draw crowds of young people. They urge those they encounter to send postcard messages to clothing companies. Postcards depicting sweatshop labor and making fun of corporate advertisements are available on-line from the Clean Clothes Campaign website. Young people find this form of activism enjoyable because they appreciate direct political messages that poke fun at authority and because they can choose the card, write a message in the appropriate textbox, choose the addressee, and then send it off. Examples of culture jamming postcards include: "Income GAP. An American Classic," a play on The GAP's logo; a card portraying Mickey Mouse with fangs and reading "BOM!!! Beware of Mickey. Disney Sweatshops in South China" which provides information on the salary level of the Disney CEO and the wages paid to Disney workers in China; another showing a picture of a man with money stuffed in his mouth and the words "The true colors of Benetton" written across his shirt, and a rewording of the Levis jeans patch "Evil Strauss & Co. $$$."

Many young people find these activities appealing because they provide a way of expressing concerns about global justice by offering immediate, counter-culture involvement with causes that research shows interest youth. These kinds of involvements have also been called life-style politics because the sharing of political messages and the engagements in political acts are embedded in everyday life. Life-style politics suits the younger generations well, as politics for them has ceased to be a separate area of life. For them, politics is utterly enmeshed with their daily life choices about how they dress, what they eat, what they buy, and which music they listen to in their free time. This is how our students have explained in class discussions their decisions to wear culture jamming clothes.

Political consumerist strategies interest young people because they allow them wiggle room to live, design, and build their own involvements. "Modding" is a term from the computer game world that characterizes this kind of youthful involvement well. Political consumerist networks allow people to "mod" (that is, to modify) political activism. Educational meetings organized by the Clean Clothes Campaign can end with participants planning their own public action days to be implemented, without central supervision, in their home towns.

Other advocacy campaigns encourage do-it-yourself involvement by providing people with a toolbox or action package to build their own activism. The Canadian anti-sweatshop network, Maquila Solidarity Network, even distributes a Sweatshop Fashion Show toolkit, which has been used by young people across the country to raise awareness about sweatshop abuses in a fun and educational way (www.maquilasolidarity.org). These tools help young people plan alternative shows whose purpose is the creation of public spectacles by questioning the politics of fashion products. Because of their alternative nature, these activities are often picked up by the media in various countries.

Political consumerist activists like the Maquila Solidarity Network also target school environments, particularly high schools. Its "No Sweat Schools" campaigns rally students together to declare their school free of sweatshop products. Their goal is to negotiate an agreement with their school stipulating that it will not purchase uniforms for students, staff, teams, and others that are made under sweatshop conditions. These campaigns are almost always initiated by students themselves, even though they are based on the mobilization and facts provided by the Maquila Solidarity network. The process of a campaign often involves raising student awareness, lobbying principals and teachers, developing a plan for change or a Code of Conduct, and lobbying the Board of Education or a local municipal council. For many pupils, this is the first time that they have engaged with the social and political institutions in their communities. During the campaign, students learn that they are more than just individualized consumers and that their actions are part of a political and economic machine with real power in the corporate and political worlds. The pupils move from the consumer-to-producer relationship to the relationship of institutional purchaser-to-supplier. Young people easily feel that their power has been increased through this shift.[10] University students in the United States have undertaken similar efforts and have even established the organization United Students Against Sweatshops (USAS), an effort considered by some to be the new student movement for the 1990s and 2000s.

Youth involvement with the global garment industry has mobilized other people, both young and old, into action and even led to institution-building efforts to follow up agreements made together with student political consumerist activists. The Workers Rights Consortium, a non-profit organization, was, for example, created by college students, university administrators and labor rights experts to make sure that university-adopted codes of conduct are effectively enforced. The "Disclosure Campaign" lobbied the Canadian federal government in 2002 for a change in its labeling regulations governing manufactured goods sold in Canada. It all started when a student in British Columbia, outraged about not being able to find sufficient information about how her clothes had been produced, cut a label out of one of her purchases and sent it to the government along with a demand for more consumer information. The physical defacement of her clothes made a powerful statement that resonated with other concerned young people across the country, who subsequently decided to join in and send in their labels as well. With the help of the Maquila Solidarity Network's website, which advertised the campaign, tens of thousands of clothing labels and petitions signed by over 20,000 Canadians were delivered to the office of the Ministry of Industry,[11] thus demonstrating that support for product transparency had gained broad public support.

CREATIVE YOUTHFUL POLITICAL PARTICIPATION

The phenomenon of political consumerism is embedded in the ongoing debate about how and why young citizens have been turning their backs on electoral politics in unprecedented numbers.[12] Indeed, much of the decline in voter turnout over the past decade can be explained by the increasing numbers of young citizens not turning up to vote at election time. In the 2000 U.S. presidential election, only 36 percent of young voters between the ages of 18 and 24 actually used their right to vote. Scattered evidence also suggests that the membership base of youth organizations is in decline, even more so than party membership in general.

Large-scale societal transformation explains young peoples' retreat from conventional forms of political involvement. They tend to dislike participation in bureaucratic and time-consuming organizations, and they typically prefer more spontaneous, informal, and egalitarian networks and organizations. This has been called the postmaterialist value shift, entailing heightened interest by younger generations in Western societies for values outside of the material world of physical safety and economic security. The phenomenon of political consumerism fits squarely into this new development. Not only does it offer new ways of political engagement outside of mainstream institutions, it also seeks to spread postmaterial values and ideas of justice, equality and fairness in all parts of the world. In one sense, political consumerism could be interpreted as evidence for the disappearance of the conventional barriers between global, national and local levels of governance in the political consciousness of young people.

Young citizens have also been found to distrust traditional or mainstream forms of political involvement (political parties, parliaments, Congress, labor unions, and so on), and they have made conscious choices to avoid them. Instead, they confront societal problems directly, as exemplified by political consumerism. A non-random survey of university students finds, for instance, that young people involved in political consumerism are also most frequently those who strongly distrust mainstream political institutions. This desire for new forms of activism also explains youth involvement in the Clean Clothes Campaign. Representatives of the Clean Clothes Campaign in Canada validate this finding. Students who join the campaign and who become active are at first very disaffected from the political process. They do not believe that voting or joining a party makes a difference.[13] Yet during a given campaign when pupils or students come into contact with government officials, they get drawn into the conventional political process.[14]

Through political consumerism, young people can directly confront transnational corporations and consumer society. They can work with their concerns about the quality of our environment and animal and human rights. Political consumerism allows them to "mod" their involvement to suit their own needs and consciousnesses. The toolkits and activity packages offer them ideas for individual and collective ways to force a variety of actors to take notice of the problems caused by our consumption patterns and corporate efforts in making us consume at an ever faster rate. Young people can decide for themselves which actors and problems to target. They can use political consumerism to call attention to the need for institutions at the global political level, the growing importance of transnational corporations, or consumer society itself.

With the help of political consumerist toolkits, young people are increasingly demanding more transparency in and control over commodity chains that seem far removed from their everyday lives. Through public performances, jokes, political messages on their clothing, and with the help of the Internet, they demand that corporations reveal the hidden politics and economic, human, ecological, and animal costs of common consumer goods and services. Young people are increasingly crying out to take responsibility for the ecological and ethical "footprints" that we all leave behind after purchasing goods at shopping malls, school cafeterias, and fast food hamburger and chicken chains. They are demanding that corporate actors share in this responsibility-taking with them.

ENDNOTES

1. Higher Education Research Institute. Findings on the American Freshmen survey. Accessed in March 2004: http://www.gseis.ucla.edu/heri/03_norms_charts.pdf.

2. Lance Bennett, "The Uncivic Culture: Communication, Identity, and the Rise of Lifestyle Politics." *P.S.: Political Science and Politics* 31 (1998): figure 6.

3. The Center for Information and Research for Civic Learning and Engagement Report: *How Young People Express Their Political Views.* Report available at http://www.civicyouth.org/PopUps/expressviews.pdf. Accessed February 21, 2004.

4. Michele Micheletti and Dietlind Stolle, "Swedish Political Consumers: Who They Are and Why They Use the Market as an Arena for Politics," *Political Consumerism: Its Motivations, Power, and Conditions in the Nordic Countries and Elsewhere* (TemaNord, 2005), 517.

5. Ungdomsstyrelsen, *Unga Medborgare* (Stockholm: Ungdomsstyrelsen, 2003), 163, 171.

6. Jørgen Goul Andersen and Mette Tobiasen, "Political Consumers and Political Investors: When Economic Agents Become Political." Paper prepared for "International Seminar on Political Consumerism," 31 May–3 June 2001, Stockholm, Sweden.

7. Dietlind Stolle, Marc Hooghe, and Michele Micheletti, "Politics in the Supermarket: Political Consumerism as a Form of Political Participation," *International Political Science Review* 26 (2005): 245–269.

8. Jonah Peretti and Michele Micheletti, "The Nike Sweatshop Email: Political Consumerism, Internet, and Culture Jamming," in Michele *Politics, Products, and Markets. Exploring Political Consumerism Past and Present,* eds. Micheletti, Andreas Follesdal, and Dietlind Stolle (New Brunswick: Transaction Publishers, 2003), 136.

9. Peretti and Micheletti, "The Nike Sweatshop Email."

10. Personal Interview by Kirsten Mercer with Ian Thomson at Maquila Solidarity Network, Toronto, 2004.

11. Ibid.

12. Dietlind Stolle and Marc Hooghe, "Inaccurate, Exceptional, One-sided or Irrelevant? The Debate About the Alleged Decline of Social Capital and Civic Engagement in Western Societies," *British Journal of Political Science* 35 (2005): 149–167.

13. Thomson interview.

14. Ibid.

*Michele Micheletti** is professor of political science at Karlstad University in Karlstad, Sweden, and **Dietlind Stolle** is associate professor of political science at McGill University in Montreal, Canada.

Michele Micheletti and Dietlind Stolle, "The Market as an Arena for Transnational Politics." New York: Social Science Research Council, 2006. http://ya.ssrc.org/transnational/Micheletti_Stolle/.

DISCUSSION QUESTIONS

1. Is political consumerism political participation, or more a method for people to express their own values and identity? Does political consumerism change the standard definition of political participation?

2. What are the benefits and limits of political consumerism as a means for interested citizens to influence public policy?

3. What factors explain why young people show interest in political consumerism as a form of political engagement?

4. Does political consumerism expand citizen policy impact by including market forces, or does it reduce policy impact by focusing on companies rather than changing public policy?

Part 4:
Inequality among Youth

Democracy is based on a principle of political equality, because citizens should have an equal opportunity to influence government. However, participation, especially in new forms of direct action and contentious politics, requires that the individual have skills and resources. New forms of direct action and contentious politics are even more demanding than voting, and thus may increase inequalities between those who possess these skills/resources and those who do not. The "one person, one vote" principle does not apply to contacting politicians, organizing a protest, or using new forms of Internet activism, where motivated individuals can participate much more than a single vote and thereby increase the inequality of participation. The essays in this section discuss different potential sources of political inequality and possible steps to address this issue. In "Youth at Risk for Non-participation," James G. Gimpel and J. Celeste Lay discuss the special challenges faced by at-risk populations, which include African Americans, Latinos, the poor, those living in single-parent households, children of the foreign-born, and those with low educational attainment. These are groups with the greatest needs for government assistance but they may be the least able to advocate for their own interests. "Civic Engagement and the Disadvantaged: Challenges, Opportunities, and Recommendations," by James B. Hyman and Peter Levine, marshals an impressive array of empirical evidence that demonstrates the participation gaps by social class, race/ethnicity, and gender. In "Gender and Civic Engagement: Secondary Analysis of Survey Data," Krista Jenkins focuses on gender differences in participation among the young. She finds that even though gender norms of participation are equalizing, young women remain distinctive in ways that are both hopeful and potentially worrisome. The ultimate question in these chapters is whether democracy benefits if overall political activism increases at the expense of a widening participation gap between the political haves and have-nots.

Youth at Risk for Non-participation

by James G. Gimpel and J. Celeste Lay*

Our findings from *Cultivating Democracy*,[1] and from our follow-up studies currently in progress, have reinforced much of the previous research that has identified poorly socialized populations. Among those most at risk for nonparticipation are African Americans, Latinos, the poor and those living in single-parent households, the children of the foreign-born, women, those with low educational aspirations, those living in noncompetitive or low-turnout political environments, the non-religious, those who are not attentive to news media, students who avoid or simply are not exposed to discussions of politics, and those who dislike their government-related courses and otherwise doubt that school authorities treat them fairly. For the respondents who possess more than a few of these risk factors, the likelihood of nonparticipation as an adult is exceedingly high. For the respondents who possess only two or three of these traits, there is the possibility that the presence of positive forces in an adolescent's environment may neutralize or overcome the ones that diminish participatory impulses.

Imagine that each risk factor is a kind of weight that adds to the inertia holding one away from moving toward the goal of responsible citizenship.[2] Those most heavily burdened may never reach the point where they even register to vote, much less volunteer for a campaign. The most burdened citizens possess a sufficiently high number of risk factors that non-involvement is the most likely outcome. Others may possess some of the risk factors, but positive forces in their environment, such as stimulating political campaigns, and adult models of participation, can help to overcome the factors that otherwise predict cynicism.

Mitigating these sources of poor socialization is a responsibility of parents. However, if parents were completely adequate to the task, we would not have such widespread non-participation among young adults in the first place. Non-participatory attitudes, like those favoring engagement, are intergenerationally transmitted. It is easy to argue that parents should assume more responsibility for civically educating their children, but getting from here to there is not a wide and straight path. One of the only places where good citizenship can be modeled for children who live in communities characterized by bad citizenship is school. Several of the stimuli to good citizenship are directly manipulable by education policymakers, including social studies education content and aspects of school climate. We believe that excellent classroom instruction about government and politics is critical for building knowledge. But exposure to civics-related coursework is not enough to make more than a marginal difference for the vast majority of students. Far more important to predicting knowledge and discussion is whether students acquire a liking for the subject matter. Students who disliked the study of government scored as much as 20 points lower on our political knowledge test than others. School-based reforms directed at increasing students' exposure to social studies, but not directed toward reshaping the content of these courses to make them more stimulating, will not accomplish much.

Our research indicates that the educational policy discussion needs to be shifted from curriculum requirements toward the development of customized curriculum content and improvement of instructional style. Experiments with curriculum reform, mentoring, guidance, and instructional method may go a long way toward uncovering techniques for teaching government that can compensate for living in neighborhoods with poor involvement. Ensuring that social studies personnel have interest in and knowledge related to classroom instruction is still another means for ensuring better citizenship education.

Exposure to television news and the amount of political discussion about current events may also be subject to curriculum modification. News media exposure, we have learned, is a stimulus for political discussion, but does not contribute directly to the basic factual knowledge that we were testing. But news sources may be a source of information gains that we did not capture in our survey. Several studies have documented that citizens do learn about politics from exposure to television campaign advertising.[3] And discussion is causally linked to knowledge, so television news is not completely without value as a tool for learning via the medium of interpersonal exchange. We conclude that exposure to television news can compensate for aspects of an adolescent's environment that have a depressing effect on discussion and knowledge, such as living in a low-turnout area with no political party mobilization.

Along with others, we have also come to view bad political socialization as part of a more general problem of adolescent development and motivation. Many students who suffer from poor school performance and low self-esteem exhibit the corresponding characteristics of low political efficacy and system support. At the same time, it is not inevitable that students with lower motivation and educational aspirations wind up badly socialized. The answer to the problem of low civic engagement is not necessarily to make everyone want to go on to a four-year college and become a physician or a professor. Many observers apparently come to believe that only people with college degrees are capable of making informed political judgments—that somehow good citizenship requires a certain requisite number of years of formal education. This makes us wonder how all of those uneducated (albeit male) masses in 19th century America managed to get to the polls and be so civically engaged.

V.O. KEY WAS RIGHT

While there is undeniable evidence that education and knowledge go hand-in-hand, and that formal education greatly facilitates political choice and decision making, it is not necessary that more years in a classroom be the only ticket to good citizenship, or that what is learned that makes citizenship more likely must be packaged with ambitions for a prestigious profession. Legions of high school adolescents remain destined for perfectly respectable working lives as metro bus drivers, stay-at-home parents, food service workers, longshoremen and bank tellers. If the only path to civic engagement is through formal education, we might as well give up on these citizens ever passing muster, to say nothing of those who wind up below them in society's socioeconomic strata.

Perhaps the connection between citizenship and formal education has been overemphasized—to the point where we fail to consider other avenues for achieving political literacy. Much of what needs to be learned to exercise competent political judgment can be picked-up from sources outside school. If our visits to rural communities have taught us anything, they have shown us that high levels of political engagement can be found among populations that are not especially well-educated or wealthy. Adolescents destined for full-time jobs after high school, and even high school dropouts, can be politically active citizens providing that they grow-up seeing models of good citizenship, or experience political campaigns that remind them that their participation is worthwhile. School is important, but it is not everything.

Writing in the middle of the last century, political scientist V.O. Key pointed to the value of partisan diversity and high turnout as driving forces behind democratic governance. The habit of nonvoting resulted in a shrunken electorate in one-party states. The limited electorate, in turn, influenced the nature of factional politics within a single party "by practically eliminating from the voting population substantial blocs of citizens whose political interests and objectives, if activated, would furnish the motive power for important political movements and demands."[4] Key went on to add that a government founded on democratic principles became some other sort of regime when large proportions of its citizens were non-voters.

Political party competition, and the associated mobilization efforts by parties and candidates, were seen by Key to be the instrument of democratic restoration. Notably, no mention is made in his landmark work of improving formal education in schools, although he does attack the anachronistic presence of suffrage restrictions in state law, which have since been ruled unconstitutional.

In the years leading up to the 2004 election, social scientists rediscovered the problem of low turnout, alarmed by the fact that in spite of the elimination of suffrage restrictions, and amazing improvements in the level of education over the course of the last century, participation rates had been steadily declining. Gerber and Green argued persuasively that turnout had dropped because people are no longer being asked to vote—and being asked face-to-face is really what counts.[5] Party and candidate mobilization efforts were reinvigorated in advance of the 2004 election, and turnout surged to levels it had not reached since 1968.

What we have found is that adolescents' sense of political efficacy and level of political knowledge is greatly enhanced in politically active areas that exhibit partisan diversity and high turnout. While we doubt that there is a lot of door-to-door campaigning going on in the highly participatory neighborhoods we visited, what we do find are adults who are interested in discussing politics with young people, and modeling good citizenship behavior by voting regularly. Even if participatory behavior is not being modeled by a teenager's parents, the adolescent can still see relatives, neighbors and other adults in the community taking elections seriously.

THE RELEVANCE OF PLACE FOR POLICIES TO IMPROVE POLITICAL SOCIALIZATION

We started under the conviction that places matter to the way young people are socialized, and we believe that our work establishes the relevance of the local political characteristics of the adult population on attitudes consistent with positive political socialization. Our work shows that political socialization does not, and should not be presumed to, work the same way everywhere, independent of contextual forces, or local distributions of opinion, that can either mitigate or aggravate individual risk factors that predict non-participation. A one-size-fits-all social studies curriculum, and an accompanying test, will not work if socialization is really more locally contingent than we have been led to believe. Rather than adopting uniform state level or national standards, standards should be locally adapted to the challenges and needs of specific populations. To the extent that forces outside of school cannot be counted upon to properly socialize young people, schools will bear more of the responsibility for teaching the values consistent with good citizenship. This is likely to place more pressure on urban school systems to reform curriculum and experiment in search of effective instructional styles. Too often we found the most creative and dedicated instructors in the schools that least needed them, where there were ample resources outside the schools that could teach the lessons of good citizenship. Suburban youth are more resilient to the presence of bad teachers than inner city youth. We need a policy initiative that will appropriately compensate and reward teachers for succeeding in the most challenging environments.

Schools in the most politically insular and isolated communities should be targeted by political party leaders of the minority party for visits that expose these students to different ways of thinking about politics and issues. For Democratic party leaders, this would involve sending representatives to the most rural and heavily Republican locations, where the homogeneity of pro-GOP views is most likely to squelch local Democratic voices, and discourage more open classroom discussions. For Republican party leaders, this would involve dispatching speakers to the most urban school systems, where the student body is often greater than 90 percent minority, and perhaps just as Democratic in their political orientation. Having a regular staff of speakers employed as part of the political party hierarchy who regularly visit schools where students tend to be of opposite political stripe will go a long way toward inculcating a respect for political difference and disagreement that is entirely absent in locations where only one side dominates. As part of the socialization process, students need to learn that there are legitimate reasons for holding opposing viewpoints, and at the same time, can benefit by having to defend their policy positions to others and to themselves.[6] At locations where dissonant views do not surface as a natural product of local diversity, dissonance must be introduced through other means.

But the other point worth emphasis is that schools are not the only answer, or even the primary one in the long term, for elevating the level of informed participation. Political parties and candidates should be more actively involved in grassroots development initiatives as part of the electioneering process, but this requires that a modicum of competition be restored to local political jurisdictions. Steps should be taken to enhance the level of political diversity at least for offices extending down to the state legislative level. In the public interest, the courts should adopt new criteria for the drawing of political district boundaries, seeking to maximize political heterogeneity and diversity, rather than allowing political officeholders to create safe election districts secure from the threat of electoral sanction. Rules maximizing political heterogeneity should apply equally to urban, suburban and rural areas, to the extent feasible to meet relaxed standards of compactness and contiguity.

POLICY DIRECTIONS

We focus our recommendations in two basic areas: policies designed to enhance social studies education and curriculum; and policies designed to promote political diversity and activism in local environments. Some of these recommendations are familiar, others less so. Some are vague, pointing only in a general policy direction. We do not pretend to be experts at implementation. We do hope that some of these ideas are discussed and that it is not the most controversial ones that are highlighted at the expense of the others.

CIVICS INSTRUCTION AND CURRICULUM

Social studies instructors need to work within curriculum guidelines that are sensitive to the needs of diverse populations and students with distinctive psychological histories. Teaching government and politics is not a one-size-fits-all proposition. Rather than centralizing standards for performance, standards are probably best decentralized and tailored to the local school population, and even sub-populations within the school. To help with this, local and state politicians and party leaders should be regularly invited to high school classes to discuss their roles and views, especially if their views are contrary to those of local populations. At the same time, programs that get students involved in their local communities may also help teachers to cater their curricula to local affairs. Service-learning programs may help in this regard.

Immigrant youth and the children of immigrant parents are often at a disadvantage when it comes to learning about the American political system. In addition to other compensatory courses for new immigrants, such as ESL, immigrant children need compensatory education in civics and social studies. They are the least likely to receive information about American government from home, and they have not been socialized with the same symbols and history lessons that children born in the United States have.

Social studies instruction should highlight the central role of conflict and disagreement in the operation of American political institutions, while showing that these disagreements are soluble and manageable. Students must be assured that disagreement and diversity can be safe, that people need not take offense when others do not agree with them, that most disputes are subject to peaceful resolution and compromise, and that more persistent disagreements can be tolerated. In some schools, there are extra-curricular activities, such as mock trial or the debating team, that help adolescents learn the value of principled dispute. However, relatively few students participate in these activities. Elements of debate and discussion should be incorporated into all social studies courses, and in many other areas of the curriculum, such as literature, philosophy, and history.

Political efficacy is as important, in many respects, as factual political knowledge. Social studies courses should not only teach the facts, but should build political efficacy. Course materials that present American political institutions and leaders as rigged and corrupt help to instill cynicism and negative attitudes about government. It is not necessary to portray American history without any of its flaws and shortcomings, but similarly, it does tremendous harm to portray it in a singularly negative light. American history and government are not "all bad" or "all good," and adolescents must learn to deal with shades of gray. Teaching the value of conflict and debate will also go a long way toward helping students learn to deal with both the positive and negative aspects of our history.

Social studies curricula should emphasize the meaning of party labels and assist students in making the connection between the major parties and the social groups that comprise the party coalitions. A critical threshold in the socialization process is crossed when youth learn which sorts of "social, economic and ideological groups affiliate with each party, while sorting out which group labels properly apply to themselves."[7]

BOLSTERING POLITICAL DIVERSITY AND ENCOURAGING ACTIVISM

To the extent possible to meet relaxed standards of compactness and maintain contiguity, election districts should be drawn so as to maximize political heterogeneity and diversity rather than to protect incumbent officeholders. Young people should be confronted with at least some elections that provide a serious partisan choice. In general, youth across many one-party locations are in desperate need of exposure to political diversity, partly to demonstrate that multiple viewpoints can coexist peacefully and that disagreement is not intolerable.

One of the best instruments of positive political socialization is responsive government, or at least government that is not widely corrupt. Working to create less discriminatory policing and a more professional, service-oriented bureaucracy are means to this end. In addition, focusing on local government, rather than national government, may also help to show that government can be responsive to those problems that are often most salient to people. Often, social studies courses and current events courses depend heavily upon national media sources and on national political issues. Examining local problems, and local solutions, can help with the perception that government is responsive.

Residential integration of ethnic minorities and white populations is another instrument for building a positive socialization experience. Conservatives would suggest that this goal is met by providing economic opportunity and upward mobility for those on the lower rungs. Liberals would suggest that fair housing policy and affirmative action are instruments to the integration of minorities with whites. We are agnostic on these options, believing that there is more than one way to achieve the same goal. Real world policy problems can rarely be resolved from within a single party's ideology or dominant policy framework.

In addition to contributing to the policy discussions on these critical topics, we hope our work contributes to the resuscitation of political socialization research in the social sciences. The time is ripe for reconsidering the findings from earlier studies. Times are changing. During the next ten years, the Depression Era generation, those who came of age during the 1930s and 1940s, will make a final exit from the electorate through mortality. The Baby Boom generation, the large post World War II birth cohort currently in its late 1940s and 1950s, will be entering retirement, and it too will begin to drop out of the electorate. Bracketing the other end of the population distribution is an enormous and fast-growing population under age 25. These are the children, and among the youngest, the grandchildren, of the Baby Boomers. In spite of the high turnout of the 2004 election, the outlook for their engagement is far from uniform. An overall decline in the level of voter participation with the passing of the Baby Boom generation would appear to lie ahead. Unless we come to a better understanding of the local forces that create good citizens, and do what we can to stimulate them in the places where they are not operating on their own, "small-d" democrats may one day be pining for the days when participation levels were at 51 percent.

ENDNOTES

1. James Gimpel, J. Celeste Lay, and Jason Schuknecht, *Cultivating Democracy: Civic Environments and Political Socialization in America* (Washington, DC: Brookings Institution Press, 2003).

2. Eric Plutzer, "Becoming a Habitual Voter: Inertia, Resources, and Growth in Young Adulthood," *American Political Science Review* 96 (2002): 41–56.

3. Stephen Ansolabehere and Shanto Iyengar, "Winning through Advertising: It's All in the Context," in *Campaigns and Elections*, eds. Candice Nelson and James Thurber (Boulder, CO: Westview Press, 1995).

4. V. O. Key Jr., *Southern Politics in State and Nation* (New York: Knopf, 1949), 508.

5. Alan Gerber and Donald Green, "The Effects of Canvassing, Telephone Calls, and Direct Mail on Voter Turnout: A Field Experiment." *American Political Science Review* 94 (2000): 653–663.

6. Diana Mutz, "Cross-cutting Social Networks: Testing Democratic Theory in Practice." *American Political Science Review* 96 (2002): 111–126.

7. Donald Green, Bradley Palmquist, and Eric Schickler, *Partisan Hearts and Minds: Political Parties and the Social Identities of Voters* (New Haven: Yale University Press, 2002), 137.

*James G. Gimpel is a professor of political science at the University of Maryland and J. Celeste Lay is an assistant professor of political science at Tulane University.

James G. Gimpel and J. Celeste Lay. "Youth at Risk for Non-participation." In Peter Levine and James Youniss, eds., "Youth Civic Engagement: An Institutional Turn." CIRCLE Working Paper 45, February 2006.

Reprinted by permission of the Center for Information & Research on Civic Learning & Engagement (CIRCLE), Tufts University.

DISCUSSION QUESTIONS

1. To increase participation by minority groups, should political parties have quotas to ensure that the diversity of society is represented in their candidates?

2. Should governments be more concerned with increasing citizen access as much as possible or with ensuring that all citizen groups participate equally?

3. Should we limit citizen participation in areas where it can be demonstrated that at-risk groups are underrepresented, such as contributing money for election campaigns?

Civic Engagement and the Disadvantaged: Challenges, Opportunities and Recommendations

by James B. Hyman and Peter Levine*

[...]

This paper was developed in the interest of extending the reach and benefits of national and community service programs to larger numbers of persons from disadvantaged populations—populations that data suggest may currently be underrepresented or underserved. In particular, this paper is intended to increase our understanding of and appreciation for the challenges and opportunities that may attend efforts to increase the participation by disadvantage groups.

In approaching our charge, we provide a broad context, showing that levels of volunteering, community service, and civic engagement vary by subgroup in the US population. Our explorations suggest that, among many variables tested in research, educational background is the clearest and most dramatic factor affecting participation: persons with more years of schooling tend to be much more involved in volunteer and service programs.[1] Thus special attention and outreach to persons without college experience (about half of the young adult population[2]) may be a fruitful and powerful direction for increasing participation in the Corporation for National & Community Service programs. Race and gender are also relevant and need to be considered, although their relationships to service and civic engagement are subtler and more complex.

This paper explores the research on these issues; generates hypotheses about what that research suggests by way of strategies for increasing participation; and finally, offers concrete proposals for strategies that might enhance the diversity and equity of participation in Corporation-supported programs.

Understanding Current Volunteering Differentials

One challenge to understanding who volunteers and who does not is our language. Conventional survey questions use the word "volunteering" without much elaboration. For example, the Current Population Supplement traditionally asks, "Since [date], have you done any volunteer activities through or for an organization?" Data obtained using this kind of question show differences by education and by race/ethnicity:

Volunteering Rates by Social Group

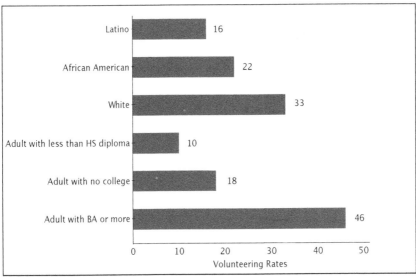

Source: Census Bureau, Current Population Supplement, 2005.

As the graph above shows, such survey questions generate results indicating that volunteer rates are positively correlated with education and that whites volunteer at rates roughly 50% higher than blacks and about twice as high as Latinos. But the survey item on which this graph is based may be misleading. To many Americans, "volunteering" means providing uncompensated service to strangers, often after school or after work. That is a form of service that fits best in middle-class lifestyles. If, for example, an adult is employed full-time and chooses to help other people's children at the local school, we call that activity "volunteering." If, on the other hand, an unemployed parent in a high-crime neighborhood spends (typically) her time carefully monitoring the community's children all day, she is unlikely to describe her activity as "volunteering," or herself as a volunteer, even though she too is providing a valued but uncompensated service to the community.

This discrepancy does not suggest that the surveys are somehow flawed. Survey items that use words such as "volunteering" and "service" actually do capture forms of engagement that Americans describe with those terms. In that sense, such survey questions do not appear to be biased per se; they produce accurate estimates of the volunteering rate for Americans of various races and ethnicities and social classes.[3] The concern however, as shown in the next section, is that such survey items tend to omit important forms of participation and engagement that Americans do not typically classify as "volunteering" or "service."

Volunteering and service are subsets of the broader concept of civic engagement. "Civic engagement" refers to individual and collective actions designed to identify and address issues of public concern. Such actions might include: joining associations, attending meetings, raising and giving money, contacting officials, and protest and/or civil disobedience. It means working to make a difference in the civic life of our communities and developing the combination of knowledge, skills, values and motivation to make that difference.[4] Placed in this broader context, real differences do exist in the rates of civic engagement among demographic groups.

Civic Engagement and Social Class

We often observe variations in the rates of civic participation by social class. Surveys consistently show that giving money, contacting public officials, working informally on community problems, and even protesting are all more common among the affluent than among the poor.[5] The American Political Science Association's Task Force on Inequality and American Democracy concluded:

> The privileged [those with more income] participate more than others and are increasingly well organized to press their demands on government. Public officials, in turn, are much more responsive to the privileged than to average citizens and the least affluent. Citizens with low or moderate incomes speak with a whisper that is lost on the ears of inattentive government, while the advantaged roar with the clarity and consistency that policymakers readily heed.[6]

To explore this further, we constructed the graph below by combining the results of two survey questions, one which queried the highest level of education that the respondent completed and another which captured the social class that the respondent considered himself or herself to be part of. The union of these questions produces our own composite measure of social class.[7] As shown below, the graph demonstrates gaps in civic engagement in a particularly dramatic way. Those who say they are both middle class and college educated are up to five times more likely to participate in all categories compared to those who say they are working class and have no college experience.

DDB (formerly DDB Needham) surveys allow us to track Americans' participation in community projects. What it means to "work on a community project" is not defined in these surveys, but we hypothesize that it means more than discrete acts of service—survey respondents may be thinking of longer

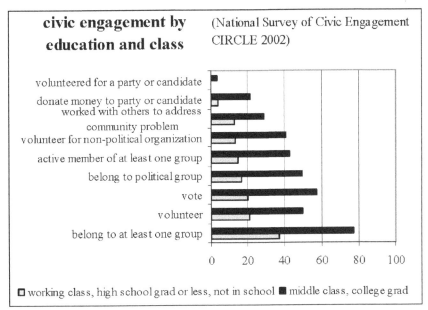

civic engagement by education and class

(National Survey of Civic Engagement CIRCLE 2002)

- volunteered for a party or candidate
- donate money to party or candidate
- worked with others to address community problem
- volunteer for non-political organization
- active member of at least one group
- belong to political group
- vote
- volunteer
- belong to at least one group

□ working class, high school grad or less, not in school ■ middle class, college grad

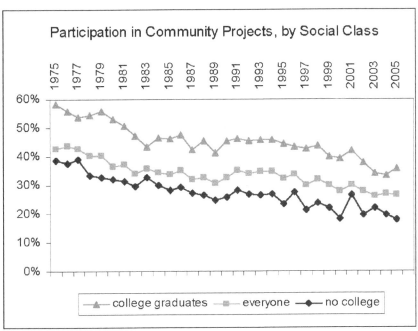

Participation in Community Projects, by Social Class

college graduates — everyone — no college

processes in which they set goals, express interests and goals, perhaps address controversies, and work to accomplish social change. Collaborating with neighbors over time to improve city services or to fight crime could be examples of community projects.

The graph on the previous page shows that Americans without college experience have been less likely than their college-educated counterparts over time to engage in community projects. And though participation has fallen for the population as a whole, it has become critically low for the less educated. This suggests that communities and neighborhoods with less well-educated residents are likely to have fewer people participating in civic projects and may, in addition, have fewer community projects underway.

Racial and Ethnic Differences

Race is also a differentiating factor, but in ways that are fairly complex.[8] Groups may participate at above-average rates in some areas of civic activity while participating at below-average rates in others. An important example can be drawn from survey questions on community projects. Those data suggest that African Americans are more engaged than all other racial/ethnic groups in working on "community projects."[9]

We suspect that these findings are coincident with the strong attachments

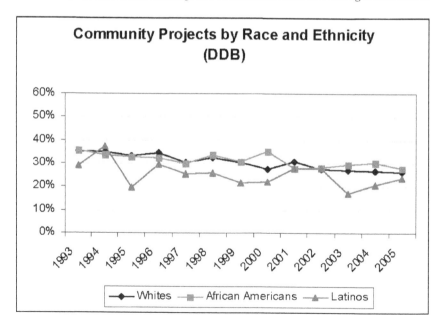

to faith traditions in the African-American community. Many of the norms and networks that connect African Americans to these community projects originate within a church. Research has shown that African Americans have higher church attendance than any other racial and ethnic group in America. In the 2004 General Social Survey, for example, 70 percent of African Americans described themselves as frequent church-attenders compared to 46 percent of Whites and 49 percent of Latinos.[10]

Interestingly, although whites are less likely than blacks to be involved in community projects and other local civic work, they are much more likely than blacks (and Latinos) to report "volunteering." It may be that whites are more likely to choose forms of participation—for example, "service" activities such as serving at a soup kitchen or tutoring a child—that are classically *labeled* "volunteering" by the Corporation and other service institutions, whereas African Americans are more likely to participate in processes that involve expressing interests and organizing for social change. Such processes are more naturally described as "working on community projects" or "addressing community problems."

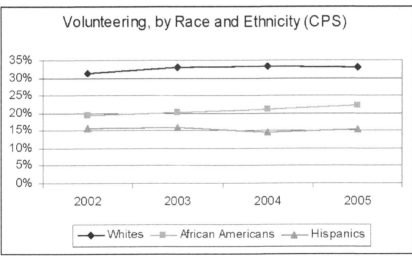

Keeter et al. find, "Much … volunteering is episodic, initiated by third parties or volunteer organizations, and decidedly nonpolitical in motivation."[11] An example would be an annual visit to a soup kitchen or to Habitat for Humanity organized by an employer without much input from the employees. By contrast, "addressing a community problem" seems to require a deeper level of ongoing participation and sometimes a more adversarial or political approach.

A 2007 report by the National Conference on Citizenship found that African

Americans are the most philosophically committed to the kind of civic participation that is collaborative and involves discussion and planning as well as action.[12] When offered a list of ways to address community needs, African Americans were the most likely to choose participating in community meetings (there was a 16-point differential on this question compared to whites), and gathering with other citizens to identify problems and solutions. This relatively political, process-oriented approach to engagement is not conventionally considered "volunteering."

Hypothesis: Participation of the disadvantaged in recognized programs will increase if/when those programs can better recognize the various forms (including process- vs. service-oriented) that civic engagement actually assumes in some disadvantaged communities.

Implications: Widening the spectrum of civic activities sanctioned by CNCS will open the Corporation's benefits to a wider audience of potential participants and sponsors in disadvantage communities.

Voter behavior also varies by race. Whites are somewhat more likely to vote than African Americans are, but the gap is not as large as one would predict based on differences in wealth and education. But this finding is somewhat nuanced by age. There is no gap at all in voter turnout between young whites and young African Americans (ages 18–25). Latino citizens vote at lower rates.

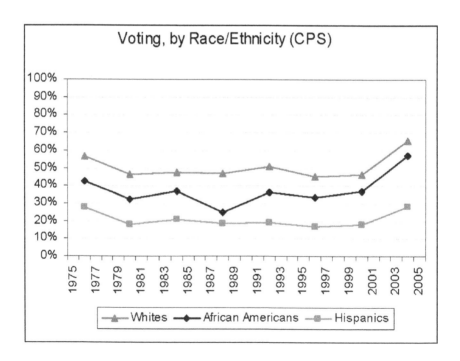

Gender

Gender is also relevant to civic engagement, although gender gaps are not especially large. Women are somewhat more likely to behave in civic ways, such as volunteering, and they also vote at higher rates than men. Men are more involved in some other political activities, such as persuading people to vote and donating money to candidates.[13]

One of the most noteworthy gaps is the relatively low level of participation by adolescent males compared to females. Girls and young women are ahead of boys and young men in most forms of voluntary community engagement.[14] They also outnumber their male counterparts in all school-based extracurricular activities except athletics.[15] Thus the engagement of young boys and young men requires special attention.

Given the differences we observe by education, race, ethnicity, and gender illustrated above, it will be a challenging for the Corporation to increase the levels of volunteering and service within disadvantaged populations, especially among Latinos and people with little or no college education. The irony here is that the marginal benefits of service both to communities and individuals will be greatest for these very groups of people who are least advantaged to start with. For instance, in their evaluation of the Teen Outreach Program (which involved service-learning), Allen and Philliber found, "The program had the greatest impact in reducing future pregnancies among the group at highest risk of such pregnancies.... For academic failure, Teen Outreach demonstrated greater efficacy for youths who had been previously suspended than for those who had not. The program was also found to be more effective for members of racial ethnic minority groups, who were also at greater risk for academic difficulty in this study."[16] This leads us to the following.

TOWARD A STRATEGY FOR INCREASING PARTICIPATION

Community Service: "Drivers" and "Inhibiters"

To meet this challenge of increasing participation, CNCS and other volunteer and service organizations need to formulate working hypotheses about the major factors that facilitate and/or impede engagement—hypotheses that they can then apply to populations of concern, disadvantaged or otherwise. To generate these hypotheses we pose two fundamental questions. The first is: What is it that determines whether individuals are more or less *willing* to volunteer? The second, and equally basic question, is: What is it that determines whether individuals have more or less *opportunity* to volunteer? We will explore these questions in turn—posing answers for each and generating hypotheses from our answers.

1.   *Disparities in Motivation/Willingness to Serve/Volunteer:* We posit three major factors that can act as drivers and inhibiters of an individual's willingness to volunteer: availability of discretionary time, personal preferences, and available personal resources. Efforts to increase participation in programs must be grounded in an understanding of both what motivates people to get involved as well as any barriers that might inhibit that involvement.

Time as a Resource: Time is the primary resource that one "spends" when engaging in volunteering and service behaviors. Time is a finite, discrete commodity in that it is limited and usually committed to only one activity "at a time." As such, choices must be made about whether or not to do an activity or, at other times, which activity to do. This suggests that time is not a "free" commodity. It has an implicit cost (i.e., the value—psychic or material—that would be derived from an alternate use [e.g., leisure, recreation, a second job, or volunteering]). Economists refer to this value as the "opportunity cost"—meaning the value of an alternate opportunity. Theoretically, people are expected to select their highest valued choice and thereby minimize their opportunity costs.

People differ in the amount of time that is truly discretionary. For example, young single mothers with school-aged children who are participating in welfare-to-work programs may simply be unable to commit time to civic engagement. Older, retired persons, on the other hand, may.

Research suggests, however, that busier people are often more civically engaged than people who might appear to be less occupied. For instance, young people who are enrolled in college full-time and who also work for a salary tend to be more civically engaged than their contemporaries who only take courses *or* who only work.[17] Several explanations are possible. It may be that student-workers are more energetic people. Alternatively, campuses and the workplaces may act as strong recruitment venues, allowing student-workers to be presented with more volunteer options and offers than their contemporaries.

Robert Putnam finds in general that working more hours does not reduce civic engagement.[18] An old adage holds that if you want something done, you should ask a busy person to do it. The implication is that scarcity of time is not always a barrier to civic participation. Indeed, we suspect that the *perception* of free time rather than the *fact* of free time is the central issue. And we further suspect that the existence of strong preferences is likely an overriding factor that can encourage individuals to "make time" for an activity—volunteering or any other.

Personal Preferences: As alluded to above, a second factor affecting motivation is the individual's "preference" or "taste"—the hierarchical order in which individuals place alternative choices—in this case, options for the use of their time. Preferences often come into play when individuals are considering several options for using their free time (as oppose reacting to a specific proposal). These preferences are determined by a myriad of factors that reflect perceptions of the associated material and/or psychic rewards.

One such factor is the *community context*. For instance, some of the typical forms of community service, such as beautifying the natural environment, may be lower priorities in communities that face pressing "institutional" and social challenges, such as poor schools and other public services, high unemployment, and the drug trade and its attendant problems. In such instances, these forms of community service may seem inadequate or irrelevant to the challenges of most concern to local residents. Consequently, preferences for "volunteering" (as typically defined) in these communities may be weaker. In fact, it is possible that the "agenda" of community priorities may be one of the factors involved in our earlier discussion about African-Americans and community projects.

Preferences for volunteering can also be influenced by *family messages* that are conveyed by parents and other family members. Keeter et al. note, "Parents and guardians, even siblings, provide critical role models for civic behavior ... Young people who were raised in homes where someone volunteered (43% of all youth) are highly involved themselves—joining groups and associations, volunteering, wearing buttons, or displaying bumper stickers at rates higher than of those who did not grow up with such examples. Youth with engaged role models are also more attentive to news of politics and government and more likely to participate in boycotts or buycotts." Among young people (ages 15–25) the volunteering rate is 31 percent if someone in their household volunteers, and 15 percent if no one does.[19]

Outside the family, preferences for engagement can also be shaped by *community messages*. There is evidence that preferences for engagement also vary among communities and cultural groups. For example, the high rate of involvement in community projects in the African-American community is thought to be partly cultural—arising from powerful norms of "giving back" that were first nurtured in the periods of slavery and segregation.[20] Various groups of Americans are taught and encouraged to participate in different ways and perhaps to different degrees. These differences may help to explain differential rates of civic participation.

In truth, considerations of opportunity costs and preferences occur simultaneously. But how these considerations combine can be complex.

Hypothesis: Persons are more likely to volunteer if they perceive they have time that they can give to volunteer activity but, regardless of these perceptions, a more powerful, potentially overriding driver of volunteer activity may be the individual's preference for the specific volunteer opportunity being presented. Exciting volunteer opportunities can cause individuals to "make time" to participate.

Implications: The availability of an array of volunteer opportunities and an effective program of information dissemination about these opportunities may be critical components of a more proactive approach to increasing volunteerism within disadvantage populations.

Personal Resources: The third factor we highlight as influencing the willingness, motivation and/or propensity to volunteer is personal resources—assets commanded by individuals that can be put to use in the volunteer activity. Two in particular are important—skills and money.

Verba et al. treat *knowledge and skills* as resources. Participating in meetings, contacting officials, and managing associations are skills that people need in order to organize volunteering efforts (which otherwise may not occur) and to engage in other forms of civic engagement, such as community problem-solving. These skills must be learned; they are not inborn.

But opportunities to learn such skills are unevenly distributed and have declined over time. Meetings, for example, are opportunities to learn skills and gain connections to other active citizens. Meeting attendance can be understood as a form of civic engagement,[21] and it may lead to further civic engagement if, for example, participants in a meeting organize a volunteering project. The following graph shows a strong link between education and meeting-attendance. College graduates are much more prone to attend meetings than high school leavers. But the graph also shows that, overall, Americans today are less likely to attend even a single meeting during the course of a given year than they were in the 1970s.

Another venue for civic "training" is education. Public schools are supposed to prepare young people for civic participation. But there are disparities in school-based civic training by income and race. Joseph Kahne and Ellen Middaugh analyzed surveys of more than 2,500 California high school seniors and a nationally representative sample of 9th graders. They found that students in schools with wealthy student bodies are most likely to report having political

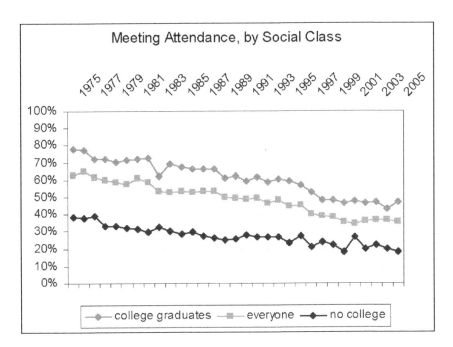

Meeting Attendance, by Social Class

college graduates — everyone — no college

debates and panel discussions. In addition, African American students are less likely than white students to have civic-focused government classes, current events discussions, and to participate in simulations of civic processes. Latino students also report fewer opportunities to volunteer, participate in simulations, and have discussion in an open classroom climate. These disparities in opportunities to learn civic skills may contribute to differentials in the rates civic engagement by social class and race.[22]

Hypothesis: Individuals are more likely to volunteer if they feel they have the skills needed to allow them be successful in making a contribution.

Implication: The Corporation should focus some of its attention on increasing opportunities for civic training in conjunction with schools, churches, nonprofits and other community agencies in poor and minority neighborhoods.

Civic engagement may also cost *money*. When we recruit volunteers we are not only asking them to commit uncompensated time but we are usually asking them to bear the cost of volunteering—an implicit contribution of cash through the costs of their transportation, meals, childcare, appropriate attire and other expenses that may associate with their participation. This too may contribute to the disparities we observe since these associated cost will be more burdensome to the poor, to the less educated, and to segments of the African-American and Latino communities. Where time and money are scarce in a household—for example, because members work long hours to pay for basic necessities—it may be harder for people to engage.

Hypothesis: Individuals are more likely to volunteer if the out-of-pocket expenses of community service are minimized.

Implication: The Corporation should explore means of covering any ancillary cost associated with its volunteer and service programs.

2. *Disparities in Opportunities to Serve/Volunteer:* The other side of our formulation concerns the extent to which opportunities for volunteering and service are equally distributed across populations and communities. Here we posit that levels of opportunity will be driven or inhibited by issues of Community Capacity, Marketing and information, and Recruitment.

Community Capacity: Many low-income and minority communities lack a robust infrastructure of non-governmental organizations capable of mounting, administering and maintaining volunteer programs. The infrastructure that does exist in these communities is more likely to be comprised of organizations oriented to the service needs of residents (e.g., housing and health services, employment and training) than organizations providing civic opportunities to youth (e.g., Scouts, Camp Fire, Boys and Girls Clubs) and adults (e.g., Lions, Kiwanis, Junior League, Elks, American Legion)[23] Moreover, because of the high needs and relatively low wealth in these communities, this infrastructure tends to be overtaxed and under-capitalized—suggesting that it contends with severe resource challenges in even meeting the community's service demands.

Some poor communities also lack adequate numbers of adults who can work with children. Daniel Hart and colleagues have found that youth volunteering rates are low in communities that have many children per adult and little wealth. In these communities (often located in inner cities), there is a shortage of adults who might run sports or mentoring programs, and there is not enough wealth to hire professional youth workers, as might be done in a suburb. Volunteering rates are higher in poor communities where there are more adults per child.[24]

Additionally, while volunteer and service programs represent net value-added to both individuals and communities, they are not without their own administrative costs and burdens. To be effective, volunteer organizations must have the people and financial resources to recruit, train, assign and monitor volunteers as well as be accountable to funding sources. These resource needs require organization have the capacity to meet them. The lack of a strong volunteer infrastructure may both reduce the number of volunteering opportunities as well as reduce the likelihood that persons are asked to volunteer.

Information and Marketing: A second challenge to increasing volunteering and service is to assure that the opportunities for and benefits of participation in programs are well-disseminated across populations and communities so they are more accessible. Information and marketing should describe both available service opportunities and the outcomes and benefits of specific volunteer and service projects in disadvantaged neighborhoods.

Recruitment: Most people who volunteer or engage in other ways (including voting) say that they did so because someone asked them to. People often develop durable commitments to service because someone asked them to serve and then the experience changed their values and preferences in favor of continuing to volunteer.[25] In fact, studies find that recruitment is an even more powerful predictor of volunteering than one's attitudes or values prior to serving.

But recruitment levels are not uniform across populations and communities. For example, research suggests that "whites are much more likely to be asked to volunteer than blacks."[26] Still as discussed earlier, African-Americans are more likely to be engaged in community projects than any other racial group—largely as a result of their relationship with the church. What is important, for our purposes, about church membership, for example, is that people are much more likely to volunteer if they belong to organizations or social networks that actively recruit members for civic engagement. Unfortunately, those organizations and networks are themselves unequally distributed, and they are also in decline.

Hypothesis: Americans' propensity to volunteer and otherwise participate in civic work depends in part on the prevalence of local civic groups and institutions that can recruit participants, market opportunities, and develop civic skills in young people.

Implication: The Corporation should direct resources to supporting non-profits in low-income communities.

OBSERVATIONS AND RECOMMENDATIONS

Our purpose in this research has been to explore issues that would increase the Corporation for National and Community Service's understanding of factors that contribute to variations in service and volunteer rates and to propose strategies that might increase participation among underrepresented groups. A first-order question, in this regard, is: which population should be of most concern? We conclude that among groups participating at lower rates, priority attention should be given to black and Hispanic people in low-income community and especially persons without college education.

Three strategic observations are made about the challenges and opportunities associated with this population.

Observation 1: We need to clarify our volunteering and service language in ways that expand to encompass the forms of volunteering and service behaviors typical of these communities—process-oriented community engagement.

Recommendation: Design service programs that are opportunities for collective problem-solving. Disadvantaged people have reasons to prefer problem-solving and meaningful, sustained projects that are aimed at serious issues that they care about. Therefore, Corporation programs should be structured so that participants have real opportunities to define and select meaningful problems and then address them collaboratively. If they are designed or advertised as "voluntary service," they will probably be less appealing. As Shirley Sagawa has argued, two factors that attract less advantaged youth to service programs are "meeting real needs" and "providing opportunities for youth leadership."[27]

Observation 2: We need to mount an array of strategies to increase the motivation and willingness to serve with an eye toward: overcoming any reluctance to commit discretionary time; and mitigating the out of pocket costs of participation.

Recommendation: CNCS should make concerted efforts to define areas of service that will appeal to community needs in areas such as education, public safety, youth development, community cleanup and others that reflect the priority concerns of disadvantaged neighborhoods and it should consider providing additional resources to sponsor agencies to subsidize the participation costs of volunteers.

Observation 3: Third, we need to construct strategies that increase the levels of opportunities available to these communities and that make those opportunities more accessible.

Recommendation: Use service programs to support mediating organizations. One of the barriers to equal participation is the decline of mediating institutions—unions, religious congregations, fraternal associations, and the like—that once were more likely to recruit members who lacked college educations. The Corporation should consider deploying volunteers to strengthen civic groups that reach working-class Americans, especially youth who have left the educational system. If the Corporation's volunteers help to strengthen organizations that involve working-class people in their meetings and other programs, numerous people will be recruited into civil society (more than just the volunteers themselves). This is a powerful form of leverage. Since many small nonprofit organizations have difficulties competing for or managing federal grants, there is a need to think about training, technical assistance, and streamlined or flexible procedures.

FINAL COMMENT

As stated at the outset, it is important that the benefits of volunteer and service programs be made available to Americans of all backgrounds. One overarching concern regards the disparities we observe by educational background. Individuals, and particularly poor minorities, with less education are less civically engaged. This presents a difficult challenge to the Corporation because of the difficultly inherent in recruiting young adults once they have dropped out of high school or have completed high school without going on to college.

Without such institutional attachments, these young people cannot be reached through counselors and teachers or recruited in their school buildings or on their college campuses. Their peer networks are smaller and more detached from adult educators. Recruiting non-college-bound youth has become even harder in recent decades as other organizations, such as unions and religious congregations, have shrunk. It is therefore crucial to recruit youth while they are all still enrolled in educational institutions.

Invest in K-12 opportunities. Consequently, and in addition to the recommendations above, we believe that early exposure to an "ethic of service" should be the cornerstone of the Corporation's strategies for increasing participation generally but particularly within poor minority neighborhoods where residents may be less likely to pursue higher education. Service organized by schools seems to have positive effects.[28] This is not necessarily an argument for mandates and requirements, because the *quality* of service opportunities might not keep pace if everyone had to participate. But it is an argument for improving the size, quality, and reach of Learn & Serve America, the Corporation's main program that serves K–12 education.

We hope these explorations and the conclusions and recommendations drawn from them prove useful to the Corporation for National and Community Service in its effort to increase the participation of underserved populations in its volunteer and service programs.

ENDNOTES

1. Cf. John Wilson, "Volunteering," *Annual Review of Sociology* 26 (2000), p. 218: "Level of education is the most consistent predictor of volunteering."

2. Mark Hugo Lopez and Karlo Barrios Marcelo, "Youth demographics," CIRCLE Fact Sheet (November 2006), using the Current Population Survey from the US Census.

3. An experiment conducted in 2004 indicated that there was little bias in traditional survey questions. The Bureau of Labor Statistics randomly asked some respondents whether they had "volunteered," and others whether they had done various specific activities. The list of activities included coaching, serving food, maintaining and building facilities, etc. By asking these behavioral questions, instead of simply asking about "volunteering," the researchers raised the apparent volunteering rate by 6 percentage points. However, the increases were very similar for all the major racial/ethnic groups and for people with different educational backgrounds. (Chris Toppe, "Measuring volunteering: A behavioral approach," CIRCLE Working Paper 43, December 2005). More research should be done using additional behavioral prompts. Questions, discussed below, about participation in community projects yield different results.

4. Excerpts from *Civic Responsibility and Higher Education*, edited by Thomas Ehrlich (Phoenix: Oryx Press, 2000).

5. National Conference on Citizenship in association with CIRCLE and the Saguaro Seminar, *Broken Engagement: America's Civic Engagement Index* (September 18, 2006).

6. American Political Science Association, Task Force on Inequality and American Democracy, *American Democracy in an Age of Rising Inequality* (2004), http://www.apsanet.org/imgtest/taskforcereport.pdf, p. 1.

7. Peter Levine, *The Future of Democracy: Developing the Next Generation of American Citizens* (Tufts University Press, 2007), p. 23.

8. Summary measures in National Conference on Citizenship, 2006.

9. This graph shows "working on community projects" over time, using DDB data. Bey's paper uses the same indicator from the 2007 Current Population Supplement and finds whites slightly ahead of African Americans. The two findings are close enough to be consistent.

10. Authors' tabulations using the GSS Cumulative Data file (1972–2006) archived by University of California-Berkeley.

11. Scott Keeter, Cliff Zukin, Molly Andolina, and Krista Jenkins, *The Civic and Political Health of the Nation: A Generational Portrait* (released by CIRCLE, 2002).

12. National Conference on Citizenship in partnership with CIRCLE and the Saguaro Seminar, America's *Civic Health Index 2007.*

13. Keeter et al., *The Civic and Political Health of the Nation*, p. 27; Mark Hugo Lopez, Emily Kirby, and Jared Sagoff, "Voter turnout among young women and men," CIRCLE Fact Sheet (January 2003, updated July 2005).

14. Karlo Barrios Marcelo, Mark Hugo Lopez, and Emily Hoban Kirby, "Civic engagement among young men and women," CIRCLE Fact Sheet (March 2007).

15. Catherine E. Freeman, "Trends in educational equity of girls & women," *Education Statistics Quarterly*, vol. 6, issue 4, table G, citing statistics from University of Michigan, Institute for Social Research, Monitoring the Future study, 2001.

16. Allen and Philliber (via NIH Public Access), pp. 9–10. Many of the impressive results from positive youth development programs have been observed in highly disadvantaged populations. Dávila and Mora do not find differences in the effects of required service on teenagers who are African American, Latino, and White, but they do find that boys benefit more than girls. This is noteworthy because girls are now achieving at considerably higher levels than girls in high school. Alberto Dávila and Marie T. Mora, "Do gender and ethnicity affect civic engagement and academic progress?" CIRCLE Working Paper 53 (2007).

17. Sharon E. Jarvis, Lisa Montoya & Emily Mulvoy, "The political participation of college students, working students and working youth," CIRCLE Working Paper 37 (2005).

18. Robert D. Putnam, *Bowling Alone: The Collapse and Revival of American Democracy* (New York: Simon and Schuster, 2000).

19. Keeter et al., pp. 30–31.

20. Richard D. Shingles, Black consciousness and political participation: The missing link, "*The American Political Science Review.*" 75 (1981): 76–91; Michelle M. Charles, Giving back to the community: African American inner city teens and civic engagement," CIRCLE Working Paper 38 (August 2005).

21. E.g., in the National Conference on Citizenship's Index of National Civic Health, via www.ncoc.net.

22. Joseph Kahne and Ellen Middaugh, "Democracy for some: The civic opportunity gap in high school," CIRCLE working paper 59 (February 2008).

23. For instance, Lochner et al. find that membership in voluntary associations (fraternal, civic, ethnic, etc.) is negatively correlated with poverty rates in Chicago neighborhoods. But the poorest neighborhoods may have various service-oriented nonprofit agencies. Kimberly A. Lochner, Ichiro Kawachia, Robert T. Brennan and Stephen L. Bukac, Social capital and neighborhood mortality rates in Chicago, *Social Science & Medicine* 56 (April 2003): 1800.

24. Daniel Hart, Robert Atkins, Patrick Markey, and James Youniss, "Youth bulges in communities: The effects of age structure on adolescent civic knowledge and civic participation," *Psychological Science* (2004) 15: 591–597; see especially p. 594.

25. K. Matsuba, D. Hart, R. Atkins, & T. Donnelly, "Psychological and social-structural influences on involvement in volunteering." *Journal of Research on Personality*, (2007) 41: 889–907·

26. Marc A. Musick, John Wilson, and William B. Bynum Jr. "Race and formal volunteering: The differential effects of class and religion," *Social Forces*, (June 2000) 78: 1554.

27. Summarized in Sejal Hathi and Bob Bhaerrman, "Effective practices for engaging at-risk youth in service," *Youth Service America* (2008), p. 16.

28. Edward Metz and James Youniss used *mandatory* service programs to test the hypothesis that volunteers are more civically engaged simply because they are motivated *before* they volunteer. They find that service increases civic engagement even when it is required. "A demonstration that school-based required service does not deter—but heightens—volunteerism," 36 *PS: Political Science and Politics* (2003): 281–286.

*James B. Hyman is an independent scholar conducting research, exploration, and analytical inquiry to improve the life prospects of poor and minority populations; Peter Levine is director of research and director of CIRCLE (Center for Information & Research on Civic Learning & Engagement) at Tufts University's Jonathan M. Tisch College of Citizenship and Public Service.

Hyman, James B., and Peter Levine. "Civic Engagement and the Disadvantaged: Challenges, Opportunities, and Recommendations." CIRCLE Working Paper 63, December 2008.

Reprinted by permission of the Center for Information & Research on Civic Learning & Engagement (CIRCLE), Tufts University.

DISCUSSION QUESTIONS

1. As long as there are large differences in social status and income between racial and ethnic groups, is real equality of participation possible? How do these inequalities affect the workings of the democratic process?

2. To increase volunteering by lower social status individuals, should all high schools mandate voluntary activity in a community project as a requirement of graduation?

3. To support civic engagement among all citizens, should the government and private foundations have special programs that support non-profit organizations only for low-income communities?

Gender and Civic Engagement: Secondary Analysis of Survey Data

*by Krista Jenkins**

Increasing attention is being paid to understanding the political behavior of the newest age cohort to enter the electorate. Following on the heels of the "Slacker generation" (that is, Generation X), this new generation, often labeled Generation DotNet, Generation Y, Millennials, or the "Echo Boomers," is commonly understood to include young adults born after 1976. It appears that DotNets are behaving in ways that are both a departure from and continuation of the behavioral and attitudinal patterns of Xers. Along with Xers, they remain among the least engaged in the world of electoral politics. Yet, at the same time, their impressive amount of civic activism suggests they may see volunteering and other civic behaviors as an alternative to more system-directed activities that are designed to influence the formal political process.[1]

Despite a flurry of research on this new cohort,[2] little, if any, attention has been paid to young women's political distinctiveness—or lack thereof. Although it may seem reasonable to expect that egalitarian trends in the education and socialization of today's youth should mitigate the importance of gender on citizen engagement, it is nonetheless a bit premature to assume the effects of sexism, stereotypes, and patriarchy have been vanquished. Politics is still largely the province of white men. Young women are likely to be internalizing this norm throughout the development of their political identities since research shows that political socialization in early adulthood has far-reaching consequences on attitudes and behavior later in life.[3] Although patterns rooted in adolescence are not impervious to change in adulthood,[4] knowing how a young woman is socialized can provide insight into her later attitudes and behavior. So, for example, if the political process appears to resonate less with young women than young men today, efforts can be made now to promote equality when behavior and attitudes are more malleable.

What follows is an overview of findings from research that addresses whether, and to what extent, gender is salient in the development of norms of citizen behavior and key precursors to citizen engagement. A variety of data will be used to illuminate the complexity of gender's relationship to citizen engagement among today's youth. The bulk of the analysis, however, is drawn from the National Citizen Engagement Study (NCES).[5]

Across some key indicators, the story is about the same regardless of sex. Young women and men appear to be receiving the same cues about politics, elected officials, and the political process. They are also responding in much the same way—that is, tuning out and doing little. However, young women are also demonstrating their distinctiveness in ways that are both hopeful and potentially worrisome. Thus, the picture to emerge is one that cannot be easily summarized by either sameness or difference.

Gender, Youth, and Citizen Engagement: Expectations

A variety of forces converge in a young person's life that help to shape her early political identity. Among these is formal education. The benefits of formal education are amply documented in regard to the development of healthy norms of citizen engagement, such as voting and paying attention to what is going on in the world of government and politics.[6] Whereas past generations of young women were disadvantaged by a gender gap in formal education, since either women were thought incapable of the rigors of higher thought or such an endeavor was deemed unnecessary for domestic caretaking, the same cannot be said today. Record levels of young women attend college and, among some demographics, their numbers exceed those of young male undergraduates.[7] From 1970 to 2000 the number of women attending college rose by 136 percent, and women's attendance in graduate school increased by 168 percent. Today women make up approximately 56 percent of all undergraduates and they outnumber men by 1.7 million in colleges and universities.[8] Clearly the gender gap disadvantaging women in higher education is no more and, in fact, young men are now the group most likely to come up short in formal education. The egalitarian trend in formal education should translate into more political socialization for young women. As a result, it is possible that today's activism among youth is characterized by no less than parity across the sexes in expressions of citizenship.

However, at the same time it is important to consider the possibility—indeed probability—that education alone is not the panacea for disparities in engagement between the sexes. Theories abound as to why women in general are not drawn to politics as much as men are. These include the extent to which women are socialized to understand politics as a "man's game." Although the contemporary women's movement has helped achieve sizable gains in the number of women elected to public office and appointed to powerful positions in government (e.g., Condoleezza Rice, Madeleine Albright, Janet Reno), it is still the norm for women to be underrepresented or absent when public policies are made. If the images that young women continue to see are of politically powerful men, politics and government will likely not resonate to the extent that they do with young men, regardless of education.

There are also arguments concerning female disinterest in "rules of the game" and notions of abstract justice, principles tied closely to the political process. Politics is about power, authority, and the allocation of scarce resources. It is often rife with conflict and there are often clearly understood "winners" and "losers." Dialogue and consensus are clearly not the norm when cable and TV news present information about the political process. The screaming matches of political commentary shows simply serve to reinforce the stereotype of politics being about dominance and control. Rather than plunging into the "who gets what" world of politics, young women—we are told—are more likely to spend their time focusing on more immediate, personal, and consensual concerns. Regardless of whether politics is accurately reflected in cultural and media discourse, its representation may alienate young women.

Thus, there are reasons to suspect that young women today are not embracing politics to the extent that young men are. Although disparities in education have certainly lessened, there remain structural and sociological impediments to getting young women interested in and engaged in the world of politics. What follows is a close look at how young women are doing on their way to becoming engaged and informed citizens, beginning with an overview of what young women are doing—and not doing—with regard to involvement in public life.

WHAT ARE YOUNG WOMEN DOING?

The National Civic Engagement Survey (NCES) represents the best survey in recent years to examine rates and types of activism among both young women and men. It is rich with questions about a variety of ways people can influence politics and their communities. These range from activities designed to influence the formal political process, such as voting, to more private activities such as community problem-solving and using one's might as a consumer to reward or punish a company for its social or political values.

Scott Keeter and his colleagues—the authors of this survey—have divided their 19 core indicators of behavior into three distinct areas of engagement.[9] Electoral engagement comprises actions people take to influence the formal political process, such as voting, donating money to a campaign or political party, volunteering for a candidate or political organization, displaying campaign buttons, signs, or stickers, and trying to persuade others politically during an election. Civic activism includes activities such as working informally with others to solve a community problem, volunteering for a non-political group, engaging actively as a member of a group or organization, and charitable fundraising, whether through participation in a walk/run/bike event or another type of fundraising. Finally, there is what the survey authors classify as "political voice" activities— actions people take to express themselves outside the formal channels of political participation. These include contacting elected officials, consumer activism, protesting, contacting the print or broadcast media, canvassing, and signing petitions (both written and email).

ELECTORAL ENGAGEMENT

Regardless of sex, today's youngest generation is only minimally engaged in activities that are designed to influence the formal political process. Regular voting in local and national elections, or what some might argue is the sole responsibility of citizenship, is reported by only about one in four women and men between the ages of 20 and 25. Among those who were too young to describe their past electoral participation (those between the ages of 15 and 19), their prospective participation looks a little better than what their older counterparts actually report. Thirty-eight percent of young women report intending always to vote in local and national elections when they are old enough, compared to 42 percent of young men.[10]

Table 1. Electoral Engagement

Percent of those 15–25 who report ...	Women	Men
Persuading others politically	34	37
Always voting in local and national elections	23	26
Displaying a campaign button, sign, or sticker	23	19
Working for a party or candidate	4	2
Contributing money to a party or candidate	4	6

Source: National Citizen Engagement Survey, 2002.

Both sexes do slightly more when it comes to activities that are arguably easier than voting, such as trying to persuade others to vote for or against a candidate during an election (about a third for both women and men) and displaying a button, sign, or sticker in support of a candidate (about one in five among each sex). Not surprisingly, a meager percentage of young women and men aged 15 to 25 report contributing money to a candidate, a political party, or any organization that supported candidates or volunteering for a party or candidate in the past 12 months.

CIVIC ENGAGEMENT

When the focus turns to the more private sphere of civic engagement, young women seem slightly more engaged in some activities than young men, and youth in general are considerably more active than in electoral politics. Today's generation of young women is clearly engaged in helping to solve society's problems through volunteering with a variety of organizations. Almost half of all young women between the ages of 15 and 25 (45%) report volunteering for at least one type of nonpolitical group in the past 12 months. Of those young women who reported volunteering, almost half spent time with a religious group (49%), about one in five worked for an environmental organization (21%), 59 percent donated time to a civic or community group involved in health or social services, and three-quarters worked for organizations that improve the lives of youth and the quality of education (76%). Compared to the percentage of young men who said they volunteered for a non-political group in the last 12 months (36%), young women's activism in this area looks healthy.[11]

Table 2. Civic Engagement

Percent of those 15–25 who report...	Women	Men
Volunteering for a non-political group	45	36
Raising money for a charity	29	27
Working with others informally to solve a community problem	21	21
Active membership in a group or Organization	20	24
Participating in a bike/run/walkathon for charity	16	15

Source: National Citizen Engagement Survey, 2002.

As for the other civic behaviors, the differences among women and men are less compelling. About equal numbers of both sexes report participating in some act of charitable fundraising in the past 12 months (29% of young women; 27% of young men). And about one in seven young women and men say they have participated in a walk/bike/runathon for charity in the past 12 months. Similar numbers of both sexes report doing one or the other—raising money or participating in an event—in the recent past. About 20 percent of both young women and men report that they have recently worked informally with others to solve a community problem. Similarly, about a fifth of both young women and men say they are actively involved in a group or organization.

POLITICAL VOICE

The list of nine "political voice" activities ranges from consumer activism to contacting an elected official to signing email or written petitions. Virtually no differences separate young women from men in their rates of political voice activism. Among young women and men, the most common political voice activity is participation in consumer boycotts and buycotts. Similar numbers of young women and men say they chosen NOT to buy (that is, boycotted) something in the past 12 months because of conditions under which the product is made or because they dislike the conduct of the company that produces it. The same is true for "buycotting," consumer behavior designed to reward a company for its social or political values through a purchase. Slightly more men (52%) than women (48%) report boycotting and/or buycotting something in the recent past, but the percentage difference is not big enough to warrant a credible claim that consumer behavior is linked to gender among youth. While it is not clear what kind of products and services young women and men are choosing to reward and punish, they are clearly aware of their power as consumers and do take advantage of their perceived influence.

Table 3. Consumer Activism

Percent of those 15–25 who report...	Women	Men
Participating in a consumer boycott	36	40
Participating in a consumer buycott	33	38
Participating in a consumer boycott and/or buycott	48	52

Source: National Citizen Engagement Survey, 2002.

The next most frequent type of political voice activity in which young people, regardless of sex, report that they engage involves signing written and email petitions. A little more than one in ten young women and men say they signed an email petition in the past 12 months, and a fifth of both sexes report signing a written petition. The numbers of both young women and men drop considerably for engagement in the remaining types of political voice activities. Ten percent of both women and men say they contacted or visited a public official in the past 12 months to ask for assistance or to express their opinion. The same percentage of both contacted a newspaper or magazine to register their opinion on an issue. Smaller numbers—still similar across the sexes—reportedly called in to a radio or television talk show to express themselves, protested, or worked as canvassers in the past 12 months.

Table 4. Political Voice

Percent of those 15–25 who report...	Women	Men
Signing a written petition	20	20
Signing an email petition	16	13
Contacting a public official	10	10
Contacting the print media	10	10
Contacting the broadcast media	8	7
Participating in a protest	7	7
Canvassing	2	2

Source: National Citizen Engagement Survey, 2002.

CATEGORIZING YOUTH

Based on these finding, the story that emerges concerning the activism of today's generation of young people does not appear to implicate the role of gender. There is no big "gender gap" in citizen engagement among today's youth. Across most of the options for participation in public life, the sexes are remarkably similar in both what they choose to do and what they tend to avoid (or at least have not yet considered doing). Although there are some interesting differences—such as rates of voluntarism—gender does not appear to be playing any significant role in shaping citizen engagement among youth.

Figure 1. Engagement among Men 15–25 Years Old

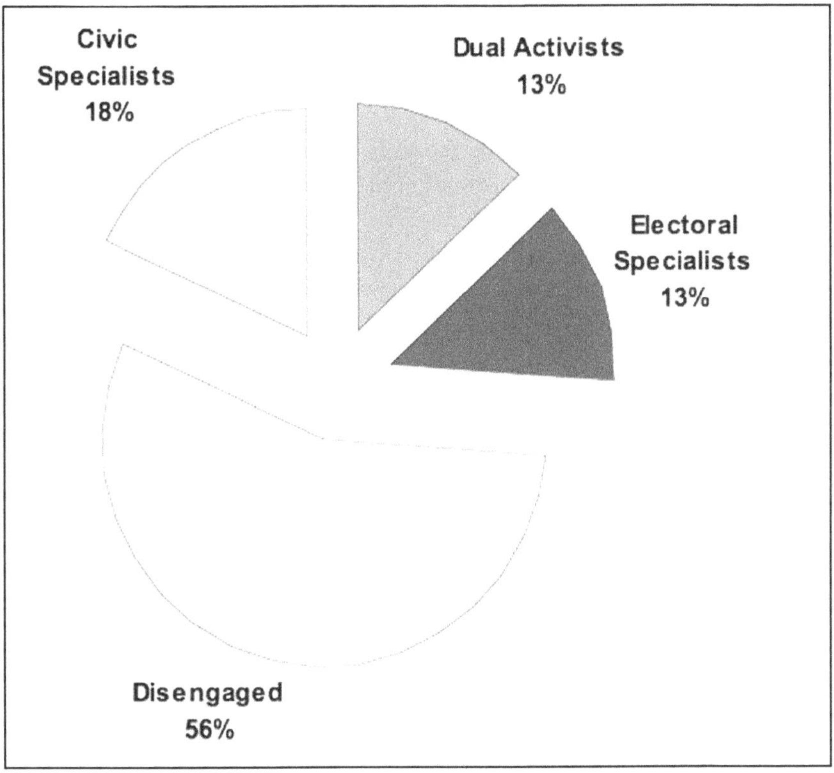

Civic Specialists 18%

Dual Activists 13%

Electoral Specialists 13%

Disengaged 56%

Source: National Civic Engagement Survey, 2002.

A typology of engagement arrived at by Keeter and his colleagues helps to further demonstrate the similarities between young women and men.[12] The typology divides people into four categories—those who engage in mostly civic or electoral behavior (civic or electoral specialists), those who do both (dual activists), and those who are largely disengaged. In order to be classified as a civic specialist, an individual had to engage in two or more civic activities but fewer than two electoral activities. Electoral specialists reported two or more electoral activities but fewer than two civic activities. Dual activists reported two or more civic AND electoral activities. And finally, the disengaged reported fewer than two civic AND electoral activities.

Using these criteria, the vast majority of today's youth are not very engaged. Indeed, more than half of today's youth—regardless of gender—fall among the disengaged. This means that many youth today demonstrate behavior that by most standards falls short of what it takes to be an engaged citizen. Relatively few are specialists in either the civic or electoral worlds. And only about one in ten is among the most engaged, regardless of gender.

THE ROLE OF EDUCATION

Education does little to change the story. The early evidence suggests that education is indeed an important part of getting young people engaged, both psychologically and in public activities. Across all of the core behaviors that make up citizen engagement, college attendance helps to boost the activism of young women and men. Moreover, educated young women and men demonstrate similar levels of involvement in public life.

For example, education's positive influence on electoral engagement can be seen for both sexes, but small gender differences still remain. Twenty-seven percent of young women with a history of college attendance report always voting in local and national elections, compared to just 18 percent of same aged women (i.e., 20–25) who never attended college. Among young men, the percent increases from 19 to 31 once college attendance is accounted for. Attempts to persuade others politically also seems to get a sizable boost through college attendance. About a quarter (26%) of young women with no formal education say they attempt political persuasion compared to over a third (35%) of college educated young women. Among young men the same nine percentage point difference distinguishes the non-college (33%) from college educated (42%).

Table 5. Education and Citizen Engagement

Percent of those 18-25 who report ...	College		Noncollege	
	Women	Men	Women	Men
Persuading other politically	35	42	26	33
Always voting in local and national elections	27	31	18	19
Volunteering for a nonpolitical group	42	33	29	19
Participating in a consumer boycott	45	52	31	33
Signing written petitions	30	32	15	14

Source: National Citizen Engagement Survey, 2002.

Similar patterns are found when considering the role of education in promoting civic engagement. Forty-two percent of young women with a history of college attendance report volunteering for a non-political group in the recent past compared to only 29 percent of their peers who never attended college. And while the benefits of education among young men are apparent as well, it still looks as if gender is important for inspiring this kind of behavior since women volunteers outnumber their male peers regardless of education.

College attendance, not surprisingly, also encourages more frequent expressions of one's political voice. Reports of written petition signing double for both sexes once formal education is accounted for. And taking part in consumer boycotts increases too, although young women appear to fall slightly behind their male peers once they move into college. For other political voice activities, the pattern remains the same. Education gives a sizable boost to the activism of both men and women, but few gender differences are apparent regardless of college attendance.

In short, regardless of whether the focus is on the amount or content of citizen engagement among youth, the evidence points to the insignificant role gender seems to be playing. Depending on how one interprets the level of activism among today's youth, young women are doing either just as well or just as poorly as young men.[13] But, at the same time, gender's importance cannot be so easily dismissed. There are meaningful and important differences across key behaviors that distinguish young women from men. In some cases, young women are doing more, but for other behaviors, young women are coming up alarmingly short.

IMPORTANT DIFFERENCES: THE GOOD AND THE BAD

Voluntarism

Looking at volunteer activities, an almost ten percentage point difference separates young women from men. Forty-five percent of young women, compared to 36 percent of young men, say they volunteered at least once in the past 12 months for a non-political group.

To some extent, the explanation is clear. The Council for Excellence in Government recently conducted a survey of youth which included a question about what kinds of things citizens should do to stay engaged in politics and their communities. Although both young men and women deem volunteering more important than political involvement, young women are more firmly committed to donating time to help others. Almost two-thirds (62%) of women believe volunteering is the most important thing for citizens to do, compared with slightly fewer young men (55%).

Table 6. Correlations between Volunteering for a Non-Political Organization and ...

	Women	Men
...Electoral engagement	.29	.19
...Civic engagement	.39	.40
...Political voice engagement	.24	.20

Source: National Citizen Engagement Survey, 2002.

Additionally, some evidence suggests that female volunteers are more engaged in activities that are expressly political. For both women and men, volunteering is significantly correlated with all types of engagement. But when it comes to the relationship between volunteering and electoral engagement, the coefficient is notably stronger among young women than it is among men.[14] The data suggest that young female volunteers are more apt than male volunteers to be engaged in a variety of activities designed to influence the political process.

To some extent, it appears that volunteering among young women is more consequential for engagement—and in particular electoral engagement— than it is for young men. Could it be that young women who volunteer are more likely to see the connection between the problem their work addresses and the role that government should also be playing? If so, it would make sense to find a stronger connection between electoral engagement and volunteering among young women. In short, volunteering may be politicizing young women which, in turn, encourages them to get involved in influencing the political process.

Unfortunately, however, there do not appear to be any significant gender differences in the motivations young people give for volunteering. The NCES asked those who volunteered if they were doing so to address a social or political problem, to help other people, or for some other reason. As it turns out, the vast majority of young female and male volunteers said they were motivated by things other than helping to solve a social or political problem (91 and 88 percent, respectively). Thus, the data do not support claims about the greater tendency of young women to link their volunteer efforts with political problems.

Cognitive Engagement

Another area where gender differences are significant is political attentiveness. But in this case, unlike voluntarism, young women are coming up short in comparison to young men. The NCES found that a quarter of all 15–25 year-olds (25%) report regular attentiveness to politics and public affairs. However, a seven percentage point difference distinguishes young women from young men in this important precursor to engagement (21 versus 28 percent, respectively). Expanding the definition of attentiveness does little to change the story. Young women are consistently, and at times significantly, less tuned in than their male peers. For example, four in ten young men report regularly reading the newspaper, compared with a third of young women (34%). A similar percentage point difference separates the sexes when it comes to watching the nightly news on television on a regular basis (49% for men versus 42% for women).[15]

Thus, across a variety of behaviors, both sexes display more inattentiveness than attentiveness. However, young women are the least engaged. Going a step further, it is no surprise that women outnumber men among those who are completely inattentive, at least as measured by a variety of relevant behaviors—following politics and government most of the time, engaging in frequent discussions about politics and public affairs with family and friends, and regularly reading the newspaper or watching the nightly news on television. More than a third of all women between the ages of 15 and 25 (35%) qualify as cognitively disengaged, compared with only a quarter of all young men (25%).[16]

Figure 2. Political Knowledge

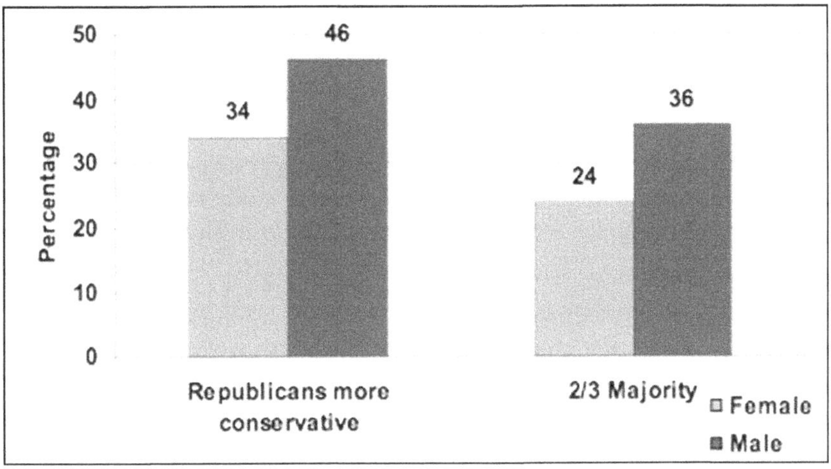

Source: National Citizen Engagement Survey, 2002.

Given the gendered trend in inattentiveness, it is no surprise that young women also know less about politics, government, and the political process. Across a variety of surveys that include questions designed to gauge a respondent's political knowledge, young women consistently turn up among the least knowledgeable. For example, almost half of all young men (46%) know that Republicans are the more conservative party at the national level compared to barely a third of young women (34%). Similarly, 36 percent of young men know it takes a two-thirds majority in Congress to override a presidential veto compared to just 24 percent of young women. The trend continues even across questions that are about politics closer to home. A recent survey by the National Council of State Legislatures (NCSL) found that significantly more young men can correctly name the governor's party affiliation in their own states than can young women (54 versus 43 percent). And an 11 percentage point difference separates the sexes in knowing which party has a majority in the lower house of the respondent's state legislature (28 versus 17 percent).[17]

ATTITUDES, BELIEFS, AND RESPONSIBILITIES

Are young women more apt to endorse active definitions of citizenship? How does gender relate to views of the political process and the workings of government? In short, do young women distinguish themselves in their psychological orientation to politics, or are we looking in vain for a gendered story in much the same way that sex appears to have little to do with engagement among youth? The answer, it seems, is largely an echo of what was found when the focus was on behavior.

Cynicism toward government is the norm, and a great many of today's youth are distrustful of the power and influence of our institutions and leaders. The NCES found that about half of both young women and men believe that the political system works to give special favors to some at the expense of others (56 versus 52 percent, respectively) and that politics is a way for the powerful to keep power to themselves (48 versus 53 percent, respectively).

Yet, at the same time, young people—regardless of gender—also demonstrate attitudes that suggest they are not entirely comfortable with writing government off. Slightly more young women than men believe that government regulation of business is necessary to protect the public interest (68 versus 61 percent, respectively). And similar numbers believe that government often does a better job than people give it credit for (68% women; 62 % men).

However, whereas gender does not seem to make a difference in what young people think about the workings and responsibilities of government, there does appear to be a slight trend among young women to believe that more rather than less is required of good citizens. For example, significantly more young women believe that it is their responsibility, rather than their choice, to get involved to make things better for society. In fact, it is only among young women that a majority sees engagement as a responsibility of citizenship (51 versus 43 percent, respectively). When it comes to believing that individuals, as opposed to government and others, are responsible for making things better in society, young women have a slight edge over young men (51 versus 42 percent, respectively).[18]

Figure 3. Views of Personal Responsibility

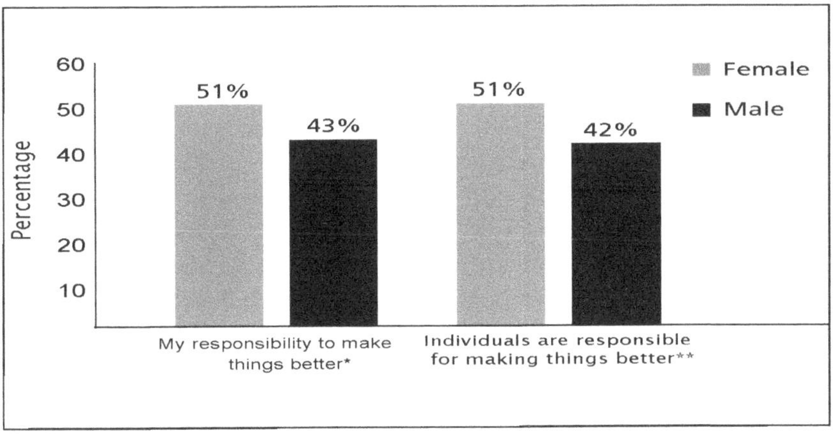

*Source: National Citizen Engagement Survey, 2002.
**Source: National Council for State Legislatures Survey, 2004.

REASONS FOR NOT VOTING

Why don't young people vote? Or, more specifically, why aren't more young women turning out to vote on election day? Are their reasons for remaining on the sidelines similar to those of young men? Or do young women have a difference of opinion with their male counterparts when it comes to their political abstinence? The data allows us to examine a few reasons often cited for non-voting among youth with a specific eye toward the role of gender.

First, mobilization has proven time and again to be instrumental in motivating voters. Simply put, those asked personally by someone to cast a vote on election day are more likely to do so than those left off the invitation list. Parties and candidates are prone to ignoring young voters and their interests. As a result, young people fail to turn out on par with older adults, in part because they are simply not asked to participate. Election year 2004 offered a hint of what can happen when young women do receive explicit invitations to get involved; while just over a third of young men aged 18-24 reportedly cast a vote in the presidential election (37%), close to a majority of young women turned out (46%).

Still, young people—regardless of gender—are less likely than older voters to have received a personal invitation to work for or contribute money to a candidate, political party, or any other organization that supports candidates in the recent past. Only about one in ten 15 to 25 year-olds report being invited compared with about a third of all those 26 and older (30%). Moreover, no gender differences materialize when considering the potential payoff that parties and candidates get by mobilizing youth. Among those 30 and younger, women are not significantly more likely to have followed through with making a campaign contribution if asked than are men.[19]

Another explanation for youth's inconsistent voting record concerns their dislike for politics and the political process. Having grown up in an age of media cynicism toward politics, young people may have decided that they would rather not involve themselves in such a distasteful process. Sentiments like these motivate young men to stay away from politics more than young women. The NCSL survey found that among eligible non-voters 18 and older, young women are more likely to give reasons for their non-voting that have nothing to do with their feelings toward politics. Rather, they give reasons that have to do with a lack of interest, feeling uninformed, and not having enough time or feeling inconvenienced. Young men, however, give slightly different reasons. Most notably, a top explanation for young men was dislike for politics and government. Whereas 35 percent of young men who do not vote said they either dislike politics and government or they simply "don't do" politics, only 16 percent of young women said the same thing.

Table 7. Top Three Reasons for Non-Voting Among Young People 18 Years of Age and Older

Women	Men
...I'm not interested in politics	...I'm not interested in politics
...I'm not informed enough to make a decision	...I dislike politics and government/I don't do politics
...I don't have time/I'm often away/It's inconvenient	...It's hard to get reliable info about the candidates

Source: National Council for State Legislatures Survey, 2003.

Taken as a whole, it is hard to argue for the importance of gender in keeping young women away from the polls. Although young female nonvoters are not as likely to be consciously rejecting politics, their lack of interest matches that of their male peers. Moreover, gender does not appear to be central in explaining which youth are invited to participate. While gender appears to be occasionally notable in a few behaviors and attitudes, there is not an abundance of evidence to suggest that today's generation of young women are very distinct from young men with regard to behaviors and beliefs consistent with active participation in public life.

DIFFERENT PATHWAYS?

In addition to being rich with behavioral questions, the NCES includes questions that measure potentially important characteristics and precursors to engagement. These range from things having to do with religion, the extent of social networks, attitudes toward citizen responsibilities, and many other useful questions. Using a technique known as ordinary least squares regression to account for a variety of influences simultaneously, it's possible to see whether young women are motivated by the same or different things than young men.

[...] When it comes to understanding what motivates youth to become involved in public life, young women are influenced to a greater degree by socializing experiences at home.[20] Among all of the precursors that demonstrate a significant relationship to a summary index of participation (i.e., electoral, civic and political voice activities), the sexes differ in the importance derived from things such as maternal education, having family political discussions, and growing up with a parent or guardian who volunteered. Young women get a boost from exposure to these kinds of experiences whereas young men appear to benefit from other experiences.

Table 8. Motivators to Citizen Engagement

Women		Men	
Cognitive engagement	2.29*	Television avoidance	2.92*
Mobilization	1.64*	Cognitive engagement	2.34*
Age	1.55	Social network	1.78*
Television avoidance	1.51	Mobilization	1.60*
Mother's education	1.06*	Religious attendance	1.50*
Internet use	.92*	Age	1.25
Social network	.92	Individual efficacy	.96*
Parent/guardian volunteer	.90*	Internet use	.84*
Discuss politics while growing up	.86*	Political knowledge	.74
Citizen duty	.85*	Discuss politics while growing up	.68
Religious attendance	.79*	Strength of partisanship	.64
Individual efficacy	.78*	Citizen duty	.55
Political knowledge	.38	Mother's education	.53
Length of residence	.29	Generational identity	.42
Generational identity	.24	Parent/guardian volunteer	.33
White	.01	White	.25
Strength of partisanship	.00	Interpersonal trust	.09
Family income	-.04	Family income	.04
Role of government	-.14	Length of residence	-.19
View of politics	-.22	Role of government	-.34
Interpersonal trust	-.41	Education	-.39
Education	-1.33*	View of politics	-.45*
Adjusted R Square	.34	Adjusted R Square	.37

* Significant at .05 level.

Note: OLS unstandardized coefficients; all variables are coded on a one-point range.

Source: National Citizen Engagement Survey, 2002.

Other differences in precursors across the sexes include strong endorsement of civic norms, views of politics, television avoidance, and education. As was found earlier, young women are more likely to believe in the importance of individual efforts to improve society. These attitudinal differences are apparent here as well, since young women are more motivated by civic norms than young men. However, when it comes to attitudes toward politics and the political system, young men who are critical are more apt to be engaged, whereas the same cannot be said for young women. What a young woman thinks about politics does not affect her activism in public life. Education, however, does. Unlike what was found previously when education seemed to promote electoral activism among young women in a simple bivariate relationship, controlling for the effects of other precursors in a model that accounts for citizen engagement writ large changes the story a bit. It appears that better educated young women participate slightly less than young women with fewer years of education behind them. Finally, fewer hours spent watching TV works to spur more involvement among young men, but television use is not a significant factor in young women's activism.

Attentiveness helps to spur participation for both sexes, which makes the previously discussed gender gap in this area of more concern. If young women continue to come up short on measures of cognitive engagement, fewer young women will benefit from this important precursor. Religious attendance, being asked to participate, believing in the usefulness of individual action for improving things in society, and Internet use are also factors that help to encourage more participation among both sexes.

In short, the most significant story to come from this analysis is the importance of early socializing experiences for young women. More family political discussions and parental modeling of good behavior appears to go a long way toward inspiring young women to be active and engaged citizens. While today's young men and women are motivated by many of the same precursors to engagement, it is equally important to recognize where young women differ and note the ways in which their activism can be encouraged. Young men can get a sizable boost simply by turning off the television. For young women, however, having good role models proves key to encouraging more citizen engagement.

CONCLUSION

Taking a close look at gender and citizen engagement among youth has yielded insights both encouraging and discouraging for young women's involvement in public life. On the one hand, young women do not enter adulthood with tendencies that make them any less likely to be engaged citizens than young men. Sameness, rather than difference, is what distinguishes gender's importance for understanding young people's involvement in public life. On the other hand, young women are distinguishing themselves from young men on some key precursors to engagement, particularly attentiveness and knowledge. The fact that young women come up short in this area is not inconsistent with what has been found among older women.[21] At least for now, society is poised to witness another generation of young women entering adulthood with norms of attentiveness that put them behind men. The trend can certainly be reversed, but it requires changes in the socialization of women that goes beyond the influence of formal education.

For its part, the Center for American Women and Politics is seeking to alter the equation with its NEW Leadership™ programs, which teach college and university students about women's political participation and encourage them to get involved. With more than a dozen NEW Leadership™ summer institutes already in place or in the planning stages at institutions around the country, CAWP aims to increase young women's attentiveness to politics and to show them how they can be more powerful forces for community change by linking their interest in volunteering to political action.

ENDNOTES

1. For a more thorough analysis of citizen engagement among all age groups, see Scott Keeter, Cliff Zukin, Molly Andolina, and Krista Jenkins, "The Civic and Political Health of the Nation: A Generational Portrait." Available online at www.civicyouth.org.

2. The Center for Research on Civic Learning and Engagement (CIRCLE) represents the best source for information on youth, citizenship, and politics. Its collection of reports and fact sheets is available online at www.civicyouth.org.

3. M. Kent Jennings and Richard G. Niemi, *The Political Character of Adolescence: The Influence of Families and Schools* (Princeton: Princeton University Press, 1974); M. Kent Jennings and Richard G. Niemi, *Generations and Politics: A Panel Study of Young Adults and Their Parents* (Princeton: Princeton University Press, 1981); Roberta Sigel and Marilyn Hoskin, *The Political Involvement of Adolescents* (New Brunswick, NJ: Rutgers University Press, 1981); Roberta Sigel and John Reynolds, "Generational Differences and the Women's Movement," *Political Science Quarterly* 94 (1979–80): 635–648.

4. Roberta Sigel, ed., *Political Learning in Adulthood: A Sourcebook of Theory and Research* (Chicago: University of Chicago Press, 1989).

5. The National Civic Engagement Survey (NCES) is a nationally representative telephone survey of respondents aged 15 and older (N=3246). The survey, conducted in the spring of 2002, contains oversamples of the two youngest age cohorts, DotNets (aged 15 to 25) and Generation Xers (aged 26 to 37) (N=1001 and 1000, respectively). The NCES measures a wide array of behaviors ranging from traditional acts of participation (i.e., voting) to new activities (i.e., consumer activism), as well as attitudes toward politics, government, the responsibilities of citizenship, and a variety of other relevant subjects.

6. Sidney Verba and Norman H. Nie, *Participation in America: Political Democracy and Social Equality* (New York: Harper and Row, 1972); Raymond Wolfinger and Steven J. Rosenstone, *Who Votes* (New Haven: Yale University Press, 1980); Sidney Verba, Kay Lehman Schlozman, and Henry Brady, *Voice and Equality: Civic Voluntarism in American Society* (Cambridge: Harvard University Press, 1995); Norman Nie, Jane Junn, and Kenneth Stehlik-Barry, *Education and Democratic Citizenship in America* (Chicago: University of Chicago Press, 1996).

7. "Black Men Falling Behind," USA *Today*, February, 2005.

8. Marshall Poe, "The Other Gender Gap," *The Atlantic Monthly* 2004, 293(1).

9. Keeter, Zukin, Andolina, and Jenkins, "The Civic and Political Health."

10. However, while gender is seemingly unimportant in inspiring more regular voting, it appears that when it comes to turnout in specific presidential elections, young women are slightly more likely to report voting than young men. A recent report by the Center for Information and Research on Civic Learning and Engagement found that the downward trend in voting among youth is more pronounced among 18–24 year old men compared to women. For example, in 1996, 42 percent of young women reported voting compared to 37 percent of young men. While the percentage difference shrunk a bit in 2000, there still remained a statistically significant three percentage point disparity between 18–24 year old female and male voters (43 and 40 percent, respectively). Analyses of 2004 exit poll data suggest the disparity among young men and women widened in this past election. While barely a third of young men aged 18–24 reportedly cast a vote in the presidential election (37%), close to a majority of young women turned out for the historic election (46%).

11. Gender differences in voluntarism do not appear to be a new phenomenon. Every year UCLA's Higher Education Research Institute (HERI) surveys college freshmen about a variety of topics related to their interests and activities including whether they performed volunteer work in the past year. Since 1984—the first year students were queried about this activity—young men have lagged behind young women an average of four percentage points in their reported voluntarism (78 for female freshmen versus 74 percent for male freshmen). Thus, it looks as if today's generation of young adults are continuing the gendered trend of women volunteering more. It is important to note that the gender gap in non-political volunteering all but disappears once regularity of volunteering is accounted for. That is, among young women who say they regularly volunteer for a non-political group, the percentage drops to 24. A similar percentage of young men (21%) tell interviewers that their volunteering happens on a regular basis also. It is hard to tell why gender differences disappear once regularity is accounted for. It could be that young women are simply more engaged in sporadic instances of volunteering than are young men, but also consistently volunteer about on par with their male peers. Unfortunately, data are not available to examine the reasons behind these gender disparities in voluntarism.

12. Keeter, Zukin, Andolina, and Jenkins, "The Civic and Political Health."

13. Another way of assessing gender's importance for citizen engagement among youth is to consider a variety of relevant precursors—including gender—simultaneously in a model that helps to explain participation. Four separate ordinary least square regression analyses were conducted, one for each type of citizen engagement and another that used a summary index of participation comprised of all of the 19 core indicators of behavior that were included on the National Citizen Engagement Survey. Each analysis demonstrated the insignificance of gender in helping to explain who participates and who does not.

14. Volunteering for a non-political organization has been removed from the combined index of citizen engagement and civic engagement.

15. Regularity of news consumption through reading a newspaper or watching the nightly news on TV is defined as using that source at least four days per week.

16. It is also important to note that the gender gap among youth in attentiveness does not appear to be a new phenomenon. While the question is not exactly akin to those that ask about behaviors, the Higher Education Research Institute's annual survey of college freshmen has consistently found young men to be more likely to believe that keeping up to date with political affairs is "very important." While the difference has waxed and waned over the years, female undergraduates generally express less interest in keeping up to date with political affairs.

17. Unfortunately the tendency of young women to be less attentive and informed about politics and government persists even during the college years. Young women—regardless of exposure to formal education—are significantly less likely than young men to say they follow politics and government regularly. About a ten percentage point difference separates the sexes among the college and non-college educated on a basic cognitive engagement question. Not surprisingly, political knowledge mirrors these findings as well. Young women, regardless of education, are less likely to answer correctly a variety of questions that assess political knowledge.

18. While the gender differences in this area are important to note, one should not overlook the rather bleak state of youth attitudes toward their understanding of citizen responsibilities. Indeed, the NCES found that clear majorities of both sexes believe that "simply being a good person is enough to make someone a good citizen" (59% women; 57% men) as opposed to "being a good citizen means having some special obligations" (38% women; 39% men).

19. Unfortunately data are not available that would allow us to tell if young women are more likely to work for party or candidate if asked.

20. Numbers marked with an asterisk indicate precursors that have a statistically significant influence on participation. The bigger the number, the greater the influence.

21. Michael X Delli Carpini and Scott Keeter, *What Americans Know About Politics and Why It Matters* (New Haven: Yale University Press, 1996).

*Krista Jenkins is an associate professor of political science at Fairleigh Dickinson University.

Jenkins, Krista. "Gender and Civic Engagement: Secondary Analysis of Survey Data." CIRCLE Working Paper 41, June 2005.

Reprinted by permission of the Center for Information & Research on Civic Learning & Engagement (CIRCLE), Tufts University.

DISCUSSION QUESTIONS

1. In which ways are young men and women distinctive in their participation patterns? What are the implications of these differences?

2. Should democracy's goal be to provide equal opportunities for participation by men and by women, and other minority groups, or should the goal be to ensure that they participate equally?

3. Many European political parties have a quota requiring a certain percentage of women candidates. Should that be required for American political parties? Is that constitutional?

Part 5:
Reforms to Increase Youth Activism

What is to be done? We generally believe that active participation in politics will strengthen the democratic process, and the changing situation of young people will require new approaches to maximize their participation in politics. The essays in this section discuss various alternatives for increasing citizen participation, especially for younger citizens. "Building a Better Citizen," by David Villano, summarizes the worries about declining participation in America and then discusses how municipal governments are taking steps to reengage their citizens. Other reforms can engage citizens in deliberations over government policy. Villano emphasizes the need for government to take positive steps in responding to participation trends. Peter Levine's "Civic Learning in School" turns to the ways that schools can be a breeding ground for good citizenship, but only if they value meaningful participation and provide an appropriate environment. He offers a range of reforms that schools, parents, and students can use to democratize education. Finally, in an excerpt from "Youth Civic Engagement in Canada: Implications for Public Policy," Dietlind Stolle and Cesi Cruz discuss how other nations are creating best practices to respond to the changing orientations of their citizens and to develop a more participatory public. Democratic participation can be increased and enriched, but it requires an active effort by families, schools, communities, the workplace, and government to expand the skills and norms of a participatory citizenry.

Building a Better Citizen

by David Villano*

In the late 1980s, Hampton, Virginia, faced the challenges of many blue-collar cities along its stretch of the southern Chesapeake: rising unemployment, a stagnant economy and the flight of young families to seek better jobs and fuller lives elsewhere. City leaders gambled on a novel response. They would target young people, hoping to cultivate a generation of citizens committed to Hampton's long-term vitality. In 1990, the city launched Hampton Youth Civic Engagement, a program to instill community pride and leadership skills in young people and engage them in governance.[1] The program was systematic, first fostering civic awareness through local service projects, then building collaboration and leadership skills through involvement with city boards and commissions on issues of increasing complexity. Young people contributed ideas—on better policing, school reform, job training—and helped with policy implementation.

Nearly two decades later, the program is still in operation and recognized as a national model for fostering civic engagement. A study of Hampton's college-age residents has found they outperform peer groups in three key measures of citizenship: the ability to engage in civic discourse, passion for their community and leadership skills. Fewer families are fleeing the city, crime is down and Hampton's voting rate is about 20 percent higher than similar communities. In 2005, the city received the Harvard Kennedy School of Government's annual Innovations in American Government Award. In 2007, *Money* magazine rated the city as one of the "Best Places to Live" in the U.S.

"What Hampton shows us is that local government can prepare its leaders of tomorrow, but it also shows that government can engage people, of all ages and backgrounds, to bring real value—things of substance—to the community today," says Carmen Sirianni, a professor of sociology and public policy at Brandeis University, whose new book, *Investing in Democracy: Engaging Citizens in Collaborative Governance*, provides an in-depth case study of the Hampton program.[2] "Enlightened leaders recognize that public issues are getting more complex. Civic engagement today is far more complicated than just showing up at a city council meeting and raising your hand."

To be sure, Hampton's experiment in civic engineering is rarely repeated. Even rarer is the source of the inspiration—elected officials, who often view public participation in decision-making as anathema. But a growing body of evidence and the culture shift accompanying the election of President Obama are prompting policymakers at all levels of government to consider programs and policies that strengthen the skills and character traits that promote good citizenship: pride in community, trust in individuals and institutions, the ability to work in groups, membership in service organizations, and even social interaction among neighbors. Political scientists and others who study the democratic process are finding that those skills and traits often correlate with the positive policy outcomes public officials routinely hope to foster, including lower crime rates, higher academic achievement, the creation of jobs and improved health care delivery. In essence, some experts are arguing that good citizenship should not simply be a means to an end; it should, by itself, be a policy objective. "Why not?" Sirianni asks. "Government invests in a lot of things. Why not civic engagement?"

In 2000, Harvard political scientist Robert Putnam rode the talk show circuit plugging his best-seller, *Bowling Alone: The Collapse and Revival of American Community*, a data-driven analysis of civic interaction in the U.S. over the past half-century or so.[3] Putnam coined the term "social capital" to describe the intangible, value-laden benefits of a strong network of community relationships. In short, he argued, things like trust and cooperation—the building blocks of democratic governance—are products of positive, sustained social interaction. "Bowling alone" was the metaphor for Americans' growing isolation.

Putnam's research revealed that communities where social capital is high are more likely to experience lower school dropout rates, less crime, fewer hospitalizations and higher rates of economic growth, among myriad indicators of personal and societal well-being that are positively correlated with strong community relationships. His 2003 follow-up book, *Better Together: Restoring the American Community* (co-authored with philanthropy expert Lewis M. Feldstein) grew from a series of round-table meetings—The Saguaro Seminar at Harvard's Kennedy School—where academics, industry officials and political leaders discussed strategies to replenish America's dwindling stock of social capital.[4]

Among the seminar's early participants was Barack Obama, then an Illinois state senator.

While some researchers say Putnam overlooked the impact of online relationships and other emerging forms of community interaction, his basic thesis has held up to scrutiny. One study found that rates of heart disease decline when neighborhood bonds are strong, even when factoring out material wealth and other socioeconomic variables; another showed that social connectedness is a stronger predictor of perceived quality of life than income or educational level. A wide-ranging Knight Foundation study released last fall found a strong correlation between levels of civic engagement and cities' rates of economic growth.[5] And a number of studies have shown that public corruption declines as social capital goes up, prompting The World Bank to encourage civic engagement as a business development strategy.

"Good citizenship makes a big difference. That we know," says Peter Levine, director of The Center for Information & Research on Civic Learning and Engagement at Tufts University's Jonathan M. Tisch College of Citizenship and Public Service. "Government functions better; public health outcomes are better; higher civic engagement among teens correlates with greater academic achievement."

Yet, as Putnam has noted, indicators of citizenship in America continue a long and, in some cases, precipitous decline, leading Levine and others to question why government officials aren't more receptive to programs that invigorate their citizenry. Over the past 50 years or so, studies show, Americans have become less knowledgeable of local and national affairs, less likely to engage in public discourse, less willing to join a group or civic organization, less likely to interact with neighbors and more likely to perceive fellow citizens as dishonest and immoral. Three years ago, the National Conference on Citizenship (NCoC), a congressionally chartered nonprofit advocacy group that measures, tracks and promotes civic participation in the U.S., produced its first national Civic Health Index, a comprehensive assessment of civic well-being compiled from 40 indicators such as voting rates, frequency of public meeting attendance and confidence in government.[6]

Despite recent gains in some categories, like volunteering and political expression, the overall trend line over 30 years shows a steady decline.

Most troubling, NCoC executive director David Smith notes, is an ongoing erosion of what he believes to be the most fundamental indicators of good citizenship: trust in neighbors and institutions and connectedness to community and religious organizations. Trust and connectedness is lowest among the so-called Millennial group—14-to-29-year-olds. "To me this is one big red flag," Smith says. "The very foundations of our democracy are threatened if our youngest citizens do not maintain the fabric that has connected us the past 200 years."

Smith and others in the field attribute declining trust levels and other civic health indicators to a host of U.S. labor and lifestyle changes over the past half-century, including the rise of women in the work force, the explosion of television viewership and Internet use, and the isolating nature of suburbia. In short, they say, there is less of the face-to-face interaction that builds interdependence and encourages collective problem-solving within society.

Putnam's research also suggests, controversially, that rising rates of neighborhood diversity may exacerbate the trend. His latest study, based on interviews of nearly 30,000 people across the country, shows that as diversity within a community goes up, virtually every measure of civic health goes down: Fewer people vote and volunteer, they give less to charity, and they are less inclined to work on community projects. In the most diverse communities, trust among neighbors is about half the level of the most homogenous settings.

Tufts' Levine says government also bears blame for the erosion of our civic fabric by responding with increasing suspicion to citizen initiatives. Levine laments the dwindling number of civic associations and citizen boards on which people could develop the habits of collective engagement necessary for a strong democracy. In one striking example, the raw number of school board seats across the country (not per capita) has declined 80 percent since 1930. Levine faults government, at all levels, for a "strong technocratic urge" that discourages citizen engagement.

"The attitude from government is that 'we're experts so we know best,'" Levine says. "Citizen participation can be quite costly and cumbersome. But we're seeing that it can be even more costly when people feel they are not part of the process."

Brandeis' Sirianni, who studies civic engagement programs in cities around the U.S., says research is beginning to support that argument. "Neighborhood empowerment, citizen involvement—in the long run this saves money by providing better policy outcomes," he says.

For their part, Americans seem ready to re-engage, but they also, somewhat paradoxically, expect government to pave the way. The National Conference on Citizenship's 2008 Civic Health Survey found that Americans overwhelmingly support laws and policies to improve citizenship. Among the initiatives researchers tested for public support: civics education in schools, service learning and tuition-for-service programs, and town hall-style gatherings to deliberate on issues of local or national importance. In other words, Americans need cajoling. Last year, for example, 67 percent of survey respondents said volunteering was personally important to them, but only 27 percent actually do volunteer.

Smith says Americans want improved citizenship like they want improved gas mileage—through government mandates and incentives: "People say they'll gladly buy cars that get 40 miles to a gallon, but only when the government tells them they have to."

A few U.S. cities are crafting programs that provide just those kinds of mandates and incentives. Some, like San Francisco's Youth Commission, focus on connecting young people to their communities and government.[7] Others, like the 10-year-old Boston Indicators Project, are more comprehensive, fostering discussion of critical issues and tracking progress on shared goals.[8] And last fall, the Minneapolis City Council created the Neighborhood and Community Engagement Commission, a mechanism to stimulate interaction between the government and citizens.[9]

The most widely cited example of a municipal government overtly fostering better citizenship may be Seattle – another recipient of Harvard's Innovations in American Government Award—where semi-autonomous neighborhood councils can enact policy and allocate public money. Begun more than 20 years ago in response to citizen concerns over crime, drugs and growth management, the program was designed to provide residents a greater say in the allocation of tax dollars.

Since then, residents have leveraged city matching funds with their own resources and labor to create more than 3,000 community projects, including new playgrounds and art installations. An unintended consequence of the neighborhood councils seems to be an informed, engaged public that routinely scores higher on measures of civic health than is the case in comparable cities. "We've been able to build a much stronger sense of community here," says Jim Diers, author of *Neighbor Power: Building Community the Seattle Way* and founding director of the city's Department of Neighborhoods. "And in the process, our attitude toward city hall has changed, our sense of government has changed. It's not just something that spends our tax dollars; it's something that's an extension of who we are as citizens."

Such cases of systemic overhaul are rare and certainly not the only approach to invigorating citizens. Diers, who now teaches community organizing and community-driven development at the University of Washington, says government can take plenty of less-comprehensive steps that influence the key civic health indicators.

A starting point, Diers says, is for public officials to acknowledge that civic health matters and can be influenced by government policy. Diers advises public officials who want to improve citizen participation to keep it simple in the beginning, monitoring concrete activities like voting rates, meeting attendance and participation on boards and committees. Measurements of social capital and civic health reflect broader accumulations of data and are more difficult to interpret. "Conversation is a first step but sometimes a difficult one to reach," Diers says. "In Seattle, civic well-being is a priority because we've all been talking about it for a long time."

To take the conversation up a level, some experts recommend a little-used measurement tool called a "social capital impact assessment" that gauges the effects of public policy initiatives on civic life. In one instance, a group of small towns in southern New Hampshire requested such an assessment before backing a widening project of I-93. The assessment asked how neighbors would be disconnected, if church and meeting attendance would decline and whether trust would be reduced as a result of the highway project. Satisfied with the results of the assessment, local officials signed off on the widening, which is now under way, but secured state funding for a five-year state program to help the affected towns address the challenges of disruption and dislocation, and to prepare for an influx of new residents once the widening is complete.

Government can also influence civic health indicators by attending to scale. Research shows that smaller is generally better as it relates to physical and social environments. Tufts' Levine says studies show that academic achievement is inversely proportionate to school size—at least, to a point. Although some researchers are unconvinced, the argument, he says, is simple: In smaller settings, children are more likely to participate in clubs, sports and other extracurricular activities that constitute the training ground for adult civic engagement. Scale also affects trust, meeting attendance and feelings of community connectedness, Levine says, explaining why civic health tends to be higher in small towns or in larger cities—such as Seattle and Minneapolis—where neighborhood-level governance is in place.

Although the overall Civic Health Index has shown a steady decline in recent decades, two closely watched indicators used in that index—voting and volunteerism, especially among younger age groups—are up. Smith attributes this to post-9/11 programs and policies that mandate community service within many schools, and to unprecedented voter-registration and get-out-the-vote drives, especially aimed at young people and minorities. Even the parents of children who participated in the Topeka, Kan.-based Kids Voting program were 10 percent more likely to vote than parents of non-participants.

But voting and volunteerism are the low-hanging fruit of citizenship. More vital, Smith and other researchers say, is a mindset of concern, a sense of pride and responsibility toward one's community that is less easily engineered and measured than a trip to the voting booth. Archon Fung, the Ford Foundation Professor of Democracy and Citizenship at Harvard's Kennedy School, says the keys to fostering a citizen mindset are genuine opportunities to participate in policymaking. In previous generations, he argues, those opportunities were found in neighborhood associations, churches, civic clubs and other membership organizations. Today, he says, government is centralized. Elected and appointed leaders focus inward, diminishing the relevance of membership associations and reducing opportunities for citizen partnerships.

Like a growing number of experts in government process, Fung is an advocate of "deliberative democracy," a hybrid of direct and representative democracy in which citizens gather to establish public policy. Unlike the traditional town-meeting style of governance (often associated with New England) in which all residents are invited to debate and vote on taxes, the budget and other issues, the deliberative democracy model relies on participant assemblies, often randomly selected, which advise public officials rather than set binding policy.

During his 2008 presidential campaign, John Edwards popularized the general notion with his "Citizen Congress" proposal to regularly convene 1 million Americans in national deliberations on critical policy issues as complex and diverse as foreign relations, taxes, job creation and campaign-finance reform. The challenges of facilitating such deliberative processes are daunting, but Fung believes the very complexity of our policy issues may provide the incentive for government officials to experiment. "Let's focus on the most intractable problems—where things are broken, and we seem to make little or no progress in fixing them, like health care," Fung argues. "When nothing else seems to work, politicians might give (deliberative democracy) a try."

A few years back, British Columbia randomly selected 160 voters for a citizens' assembly that convened to recommend changes to the provincial electoral system. The recommendations were then put to voters in a binding referendum, essentially bypassing elected officials.

Similarly, a year ago, as Pennsylvania legislators considered a bill to ban same-sex marriage, Carnegie Mellon University's Southwestern Pennsylvania Program for Deliberative Democracy assembled a randomly selected group of 400 voters from around the state to research and discuss the issue.[10] At the end of the daylong event, facilitators released a "deliberative poll" showing that 70 percent of state voters support the recognition of same-sex unions. Lawmakers rejected the same-sex marriage ban.

Fung believes such communal exercises not only produce sound policy but also reignite the citizen impulse to remain informed, concerned, engaged and trusting— the social-capital measures most in decline. In many European countries, Fung adds, governments routinely target citizen engagement and other indicators of citizenship as policy objectives. Government rarely does so here, in spite of—or perhaps due to—a belief that the gold standard of democracy is practiced in America.

Fung blames "an indifference born of complacency and self satisfaction" for the reluctance of politicians and public officials to push policies that promote civic engagement. Like automakers chasing innovations or technology companies with a constant eye on the horizon, he says, government process must evolve to reflect changing conditions—or risk losing the support of its customers.

Last May, President Obama signed a directive that was little noticed outside the beltway but applauded by those who study social capital and citizenship. With his signature, the White House Office of Public Liaison—historically, a kind of gatekeeper for interest groups seeking access to the Oval Office—became the White House Office of Public Engagement.[11] "This office will seek to engage as many Americans as possible in the difficult work of changing this country through meetings and conversations with groups and individuals held in Washington and across the country," Obama said in a video announcement. The directive coincided with the release of his transition team's *Citizen's Briefing Book*—a collection of the best ideas and proposals submitted by ordinary Americans for addressing the nation's challenges.

It was not Obama's first step to re-energize citizens. In April, he signed the $6 billion Edward M. Kennedy Serve America Act, greatly expanding AmeriCorps and other volunteer service programs.

The extent to which Obama's programs and policies have affected citizenship in America is not clear. Typically, Smith explains, civic health declines during recessions as people hunker down, turning inward. But despite difficult economic conditions, many measures of civic health seem to be inching up. Smith stops short of attributing the findings to the Obama presidency, but he believes a canon of populist inclusivity—preached by both candidates during last year's campaign—has inspired citizens to stay informed and get involved, even after the election. "We know that Americans are eager for meaningful engagement in civic life," Smith says. "That's a very good thing. Now we need for our leaders to recognize that government can help make that happen or it can get in the way of it."

ENDNOTES

1. http://www.hampton.gov/foryouth/youth_youth.html

2. Carmen Sirianni, *Investing in Democracy: Engaging Citizens in Collaborative Governance* (Washington, DC: Brookings Institution Press, 2009).

3. Robert Putnam, *Bowling Alone: The Collapse and Renewal of American Community* (New York: Simon & Schuster, 2000).

4. Robert D. Putnam and Lewis Feldstein, *Better Together: Restoring the American Community* (New York: Simon & Schuster, 2003).

5. Knight Foundation, Soul of the Community (http://www.soulofthecommunity.org).

6. http://www.ncoc.net/index.php?tray=topic&tid=top5&cid=9

7. http://www.sfbos.org/index.aspx?page=5585

8. http://www.bostonindicators.org/Indicators2008/

9. http://www.ci.minneapolis.mn.us/ncr/NCEC_Home.asp

10. http://caae.phil.cmu.edu/caae/dp/

11. http://www.whitehouse.gov/administration/eop/ope

*David Villano is an award-winning, Miami-based journalist.

Villano, David. "Building a Better Citizen," *Miller-McCune*, November 2, 2009.

Used by permission.

DISCUSSION QUESTIONS

1. Would randomly selected panels of citizens to advise the government on policy issues be a good way to expand democratic representation, or would it give too much power to a handful of non-elected individuals?

2. Another option is to create special panels or committees to represent youth and engage them in the political process. Is it appropriate and fair to set up special means of political participation for just one age group? (See the information on the UK Youth Parliament in the introductory chapter and the appendix at the end of this book.)

3. If public service strengthens good citizenship, should all young people be required to spend a year in public service, such as the military, health care, schools, or other public service?

Civic Learning in School

by Peter Levine*

Schools are not the only venues for civic development, but they are important. They alone reach everyone, including disadvantaged students and students who would not be inclined to volunteer or participate in civic projects. A study of civic education in Chicago found that students gained commitment to civic participation if they experienced service-learning in school, were required to follow the news, or participated in open discussions of current events in their classrooms. After-school and community-based programs also had significant positive effects, but the impact was much smaller. This contrast may be surprising, because Chicago is a hotbed of excellent community-based civic projects, whereas the Chicago public schools do not have a reputation for general excellence. However, the community-based projects draw volunteers who are already committed to civic engagement before they sign up; these projects are hard pressed to *increase* commitment or engagement. In contrast, even when school-based civic education is of mixed quality, it may have strikingly positive effects—presumably because even disengaged students are regularly exposed to civic and political ideas and opportunities.[1]

Schools have inadequate funding in many communities. Nevertheless, they have enormous resources that they can use for civic education: 3.7 million teachers, 116,000 school buildings, and 78,411 libraries in the public sector alone, not to mention countless hours of time that children are required to spend in their care.[2] They have a civic mandate dating back to their founding in the nineteenth century. Finally, deliberate education for democracy in K-12 schools *works*: "If you teach them, they will learn."[3]

This essay discusses several ways that schools can be used to improve civic education in America: courses, student voice in school, service-learning, extracurricular activities, and simulations. The goal of these reforms is to use the schools to improve the quality of democratic citizenship.

COURSES

Until recently, the "accepted wisdom in the political science profession" held that courses on civics, government, and American history had "little or no effect on the vast majority of students."[4] That conventional wisdom was based on a few studies from the 1960s, plus a widespread assumption that political participation was a function of social class or other large social forces, not amenable to direct intervention in the classroom.

However, researchers have conducted several large studies since the 1980s, including the National Assessment of Education Progress (NAEP) Civics Assessment; the International Association for the Evaluation of Educational Achievement (IEA) Civic Education Study, a detailed survey of 14-year-olds conducted in 27 countries, including the United States; and several polls that ask young adults about their own civic education as well as their current civic activities. Consistently, these studies find positive correlations between taking a class on civics, government, or American history, on one hand, and possessing civic knowledge, confidence, and attitudes, on the other.[5]

For example, an analysis of the NAEP Civics Assessment, which measures factual knowledge and cognitive skills, found that course-taking has a positive relationship with knowledge and skills even after controlling for other factors.[6] Gimpel and colleagues found that taking a course on government slightly improved Maryland students' habits of discussing politics, political knowledge, and feelings of personal efficacy. Taking a government course also slightly lowered students' confidence in the responsiveness of government.[7]

Other researchers found correlations between taking civics classes and behavior, perhaps because people need knowledge in order to take action, or perhaps because students are inspired by their courses to participate later in life. In a 2003 poll, young people who said they had taken a civics class were twice as likely to vote, twice as likely to follow the news, and four times as likely to volunteer for a campaign than those who had never taken civics courses.[8]

That finding does not prove that a single course doubles voter turnout; the relationship is more complicated than that. People might choose to take courses because of a pre-existing interest in politics; or having learned that civic engagement is valued, they might become prone to exaggerate how much they participate; or they might be more likely to *remember* taking a class because they are politically involved. However, controlling for other factors (such as race, family income, geographical location, and ideology) in the survey, we still found very strong positive relationships between course-taking and behavior.[9]

Melissa Comber examined the link between course-taking and civic skills among American ninth-graders. She found that taking courses had a substantial positive effect on interpreting political texts, following the news, and discussing politics with parents.[10]

One might assume that students gain information from courses but then gradually forget what they have learned—much as I have forgotten the content of my high school chemistry course. However, there is another reasonable hypothesis: perhaps obtaining a foundation of knowledge in adolescence allows a person to understand news articles and broadcasts and to participate in political conversations. By following and discussing the news, the citizen who starts with a base of knowledge gradually increases his or her understanding. This is a theory of education as investment instead of knowledge as a temporary response to a stimulus.

There is suggestive evidence that supports this investment hypothesis. For example, two years after they completed the Kids Voting program (which combines discussions of current issues with a mock election), students who participated were still more likely than their counterparts to discuss issues outside of class and to follow the news.[11] Furthermore, Eric Plutzer showed that voting follows an investment model. Once a citizen casts a first vote, a habit forms. Even if the positive stimulus is removed, the citizen tends to vote in subsequent elections.[12] People become more likely to vote as they grow older, quite apart from any specific events that take place, such as getting married, graduating from college, having children, or buying a home.[13] The authors suggest that political knowledge gradually accumulates and makes it easier to vote. In that case, politics differs from subjects like chemistry, where our understanding tends to decay over time unless we deliberately renew it. Starting adolescents with better knowledge would put them on a higher trajectory for life.

Thus, research argues that students should study some combination of civics, government, and social studies because that will make them more knowledgeable and engaged later in life. This finding raises two further questions: What topics should students study? And how should the material be presented to them? At least since 1900, strikingly similar debates about the content and pedagogy of social studies have recurred. Some people think that civics should be patriotic and affirm the value of American institutions; others, that civics should help students detect and oppose injustice. Some people think that civics should focus on issues of immediate relevance to students, especially problems in their local communities and opportunities for direct action; others believe that the core of civics ought to be perennial themes, such as liberty, equality, and rule of law. Some argue that civics class should be highly interactive, with opportunities for students to debate, conduct research, and go out into the community. Others emphasize the need to impart core knowledge, including challenging facts and concepts that the teacher has and the students initially lack.[14] Some believe that teachers should be rigorously neutral on all controversial issues; others think it is useful to demonstrate that teachers, as thoughtful adults, hold and defend positions.

Much has been written about these debates, which are inevitable in a pluralist democracy. Because civic education is intended to reproduce and improve our democratic culture, it will always be controversial. However, it is important not to let arguments about content overwhelm the evidence that civics classes are useful.

Because education about politics and issues is intrinsically controversial and ideological, it would be improper and counterproductive to try to impose a single model on all communities. Inevitably, government and politics will be taught differently in Philadelphia, PA, than in Philadelphia, MS. A broad framework for factual knowledge can attract national consensus, as shown by the NAEP civics assessments, which have been written on several occasions by ideologically diverse committees. However, many controversial questions about what young citizens should learn and do should not be settled at the federal level.

Despite the need for pluralism, many experts propose two overarching principles. First, students should learn about great, perennial ideals and concepts such as those presented in the Declaration of Independence, the Constitution, and the Gettysburg Address. Those foundational concepts, however, should be connected to practical, current, real-world issues. Second, education for citizenship should be at least partly experiential. That does not mean that lectures and textbooks are useless, but it is important to avoid a scene that has been replicated in classrooms since the 1800s, in which a teacher instructs students about the mechanics of government without giving them any opportunity to debate, conduct research, experiment, or create.[15]

Gimpel and colleagues derive two additional recommendations from their study. They find that students who *like* studying government and politics are dramatically more likely to discuss politics, feel more efficacious, and be more knowledgeable than their peers.[16] Enjoyment of the subject matter may arise from students' prior interests and temperaments, in which case it will be hard to change. However, it may also be that enjoyable courses increase students' interest in politics, whereas boring courses turn them off. Given the importance of increasing civic motivations (not just factual knowledge), it is worth trying to make civics courses especially enjoyable instead of especially dull—which is their reputation. That argues for activities such as field trips, visitors from the community, debates, skits, and art projects.

Gimpel and colleagues find that most social studies classes, "fail to develop in students an appreciation for the importance of conflictual aspects of American political history. Students often come to view disagreement and conflict as negative, as something to be avoided, and that no good can come of it." Students who disliked government and politics expressed "open contempt" for disagreement, as portrayed in news about Congress and the presidency.[17] This is a problem, since the country is always divided about important matters of principle and interest, and politics is our means of resolving such differences peacefully. Other research has found that many Americans do not acknowledge that there are real public disagreements. They see clashes between liberals and conservatives in Washington as unnecessary and artificial—motivated by sheer partisan competition. This resistance to conflict alienates people from participating in politics.[18] It would therefore be helpful if students learned about disagreements and practiced taking sides without demonizing opponents.

STUDENT "VOICE" IN SCHOOLS

Although topical discussions are part of good civics teaching, they deserve separate consideration. They can occur in venues other than social studies courses. For example, analyzing a novel in an English class can stimulate a current events discussion, as can certain topics in science, health, foreign languages, and even mathematics. Extracurricular clubs, school-wide meetings, and homeroom classes can also be opportunities for such discussions.

In addition to talking about broad public issues, such as war in the Middle East or homelessness in America, students can also seriously discuss issues that arise within their own schools. For example, the institution's rules, its array of courses and extracurricular activities, and its lunch menu are almost inevitably topics of informal discussion. However, the response of schools to such conversations varies. At one extreme, adults could try to suppress any talk about school issues, viewing such discussions as subversive. At the opposite extreme, students could govern a whole institution through a completely democratic process. There have been scattered experiments with truly democratic schools, such as Sudbury Valley in Massachusetts, which is an independent nonprofit corporation governed by an assembly in which every person—whether a student, teacher, or another kind of adult worker—has one vote. These models offer welcome opportunities for experimentation and learning, but they would be difficult to implement in public school systems that understand "democracy" as governance by elected municipal, state, and federal officials.

The most fertile ground lies between democratic schools, such as Sudbury, and those that actively discourage student voice. Some schools grant formal advisory roles to selected students, such as the leaders of the student government. Some organize "town meetings" and other deliberations that have some impact on policy. In some schools, the student newspaper is an influential forum for discussing common issues, and the administration takes it seriously. Certain schools have no formal structure for student input, yet youth feel that adults care what they think. The culture of such institutions encourages discussion. That norm may depend on day-to-day choices, such as whether to allow adequate time for discussion when school policies arise, whether to encourage everyone to speak, and whether to act on reasonable advice that comes from students.

Two recent projects have tried to move participating schools toward greater levels of student voice. The First Amendment Schools is a network of about 100 schools that receive modest funding to increase students' constructive influence on their own school's policies. This initiative tries to enhance young people's support for civil liberties, but the tactic is to make free expression consequential inside schools. In Hudson, Massachusetts, a new high school was physically designed to permit students to meet in clusters of 100–150 to deliberate school issues weekly. An evaluation found a rapid increase in the school's volunteering rates that seems to have resulted from the weekly meetings. Apparently, students were empowered or motivated by their experience of "voice."[19]

Broader evidence comes from surveys that ask students whether they believe that their opinions about school issues are welcomed. The IEA study found positive relationships between students' knowledge of politics and interest in current events, confidence that that could make a difference in the way their own schools were run, and their belief that the student council had an impact on school policies. These effects also appeared in a sub-sample of schools where educational outcomes were generally poor, suggesting that student "voice" may have important benefits for less advantaged students.[20]

Other studies find correlations between students' confidence in American democracy and their belief that their own schools are equitable and tolerant communities.[21] Specifically, students' confidence in democracy is higher if they think that their teachers "hold the same high standards for and respect the ideas of all students" and "insist that students listen to and respect one another." In several countries, students were more likely to commit to serving their communities and nations if they felt that their own schools were institutions "where caring transcended the borders of social cliques."[22] This research moves us beyond deliberations about school-wide policies into the subtler but essential realm of school *climate*.[23] If, for example, bullying is treated as a problem that deserves adult attention, and if students are trained so that they can help to resolve it, then they are more likely to view their schools as equitable and tolerant institutions. In contrast, if schools either ignore bullying or develop "zero-tolerance" policies that turn all threats into disciplinary cases, the school climate will be less favorable.[24]

SERVICE-LEARNING

"Service-learning" means an opportunity for students to serve in their communities while they study, discuss, or reflect upon their service. It implies a deliberate combination of academic study and practical work. Service-learning has a long heritage in the United States and in many other countries. In the mid-twentieth century there were some excellent programs that we would now call "service-learning." For instance, the city planning commission of a small city in the northeastern United States asked social studies teachers to recruit high school seniors who in turn designed and conducted community surveys, produced maps, and wrote recommendations.[25] An earlier example is the formal civic education programs connected to service work that the Civilian Conservation Corps established in the 1930s.[26] In 1999 about half of American high schools claimed to offer service-learning opportunities.[27]

In practice, both the service and the learning in "service-learning" differ widely. "Service" may mean tutoring, visiting elderly people, raising money for charity, cleaning up public spaces, taking soil or water samples for environmental monitoring, creating Web sites or broadcast segments, or organizing communities for political action. "Learning" may mean discussing a service experience in class, writing journal entries about underlying issues, or even conducting elaborate research studies.

There is no doubt that the best service-learning works. It not only enhances students' skills and interests but changes their fundamental identities, so that they become—and see themselves as—active citizens.[28] The best evidence that *average* service-learning has positive effects comes from a longitudinal study in the Chicago schools, which found it had a very substantial impact on students' commitment to civic participation.[29] Other research concluded that students were more likely to finish high school and graduate from college if they had taken high school courses with mandatory community service—a rough proxy for service-learning.[30] However, in the context of real public schools, service-learning often degenerates into cleaning the school playground and then briefly discussing this experience (or even making photocopies for the principal and *not* discussing it with anyone).

A 2005 research project found that average service-learning classes had slightly better civic outcomes than average social studies classes. Students who had been exposed to service-learning gained more knowledge of civics and government and felt more confident about their own civic skills, compared to students who had taken conventional social studies classes. However, the apparent effects of service-learning were not positive for students' sense of their own community attachment or their own ability to make a difference. (Possibly, the difficulty of the projects they undertook turned them into pessimists about achieving social change.) In any case, there were also very large differences between the best and worst service-learning. Some classes that claimed to use service-learning produced notably poor results.[31]

In a public school setting, service-learning may degenerate for two reasons. First, to develop ambitious service projects is difficult and time consuming; it requires skills, local knowledge, logistical support, patience, and energy. Second, public schools court controversy whenever their students engage in political advocacy and/or "faith-based" community action. Yet eliminating politics and religion as activities drastically narrows the range of discussion and action; as a result, service-learning often becomes trivial.

Many of the best programs are found in Catholic high schools, where service experiences are connected to a challenging normative and spiritual worldview: post-Vatican II Catholic social thought. As Anthony Bryk and colleagues observe, "The formation of each student as a person-in-community is the central educational aim of [American Catholic] schools. From this perspective, schooling involves more than conveying the acquired knowledge of civilization to students and developing in them the intellectual skills they need to create new knowledge. Education also entails forming the basic disposition for citizenship in a democratic and pluralist society."[32] Thus service-learning in Catholic schools is combined with searching moral reflection, exhortation, and examples of commitment. There is no evidence that such programs cause their graduates to agree with the main doctrines of Catholic theology; but students do develop lasting engagement with their community.[33] However, the Catholic model cannot be replicated in public schools, which must be more normatively neutral and respectful of pluralism.

Service-learning is an example of an educational strategy that has strongly positive effects at its best. Most of the best examples occur when teachers (and sometimes also students) are self-selected and highly motivated to try service-learning. Such people need to be supported and rewarded, but we should not try to increase the prevalence of service-learning by mandating it or providing very generous funding for it. Rapidly increasing its frequency will simply reduce its quality. Instead, we should try to enhance quality and quantity simultaneously, by linking together motivated volunteers, studying what particular practices work best, rewarding and recognizing the excellent practitioners, and making sure that there are sufficient funds to support the best programs and to launch willing novices.

If a school superintendent asked me what the research shows about service-learning, I would say that it supports creating a small competitive grant program and providing voluntary opportunities for teachers, such as seminars on how to organize a community service class. However, it does not support allocating a lot of money for service-learning or setting a high target for the rate of student participation. In this respect, service-learning differs from social studies teaching. Thus I would advise a superintendent or a state official to mandate social studies classes for all students (while also trying to support or weed out the worst teachers and reward the best ones). Service-learning should be cherished and admired when it is done well, but it should not be mandated.

One form of service-learning seems especially promising to me—based on my experience with it over several years—although it has not yet been rigorously evaluated. It is variously called public-interest research, community-based research, or youth-led research. Conducting research is consistent with the express purposes of public schools, so it is less controversial than political action. Yet research on public issues can be deeply motivating; it can influence identities and attitudes, not just knowledge. By asking students to study their own communities, we can help them to experience and prize the values of public service, empirical rigor, and critical inquiry. If they give away the fruits of their research, that is a rewarding form of "service."

EXTRACURRICULAR ACTIVITIES

They also serve who serve at home: for example, within their own school buildings. Almost any school houses a "civil society" composed of organized groups and various informal networks and interest groups. In CIRCLE's 2006 omnibus survey, 62 percent of high school students said that they were currently participating in an organized school group or club such as a sports team, band or chorus, language club, or the like. However, all the most common types of groups (athletics, cheerleading, music, drama, debate, newspaper, yearbook, student government, subject matter clubs, and vocational clubs) drew smaller proportions of the high school population in 1992 than they had 20 years earlier—evidence of a decline in high school civil society during that period.[34]

All students should have opportunities to choose among groups that have serious functions and that are adequately supported with money, equipment, and adults' time. Many longitudinal studies have found lasting relationships between participation in school groups and voluntary membership in adulthood. In some studies, membership in school groups turns out to be a better predictor of adult engagement than is education or income.[35] Thus, to recruit students into satisfying extracurricular activities may help make them civic activists, news consumers, and voters, thirty or fifty years later. Presented with this argument at a meeting of the Campaign for the Civic Mission of Schools, Sandra Day O'Connor recalled that she had been a shy high school student until she joined a school group. She was then on a path to become an attorney, an influential state legislator, and the first woman associate justice of the United States Supreme Court.

There are several plausible reasons for the link between extracurricular participation and lifelong civic engagement. Belonging to school groups may build confidence, or it may be sufficiently satisfying that members develop a taste for participation. People may form networks in school groups that keep them connected to associations as they age. Not least is the educational value of extracurricular activities. In Reed Larson's terminology, students can obtain opportunities for "initiative" by participating in voluntary, purposive, collective activities such as publishing a school newspaper or organizing a dance.[36] Extracurricular participation can teach people how to keep records and chair meetings, how to respond when some members shirk their duties, how to handle a budget, how to persuade groups of peers, and how to advertise the benefits of an association to outsiders. Once these skills are learned, they will enhance participation in civil society.

Although we are primarily interested in whether extracurricular participation helps make students into active and responsible democratic citizens, it is worth noting that active civic participation in school helps young people succeed in other aspects of life. That argument may persuade school officials who are not focused on civic education to provide adequate extracurricular opportunities. For instance, "involvement in student government between 1990 and 1992 increased the odds of being a college graduate by 2000 by nearly 18 percentage points."[37] Eccles and Barber found strong and lasting correlations between participating in school groups and healthy development: namely, completing high school, succeeding in college, and avoiding drugs and alcohol.[38]

Several studies have drawn a distinction between "instrumental" groups, which exist to complete a task, such as publishing a yearbook or a newspaper or organizing student events, and "expressive" groups, whose purposes are more intrinsic, such as athletics, cheerleading, music, and hobby clubs. I am not sure whether this distinction is conceptually clear, membership in groups classified as instrumental predicts political participation, whereas membership in expressive groups does not. One explanation is that students who have to work together to fulfill a function for their community are most likely to develop civic skills.[39]

That finding argues that students should be asked to conduct important school business through voluntary associations such as a student government and school media. However, a recent study found positive relationships between team sports and volunteering, registering to vote, voting, watching the news, and feeling comfortable making statements at public meetings.[40] Apparently, sports are good for civic participation, contrary to some previous scholarship that was critical of athletics.

Nonetheless, special attention should be given to activities with the explicit goal of enhancing civic development, especially scholastic journalism and elected student government. Evidence is strong that these activities build civic skills and values for their own members, although it is less clear that they benefit the whole student population. For example, research finds that students who work for scholastic newspapers hold more positive attitudes toward the press and free speech and consume more news.[41] But whether a school has a student newspaper has no positive effects on average students' attitudes. In the large, comprehensive, public high school where I have worked on after-school projects, members of the newspaper and government are almost completely insulated from the rest of the student body, which pays no attention to them. Nonetheless, a student government and newspaper *could* be important civic resources for all members of a school community, promoting discussion of public issues and supporting other student groups.

In some schools, every student has a roughly equal opportunity to participate; in others, most are left out. In some schools, voluntary groups bridge race, ethnicity, culture, and class; in others, they divide students along those lines. In a given institution, the biggest and most influential groups may emphasize athletic competition, school pride, service, artistic creativity, cultural diversity, or political activism. However, if we treat a school's collection of clubs as a microcosm of civil society, then some propositions about the adult nonprofit sector ought to apply. For adults, pluralism and choice are valuable; people cannot be "shepherded" into groups that others may consider most valuable.[42] Even more than adults, adolescents must experiment in order to develop their interests and identities; they should be able to try various roles, even if we might not fully approve of them.[43] But even though individuals must be allowed to choose their groups, it is better when civil society cultivates what Robert Putnam calls "bridging social capital," not only "bonding social capital." That is, people ought to learn to work together with those different from themselves and develop trust and useful networks that "bridge" differences; they should not merely use associational membership to differentiate in-groups from out-groups.[44] In American schools, voluntary associations tend to be exclusive. Without being overly manipulative, adults should foster "bridging" activities and groups, such as dramatic productions that draw from several subcultures within a school, or service events that include everyone.

SIMULATIONS

Service-learning and membership in school groups are ways for students to perform actual public work. Another model asks young people to play *simulated* civic roles. Traditional examples include moot trials, mock elections, model legislatures, and the Model United Nations program. More than half a million students cast ballots every four years in Scholastic's mock presidential election.[45] In one classroom experiment with an imaginary society, students became more tolerant when they observed the unfair effects of simple majority rule.[46]

More recently, computers help students simulate political situations. In one form of simulation, an individual student plays a leadership role in a historical or hypothetical situation, using software that someone else has written for that purpose. For example, in Oregon Trail players pretended to be pioneers moving west from Independence, MO, in 1848. They presumably learn some facts about American history and some civic skills, such as how to negotiate with others (in this case, with computer-generated characters). Another illustrative title is the popular SimCity series, in which a player runs an imaginary town by setting the zoning rules and building the public infrastructure. The computer simulates the response of the private sector. To win is to achieve growth and prosperity with low crime.

In another genre of computer-assisted game, many human players interact via networked machines. These games can resemble traditional, face-to-face simulations (such as Model U.N.), but there are important potential differences. Thanks to computers, many more people can play simultaneously, the players can be strangers who are distributed across the globe, participants can face randomly generated events of some complexity, and the visual environment can be rich and complex. In ICONS (International Communication and Negotiation Simulations), students from various countries simulate diplomatic exchanges. A careful evaluation found that ICONS improved students' sophistication and complexity of thinking.[47]

In recent years, massive multiplayer role-playing games have become popular. Hundreds of thousands of students interact in simulated "worlds," such as Second Life. Such simulations can be deliberately designed to teach civic skills. For example, they can have realistic political and economic systems, and winning can require working constructively with others. As an alternative, students could be encouraged to behave in civic ways within standard commercial games as part of class projects. The so-called first-person shooter games are famous for their high rates of violence. But Joseph Kahne and colleagues find that video games overall do not depress civic engagement and that activities connected to video-game play, such as helping other players and discussing ethical issues that arise within the game, are positively related to civic engagement. Their study investigates widely available, commercial games that adolescents choose to play in their free time. Given the somewhat positive results, they argue that there is enormous potential for the design and promotion of new games that are better for civic education.[48] However, there is a theoretical argument against using simulations for civic engagement. If young people have actual civic assets, then they should be called upon to play real roles in their communities, thereby learning that they can address serious issues. Asking them to pretend that they are legislators, diplomats, or litigators implies that they are not ready for real citizenship. Besides, those roles are rare enough that most students will not grow up to play them. A simulation might teach them that politics is remote from their real lives and prospects.

That argument should be weighed against the important advantages of simulations. By creating controlled, imaginary environments, educators can ensure that players encounter complex, intellectually challenging problems, tailored to their developmental needs or to educational standards. I often recall sitting on a curb with a group of high school students, waiting in 100-degree heat for a bus to take us to a service site. We were trying to accomplish real social change, but the failure of the bus ever to appear meant that we mainly experienced frustration. If we had remained inside the high school pretending to be lawyers, members of Congress, or delegates to the United Nations, we might have learned considerably more.

IMPLICATIONS FOR POLICY

I have argued that it is important to preserve and expand civics courses, service-learning programs, and extracurricular organizations in schools and to give students appropriate "voice" in their own education.[49] The sheer number of opportunities is not the only important question; *quality* also matters. We need service-learning programs that truly stretch the minds of students and address authentic issues; extracurricular activities that engage a broad range of students in meaningful activities and connect them to voluntary associations; and teachers who are prepared to explore perennial and emerging issues of politics and justice and to use experiential methods such as projects, debates, and simulations. It is also important to continue teachers' education about democracy after their careers have begun.[50]

When Americans discuss what makes a civics class or service program good, they disagree about matters of principle, such as whether teachers should promote patriotism and other values. I think that we should be pluralists and federalists and welcome a fair amount of diversity in civics curricula and teaching across the country. Most important is to invest schools' time and money in courses, service opportunities, and extracurricular activities and to encourage teachers and other educators to think and care about civic themes.

We must worry about *equality* as well as quantity and quality. Civic education is preparation for a democratic system in which all are supposed to be equal. Kahne and Middaugh find, "A student's race and academic track, and a school's average socioeconomic status (SES) determines the availability of the school-based civic learning opportunities. High school students attending higher SES schools, those who are college-bound, and white students get more of these opportunities than low-income students, those not heading to college, and students of color."[51] As a result, there are stark differences in civic knowledge by social class.[52] Some programs mainly serve high-performing schools with college-bound students. They may improve the quantity and average quality of civic education but lower equality.

As we seek to promote the civic mission of schools, we must confront the most powerful trend in education, which is the standards-and-accountability movement. This movement calls for students to be regularly tested in core academic subjects, especially reading, writing, mathematics, and science. The movement culminated in the No Child Left Behind (NCLB) Act of 2002. Among other things, NCLB requires all students to be tested annually in reading and mathematics—and regularly in science.

There are arguments in favor and against standardized tests as a means of enhancing student outcomes in reading, math, and science. If it is successful, the program will benefit democracy, because basic educational success predicts political participation. I am not sure whether it will achieve its explicit purposes. However, for purposes of *civic* education, standardized tests raise at least four serious obstacles.

First, teachers and schools spend time on topics that are on standardized tests, especially if the tests have high stakes. NCLB requires testing in three major subject areas but not in civics, history, or government. There is evidence that school districts are cutting those subjects to devote time to the material mandated for regular high-stakes exams, especially in the early grades.[53] This trend puts advocates of civic education in a bind. Students are already spending so much time on pencil-and-paper tests—and schools are facing so many unfunded mandates from the federal government—that it seems irresponsible to add a civics test to the national requirements. On the other hand, if there is no required civics test, courses will be phased out in many schools.

Second, pencil-and-paper tests measure only skills and knowledge, but we should also seek to impart attitudes, values, habits, and behaviors. Adding questions about values to high-stakes written tests is not the answer, since students could easily provide the desired answers without actually holding the desired values, which makes the tests unreliable. There is also an ethical problem with testing values. I think, for instance, that we should teach young people to vote, yet we should not penalize those who oppose voting because they hold religious or political objections to the current regime.

Third, the whole idea of high-stakes testing embodies a "deficits" approach. Schools are required to identify students who are failing and intervene to correct their problems. Yet, Federal law does not require anyone to provide positive opportunities, even though the theory of positive youth development suggests that some of the government's explicit goals (such as reducing the high school dropout rate) would be better served by making sure that every student had opportunities to serve, create, collaborate, and lead.

Fourth, high-stakes standardized tests constrain the choices that are available to schools and local communities. Federal law now demands a set of essential goals: students must pass written tests in a limited set of subjects. But most Americans place *other* goals higher on their own agendas for schools.[54] If parents, teachers, other citizens, and students wish to deliberate about what they want their local schools to accomplish, they may find that this discussion is moot; the national government has already decided. That is unfortunate because a discussion about goals and priorities would itself be a form of civic education, especially if students were encouraged to participate.

In my view, the basic structure of NCLB is likely to remain in place for at least a decade. It is the outcome of powerful political vectors from both the

Democratic and the Republican side. Despite continued opposition to it, I do not expect NCLB to be repealed. Besides, it is at least plausible that the act, suitably revised and better funded, would increase students' basic academic performance and reduce educational inequality.

Thus, I believe we need creative and constructive ways to enhance civic education *within* the basic framework of high-stakes testing. One idea is to add a mandatory civics examination without increasing the net amount of testing that any student faces during his or her school career. Although the federal government could allow states and localities to meet that mandate in several ways, two approaches are obvious. A civics test could replace one of the subjects that are now mandatory at a particular grade level. Alternatively, existing tests of reading, writing, and mathematics could be revised to incorporate enough questions about political and historical themes to derive a reliable "civics" score for each student. This reform would motivate schools to enhance students' civic knowledge but not their civic values, habits, or attitudes. However, knowledge is worth enhancing because it is intrinsically valuable as well as an important precondition of effective civic action.

A second idea is to argue that schools should use civic *means* to attain the existing *ends* of federal law. For example, NCLB requires all American students to pass reading examinations. Those tests already include passages about history and social issues. Some research finds that students need specific experience in interpreting material about politics, history, or social issues before they can handle it on an examination. Partly because of the emphasis on "decoding," and partly because textbook publishers are afraid of controversy, almost all political and social themes have been stripped out of elementary reading texts, which are mostly stories about furry animals or small children in domestic settings. However, it is not enough to have read anodyne fictional texts if one is confronted with a passage about Martin Luther King Jr. or World War II on an exam. Such passages will use specialized vocabulary and allude to background knowledge that make it difficult for students to comprehend.

In order to motivate students to read and understand texts (fictional or non-fictional) about social and political themes, the instruction should be experiential, with mock elections, field trips, and service projects. Besides providing motivation, experiential civic education is a way to meet the current federal mandates in reading.[55]

Civic education could also help meet the NCLB requirement to raise high school graduation rates. According to the theory of positive youth development, students are more likely to graduate if they engage in extracurricular activities and service projects and have opportunities to exercise "voice" in their schools.

However, with civic education a relatively low priority for policy makers, it is no easy task to recover the civic mission of schools. The two most important reasons to do so are political equality and educational success. The loss of engaging, interactive forms of civic education has fallen hardest on young people from disadvantaged backgrounds. Gaps in voting and other forms of civic participation by social class are unjust, and can be reinforced by inequalities in education.[56] At the same time, students benefit educationally when they are given opportunities to engage with serious public issues in school. Civic learning requires them to engage with complex issues, to collaborate, to interact with adults, and to form medium- or long-range plans. Such work can enhance students' academic attainment, with the greatest benefits accruing to disadvantaged youth.[57] This is all the more reason that every American student must have an inspiring civic education.

ENDNOTES

1. Joseph Kahne and Susan Sporte, *Developing Citizens: A Longitudinal Study of the Impact of Classroom Practices, Extra-Curricular Activities, Parent Discussions, and Neighborhood Contexts on Students' Commitments to Civic Participation* (unpublished paper October 2006).

2. Gregory Strizek et al., *Characteristics of Schools, Districts, Teachers, Principals, and School Libraries in the United States, 2003–04* (Washington, DC: National Center for Education Statistics, April 2006), table 1, 13.

3. Carnegie Corporation of New York and CIRCLE, *The Civic Mission of Schools* (Washington, DC: CIRCLE, 2003), 23. Experts representing diverse ideologies, professions, and disciplines (including political science, psychology, education, law, and philosophy) examined the civic mission. The report remains a useful template for discussing civic education within K–12 schools.

4. Richard Niemi and Jane Junn, *Civic Education: What Makes Students Learn* (New Haven: Yale University Press, 1998), 16.

5. Melissa Comber, "Civic Curriculum and Civic Skills: Recent Evidence," CIRCLE Fact Sheet (November 2003).

6. Niemi and Junn; Jay Greene, review of "Civic Education: What Makes Students Learn," *Social Science Quarterly* 81 (2000): 696–697.

7. James Gimpel, J. Celeste Lay, and Jason Schuknecht, *Cultivating Democracy: Civic Environments and Political Socialization in America* (Washington, DC: Brookings Institution Press, 2003), 149.

8. Karl Kurtz, Alan Rosenthal, and Cliff Zukin, "Citizenship: A Challenge for All Generations" (Denver: National Conference of State Legislatures, 2003), 6.

9. Comber, *Civics Curriculum*, 5.

10. Melissa Comber, "The Effects of Civic Education on Civic Skills," CIRCLE Fact Sheet (October 2005); see California Campaign for the Civic Mission of Schools, The California Survey of Civic Education (2005), 9 (http://www.cms-ca.org).

11. Michael McDevitt and Spiro Kiousis, "Experiments in Political Socialization: Kids Voting USA as a Model for Civic Education Reform," CIRCLE Working Paper 49 (August 2006).

12. Whether one voted last time is a positive correlated in a current election, even once other variables are controlled. See Eric Plutzer, "Becoming a Habitual Voter: Inertia, Resources, and Growth," *American Political Science Review* 96 (2002): 41–56.

13. Benjamin Highton and Raymond Wolfinger, "The First Seven Years of the Political Life Cycle," *American Journal of Political Science* 45 (2001): 202–209.

14. Bruce Frazee and Samuel Ayers, "Garbage in, Garbage Out: Expanding Environments, Constructivism, and Content Knowledge in Social Studies." In James Leming, Lucien Ellington, and Kathleen Porter-Magee, eds., *Where Did Social Studies Go Wrong?* (Washington, DC: Fordham Foundation).

15. Carnegie and CIRCLE, *Civic Mission*.

16. Gimpel, Lay, and Schuknecht, 150–152.

17. Gimpel, Lay, and Schuknecht,153–154, 212.

18. John Hibbing and Elizabeth Theiss-Morse, *Stealth Democracy: Americans' Beliefs about How Government Should Work* (New York: Cambridge University Press, 2002).

19. Hugh McIntosh, Sheldon Berman, and James Youniss, "A Five-Year Evaluation of a Comprehensive High School Civic Engagement Initiative," CIRCLE Working Paper 70 (March 2010).

20. Carnegie and CIRCLE, *Civic Mission*, 27.

21. In the California Survey of Civic Education, the only approach to civic education that enhanced students' trust in others and confidence in institutions was giving them voice in their own schools (California Campaign for the Civic Mission of Schools, 9).

22. Flanagan, Constance, and Nakesha Faison, "Youth Civic Development: Implications of Research for Social Policy and Programs," *Social Policy Report* 15, 1 (2001): 4, 7.

23. Gary Homana, Carolyn Henry Barber, and Judith Torney-Purta, "School Citizenship Education Climate Assessment" (Denver, CO: Education Commission of the States, 2006).

24. Flanagan and Faison, 5–7.

25. James Beane et al., "Long-term Effects of Community Service Programs," *Curriculum Inquiry* 11 (Summer 1981): 145–146.

26. Gary Daynes and Nicholas V. Longo, "Jane Addams and the Origins of Service-learning Practice in the United States," *Michigan Journal of Community Service Learning* 11 (2004): 5–13; Melissa Bass, "National Service in America: Policy (Dis)Connections over Time," CIRCLE Working Paper 11 (2004); Melissa Bass, "Civic Education through National Service," CIRCLE Working Paper 12 (2004).

27. U.S. Department of Education, National Center for Education Statistics, "Service Learning and Community Service in K–12 Public Schools" (September 1999), table 1.

28. James Youniss and Miranda Yates, *Community Service and Social Responsibility in Youth* (Chicago: University of Chicago Press, 1997).

29. Kahne and Sporte, *Developing Citizens*.

30. Alberto Dávila and Marie Mora, "Civic Engagement and High School Academic Progress: An Analysis Using NELS Data." CIRCLE Working Paper 52 (2007)

31. Shelley Billig, Sue Root, and Dan Jesse, "The Impact of Participation in Service-learning on High School Students' Civic Engagement," CIRCLE Working Paper 33 (2005), 26–27. The California Survey of Civic Education found that service learning increased students' civic skills, but service learning did not enhance interest in politics, political knowledge, or intentions to vote.

32. Anthony Bryk, Valerie Lee, and Peter Holland, *Catholic Schools and the Common Good* (Cambridge, MA: Harvard University Press, 1993), 289.

33. Yates and Youniss, 141 and passim; David Campbell, "Making Democratic Education Work." In Paul Peterson and David Campbell, eds., Charters, Vouchers, and Public Education (Washington, DC: Brookings Institution Press, 2001), 241–267.

34. Patricia Green, Bernard Dugoni, and Steven Ingels, "Trends among High School Seniors," *Statistical Analysis Report* (Washington, DC: National Center for Education Statistics, 1995).

35. Mary Kirlin, "The Role of Adolescent Extracurricular Activities in Adult Political Participation," CIRCLE Working Paper 2 (March 2003) summarizes eight studies that find positive correlations between extracurricular activities and adult civic participation. See Michael Hanks, "Youth, Voluntary Associations, and Political Socialization," *Social Forces* 69 (1981): 211–223; Paul Beck and M. Kent Jennings, "Pathways to Participation," *American Political Science Review* 76 (1982): 94–108; Elizabeth Smith, "The Effects of Investments in the Social Capital of Youth on Political and Civic Behavior in Young Adulthood," *Political Psychology* 20 (1999): 553–580; Jennifer Glanville, "Political Socialization or Selection? Adolescent

Extracurricular Participation and Political Activity in Early Adulthood," *Social Science Quarterly* 80 (1999): 279–290; M. Kent Jennings and Laura Stocker, "Social Trust and Civic Engagement across Time and Generations," *Acta Politica* 39 (2004): 361–363.

36. R. W. Larson, "Toward a Psychology of Positive Youth Development," *American Psychologist* 55 (2000): 170-183; Eccles and Barber, "Student Council, Volunteering, or Marching Band."

37. Dávila and Mora, "Civic engagement and high school academic progress."

38. Jacquelynne Eccles and Bonnie Barber, "Student Council, Volunteering, Basketball, or Marching Band," 14 *Journal of Adolescent Research* (1999): 38; Bonnie Barber, Jacquelynne Eccles, and Margaret Stone, "Whatever Happened to the Jock, the Brain, and the Princess? Young Adult Pathways Linked to Adolescent Activity Involvement and Social Identity," *Journal of Adolescent Research* 16 (2001): 429.

39. Kirlin, "The Role of Adolescent Extracurricular Activities in Adult Political Participation," 15.

40. Mark Hugo Lopez and Kimberlee Moore, "Participation in Sports and Civic Engagement," CIRCLE Fact Sheet (February 2006); Robert Fullinwider, "Sports, Youth and Character: A Critical Survey," CIRCLE Working Paper 44 (February 2006).

41. Mark Hugo Lopez et al., "Schools, Education Policy, and the Future of the First Amendment," in Progress.

42. Nancy Rosenblum, "The Moral Uses of Pluralism." In Robert Fullinwider, *Civil Society, Democracy, and Civic Renewal* (Lanham, MD: Rowman & Littlefield, 1999), 261.

43. Erikson, "Eight Ages of Man," *International Journal of Psychiatry* 2 (1966) 290.

44. Robert Putnam, *Bowling Alone: The Collapse and Revival of American Community* (New York: Simon and Schuster, 2001), 22–24.

45. http://teacher.scholastic.com/scholasticnews/indepth/election2008.htm.

46. Patricia Avery, "Teaching Tolerance: What Research Tells Us," *Social Education* 66 (2002): 273.

47. Judith Torney-Purta, "Cognitive Representations of the International Political and Economic Systems in Adolescents." In H. Haste and J. Torney-Purta, eds., *The Development of Political Understanding* (San Francisco: Jossey-Bass, 1992), 11–25; J. Torney-Purta, "Conceptual Changes in Adolescents Using Computer Networks in Group-mediated International Role Playing." In S. Vosniadou et al., eds., *International Perspectives on the Design of Technology Supported Learning Environments* (Hillsdale, NJ: Erlbaum, 1996).

48. Joseph Kahne, Ellen Middaugh, and Chris Evans, *The Civic Potential of Video Games* (Cambridge: MIT Press, 2009).

49. I also realize there are controversies in how these reforms are enacted. See Peter Levine, *The Future of Democracy: Developing the Next Generation of American Citizens* (Medford, MA: Tufts University Press, 2007), chap. 7.

50. Torney-Purta and colleagues find "a statistically significant and relatively substantial effect" on students when educational programs are aimed at practicing teachers; Judith Torney-Purta, Carolyn Henry Barber, and Wendy Klandl Richardson, "How Teachers' Preparation Relates to Students' Civic Knowledge and Engagement in the United States: Analysis from the IEA Civic Education Study," CIRCLE Fact Sheet (April 2005).

51. Joseph Kahne and Ellen Middaugh, "Democracy for Some: The Civic Opportunity Gap in High School," CIRCLE Working Paper 59 (2008).

52. Judith Torney-Purta and Carolyn H. Barber, "Strengths and Weaknesses in U.S. Students' Knowledge and Skills: Analysis from the IEA Civic Education Study," CIRCLE Fact Sheet (2004).

53. Peter Levine, Mark Hugo Lopez, and Karlo Barrios Marcelo, *Getting Narrower at the Base: The American Curriculum after NCLB*. CIRCLE monograph (December 2008).

54. David Mathews, *Reclaiming Public Education by Reclaiming Our Democracy* (New York: Kettering Foundation Press, 2006), 16–17.

55. Nell Duke, S. Bennett-Armistead, and E. M. Roberts, "Filling the Great Void: Why We Should Bring Nonfiction into the Early-grade Classroom," *American Educator* 27 (2003): 1–8; Mariam Dreher, "Motivating Struggling Readers by Tapping the Potential of Informational Books," *Reading and Writing Quarterly* 19 (2003): 25–38; J. Flood and D. Lapp, "Types of Text: The Match between What Students Read in Basals and What They Encounter in Tests," *Reading Research Quarterly* 21 (1986): 284–297.

56. Peter Levine and Constance Flanagan, "Youth Civic Engagement during the Transition to Adulthood." In Mary Waters, Gordon Berlin, and Frank Furstenberg, eds., *Transition to Adulthood* (Special issue of *The Future of Children*), 20 (Spring 2010): 159–180.

57. Britt Wilkenfeld, "Does Context Matter? How the Family, Peer, School, and Neighborhood Contexts Relate to Adolescents' Civic Engagement," CIRCLE Working Paper 64 (2009).

*Peter Levine is director of research and director of CIRCLE (Center for Information & Research on Civic Learning & Engagement) at Tufts University's Jonathan M. Tisch College of Citizenship and Public Service.

DISCUSSION QUESTIONS

1. If you are a student, how does the school directly involve students in decision making about things that affect campus life? What could be done to further democratize your school? Do you think it would affect how you view politics outside of school?

2. Should every state mandate a meaningful service learning experience as a requirement for high school graduation?

3. Should civics courses involve debates about conflicting national issues, or should they focus on the values we share and agree on?

Youth Civic Engagement in Canada: Implications for Public Policy

by Dietlind Stolle and Cesi Cruz*

[...]

FACTORS AND PROGRAMS THAT FOSTER YOUTH CIVIC ENGAGEMENT

The question for policy makers concerned with the state of youth civic engagement is how best to mobilize youth and maximize the benefits from their participation. Verba et al. and several other participation scholars identified three main factors that determine civic and political participation: resources, interest, and recruitment.[1] Resources refer to economic resources, such as time and money that enable participation; interest refers to the political and civic stimulation and the sense of political efficacy that facilitates involvement; and recruitment refers to social networks that serve to mobilize citizens and promote participation.

This work suggests three broad strategies of policy and program development to promote civic participation. The first would be to ensure a more equitable distribution of resources, or to mitigate the impact of unequal access to resources by removing institutional, administrative, or socio-economic barriers to participation, such as residency requirements. A second broad strategy focuses on youth engagement efforts and increasing political interest. Many programs have concentrated on developing civic education as a means of addressing apathy or a diminished sense of political efficacy, but some programs work better than others. The third strategy develops social networks that will help in recruiting youth into civic life and sustain their involvement even when they become adults. This section outlines strategies for achieving these civic engagement goals in different arenas of everyday experience of youth: homes, schools, communities, and workplaces.

The Home

Although there are many different paths to civic engagement, most scholars agree that these paths all begin in one place: the home. In addition to recognizing the importance of family socialization, home-based approaches to fostering youth engagement focus on providing resources and developing basic civic skills and political interest. To meet these goals, many successful programs promoted resilience in youth through supportive relationships with parents and other family members, helped parents or adult family members become civic role models for youth, and provided children with the capacity to reinforce their parents' engagement.

Building Social Attitudes and Support Networks for Youth

One approach to fostering youth engagement in the home focuses on promoting positive relationships within the family to develop both social attitudes and support networks that youth can draw on throughout their lives. After all, the first lessons in social behaviors and values (such as norms of trust and reciprocity) are learned in the home through relationships with parents and other family members. Generally, children who are provided with a positive and open home environment and who are socialized in a self-respecting and tolerant atmosphere are more likely to be co-operative and socially active.[2] Steinberg showed that children with parents who talk to them about school and take an interest in their lives are more willing to engage in the community.[3] Research also shows that the building of trust and co-operation in children is closely related to principles of consistency. Trust and co-operative attitudes in children flourish in a predictable and stable environment.[4] In other words, the family atmosphere and parent-child interactions matter.

At the same time, one research area needs further support and future investment. Paradoxically, although this is one of the most complex and least understood ways of promoting youth engagement, it is an area where the amount of resources invested in youth can potentially provide the most far-reaching and long-term effects. Current research in Canada, the United States and Germany examines child-rearing techniques, the family atmosphere and parents' support for their children's networks in their potential to develop "civicness" in children and youth.[5] Policies resulting from this research might include government-offered tutorials for parents and special TV programs for parents on successful child-rearing techniques.

Providing Parents with the Resources to Become Civic Role Models for Youth

Many home-based approaches to fostering youth engagement focus on the importance of the family for providing youth with role models for civic engagement. Our earlier discussion has shown how parental engagement usually fosters the involvement of children. The MotherRead/FatherRead programs provide an example of a resource-based approach in the United States, which encourages parents to take books home and read to their children and discuss themes of the books. In addition to providing literacy resources to households with children, these programs promote discussion and debate in the home. This program has the advantage of learner-centred instruction, which tailors the curriculum to each group of program participants. For immigrant families, for example, there is the My United States program, which uses the MotherRead/FatherRead curriculum to teach families about US history and government, and to prepare them for citizenship and naturalization.

One other example that has become a trend in recent years is family volunteering, which is promoted and supported by many organizations in the United States and Canada, such as the Points of Light Foundation. Family volunteering is encouraging families to volunteer together. The goal is to get the whole family involved, which is seen as a way to encourage long-term volunteering (especially among busy parents who want to spend quality time with their kids) and boost volunteer rates/numbers. Family volunteering is seen as a way to foster civic engagement by providing youth with role models, promoting positive attitudes toward service, family cohesiveness, and communication. A survey of voluntary organizations in Canada found that 60 percent of respondents reported having family volunteers, and 16 percent offered special volunteering programs specifically geared toward families.[6]

Engaging Adolescents and Their Parents Together

Although many home-based approaches focus on transmitting civic skills, attitudes, and values from parents to children, fostering civic engagement in the home is not simply a parent-to-child process. The participation of children can also promote parent engagement. As a result, home-based approaches can be particularly effective when they enable parents and children to reinforce and promote each other's civic skills and attitudes.

One example of such a program is Kids Voting USA, which uses a multipronged approach to teach students about democracy.[7] The curriculum promotes voting and political engagement, which is extended to the community in a service learning component and a parallel student election held on Election Day. Youth are engaged in the political process on many levels, culminating in youth participation in national and local elections.

Kids Voting USA can promote youth engagement in politics: research conducted in 1996 in Kansas showed a strong correlation between participation in Kids Voting USA and registration and voting as a first-time voter. In addition, McDevitt and Chaffee also found that Kids Voting USA increased turnout for parents whose children were participating in the program. This suggests the possibility of a "trickle-up" effect associated with promoting engagement: not only do parents serve as civic role models for their children, but it seems that children can also set a civic example for their parents as well.

Another program fosters family relationships with schools and communities. Families and Schools Together Canada (F&ST) is a set of programs at different levels of child development that brings families together to participate in activities meant to enhance family relationships and support communities. This approach focuses on the home by creating linkages among families, schools, and communities. In surveys conducted by F&ST, 86 percent of parent participants reported making new friends through the program, and 91 percent reported that the program encouraged them to become more involved with the school community.[8]

At School

As the "only institutions with the capacity and mandate to reach virtually every young person in the country," schools tend to take the lead in establishing programs to foster youth engagement.[9] In earlier socialization research, the effect of civic education programs has been mixed. This was mostly due to the top-down character of civic education programs in which students were asked to learn facts about their political systems. However, recent research has contributed to a new innovative and interactive approach that can help develop political knowledge and civic skills in youth. In meeting these goals, two strategies have been particularly successful: encouraging discussions in classrooms and integrating civic skills, such as letter writing or debating, into the curriculum; and establishing youth-led service-learning or volunteering programs.

Encourage Discussions in Classrooms and Integrate Civic Skills into Curriculum

According to Niemi and Junn, learning about government and citizenship merely by memorizing facts is not as effective as participatory or interactive programs.[10] Students who report that their teachers encourage open discussions on politics and national issues tend to score higher on civic engagement scales than other students.[11] Classroom discussions can also increase the effectiveness of other programs aimed at fostering youth engagement. Andolina et al. found that encouraging student volunteers to discuss their experiences in class makes them twice as likely to continue volunteering later in life.[12] Sixty-four percent of student volunteers who discussed their service work in class continued to volunteer regularly, as compared to only 32 percent of student volunteers who did not have the opportunity to discuss their service work in class.[13]

Schools can also foster engagement by encouraging the development of specific civic skills, through hands-on activities. However, the emphasis on different skills varies: 80 percent of high school students have been required to give a speech or oral report, but only 51 percent have taken part in a debate.[14] According to Andolina et al., "students who have been taught these skills, especially letter writing and debating, are much more likely than those lacking such education to be involved in a range of participatory acts inside and outside the school environment, even when other factors are taken into account."[15]

An example of a successful civic education program is the national Youth Leadership Initiative (YLI) in the United States,[16] which is "designed to involve students in the American electoral and policymaking process and to foster greater community awareness and participation."[17]

This program combines in-class and electronic sessions for students to learn about local politics and civic duty. Strengths of the program include flexibility to tailor programs to fit local interests, ability to foster discussion and debate, and use of hands-on learning. The focus on local politics encourages students to become involved in issues that directly affect them. For example, students study how campaign advertisements influence people by selecting a local advertisement, analyzing the possible meanings—both intentional and unintentional—and discussing the reasons why certain advertisements are targeted to particular groups of people. The program also fosters discussions and debates among students. Students study and discuss the meanings behind Norman Rockwell paintings about civil and women's rights, and read and discuss Locke's theories on universal human rights. The program also emphasizes participation to teach students about politics. For example, to learn about elections and the differences between political party ideologies, students participate in an on-line "e-campaign" where they can run in a local gubernatorial or presidential race. During this simulation, the students get hands-on experience with local political issues, participating in debates and, ultimately, going through the election itself.

An example of a successful program in Canada is Student Vote 2004, which partnered with Elections Canada and the Department of Canadian Heritage to hold parallel federal elections among youth under the voting age in schools to raise civic awareness. The non-partisan program is intended to foster a "habit of electoral and community participation among students."[18] Over a quarter million students participated in this initiative, from more than 1,100 schools throughout the country.[19] Student Vote 2004 conducted surveys in addition to administering the parallel election. Before May 27, 2,915 students participated in a pre-election survey that showed 68 percent would vote if the election were held that day and 34 percent kept informed about issues, government, and politics. In addition, students participating in the pre-election survey could name an average of four political parties. After the Student Vote in their school, a post-election survey with 1,401 student respondents indicated that 87 percent would vote if the election were held that day and 53 percent kept informed of issues, government, and politics. Students in the post-election survey were also able to name an average of five political parties. This partnership illustrates ways to mobilize nongovernmental organizations to address the problem of non-voting youth.

Establish Youth-Led Volunteering Programs

The practice of service learning is widespread in the United States and Canada. In the United States, a recent survey by the National Center for Education Statistics showed that 83 percent of high schools offered community service opportunities in their curriculum, compared with only 27 percent in 1984.[20] It is widely believed that the volunteering experiences in service learning contribute to the development of a civic identity in youth.[21] The task here is to create programs that leave a lasting impact on young citizens. In particular, school-based programs need to address the fact that volunteering rates diminish after high school. Unfortunately, programs can vary widely both in goals and in how they are implemented, giving rise to mixed results. Service learning tends to be most successful when two broad goals are kept in mind: using student-led volunteering to foster civic skills, and making the links between individual actions and broader governmental and societal outcomes.

One example of student-led volunteering is the Peace Corps Partnership Project, which uses several strategies for encouraging youth engagement through service learning. First, the program emphasizes student ownership of projects. Students are involved at every step of the process, from evaluating needs, raising funds, and implementing solutions. Jim Miller, a teacher at Corcoran High School, described the process of choosing a project as "a tremendous learning experience, as students compare and discuss the various merits of the projects, how much money is to be raised, and the relative needs among the projects."[22]

Second, the program is integrated into the curriculum. Students exchange letters, drawings, and photographs with Peace Corps volunteers, which are used as hands-on learning tools in the classroom. Third, the program reinforces membership in other school clubs and activities. Peace Corps Partnership programs within the school are co-ordinated by student members of the school's International Relations Club. Club members are also encouraged to present workshops about the program and their current fund-raising projects. Fourth, participation in the project encourages students to get involved in their communities. As part of their involvement, high school students pair up with and teach younger students at the neighboring elementary school. In addition to learning about the cultures of the different places the Peace Corps is involved with, the younger students are encouraged to participate in the fundraising programs.

Service learning is also more successful when it explicitly establishes the link between citizen action, government policies, and socio-political outcomes.[23] Students may be serving food in soup kitchens, for example, but they aren't necessarily making the link from their individual role to government policies that address the problem of poverty from an institutional standpoint. Yet several successful examples of service learning programs make this link between individual action and policy outcomes. One group studied the causes of domestic violence and held workshops for other high school students to educate them about domestic violence; another group worked with a community to halt the construction of a hazardous waste-disposal plant. According to Westheimer and Kahne, such programs "use the power of experiences helping others to teach students to address complex social problems and their causes."[24]

Communities and Social Networks

For youth making the transition from childhood to young adulthood, communities are particularly relevant for developing civic skills and attitudes. Young people spend lots of time in their social networks, and they offer a variety of avenues for mobilizing youngsters into civic attitudes and behaviors. There is much research on the effect of voluntary associations for adults, which shows that members of organizations and associations exhibit more democratic and civic attitudes as well as more active forms of political participation than non-members. Almond and Verba found that members of associations are more politically active, more informed about politics, more sanguine about their ability to affect political life, and more supportive of democratic norms.[25] Others have noticed that the number and type of associations to which people belong, and the extent of their activity within the organization, are related to political activity and involvement.[26] In later research, Verba and his colleagues found that members of voluntary associations learn self-respect, group identity, and public skills.[27]

To these findings, the social capital school adds the insight that membership in associations should also facilitate the learning of co-operative attitudes and behavior, including reciprocity. In particular, membership in voluntary associations should increase face-to-face interactions between people and create a setting for the development of trust. This in-group trust can be used to achieve group purposes more efficiently and more easily. Furthermore, via mechanisms that are not yet clearly understood, the development of interpersonal trust and the co-operative experiences between members tends to be generalized to the society as a whole.[28] In this way, the operation of voluntary groups and associations contributes to the building of a society in which co-operation between all people for all sorts of purposes—not just within the groups themselves—is facilitated.[29]

Most recently, social capital research has emphasized that not all associations are alike and that we should make distinctions between various types of groups.[30] For example, it has been argued that the composition of the groups matter for positive socialization results. Groups constituted by a wide variety of people from various (ethnic, racial, socio-economic) backgrounds are assumed to have more beneficial effects on the learning of tolerance and civic attitudes, such as generalized trust.[31] Diversity in groups with positive co-operation experiences might be the most useful tool in fostering and maintaining social capital, civic orientations, and an interest in society and politics more broadly.

Socialization research has shown that associational experiences are even more powerful and lasting for young citizens. For example, participation in extracurricular activities is related to a host of positive outcomes for youth. Children and youth who participated generally had stronger academic skills, higher self-esteem, and better health than those who did not participate.[32] Longitudinal studies like the Jennings and Niemi panel survey suggest that participation at a young age has lasting effects on subsequent political attitudes and behaviors.[33] In an analysis of the Canadian National Longitudinal Study of Children and Youth (NLSCY), Harell and Stolle found that youth engagement in community groups and other types of clubs is one of the most important predictors of club membership, volunteering and willingness to take on special responsibilities in an organization four years later.[34] Moreover, dropping out of these club activities has negative effects.

Social groups provide networks, especially at the local level, that can be used for various mobilization efforts later on in life.[35] According to Keeter et al., one in five volunteers aged 15 to 24 (born after 1976) reported getting involved because "someone else put us together," compared to 14 percent of those born between 1964 and 1976, 6 percent of those born between 1946 and 1964, and 11 percent of those born before 1946.[36] In sum, social networks and groups are important particularly for youth, because they shape attitudes, co-operative behaviors, and provide networks for mobilization.

Unfortunately, the study of adolescents' social environments and their involvement in various forms of social interaction—although one of the most promising avenues for socialization research—is one of the most understudied areas. It is interesting to observe that socialization studies remain largely focused on the realm of education. Only recently have we seen a move to integrate more aspects of the actual interactions in school, such as classroom atmosphere and the opportunity to talk freely in class, into such research designs. Stolle, Gauthier and Harell are developing a new longitudinal study with 16 to 17 year olds in Quebec and Ontario, in which they focus specifically on the character of the social networks in which young citizens are embedded.[37] They examine how the diversity and intensity of the networks contributes to the development of civic attitudes and behaviors.

Relying here on the existing, although incomplete, research on the effects of youth networks, we highlight the following strategies from which communities would benefit: actively recruiting youth to participate in and promoting networks, and fostering youth leadership in organizations.

Promoting Outreach through Networks

Programs aimed at promoting youth engagement are more likely to have lasting effects if they are able to foster and develop the networks created by their participants even after they are no longer participating. After all, participation is generally high among young children: 87 percent of Canadian children aged 4 to 15 participated in organized extra-curricular activities.[38] Yet the role for a network-based approach to social capital must be to maintain the benefits of this early engagement in extra-curricular activities throughout adolescence and into adulthood by taking advantage of the social networks created by organizations and clubs to mobilize and facilitate engagement later in life. Usually, engagement in such social activities is supported somewhat during the school period, but then drops off sharply.

It is also worth mentioning here that Swedish municipal governments offer financial support to youth and sport-related organizations. These financial resources are used for the organizational infrastructure, member meetings, and events. Interested youth can get together and apply for financial resources in their communities. Since Sweden has fewer problems with the decline of youth engagement, such strategies might be worth consideration.

Not only peer networks are important; adolescent-adult contacts add a useful dimension to fostering civic spirit. Our example here results again from the Swedish context, where we can find community networks designed to establish useful contact between adults and adolescents. The idea is that parents form loose neighborhood groups which go on night walks to be in touch with the kids in their communities.[39] A non-profit umbrella organization called Fathers and Mothers in the City provides the necessary infrastructure for interested parents and adults to participate. Whereas some have criticized such programs as a form of social control, interviews have revealed that the resulting contacts between adults and youth have been extremely useful in preventing youth-related crime, and in fostering youth-adult activities as well as further societal engagement in communities.

In Canada, programs to promote long-term engagement have benefited from a multi-faceted approach to creating and sustaining social networks for youth. One example is the Aboriginal Youth Research program of the Centre of Excellence for Youth Engagement (CEYE), which promotes youth health outcomes by building community-wide networks of knowledge inquiry and exchange.[40] The Centre's numerous partnerships with organizations and communities allow it to promote the continued engagement of youth by encouraging involvement in other related youth programs and conferences. For example, as part of a community-based effort to promote engagement among Aboriginal youth, the CEYE encouraged participants to present their work to nationwide conferences for Aboriginal youth. The Centre also employed youth from the community to assist in research development, strengthening the ties between the CEYE and the community. The linkages between youth, researchers, schools, government, and the community promote skill building and knowledge sharing even after the formal program ends.

Fostering Youth Leadership and Participation within Organizations

Promoting youth engagement in the community is often as simple as offering young people a seat at the table: youth-oriented foundations and non-profit organizations have recognized the value of establishing youth advisory boards. These organizations benefit from youth input to improve the effectiveness of their programs. In addition, the experience of participating in youth advisory boards fosters community values in youth, and allows them to develop leadership and civic skills.

In Canada, the CEYE has taken the lead in promoting youth participation within organizations. It brings together the research on building effective programs for youth engagement, and uses these resources to help improve organizations and programs in their network. In promoting youth participation and youth leadership within organizations, the CEYE also practices what it preaches: in 2002 there were 76 youth trained to carry out CEYE research.[41] Youth are also involved in all aspects of the CEYE's activities. In addition to being the focus of the CEYE's programs, young people also serve as program co-ordinators, advisors and evaluators, researchers, and conference participants.

Worldwide, youth advisory groups are giving young people a voice in government policy at local, national, and international levels. One example, Voces Nuevas in Peru, specifically allows youth representatives to join discussions about the government's poverty reduction programs. Another model, called the co-management approach by the Advisory Council on Youth in the European Union, makes youth equal partners in the formulation of regional policies. Similar programs of national youth councils in many other developing countries have evolved with representatives from the established networks of scouts, young politicians, and youth in media, drama, and sports, etc. Because many of these youth networks and councils are often invited to participate in global forums, in addition to promoting engagement among their youth participants, they have also become significant contributors to government policy decision making.

Workplaces

Unfortunately, the workplace has been largely ignored by efforts and programs to encourage youth engagement, which is reflected by a similar omission in the literature on adult workplaces.[42] The workplace, however, plays an important role in young people's lives: workplaces constitute a social environment for building networks and developing skills and attitudes. The problem is that most civic outreach programs focus on the school population, excluding young adults who drop out of schools or who complete their education early. It is, therefore, no wonder that we find particular strong engagement gaps between those youth who continue with their education and youth who have started to work disproportionately early. To encourage youth engagement in the workplace, several strategies stand out: ease the school-to-work transition through outreach and mentoring, and reward and recognize youth participation.

Outreach and Mentoring

Traditionally, the paths youth could take from school to work were straightforward and simple: from high school to work, or the option of post-secondary education in between. In recent decades, however, this passage has become increasingly complicated and non-linear, because of a number of factors, such as the difficulties of finding employment, the rise of non-traditional jobs, and increased student debt.[43] Youth today can find themselves repeatedly going back and forth from school to work or combining work and school. In this context, mentoring and outreach programs ease the school-to-work transition.

Examples of such initiatives could include having youth choose adults in their field of interest to "shadow" adult activities including in the civic sphere or establishing internship programs that allow youth to get hands-on experience (as opposed to doing administrative or clerical tasks).

Rewarding Youth Participation

One effective way that workplaces can encourage youth engagement is to acknowledge the skills youth can develop through involvement in organizations and volunteering as an important part of their work experience. This allows youth to benefit from their contributions to community and gives companies the advantage of hiring youth with specific skill sets, such as leadership or hands-on experience with working as part of a team.

Millennium Volunteers (MV) in the United Kingdom allows youth between the ages of 16 and 24 to gain recognition for their achievements in service. The program evaluates and tracks youth service by issuing awards for 100 and 200 hours of community service. According to the program, over 40,000 program participants have received awards for 200 hours of service. Through partnerships with the private sector, MV promotes awareness of the value of skills acquired through volunteering. For employers, the program provides a standard for identifying the achievements of youth volunteers, and the MV distinction has become widely recognized and valued among employers. The MV program has two positive outcomes for youth: promoting youth personal development through civic engagement and easing the school-to-work transition by connecting employers with youth.

THE POTENTIAL FOR FUTURE POLICY AND PROGRAM DEVELOPMENT

In contemplating future policy and program development to foster youth civic engagement, there are two main strategies for government action: focus efforts on the most beneficial forms of political and civic engagement, and target programs to disengaged youth.

Focus Efforts on the Most Beneficial Forms of Engagement

While youth engagement is beneficial for youth themselves, the community, democracy, and the economy, the impacts can vary. Generally, different forms of engagement and participation are not equally desirable. As Tossutti emphasized in her study, there are significant "qualitative differences between different types of involvements and the very different political outcomes that can result."[44] Similarly, Jennings noted that not all forms of political activity are equal in terms of fostering civic attitudes and political engagement.[45] As a result, government should concentrate on promoting forms of engagement that result in payoffs for the larger society and encourage individuals to reinvest the returns of participation for their own benefit. Government policies for promoting beneficial forms of engagement include supporting programs that encourage youth to work toward common goals and diverse youth networks, and providing work-related incentives for youth engagement, and financial and infrastructural support for youth community groups.

Support Programs that Encourage Diverse Networks and Co-operation Toward a Common Goal

In general, extra-curricular activities and the participation in social groups are important for youth participation, because they provide a context for youth to engage with one another and develop civic skills, such as teamwork. At the same time, these positive outcomes for engagement increase when activities promote youth co-operative efforts toward a common goal. In addition, recent research has found that diverse networks might be better for developing civic attitudes and tolerance than groups that bring together people from similar backgrounds. Positive co-operation experiences in diverse groups develop norms of generalized reciprocity, tolerance and, most likely, generalized trust, and mobilize youth into thinking differently about their society.[46]

Governments can focus on providing more opportunities for extra-curricular activities and youth groups, especially those that encourage youth to co-operate toward common goals. Geographic exchange programs and youth partnerships (such as Big Brother, Big Sister) that bring diverse youth together for collective experiences might be particularly fruitful here.

Governments can also explore ways to link the notion of achieving common civic goals, through less civic-oriented activities that are more popular among youth, such as art, music, sports, and other similar activities. Sport participation is a particularly promising example for Canada, because young people participate in sports at higher rates than any other age group. According to Sport Canada, among 15 to 18 year olds, 80 percent of males and 64 percent of females participated regularly in sports activities.[47] The networks created by widespread youth participation in sports can be mobilized by government toward youth civic engagement efforts. For example, the government can encourage youth soccer teams to have civic-oriented goals, through activities, such as fund-raising drives to collect soccer equipment to donate. Sports are also an area where the government can encourage youth to help each other through youth-led participation. Youth soccer players on organized teams can help teach and coach special soccer clinics to promote participation among disadvantaged youth.

One example of a program in Canada that uses sports to achieve civic engagement goals is the Legacy program associated with the 2002 North American Indigenous Games. This program uses the context of the Games to promote Aboriginal youth engagement and empowerment, through sport-related activities. Aboriginal youth volunteer to construct traditional Red River carts to take part in a ceremony for the games, under the guidance of a Metis elder.

Providing Work-Related Incentives for Youth Engagement

One of the most promising roles for government in encouraging youth engagement is to provide incentives for youth engagement through work. The advantages governments have in influencing the school-to-work transition can be mobilized specifically to promote youth engagement by linking youth service to broader employment opportunities. Governments can provide incentives for youth engagement in several ways, such as educating and forming partnerships with businesses, or establishing programs to give priority to hiring youth with service experience for government positions.

Governments have the resources to create and publicize job databases for youth, and fund internship programs and summer job initiatives. Canada's Youth Employment Strategy is an example of a multi-faceted approach to promoting youth in the work force. Programs in the Youth Employment Strategy include Young Canada Works (YCW), a joint initiative of the Department of Canadian Heritage and Parks Canada, which provides grants, in the form of wage subsidies for summer jobs and internships. The two internship programs, Building Careers in Heritage and Building Careers in English and French, allow young Canadians to develop valuable work skills and experience, while learning about and promoting Canadian heritage.

Support to Youth Community Groups

A more costly alternative for governments is to support youth groups with financial help and aid in infrastructure. Local governments might be able to distribute financial resources to youth groups, and might support such groups by providing meeting space in (youth) community centers. The provision of space that lends itself to social interactions is an important issue for fostering social networks in communities.[48] Since space for youth groups would allow for better partnerships between youth, the parents in the community and other adults, it might not only help in shaping youth networks, but it might also help to prevent delinquent behavior.

Target Efforts to Specific (Disengaged) Groups

Since our analysis has found that certain groups of youth are more disaffected than others with the trend indicating a widening gap between the participants and the bystanders, government policies can also be designed to target specific disengaged groups within the youth population. In particular, governments can recruit minority youth, such as Aboriginal and immigrant youth, and re-engage older youth, especially those in the work force.

Minorities

For government, the integration of minority youth who are disproportionately disengaged in political and public affairs is a central issue. One promising avenue for encouraging participation among youth members of disadvantaged groups is through government funding and promotion of what are considered to be best practice programs. These programs continually empower youth to partake in decisions that affect them directly. Good programs allow youth full access to knowledge and information about policy issues, and about conditions in the economy that determine their employment and livelihoods. These programs also provide the venues for youth to voice their concerns about government programs and policies. Last, a program is a best practice when it makes governments more accountable for their actions, allowing youth to assist in monitoring and evaluating public programs.

One example of a best practice program in Canada is the Department of

Canadian Heritage Urban Multipurpose Aboriginal Youth Centres (UMAYC). The centerpiece of UMAYC is the creation of a network of youth centers that provides the Government of Canada with a starting point for creating programs for Aboriginal youth. According to Canadian Heritage, these centers will provide "Aboriginal community-based, culturally relevant and supportive projects, programs, services and counseling to urban Aboriginal youth."[49] The UMAYC programs fit the best practice criteria, because of their emphasis on a multi-dimensional and multifaceted approach to empowering Aboriginal youth. Another example is Elections Canada's Aboriginal Elder and Youth Program (AEYP). While aimed at increasing voter turnout among Aboriginal voters in general, it fosters civic skills and attitudes among youth by engaging them in assisting, interpreting for, and providing information to fellow Aboriginal electors. The Program also provides youth with an opportunity to monitor and evaluate the government.

In addition to promoting best practice programs, it is important for policy makers to deal with the problems associated with minority status, but also to address the issues specific to minority youth. This task is especially difficult, because of the wide range of experiences and cultures within the demographic group. For example, immigrant youth from different countries can face different linguistic or cultural barriers to civic engagement. At the same time, culture can also play a role in facilitating integration. A cultural emphasis on family and educational achievement, for example, can actually help the integration of youth into society.[50] Therefore, programs to meet the needs of immigrant youth are most effective when they recognize and build on existing cultural traditions and family structures.

Similarly, addressing the needs of Aboriginal youth is important for developing successful programs. In Australia, for example, youth volunteering was identified as a particularly relevant issue, as 56 percent of indigenous volunteers were under 34 years of age, compared to 27 percent of volunteers in the general population of Australia.[51]

To foster youth volunteering, the Australian government funded environmental programs, such as the Green Corps, for young people aged 17 to 20. Overall, five percent of Green Corps participants identified themselves as indigenous, a comparatively large percentage, because indigenous youth are only 2.97 percent of the overall population of 17 to 20 year olds.[52] Furthermore, more recent projects have shown participation rates of indigenous youth to be as high as 9 percent. According to the Green Corps, its success in encouraging indigenous youth to participate in its programs stems from an emphasis on indigenous history and land use of the area. The Green Corps also forms partnerships with local indigenous people and organizations for their projects.

Reducing the Participation Gap

One of the most troubling trends in Canada is the widening gap in participation between the most and least educated youth. In the last decade, voter turnout "has fallen over 30 points among those with less than a high school education and 15 points or more among those who have completed high school and/or some college. Meanwhile, turnout has held steady among young university graduates."[53] Consequently, pure university-based efforts for voter registration, may be reinforcing this gap in turnout by encouraging those youth most likely to vote anyway. Government efforts need to be directed at reducing the participation gap between the youth who are tuned out and those who remain active.

One successful Australian program ties provisional voter registration lists with secondary school-based registration drives. Australia has special agreements with high schools for funding tied to the number of students registered on the list of electors.[54] Provisional registration is important, because many high school students are below voting age, and provisional registration allows registration efforts to begin in high schools instead of college or university. This has the advantage of being able to reach a broader segment of youth.

Volunteering is another area where inequalities in participation among youth matter for the design of government programs. Those 15 to 19 years old volunteer at a higher rate and contribute more time to volunteering than the average for all age groups. In 2000, 37 percent of 15 to 19 year olds volunteered, contributing an average of 136 hours, compared to only 22 percent of 20 to 24 year olds, contributing an average of 121 hours.[55] In other words, programs need to focus on creating skills and capacities, and foster the social networks that will enable youth to continue volunteering. Simply requiring students to volunteer only boosts the numbers of student volunteers in high schools; promoting long-term engagement is only achieved when volunteering is linked to broader societal issues and public policies. In addition, government efforts to increase volunteering among youth should also focus on youth aged 20 to 25. Examples include promoting company-sponsored initiatives and volunteering at the undergraduate and postgraduate levels.

Finally, we propose that governments support research particularly in the area of how to mobilize disadvantaged youth, particularly marginalized youth without employment and low levels of education; immigrant youth, and

Aboriginal youth. How can society reach and mobilize such youth? Which themes and styles of participation get them involved? How can the importance of the maintenance of cultural heritage of Aboriginal and immigrant youth be linked to mobilization in the wider society? How can diverse ties between majority and minority youth be established in natural ways? How can the lack of resources for some youth be overcome to bridge the participation divide? The most promising avenue here is to undertake quasi-experimental research with disadvantaged youth, in which different mobilization strategies are tested in controlled settings.

CONCLUSION

This report has examined the status of youth civic engagement in Canada. Canadian youth are more disengaged than older age groups, particularly in voting, party membership, and political knowledge, and they are less involved in traditional political activities than earlier generations at the same age. We should note that young citizens have found many more expressions and action repertoires to communicate their political and societal views, such as political consumerism, protest and life style politics; however, this development—although important—does not substitute for the loss in traditional forms of participation. The trend of youth disengagement is visible in several western democracies, particularly in the United States. Besides a general decline in overall "civicness" in the population as a whole and in the young generation, we observed a remarkable process, which is the widening gap between marginalized youth with fewer resources and those young people who go to college and receive higher levels of education. If this trend continues, our democratic systems will become less and less representative of all the diverse opinions and experiences of the Canadian population.

Not all the causes of these societal trends are well understood. Our report has therefore attempted to focus on those factors that are beneficial for fostering youth engagement in society and politics. Besides the role of socio-economic resources that are looming, we have highlighted the role of social networks and groups, in which young citizens learn civic skills, experience co-operation with others, learn trust and reciprocity, and become mobilized into further action. Social networks are particularly useful when they are composed of diverse individuals who bring different views and experiences to the group life. In addition to networks, we have discussed here the role of civic educational programs that should include hands-on experiences and actual problem solving in the communities in which youth live. Finally, governments' attempts to foster youth engagement should also integrate the findings that youth practice a variety of new action repertoires that are driven by life-style politics, embedded in horizontal (as opposed to vertical) networks, motivated by private concerns. In addition, if societal and political issues relate more directly to the experiences of adolescents, youth mobilization should be more successful.

ENDNOTES

1. Sidney Verba, Kay Schlozman, and Henry Brady, *Voice and Equality: Civic Volunteerism in American Politics* (Cambridge: Harvard University Press, 1995).

2. Eric Uslaner, *The Moral Foundations of Trust* (New York: Cambridge University Press, 2002).

3. L. Steinberg, *Beyond the Classroom: Why School Reform Has Failed and What Parents Need to Do* (New York: Simon & Schuster, 1996).

4. J. Rempel, J. Holmes, and M. Zanna, "Trust in Close Relationships," *Journal of Personality and Social Psychology* 1 (1985): 95–112; K. Rotenberg, "A Promise Kept, A Promise Broken: Developmental Bases of Trust," *Child Development* 51 (1980): 614–617.

5. Dietlind Stolle, "The Family Roots of Social Capital." Unpublished manuscript, 2005.

6. Volunteer Canada, *Family Volunteering: The Final Report* (2002). <http://www.volunteer.ca/volunteer/ pdf/ fvfr_eng.pdf>.

7. M. McDevitt and S. Kiousis, *Education for Deliberative Democracy: The Long-Term Influence of Kids Voting*. USA Center for Information and Research on Civic Learning and Engagement, Working Paper 22 (2004).

8. F&ST (Families and Schools Together Canada). 2004. <http://www.familyservicecanada.org/fst/index_e. html>.

9. Carnegie Corporation of New York and CIRCLE, *The Civic Mission of Schools* (Washington, DC: CIRCLE, 2003).

10. Richard Niemi and Jane Junn, *Civic Education: What Makes Students Learn* (New Haven: Yale University Press, 1998).

11. Scott Keeter et al., "The Civic and Political Health of the Nation: A Generational Portrait" Center for Information and Research on Civic Learning and Engagement (2002): 32; see also Judith Torney-Purta, "Civic Knowledge, Beliefs About Democratic Institutions, and Civic Engagement Among 14 Year-olds," *Prospects* 31 (2001): 279–292.

12. M. Andolina et al., "Habits From Home, Lessons From School: Influences on Youth Civic Engagement," *PS: Political Science & Politics* 36 (2003): 275–280.

13. Ibid.

14. Ibid.

15. Ibid., 278.

16. The YLI is a particularly useful model for future programs, because its effects on youth engagement have been rigorously assessed in several quasi-experimental studies. In one such study, Stroupe and Sabato found that YLI programs have a substantial and positive effect on students' levels of political knowledge, and that these effects hold even when other factors were considered. Students involved in the YLI program performed better than non-YLI students when answering 17 political knowledge questions. The mock election component of the YLI program, in particular, was found to be effective. According to Stroupe and Sabato, "the more exposure students have to the political participation exercises involved in the mock election aspects of the YLI program, the more likely they were to show increased positive outcomes" (7). Students who participated in the mock election were more likely to agree with statements that reflected political efficacy (an average of 2.20 items out of 5 on the index) compared to students whose classes did not have this program (an average of 2.06). In terms of political knowledge, mock election participants scored an average of 11.15 out of 17 questions, compared to only 9.87 for students.

17. K. Stroupe and Larry Sabato, "Politics: The Missing Link of Responsible Civic Education," Center for

Information and Research on Civic Learning and Engagement Working Paper 18 (2004). In this study, individual civics classrooms randomly sampled for inclusion in treatment groups were chosen from schools with at least one teacher who planned to use the YLI resources. Participating teachers were instructed to administer the survey to their earliest class of the day, to ensure random distribution at the respondent level. The control (non-treatment) groups in the study were randomly selected among schools registered with the National Council for Social Studies and from a random selection of schools generated from a national list provided by MDR Market Data Retrieval.

18. Student Vote 2004. 2004. <http://www.studentvote2004.ca/sv04/summary.html>.

19. Canada NewsWire, 265,000 students under the voting age vote in parallel federal election. June 25, 2004. <http://www.newswire.ca/en/releases/archive/June2004/25/c8562.html>.

20. J. Westheimer and J. Kahne, "Educating the 'Good' Citizen: Political Choices and Pedagogical Goals." Democratic Dialogue: A University of Ottawa online forum, 2004: 2. <http://www.democraticdialogue.com/DDpdfs/WestheimerKahnePS.pdf>.

21. J. Youniss et al., "Youth Civic Engagement in the Twenty-first Century," *Journal of Research on Adolescence* 12 (2002): 121–148.

22. J. Miller, "The Peace Corps Partnership at Corcoran High School and John T. Roberts School." World Wise Schools, 2005. <http://www.peacecorps.gov/wws/service/projideas/jim_miller_article.html>. Accessed February 2005.

23. Westheimer and Kahne, "Educating the 'Good' Citizen."

24. Ibid., 3.

25. Gabriel Almond and Sidney Verba, *The Civic Culture* (Princeton: Princeton University Press, 1963); see also M. Hanks and B. Eckland, "Adult Voluntary Associations and Adolescent Socialization," *Sociological Quarterly* 19 (1978); Sidney Verba and Norman Nie, *Participation in America* (New York: Harper and Row, 1972).

26. D. Rogers, G. Bultena, and K. Barb, "Voluntary Associations Membership and Political Participation: an Exploration of the Mobilization Hypothesis," *Sociological Quarterly* 16 (1975): 305-318.

27. Sidney Verba, Kay Schlozman, and Henry Brady, *Voice and Equality: Civic Volunteerism in American Politics* (Cambridge: Harvard University Press, 1995); see also P. Dekker, Ruud Koopmans, and A. van den Broek, "Voluntary Associations, Social Movements and Individual Political Behavior in Western Europe," in *Private Groups and Public Life*, ed. Jan van Deth (London: Routledge, 1997); George Moyser and Garriant Parry, "Voluntary Associations and Democratic Participation in Britain," in *Private Groups and Public Life*, ed. Jan van Deth (London: Routledge, 1997).

28. C. Boix and D. Posner, "Making Social Capital Work: A Review of Putnam's Making Democracy Work," Working Paper No. 96-4. Center for International Affairs, Harvard University (1996).

29. For empirical evidence regarding this relationship, see Almond and Verba, *The Civic Culture*; J. Brehm and W. Rahn, "Individual Level Evidence for the Causes and Consequences of Social Capital," *American Journal of Political Science* 41 (1997): 999–1023; M. Hooghe and D. Stolle, eds., *Generating Social Capital: Civil Society and Institutions in Comparative Perspective* (New York: Palgrave, 2003); D. Stolle and T. Rochon, "Are All Associations Alike? Member Diversity, Associational Type and the Creation of Social Capital," *American Behavioral Scientist* 42 (1998): 47–65. Although association members consistently exhibit more civic attitudes and behaviors than non-members, it has not been shown that the experience within the association per se leads to these outcomes or whether more trusting and more civically oriented citizens self-select into associations more disproportionately.

30. Putnam, *Bowling Alone*; Stolle and Rochon, "Are All Associations Alike?"

31. D. Mutz, "Cross-cutting Social Networks: Testing Democratic Theory in Practice," *American Political Science Review* 96 (2002): 111–126.

32. Statistics Canada, "National Longitudinal Survey of Children and Youth: Participation in Activities." *The Daily*, May 30, 2001. <http://www.statcan.ca/Daily/English/010530/d010530a.htm>. Although the findings reported by Statistics Canada demonstrate a relationship between participation in extracurricular activities and positive outcomes for youth and children, there is not enough evidence to suggest a causal relationship. More analysis is necessary to determine whether these outcomes are caused by participation or whether the correlation between participation and positive outcomes is indicative of another underlying cause.

33. M. K. Jennings and R. Niemi, *Generations and Politics* (Princeton: Princeton University Press, 1981).

34. A. Harell and D. Stolle, "Social Capital and the Forgotten Insights of Socialization Studies." Unpublished manuscript, 2005.

35. D. Stolle, and M. Hooghe, "The Roots of Social Capital. Attitudinal and Network Mechanisms in the Relation between Youth and Adult Indicators of Social Capital," 39 *Acta Politica* (2004): 422–441.

36. Keeter et al., "The Civic and Political Health."

37. D. Stolle, M. Gauthier, and A. Harell, *Bridging Differences: Youth, Diversity and Civic Values*. Longitudinal Study under development. SSHRC and FQRSC financed, 2005.

38. Canada, Statistics Canada, "National Longitudinal Survey of Children and Youth: Participation in Activities." *The Daily* May 30, 2001. <http://www.statcan.ca/Daily/English/010530/d010530a.htm>.

39. Farsor and Morsor på stan. nd. Home page. <www.farsormorsor.se>.

40. CEYE (Centre of Excellence for Youth Engagement), *Annual Report 2002*. <http://www.tgmag.ca/centres/index_e.html>.

41. Ibid.

42. D. Mutz and J. Mondak, "Democracy at Work: Contributions of the Workplace Toward a Public Sphere." Paper presented at the annual meeting of the Midwest Political Science Association, Chicago, April 23–25, 1998; an exception is H. Brady, S. Verba, and K. Schlozman, "Beyond SES: A Resource Model for Political Participation," *American Political Science Review* 89 (1995): 271–295.

43. S. Franke, "School, Work, and the School-work Combination by Young People." Statistics Canada Research Paper, 1998.

44. L. Tossutti, "Youth Voluntarism and Political Engagement in Canada." Paper prepared for presentation at the annual meeting of the Canadian Political Science Association, Winnipeg, Manitoba, June 3–5, 2004.

45. M. K. Jennings, "Residues of a Movement: The Aging of the American Protest Generation," *American Political Science Review* 81 (1987): 367–382.

46. Rogers, Bultena, and Barb, "Voluntary Associations Membership and Political Participation"; M. Hanks, "Youth, Voluntary Associations and Political Socialization," *Social Forces* 60 (1981) 1: 211–223; J. Glanville, "Political Socialization or Selection? Adolescent Extracurricular Participation and Political Activity in Early Adulthood," *Social Science Quarterly* 80 (1999): 279–290; M. Conway and A. Damico, "Building Blocks: The Relationship Between High School and Adult Associational Life." Paper presented at American Political Science Association meeting, August 30–September 2, 2001. San Francisco, California.; Mutz, "Cross-Cutting Social Networks."

47. Sport Canada, "Sport Participation in Canada: 1998 General Social Survey." <http://www.pch.gc.ca/progs/sc/info-fact/part_e.cfm>.

48. J. Jacobs, *The Death and Life of Great American Cities* (New York: Random House, 1961).

49. UMAYC. 2005. <http://www.nafc-aboriginal.com/pages/umayc/index_e.html>.

50. P. Anisef and K. Kilbridem, *The Needs of Newcomer Youth and Emerging "Best Practices" to Meet Those Needs—Final Report*. Prepared for the Settlement Directorate, Ontario Region, Citizenship and Immigration Canada. Toronto: Joint Centre of Excellence for Research on Immigration and Settlement, 2000.

51. L. Kerr et al., "Celebrating Diversity: Experiences and Perceptions of Volunteering in Indigenous and Non-English Speaking Background Communities," *Australian Journal on Volunteering* 6 (2001): 9–17.

52. Green Corps, "About Green Corps." <http://www.greencorps.com.au/Page.asp?l1=1&l2=1>.

53. E. Gidengil, A. Blais, N. Nevitte, and R. Nadeau, "Turned Off or Tuned Out? Youth Participation in Politics," *Electoral Insight*. Elections Canada, 2003. <http://www.elections.ca/eca/eim/article_search/article.asp?issueid=8&lang=e&frmPageSize=&textonly=false>.

54. K. Archer, "Increasing Youth Voter Registration: Best Practices in Targeting Young Electors," *Electoral Insight*. Ottawa: Elections Canada, 2003.

55. D-Code, "Citizen Re:Generation: Understanding Active Citizen Engagement Among Canada's Information Age Generations." <http://www.d-code.com/pdfs/CitizenReGen2003.pdf>.

***Dietlind Stolle** is associate professor of political science at McGill University in Montreal, Canada; **Cesi Cruz** is a Ph.D. candidate in political science, University of California, San Diego.

Dietlind Stolle and Cesi Cruz. "Youth Civic Engagement in Canada." In *Social Capital in Action: Thematic Policy Studies*. PRI Project. September 2005, 98–114.

Used by permission.

DISCUSSION QUESTIONS

1. If you are the mayor of a small town and want to increase youth participation in politics, what one or two reforms would you try because you think they are most effective? Explain your choices.

2. If you are an employee, how could your employer encourage workers to be more involved in their community?

3. What are the benefits of implementing an election among young people to select a national youth legislature to lobby for youth issues (see appendix on the UK Youth Parliament)?

The UK Youth Parliament Manifesto

ABOUT THE UK YOUTH PARLIAMENT

The UK Youth Parliament (UKYP) enables young people to use their energy and passion to change the world for the better. Run by young people, for young people, UKYP provides opportunities for 11–18 year-olds to use their voice in creative ways to bring about social change.

UKYP was launched at the House of Commons in July 1999, and held its first Sitting in February 2001 in London. There are currently over 600 elected MYPs (Members of Youth Parliament) and Deputy MYPs who represent both young men and women, including young people from a variety of ethnic backgrounds, and with physical and learning disabilities.

UKYP elections take place each year across the UK. Any young person aged 11–18 can stand or vote in UKYP elections. In the past three years over one million young people have voted in UKYP elections. Once elected, MYPs work with their MPs, councillors, school and youth councils and peer group members on the issues of greatest concern to their constituents. For more information about our work please visit www.ukyouthparliament.org.uk.

ABOUT THIS MANIFESTO

Foreword by Natalie North

UKYP Yorkshire and Humberside Representative

Summer 2008 saw the UK Youth Parliament's Annual Sitting at the University of Exeter. The Sitting saw the diverse Members of Youth Parliament (MYPs) come together to plan the UK Youth Parliament's work over the coming year, and revisit and revise the manifesto.

The manifesto plays a vital part in the work of the UK Youth Parliament; it gives the public and those influential adults the voices of young people and their opinions on pressing issues. It raises awareness and gives our stance on things. Obviously it is therefore essential this document stays updated and current.

At the Sitting, additions were made to the manifesto and things were taken out. MYPs then voted on all the additions to the manifesto to ensure it reflected the view of the young people in the United Kingdom.

The past few years have seen dramatic changes within policy due to work of the UK Youth Parliament. Most recently our campaign on improving Sex and Relationships Education has resulted in Personal, Social and Health Education (PSHE) becoming a statutory part of the curriculum.

The success of this campaign highlights the importance of this document in bringing about change within society, and ensuring young people have their voice heard and acted upon, as they are the next generation!

CULTURE, MEDIA AND SPORT

A Fair Image for Young People

We believe the use of discriminatory language should be banned. It appears that it is acceptable to use language deemed as discriminatory against young people, for example "yob". UKYP believes that these terms do not reflect the majority of youths today.

UKYP believes there should be an increase of positive reports in the media based on young people. Negativity produces stereotypes and UKYP wants to ensure discrimination against young people doesn't occur.

Young people should be encouraged to take an active role in the media so their views are also represented which allows positive insight for all audiences. UKYP believes that the majority of young people should not have to suffer the consequences of the minority's actions.

Appreciating Culture

UKYP proposes a day set aside for a youth led multicultural celebration for all generations. This brings together communities and teaches about different backgrounds and beliefs. It is an opportunity for prejudice and stereotypes to be combated. These festivals should be piloted in major cities with a view to expanding into smaller areas.

UKYP also believes there should be more emphasis on a multicultural curriculum which should be compulsory. This will include respect for other beliefs. Furthermore this should be applied to adults not only young people.

Youth Sport Matters

UKYP would like to see a variety of sports made available to all young people as part of their school curriculum. These sports should be advertised widely around the community to ensure that all young people get involved because we believe there is a sport for everyone.

We believe all young people should be entitled to subsided access to all leisure facilities in their areas, including transport to those facilities. This in turn will reduce the carbon footprint due to unnecessary travelling to the facilities, which may be a consequence of individuals obtaining lifts from their parents.

UKYP would like to see a vast improvement in leisure facilities as many of these are not fully developed across the country.

EDUCATION, SKILLS AND EMPLOYMENT
Bullying

School anti-bullying policies should be written by students in consultation with teachers and relevant professionals. We believe that the policy should include:
- The necessity of having professional advice and peer support for both the victim and the bully.
- Ensuring that records kept by schools in relation to bullying are kept confidential and are not used to disadvantage the bully.

Participation

UKYP believes that there should be evidence of active and meaningful participation and student voice in all aspects of the education system.

Citizenship

Citizenship education should be radically overhauled through a youth led UK wide review. Teaching staff should be specifically trained to deliver it following the review. The review should explore the meaning and scope of 'citizenship' along the following lines:
- Political education – young people should be able to learn more about the political process, the exercise of power and political parties.
- Sex and Relationships Education (SRE)—SRE should be compulsory in all schools. It should be free of religious influence and should include issues surrounding pregnancy, sexual health and sexuality.
- Cultural awareness—schools should promote equality. The syllabus should include sign language skills on a basic level.

- Community cohesion and environment—the education system should encourage young people to participate fully and engage with communities e.g. volunteering.
- Life skills—basic life skills such as budgeting should be taught to young people from an early age.

School Environment

Large class sizes and classrooms designed for temporary use are not conducive to constructive learning. UKYP believes that class sizes should be significantly reduced and school environments should be well built, well equipped and attractive.

Higher Education

In order to make higher education more accessible, UKYP believes that university tuition fees should be abolished.

Schools should actively encourage students from all backgrounds to have knowledge about and, should they have the ability, aspire to attend the best universities.

Minimum Wage

UKYP believes that 18 year-olds should receive the same minimum wage as 21 year-olds.

Education Maintenance Allowance

UKYP believes that the threshold for eligibility for the Education Maintenance Allowance should be increased and should take into account factors other than household income, such as the number of dependent children in the household, the number of university students being supported by the household and family situations.

Underperforming Schools

The government should carefully consider the underlying issues behind schools' underachievement, for example poverty, behaviour and school leadership, and where appropriate increase investment.

Examination Boards

In order to both minimise disruption and worry during examination periods and equalise the value of qualifications, exam boards need to work more closely together to co-ordinate course specifications and exam timetables.

Personalised Learning

We believe that learning should be personalised, with young people following courses most appropriate to their skill, needs and abilities. As part of this UKYP would like to see:

- An improved range of subjects available across the board, in particular vocational routes and applied academic courses.
- The encouragement of alternative skills-training, such as modern apprenticeships, which will help to combat our current skills shortage.
- Young people not in education, employment or training being given additional support to identify and achieve their aspirations.
- Specialist schools not forcing young people to take their specialist subject at the expense of other choices; student choice is paramount.

ENVIRONMENT, TRANSPORT AND RURAL AFFAIRS
Transport for Young People

UKYP believes that young people between the ages of 11 and 18, and in full-time education, should be entitled to a national concessionary fare on all public transport.

UKYP believes that educational facilities should be provided with state support to allow free transport schemes to and from schools and extracurricular activities.

UKYP believes that public transport should be more accessible to all young people, including those with additional needs or living in rural areas. Young people have voiced the opinion that they are disadvantaged living in rural areas by the lack of services available.

If such services were improved it would break down the barriers that seem to have settled between rural and urban areas.

Global Warming

Currently, Britain creates most of its electricity using fossil fuels such as coal, oil and gas. These produce greenhouse gases which contribute to global warming. If we do nothing about this soon, it will be too late to do anything. UKYP believes that we need to use more renewable resources such as wind, solar, wave, tidal and more.

Over-packaging of products nowadays is a problem. UKYP realises that plastics are essential to pack certain products so proposes as an alternative that biodegradable plastics/recyclable plastics are used instead of non recyclable plastics.

UKYP believes that all education establishments must understand that it is their duty to promote and encourage sustainable action for the benefit of our environment. Schools in particular are able to sign to the eco schools commitment which allows their students to take on board a management role and tackle a wide range of environmental concerns, ranging from recycling to energy. This will allow the school to eventually be identified as environmentally friendly with green flag status.

Facilities for Young People

UKYP believes that young people, particularly in rural areas, should be provided with a range of activities to allow them to interact and have access to facilities of the same calibre that are provided in urban areas. This should include youth clubs, night time facilities, day time activities, and small shopping facilities that are both safe and a convenient distance to allow for rural access.

UKYP believes that young people should be consulted on the location and content of these activities and facilities which should be provided at an affordable price.

UKYP believes that all young people should have access to the best educational facilities and employment opportunities possible. This is particularly inclusive of rural areas, meaning that young people will have good educational facilities and employment opportunities within a convenient distance.

EMPOWERING YOUNG PEOPLE

Local Government

UKYP believes that all local authorities should have young people's representation on them.

National Government

UKYP believes all government publications should meet a UKYP approved standard for youth engagement.

UKYP believes that for every policy that affects young people, the government should consult young people (with a minimum engagement of 1 young person consulted for every 1,000 affected).

UKYP believes there should be exofficio seats on government select committees for MYPs (particularly the Department for Children, Schools and Families, the Department of Communities and Local Government, and Scottish Affairs Select Committees).

UKYP believes that government departments should sponsor young people's think tanks, to advise on policy development and engage young people in the political process.

Grassroots Empowerment

UKYP believes there should be a better accreditation system for young volunteers.

UKYP believes that there should be more funding streams available, both at national and local levels for running activities to engage and empower young people.

UKYP advocates the use of this model for engaging with young people in a meaningful manner.

UKYP believes all secondary schools should have an elected school council which holds regular meetings and represents all students. Furthermore, every school should have an elected student governor.

HEALTH
Mental Health

UKYP believes that mental health education should be made compulsory in PSHE lessons, covering issues and common clinical conditions including depression.

UKYP feels that the government should increase and improve the facilities and provision for young people making them accessible, affordable and age appropriate. In addition we believe that mental health professionals who specialise in the needs of young people should treat young people with mental health conditions in centres exclusively for young people.

National Health Service

UKYP believes sexual health clinics should be open on days and at times which are appropriate for young people.

UKYP calls for a clarification on doctor/patient confidentiality. SRE should be taught in a more engaging way with issues, such as becoming a teenage parent being addressed by teenage parents.

UKYP believes that professionals should be brought in to teach SRE in schools.

UKYP strongly feels that there should be more representation of young people within the NHS as they currently often feel discriminated against.

Sexual Health

UKYP's stance on SRE is based on a survey of 21,000 young people. UKYP believes that SRE should start from an early age and should be statutory in all schools.

UKYP is concerned that there is not enough education about STIs. We feel that young people should be more aware of the facts about STIs, instead of common misconceptions.

UKYP feels that teenage pregnancy awareness is not as effective as it should be amongst young people. We strongly believe that there should be an increase in information about relationships and the responsibilities of being a parent; adoption and abortion, as well as education on the possible consequences of all the above. UKYP stresses that in order for better SRE, more peer mentoring needs to be implemented in as many aspects of SRE as possible. When peer mentoring is available, there is increased engagement amongst young people.

Health and Lifestyle

UKYP believes that the media can have a detrimental effect on young people by promoting the "perfect body" such as size zero models and believe we should be promoting steps towards minimizing these stereotypical views and promoting individualism.

UKYP wants to promote the awareness of eating disorders and make it known that these conditions are often caused by stress. We support the use of informational talks in schools and youth clubs to raise awareness of these issues, and believe that the media can play a positive role in changing young people's attitudes toward themselves.

UKYP believes schools should have a greater focus on a wide range of healthy food, which doesn't just focus on pasta and bread, and would like to promote and encourage school chefs to be more inventive with school menus.

Drugs and Alcohol Awareness

UKYP believes that more drug and alcohol awareness should be delivered in schools and youth clubs.

UKYP does not condone underage drinking but we do realise that realistically it is hard to prevent, therefore young people should be made aware of the effects and consequences of binge drinking.

UKYP supports the use of shock tactics in the form of dramatic visual posters that depict the consequences of drunken violence, drug use and abuse, e.g. gun and knife crime.

UKYP believes that this will deter young people from drinking as much alcohol as they do because they are now aware of the detrimental effect it has on their health, and the lives of others. UKYP will press the government to prevent supermarkets from selling cheap alcohol to young people.

INTERNATIONAL MATTERS
Conflict

UKYP believes international disputes should be solved diplomatically and military intervention should be a last resort. Furthermore we support the nuclear disarmament of all nations.

UKYP believes we should not force other countries to adopt democracy but should instead allow them to adopt their own systems of government, providing these pose no threat to human rights and/or international peace.

The Middle East

UKYP supports our troops deployed in Afghanistan, Iraq and the rest of the world by addressing issues of inadequate equipment, living conditions and healthcare, enabling them to support citizens and the development of stable governments.

UKYP support efforts that encourage and support the continual development of democracy in the unstable parts of the Middle East, which have shown a desire to establish democratic processes; and supports efforts to secure a lasting peace in the Israeli/ Palestinian conflict.

Human Rights

UKYP believes that the UK should not ignore human rights abuses. Helping those who suffer as members of the human race is more important than a relationship with a military regime.

UKYP also believes that the UK should encourage communications between African nations to put pressure on the Mugabe regime in Zimbabwe (a country whose people have demonstrated for greater democratic rights) to respect democracy and support human rights in the country and support the Zimbabwean people.

UKYP opposes the detention of prisoners without trial in Guantanamo Bay. All of those currently held in Guantanamo Bay should be immediately released or put on trial in a civilian court.

Globalization

UKYP believes immigrants are vital to the development of the UK economy, its culture and diversity. UKYP thinks that corporations should ensure fair wages and opportunities for their workers in other countries.

Poverty, Aid and Sustainable Development

UKYP believes that we should support ethical responsibility in companies, based in More Economically Developed Countries (MEDCs) towards people living in poverty in Less Economically Developed Countries (LEDCs) (e.g. fairtrade, no exploitation and improved living conditions).

UKYP urges the UK government to ensure the Millennium Development Goals are met by 2015 and to keep the promises it made at the G8 summit in Gleneagles in 2005 relating to the cancelling of third world debt and overseas aid.

LAW AND SOCIETY

Gun and Knife Crime

Gun and knife crime has grown particularly amongst young people. Last year in the UK 27 11-19 year-olds were brutally murdered as a result of this problem. Awareness of the extreme consequences of gun and knife crime must be raised on both an individual and communal level.

UKYP believes that the current government initiatives battling gun and knife crime are not sufficient to solve the underlying causes of this crime.

UKYP believes that more should be done to address the gang culture which exists in today's society. With the support of schools, youth provisions and the local police, UKYP believes that this problem can be solved.

Mosquito Devices

The mosquito is a device which creates a high pitched noise to deter young people from congregating in certain places e.g. outside shops.

UKYP believes that this device discriminates against young people, and should be removed due to the fact that they can cause unnecessary harm and distress to young people, babies and some adults.

UKYP believes that the boxes have major negative effects and is not a long term solution to any problem.

We feel that this is definitely not the correct approach to prevent conflict and encourage community cohesion.

UKYP will continue to campaign for a full investigation into the health effects of this device and the possibility of its removal.

Equality and Discrimination

UKYP believes that all people are equal regardless of gender, disability, ethnicity, age, sexuality or faith. This means they all deserve to be treated equally.

UKYP believes that the media representation of young people is discriminatory and we will campaign for more positive representation. We feel that the society we live in today is very divided in terms of age, and conflicting opinions on young people. This is evident through the use of stereotypes in the media, specifically labelling young people as being part of a gang or referring to them as yobs or thugs.

APPENDIX   285

UKYP are concerned about discrimination in the workplace. Despite the 2006 equality act young people are paid a lower wage than their adult counterparts solely because they are younger. This is ageist discrimination, and UKYP deems this unacceptable.

UKYP will campaign for a fairer representation of young people in the media, and will condemn any situation where a young person is deemed unequal, or is discriminated against.

Britishness and Citizenship

UKYP understands Britishness to be a celebration of our individual identities, backgrounds and beliefs whilst simultaneously regarding each other as member of a united community.

We fervently believe that everyone should unite around a collective British identity to create a more harmonious and connected society. UKYP supports the government proposed consultation to strengthen British identity and unity.

UKYP believes that British society thrives on the acceptance of others, partnership and cohesion.

UKYP applauds the government for introducing citizenship education within the national curriculum. However, we believe that it now needs to be radically improved. There appears to be no clear or effective curriculum for this particular subject and thus it does not serve its purpose. This is confirmed by the fact that this subject is seldom taught by appropriately qualified tutors.

UKYP firmly believes that the government, in consultation with young people, should create a stable platform for it to be taught effectively.

Child Poverty

UKYP believes that no child should be in poverty. Every child matters and deserves a good quality of life. The government have already set targets to reduce child poverty and UKYP argues that these targets are met as soon as possible in order to remove child poverty in the UK.

UK Youth Parliament Manifesto. 2008. http://www.ukyouthparliament.org.uk/downloads/UKYP_ Manifesto_2008.pdf.